Praise for Searching for Spice

"Be careful what you pray for. . . . Megan DiMaria's *Searching for Spice* is an entertaining tale of an Everywoman who yearns for the Extraordinary—as we all do on occasion. Filled with humor, zest, and real life, this charming romantic tale will charm and delight."
—**ANGELA HUNT, author of *Doesn't She Look Natural?***

"*Searching for Spice* is a wonderfully refreshing story of one wife's refusal to let romance be held hostage by married life. I loved the voice, the characters, and the humor was terrific—everything was just so fresh. It was the perfect book for me to read at the perfect time."
—**MAUREEN LANG, author of *The Oak Leaves* and *On Sparrow Hill***

"A great look at the ordinary things that make up an extraordinary life. DiMaria shows us that sometimes life itself can be the best seasoning for love."
—**MARILYNN GRIFFITH, author of *Pink* and *Made of Honor***

"*Searching for Spice* is a fantastic read that I couldn't put down. With a grabbing main character, a cast of friends and family that makes things interesting, a story line to keep the pages turning, and writing that brought both laughter to my lips and tears to my eyes, *Searching for Spice* is a novel not to be missed. I'm looking forward to reading more from this new author."
—**ROSEANNA WHITE, senior reviewer, *Christian Review of Books***

"Debut author Megan DiMaria breaks new ground with *Searching for Spice* by putting a unique twist on one woman's desire for a bodice-ripping, lip-flaming affair . . . with her husband! DiMaria taps into the inner longing of every married woman. *Spice* stands apart from other chick-lit novels by fearlessly tackling faith-breaking trials and temptations all readers can relate to. Sharp writing and dialogue put you in Linda Revere's head, building your faith, along with hers, as she faces mountainous obstacles to her dreams and finds peace in Jesus."
—**DARCIE J. GUDGER, reviewer for www.titletrakk.com and host of www.joyinthelitterbox.blogspot.com**

Searching for Spice

Searching for Spice

Megan DiMaria

TYNDALE HOUSE PUBLISHERS, INC.

CAROL STREAM, ILLINOIS

Visit Tyndale's exciting Web site at www.tyndale.com

Visit Megan DiMaria's Web site at www.megandimaria.com

TYNDALE and Tyndale's quill logo are registered trademarks of Tyndale House Publishers, Inc.

Searching for Spice

Designed by Beth Sparkman

Edited by Lorie Popp

Published in association with the literary agency of Alive Communications, Inc., 7680 Goddard Street, Suite 200, Colorado Springs, CO 80920.

Scripture quotations are taken from the HOLY BIBLE, NEW INTERNATIONAL VERSION®. NIV®. Copyright © 1973, 1978, 1984 by International Bible Society. Used by permission of Zondervan. All rights reserved.

This novel is a work of fiction. Names, characters, places, and incidents either are the product of the author's imagination or are used fictitiously. Any resemblance to actual events, locales, organizations, or persons living or dead is entirely coincidental and beyond the intent of either the author or the publisher.

Library of Congress Cataloging-in-Publication Data

DiMaria, Megan.
  Searching for spice / Megan DiMaria.
    p. cm.
  ISBN-13: 978-1-4143-1887-5 (pbk.)
  ISBN-10: 1-4143-1887-1 (pbk.)
  1. Marriage—Fiction. 2. Spouses—Fiction. I. Title.
  PS3604.I4645S43 2008
  813'.6—dc22
                                      2007038558

Printed in the United States of America

14 13 12 11 10 09 08
7 6 5 4 3 2 1

For Carl.
Your love warms me,
your humor tickles me,
and
your encouragement
fuels me.

ACKNOWLEDGMENTS

My heartfelt thanks go out to my loving family. Carl, Dan, Kathleen, and Liz—it's all because of your love, support, and humor that I was able to make this dream come true. Thank you for letting me live in Linda's world and inhabit yours at the same time. Thank you to my beloved DiMarias in New York for your love and encouragement, especially Ann, Sal, Grace, Lou, Ruth, Joe, Patti, Tom, and Cathy. Thanks also to my parents, the late Bill and Marie McCormack, who encouraged me to pursue my dreams.

I am deeply grateful for my wonderful critique partners: Marion Bullock, Angie Poole, and Frances Devine.

The amazing authors of the American Christian Fiction Writers and the Denver chapter (His Writers) have been an incredible encouragement, and I'd like to name all who have generously given of their time and wisdom, but there's not enough room on the page.

The support of my Words for the Journey crew kept me going, especially Sharen Watson, Jan Parrish, Tonya Vander, and Heather Diane Tipton.

Donita Paul, you've been a sweet friend and mentor—thanks for always having an encouraging word for me.

To the incredible Nangie team, Angie Hunt and Nancy Rue—I couldn't have asked for more precious fairy godmothers. Thanks for helping me find my way to the ball.

Thank you, Beth Jusino, my agent, for taking a chance on an unknown author.

Thanks to my dear friend Leah Wyckoff for her invaluable medical expertise and Shaun Gloude for her legal expertise.

A big thank-you to Jan Stob and Lorie Popp, my editors at Tyndale, for bringing my dream to reality.

And thanks be to my Lord Jesus Christ, the author of life and love and dreams.

Come away, my lover, and be like
a gazelle or like a young stag on the
spice-laden mountains.

SONG OF SOLOMON 8:14

• • •

Jerry looks at me as if my head has sprouted petunias. "Linda, the half-and-half isn't cold."

I regard him through bleary eyes and swallow a yawn. His silhouette appears soft and gauzy, framed by the daylight pouring through the kitchen window, glowing like a Thomas Kinkade painting. I should have given myself an extra dose of eyedrops when I got up this morning. Ever since my LASIK surgery, I've applied a thick, Vaseline-like ointment to my dry eyes at night before dropping into bed. "What?"

He's standing in the middle of the kitchen, the questionable carton of half-and-half in one hand and a mug of steaming coffee in the other. His plaid robe hangs partway open, the belt loosely tied over wrinkled pajamas. A look of perplexity transforms his intelligent features into a caricature of a hapless sad sack. But truly nothing could be farther from the truth. My husband is a PhD chemist. So who *is* this clueless schmo standing before me?

Jerry raises the hand holding the half-and-half. "Warm."

"Is the refrigerator broken?" I launch from my seat and open the door of our five-year-old GE side-by-side fridge that I just *had* to have and, by the way, got at a fabulous discount at the scratch-and-dent sale at Sears.

The interior of the appliance is dark, the first clue that something is amiss. And come to think of it, the refrigerator's typical hum of electrical activity was absent from my morning symphony of appliances that serenades me while the coffee brews and the microwave heats my favorite tall latte mug.

I peer inside. *Oh, rats.* Condensation coats the exterior of a large jar of dill pickles on the top shelf. I put my hand on a glass casserole dish to confirm my diagnosis. "It's not working."

My dear husband is still rooted to the floor. Some people are dependent on that caffeine jolt to get them going in the morning, and he's their poster boy.

"Pour some half-and-half in your coffee, Jer. It's probably okay."

He follows my instructions and takes a seat at the table. "Well, I don't think I could stomach warm milk with my shredded wheat."

I open the freezer door and root around until I find the Sara Lee pound cake I was saving for the weekend. This cake would have been so delicious with some fresh strawberries and whipped cream. I console myself with the knowledge that I really don't need the extra calories; I'm fluffy enough. That's the loving word the Revere family uses to refer to those dreaded unwanted pounds. As in, "Don't you love to hug Grandma? She's so fluffy."

"This will have to do for breakfast. Can you run down to the basement and get the picnic cooler? Maybe we can salvage some of the frozen meat."

Jerry takes a deep swig of his legal stimulant and disappears into the basement. While I pour my tea and set the table, I hear him muttering amid the noise of boxes being shifted across the cement floor.

"What's Dad doing?" Emma stands at the top of the basement stairs, her ear cocked to the sounds coming from below. At fifteen she's still my little girl on some days, but on others I see the lovely young woman who's emerging from within.

I fill her in on the morning's tragedy.

She flips a strand of light brown hair behind her shoulder and saunters to the table. "Whatever."

Okay, so today I see that snotty teenage brat who's hijacked my little darling. Obviously she doesn't feel my pain and is clueless about the cost or inconvenience of a busted refrigerator. Ah, the bliss of youthful ignorance.

Em picks up the knife and slices a piece of cake. "No juice?"

"Help yourself."

She pushes to her feet, grabs a glass, and opens the freezer to retrieve three measly ice cubes.

Just as Jerry's emerging from the basement with the dusty cooler, our son, Nick, joins us, wearing a pair of green sweatpants and a faded T-shirt. His eyelids are at half-mast, and he has a bad case of bed head. Emma's only too happy to give him our news.

I begin to load the picnic cooler with frozen meat and toss the few anorexic ice cubes left in the freezer on top of our chicken breasts, pork tenderloin, ground beef, and frozen vegetables. "Well, this won't do the trick." Too bad it's springtime. Otherwise I could toss my food in the snow.

No one responds to my comment, so I turn to my college-age son. "Nicky, would you please run to the store and get a bag of ice?"

He grimaces, but he's maturing nicely and agrees to drive the few blocks to the store to run my errand. Emma plops herself down in front of the computer, no doubt relieved for once that she doesn't have her driver's license yet.

I paw through our junk drawer in the kitchen for the stack of business cards to find a repairman. Mechanic. Insurance agent. Day spa. Where did that come from? My nerves begin to dance like a cat on hot pavement. I don't have time for this. "Jer, who should I call?"

My honey squeezes my shoulder. Ah, marital solidarity. He moves toward the desk that sits between the kitchen and family room. "Em, may I use the computer?"

She glares at him but silently gives up her seat. In a moment,

Jerry has the telephone number of the Sears repairmen. He passes the scrap of paper to me. "Here ya go."

Great. So much for marital solidarity.

I dial the number, navigate the menu, and plead my case to the dispatch associate. "Two o'clock? Um, okay. Thanks. Someone will be here to let him in." I disconnect the call and secure the handset on its base. "Jer? What's your schedule today?"

He grunts out a reply with his back toward me while he pours another mug of coffee.

"What?"

He turns and takes a careful sip of the hot liquid. "Sorry. Faculty meeting. No can do."

Anxiety builds in my chest. Swell. As usual, *I'm* the one who has to make the appointment and alter my schedule to accommodate this fiasco.

I'm loading the breakfast plates into the dishwasher when Nick walks in bearing a twenty-pound bag of ice. He opens the back door, then drops the bag onto the brick patio.

"Nick?"

He retrieves the bag of ice and beams his killer grin—the one that made my sensibilities melt nearly twenty-six years ago when his father favored me with the same endearing smile at a gas station off the Pennsylvania Turnpike.

I have to confess it's as though Jer saw my heart soar toward the heavens in that moment and caught it in his hand. And that's where it's been ever since. I had run out of gas, and he was fueling his 1973 Volkswagen Karmann Ghia. Both Jerry and his cute little red car were about the best thing I'd seen in forever. He offered to drive me and my gallon of gasoline to my stranded car, and the rest of the story, as they say, is history.

The grandfather clock chimes from the living room, reminding me that I'm behind schedule. Being late for work at Dream Photography is a major transgression. My stomach knots to think that not only will I be late, but I'll have to leave early too. A hive of angry bees bounces off the inside of my skull, clamoring to escape, and a deep sigh drains from the bottom of my lungs.

"Mom?" Nick lays his hand on my shoulder. He is so like his father, bless him. "Chill. It's only a refrigerator."

He makes me smile in spite of my poor attitude. "I know. It's just that I'll have to leave work early, and—"

"What time is the repairman coming?"

Praise God—we must have done something right to deserve this child. "Two o'clock. Will you be home from school?"

He shakes his head. "Sorry. I need to buy a book for my history class."

Are you kidding me? My hands ball and land on my hips. "Can't you buy the book another day?"

"I really need to get going on my term paper. It's due in three weeks."

My anxiety level rises again. "Won't the bookstore be open tomorrow?"

Nick rolls his eyes. "I won't have time to stand in that line at the bookstore tomorrow." He pours the ice cubes onto the meat, ending our discussion.

I toss the lid on the cooler and scurry upstairs to get ready for work. So what's our new family slogan? Every man for himself?

• • •

I walk into the organized chaos that is Dream Photography—one of the best-known portrait studios in metro Denver. The ringing telephone provides nerve-jarring background noise for the pandemonium playing itself out.

A well-groomed toddler makes serious work of tossing neatly arranged brochures onto the floor, while his mother wipes baby spit from her infant daughter's dress. Another client is tapping her foot and checking her wristwatch. Add to that the family being escorted to the lobby to schedule their image presentation—aka sales session—by none other than Luke Vidal, my surly boss.

My tardiness is noted by Luke with a raised eyebrow and a brief tic of his head, one that goes unnoticed by our clients but hits pay dirt in my always-too-willing-to-accept-guilt gut. "Linda, can you schedule an image presentation for the Murrays?"

Sure, Luke *would* have to enlist me to wait on clients before I get the chance to clock in and get my bearings. That must be my punishment for coming in late. I hurry behind the reception desk and smile at the Murray clan—the ones who think Luke is the greatest thing since the invention of the daguerreotype.

Luke pumps the outstretched hand of Andy Murray. "The shoot went well. I think you'll love the images." He gives a peppermint-sweet grin to the rest of the family and struts from the beautifully appointed lobby of his home away from home.

I take care of business and trot to the break room to clock in and catch my breath.

My coworker Traci looks up from a pile of five-by-sevens. "Hey, girl. Where have you been?"

"Don't ask."

She puts down a print of a gorgeous bride and waits for the information she knows I'll spill. I unburden my tale of woe, and she nods and gives me the expected platitudes.

She smiles her Pepsodent grin and pats me on the back. "Isn't life grand?"

I really love Traci, but sometimes she can lay it on too thick. She passes me the day's schedule, then exits the room.

I glance at the list of appointments. *Rats*. I better get moving. The bees have begun to swarm in my brain again.

After grabbing the necessary client files and slipping into a salesroom, I power up my Mac and access the network. Within moments I've loaded my client's images and have chosen an appropriately sentimental song to accompany the slide show. I turn on the projector and dim the lights. Clients go gaga over our well-designed salesrooms—I mean, image presentation rooms. They look more like an elegant home theater than a place of business.

I race back to the lobby, discover that my nine-thirty sale has arrived, and paste a smile on my face. "Heidi, Ken, it's good to see you again. If you don't remember, my name's Linda."

They greet me, and I escort them to the salesroom, chatting with them to break the ice.

The freshly baked cookies placed on the coffee table make my mouth water and hopefully put our well-heeled clients in the mood to take an emotional journey while gazing at the incredible images produced in our high-end studio.

"Can I get anyone a bottle of water before we begin?"

"Yes, I would love some water." Heidi claims a seat in one of the overstuffed chairs. She glances toward her husband, who is inspecting the frame on one of the portraits that adorn the walls. "Ken?"

"Oh yes. Please."

I excuse myself and go to the fridge to get some of our private-label water bottles. From the first moment our customers call to schedule their appointment and until they have their portraits delivered, they're treated like royalty. Fortunately, most of them deserve such treatment.

Heidi and Ken are clients from way back. They've been through everything with us, from the old days of film to the current high-tech, all-digital studio we've evolved into.

When I return, I distribute the water and start the viewing program. The swell of sentimental music explodes from the speakers in the ceiling, and images of two adorable little girls move across the big screen. They sit in a wicker swing under a towering oak tree in a field of tall, natural grasses. The lighting illuminates the canopy of green branches above them, while they are perfectly shaded from the bright morning sun. The girls are wearing off-white linen dresses and holding lovely vintage rag dolls. The camera changes perspective, and the girls are in the foreground, framed by the leaves from the branch of a nearby tree. In the next scene they're sitting at a small, white bistro table enjoying a tea party with a rose-patterned porcelain tea set and a teddy bear for a guest.

The music plays on as the girls pose by an antique baby carriage. They both gaze off into the distance, their expressions a paragon of youthful innocence.

I'm so sick of these types of saccharine images, I could puke. But day after day, they provide the all-natural, nitrate-free bacon I bring home to my family.

Heidi sniffs and reaches for the box of tissues that sits on the table. The last image fades from the screen, and the music stops. Heidi grasps for her husband's hand. He nods and smiles.

I hand a price list to Ken, and we get down to business.

Heidi appears to suffer heart-wrenching torment as we narrow the number of images down from thirty-nine to fifteen. You'd think I'm dishonoring her cute little daughters by deleting some, but unless you've got a huge bank account, you can't buy them all.

She clutches a hand to her heart, and her husband says, "I love that expression on Olyvia's face."

I slip into sales mode. "That image is gorgeous, but look at the subjects. Your girls are beautiful."

They smile in agreement. We continue to weed through the images to find their favorites. I'm getting dizzy from comparing similar poses and going back and forth while Heidi hems and haws about the merits of each picture.

"Ah, can you pull up number twenty-two?"

I maneuver the program to display an image of the girls sitting at the bistro table.

"And can you compare it to number twenty-four?"

Could this woman say *please* just once? Would it kill her to treat me with a modicum of respect?

She turns to her husband. "What do you think?"

Poor Ken looks as though he's pulling himself out of a stupor to respond. "Uh, I don't like the way Trynity's hand is curled on the table."

Heidi stands and moves closer to the screen. "Really? I think that's cute."

He sighs. "Okay, keep that one."

"But Olyvia isn't looking in the right direction."

"Heidi, sit down so I can see the screen."

She flashes him a look that could take the merry out of Christmas. *Uh-oh.* This isn't good.

I clear my throat and try to maneuver the sale in the right direction. "What if we take Olyvia's head from image twenty-five and put it on this image?"

They both study the pictures that I put side by side on the screen.

"And, Ken, didn't you say you love that expression on Olyvia's face?"

He jerks in my direction, and I don't know if he's pleased that I'm asking for his input or annoyed. "What will this cost?"

Oh, so that's the way we're going to be, huh, Ken? "Well, there will be an extra art fee to swap out that head, but if you both love the images and you're purchasing a wall portrait, it's well worth the charge."

"How much?" Ken insists.

Heidi shifts in her seat. "Oh, it will be perfect. We could hang it in the dining room across from the china cabinet."

That Heidi, she's my kind of gal. *Press on, full steam ahead.*

"How much will it cost?"

I wave my hand to minimize the bombshell. "Oh, only about fifty dollars."

If the room were brighter, I'm sure I'd see steam floating from his ears. "Can you show us what that would look like?"

I don't know why he's giving me a hard time. He's bought images with head swaps from us before. "Sure, this is down and dirty, but it will give you an idea." My artistry is crude at best, but I do a quick swap. "Of course our imaging artists will make it look 100 percent natural. No one will know this isn't the original image."

Ken leans back in his chair, a movement I take for acceptance.

I go in for the close. "Now what size portrait were you thinking of?"

Heidi clasps her hands. "Maybe a sixteen-by-twenty."

"Okay. What size is the wall it's going on?"

She looks confused, as if I'm speaking in Mandarin.

I stand and grab a twenty-by-twenty-four-inch frame that holds a white piece of foam core. "Let's look at this size, and tell me what you think." I step into the middle of the room and center the image on the blank canvas.

They respond with the usual sigh of desire.

"You may even want to see the next size up." No sense in not trying.

"Okay, let's see. . . ."

Cha-ching. Looks like I'm well on my way to exceeding my weekly goal. By the time they're ready to leave, I can tell Heidi wants nothing more than to go home and hug her little darlings. For the amount of money I collected from their mom and dad, I want to hug the girls too.

If only the rest of my day goes as well. After the refrigerator crisis, I could use a break.

The next few hours pass with a minimum of frustrations. Sure, my boss is his usual self. I stay busy, keep my head down, and avoid any further wrath.

By one fifteen I'm itching to go home, but I'm anchored to my chair until my paperwork's complete. I'd love to see the look on Luke's face later tonight when he reviews the receipts. My sales were above average.

Daydreams of employee-of-the-month recognition fill my head. I wonder what kind of gift certificate Luke will give as a prize this month—Nordstrom would be nice or Brook's Steak House.

The sound of laughter pulls me from my reverie. Traci marches into the office, followed by Luke. They both look pleased and a little too chummy.

"What's up?"

Luke puts a hand on Traci's shoulder. "Looks like we know who's going to win the top sales prize this month."

Huh? Not me? "Really?"

Traci beams. "My last sale was over four thousand dollars."

"Great." Makes my morning seem paltry in comparison.

Luke glances my way. "What were your numbers so far?"

I push the papers toward him. "I had a great day too."

His smile cools as he rifles through the invoices, and he nods. "You're getting there. Maybe the pro here could give you a lesson."

My grin remains pasted to my face as they leave the room talking about Traci's accomplishment. Great. It's not as though I'm inept. But for all the work I do, Luke could occasionally throw me a bone. I scrape my wounded ego off the floor and clock out. If the traffic cooperates, I'll get home just in time to let the repairman in.

The warm car feels like heaven after the air-conditioned chill of the studio. I forgo the AC and roll down the windows. My '99 Ford Taurus creeps toward the freeway. Swell, I should have known better than to be so optimistic. I'm hitting every traffic light.

When I veer onto the entrance ramp, I slip in a CD and cruise to the funky tunes of Three Dog Night. Nothing helps me unwind more from a hectic day than good old seventies music. Rock on.

So much for traffic cooperating. A tractor on C-470 has emptied its cargo of canned tomatoes on the highway, paralyzing traffic. If only I had turned on the radio, I'd be cruising on County Line Road instead of playing follow the leader as traffic narrows to one lane and threads though cases of whole, chopped, and pureed tomatoes. What a mess.

The congestion practices my patience for a few more minutes; then the highway opens up, and I continue on my way.

I pull onto my street with the appliance repair truck following right behind me. After parking in the garage, I hop out of the car and walk to the side window of the truck. I gingerly knock. "Hello."

The middle-aged repairman startles and looks up from his sheaf of papers. He cranks down the window. "Yes?"

"Give me a second to grab my dog. Then you can come in."

He shrugs and pulls out a cell phone.

Three minutes later Belle, our Jack Russell terrier, is secured in the powder room. I open the front door and motion to the man in the van.

He takes his time getting out of the vehicle and carries a large tool case up my driveway. As he walks in, he thrusts out a calloused hand. "Chuck."

"Nice to meet you, Chuck. I'm Linda."

He follows me to the kitchen, glances at the silent refrigerator, and drops his tools in the middle of the kitchen floor. He looks entirely too pleased as he sets about to dismantle my refrigerator.

I head to my living room and plop down on my overstuffed love seat, where the afternoon sun will illuminate the pages of the novel I'm reading. There's nothing like the Colorado sun. Its heat warms you to your marrow.

"Uh, excuse me."

My eyes pop open. I've fallen asleep. *How embarrassing.* I haul myself into a sitting position, tugging my shirt down over the top of my pants and swiping at the wet spot on the corner of my mouth. "Are we finished?"

Chuck looks as if he's reining in his irritation and cuts short a sigh. "I'm finished."

I follow him back to the kitchen. I'm not crazy about his attitude.

He pushes the bill toward me. My gaze goes directly to the digits on the bottom right of the paper. "Four hundred and twenty-two dollars?" *Are you kidding?*

He rattles off the names of new parts that were required to bring my refrigerator back to life.

My stomach knots. "Should I have just purchased a new refrigerator?"

Chuck cocks his head. "That's not my call. I just did what was requested on the work order."

I pull my checkbook out of my purse and write a check. "Thanks." *For nothing, Chuck.*

I walk him to the foyer and lock the door behind him.

The next few minutes are spent catching up on laundry and sorting through junk mail. A dry cleaning claim ticket sitting on the counter catches my eye, and I decide to run some errands.

The dry cleaner is farthest from home, so that's my first stop, followed by the vet's to get some dog food.

The tinny tune of the "Hallelujah" chorus chirps from within my purse. I grab my bag and grope for my cell phone. "Hello?"

"Where are you?" Jerry sounds irritated.

"Running errands. A few less things to do on Saturday."

"Lin, I just called home. The troops are wondering what's for dinner."

I turn down the volume on my CD player and roll my eyes. "Do you think you could stop on your way home?"

"Uh, I'm already on our street. Why don't you grab something?"

Couldn't he have thought about dinner fifteen minutes ago? Does everything have to fall into my lap? Great. "What sounds good? Italian? Chinese?"

"Whatever you want, dear."

"Sure. See you in about twenty minutes."

He disconnects the call, and I toss my phone in my purse. I punch the CD player's volume up again and belt out the tunes of my youth.

Within a few minutes I pull into the right lane of Pine Grove Road so I can turn into the strip mall that's home to Abacus—the best Chinese restaurant west of the Mississippi.

The last time I stopped in for some food on my way home, Mr. Tang presented me with a boxed fountain pen as a gesture of appreciation for being one of his most loyal customers. Since there's no such thing as an award for the mother who serves her family the most take-out food in a year, the pen will have to do.

I place my order and sit at the bar sipping an iced tea while my dinner is prepared. I always find the background music here bizarre. Somehow, somewhere they've found old songs played with an Asian flair. Who would have ever thought "Up Where We Belong" could sound this way? I wonder what Joe Cocker and Jennifer Warnes think of this.

I grab my tea and move to a seat in the shadows of the room to indulge in one of my favorite pastimes—people watching.

A redheaded boy plays the chopsticks on the table as though it were a drum, while his parents exchange hushed, tense words. They may be speaking quietly, but their body language is screaming. No wonder that child is enjoying a world of his own making.

At another table, an older couple in their sixties incline their heads toward each other and speak tender words. At least that's what I want to think. For all I know, they could be discussing the finer points of egg drop soup. The woman looks down at her menu, and a section of gray hair escapes her black suede headband. She quickly pushes it behind her ear. As she lowers her hand to the table, her escort reaches over a meaty hand and strokes her arm. Lovely.

"Ms. Revere?" Mr. Tang calls me to the cash register. I exchange my credit card for dinner to complete our transaction.

● ● ●

When I get home, I find the table is not set. *Do I have to do everything?* "Nick? Emma? Somebody come here and give me a hand!" I gather the morning paper and drop it in the recycling bin in the garage.

Emma appears and puts a pile of plates and silverware on the table. "Don't freak out, Mom."

"Excuse me? Are you the family princess, or can you pitch in?" This girl can make me crazy. I'd like to—

"Emma, grow up." Nick begins to set the table.

"You're such a jerk! Don't talk to me like you're my parent."

Jerry finally joins us. "Knock it off."

Emma glares at him but says nothing, and Nick smiles that self-satisfied grin that I know drives his sister up the wall.

Within moments, we're all seated at the table, having divided up our vegetable fried rice, sesame chicken, beef with broccoli, and imperial shrimp. At least dinner is delicious.

"Oh, what's this?" Jerry picks up the yellow invoice.

I bet the dollar amount on the bottom of the page will take away his appetite. "The refrigerator repair wasn't under warranty."

He clutches his heart. "Guess not. Was all this necessary?"

My scalp prickles. "I don't know anything about appliance repair. If you really cared, you could have come home."

He looks as if he's about to say something but changes his mind. Wise decision.

I push away from the table and open the refrigerator. There's so little food in there, it's pathetic. But there is milk, juice, eggs, cream cheese, and half-and-half. I guess Jerry can be thoughtful sometimes. On the counter next to the fridge sits a bag of chips and a container of brownies, proof that he was hungry when he dashed into the store. This Saturday is going to be an expensive day at Wal-Mart.

When dinner is over, Emma stands and clears the table. Without being asked. *Well, wonders never cease.* I put some leftovers into a Pyrex bowl for lunch tomorrow.

The rest of the family gravitates toward opposite ends of the house, and I'm left in the kitchen with no one but Belle to keep me company. The hum of the refrigerator sounds real good as I sponge the sticky Asian sauces off my pine table.

It's been a long, expensive day. I trudge upstairs and find Jerry watching *Everybody Loves Raymond* reruns on TV. As I pass through our bedroom to the bathroom, he laughs. Music to my ears.

I stride into my walk-in closet and exchange my work clothes for a flannel nightgown. It's wonderful to peel away the worries of the day and slip into my comfort zone.

Jerry grins at me as I place my large reading pillow on my side of the bed and settle into its welcoming softness. He flips through the channels, and I read a novel. Neither of us speaks. But aren't most couples like that? Isn't the end of day when folks wind down and relax?

After a while, I lay aside my book and reach for my Bible. I flip through Psalms for nourishment for my weary soul. Some days seem to last forever. While I soak up encouragement, Jerry changes into his pajamas and goes downstairs to let Belle out before tucking her into her kennel for the night.

The clock downstairs chimes the end of the day. I move to the vanity and squeeze some of my night ointment into my eyes, set the alarm, slide under the sheets, and turn out the light.

"I'm meeting Deb for lunch tomorrow," I say.

"That's nice."

"We're going to TeaTime. Do you want me to bring home some scones for you?"

"No. That's okay." Jerry tugs at the blankets, a nightly ritual.

I hang on to my share for dear life. "Night, Jerry."

He mumbles something unintelligible and pats my arm.

My eyes slowly adjust to the dim room. The soft shadows are familiar, and the sound of Jerry's deep breathing is comforting. So why do I feel disquieted?

The bed bobs while my husband rolls over and settles farther into slumber.

I'm a thousand miles away from sleep. My mind wanders, and I recall that loving couple at Abacus. Are they married? How long have they been together? They seemed so tender toward each other.

I remember when Jerry used to kiss me good night. Now all I get is mumbles.

What has happened to our marriage?

3

The security alarm chimes as I push my way through the entry. I always thought having a charming little bell attached to the door would be a more suitable accessory for an English tearoom, but you can't deny the march of technology.

The owner of TeaTime smiles while she delivers lunch to a table of well-dressed young women.

A few of the ladies move their designer handbags to make room for their soup and sandwiches. The early afternoon sun stretches across their laps, bathing them in an ethereal golden splendor. With that amount of bling on their hands, they would shine regardless of the atmospheric conditions. One girl's ring is so large it looks like something that came out of a goodie box at the pediatrician's office.

How *does* she maintain her balance with that thing hanging off her hand? And under the right circumstances, the sparkling gems that rest against their emaciated necks could be blinding.

Now, I'm no slouch, but the contrast between myself and these ladies who lunch is just too apparent. Fortunately the rest of the patrons look like good old regular folks.

I wait while the owner buses a table by the window.

"Hello, sweetie. Are you alone?"

"No, a friend will be joining me."

She nods as if she knew that all along. "Alrighty, then."

I stand aside so the cheerful woman can do her job, then sink into the contemporary teal and brown upholstered chair as soon as she's on her way.

One glance at my plain gold Timex confirms what I suspected—Deb's late as usual. I place my purse on the floor by my chair and take in the scene. On the table next to me sits a glossy magazine. Except for the periodical, the table is empty. No teapot, no purse, no sign of occupancy.

I gaze around to see if maybe the magazine's owner is strolling through the charming café. Perhaps she's checking out the shelves of novelty teapots in the shapes of whimsical farm animals or replicas of stacked books or elaborate cupcakes. But the other patrons are all quietly talking to their companions.

The magazine's bright cover is consumed with the digitally enhanced image of a beautiful Hollywood starlet. I know better than to believe what I see. No one is that gorgeous. It probably took a skilled imaging artist at least thirty minutes to smooth out that complexion and remove the dark circles from those jaded young eyes.

Waiting without reading material is such a waste of time. And that magazine is just screaming to be read. I tarry a moment longer to see if someone is going to exit the restroom and casually turn my head to make sure no one is looking. My furtive glance assures me I'm being ignored, so as fast as a gazelle, I snag the orphaned periodical.

I page through the magazine until a quiz catches my eye: "Do You Have a Passionate Marriage?" Well, let's see.

Okay, question one: "Do you ever slip a note to your spouse telling him that he still gives you butterflies?"

Uh, I don't think so. Do people really do that sort of thing?

Question two: "Do you make your husband his favorite dish?"

This one's easy—yes. Not that lasagna is a snap to make, but it sure puts a delicious grin on my sweetheart's face.

Question three: "Do you often wear clothes that will turn his head?"

No, not unless you count the times when Jerry tucks in the labels that stick out of my neckline after I rush to dress for work. He just hates it when I'm tag challenged or a bra strap escapes its rightful place.

Question four: "Do you kiss your husband spontaneously in public?"

Gracious, no. Jerry would have a heart attack.

Right now I'm one for four, not exactly a glowing indicator of marital bliss.

Question five: "Do you hold your husband's hand while watching television?"

Oh, come on. If you hold hands, how do you eat popcorn or surf the channels?

I have a sinking feeling in the pit of my stomach, and I don't think it has anything to do with being hungry.

Has my marriage lost its passion?

I glance up from the wretched quiz as a car carrying a young couple enters the parking lot and pulls up to the door. The animated young woman, wearing a teal TeaTime shirt, says something, and her companion throws back his head and laughs. She smiles a smug response. I watch with interest as the boy stretches his right arm over and, with obvious affection, tousles her curly brown hair. The girl releases the seat belt, moves closer, and then . . . holy cow. They lock lips like there's no tomorrow. She draws away from him, then playfully leans in again for a follow-up smooch.

"Earth to Linda."

I'm startled from my gawking as my best friend pulls out a chair and joins me. "What are you staring at?"

I smile, raise my eyebrows, and shrug as the young waitress, still glowing from her passionate kiss, cruises by our table. I sigh. "Young love. Wasn't it wonderful?"

"Hey, old love's not so bad either." She settles in her chair, and I can see the wheels in her head turning.

Deb Hinesley is one of those women who is beautiful at any age. When she was younger, she instinctively knew which fads to embrace and which to ignore, incorporating the best fashions of each decade into her wardrobe. Her dark blonde hair displays subtle highlights, and her nails are trimmed to sport length and polished a perfect shade of dusty rose to coordinate with the earth tones she prefers to wear.

Behind her wire-framed Kate Spade glasses, her eyes warm with the slow grin that creeps across her face. I know she's thinking of her husband when I see that Mona Lisa smile. According to Deb, Keith really knows how to treat a woman. On Valentine's Day he told Deb to meet him for a late lunch at The Brown Palace Hotel in Denver. What he didn't tell her was that it would be a long lunch—one that lasted until far into the evening—and he booked the hotel's Tranquility package, complete with chocolate-covered strawberries, a one-hour massage, and rose-petal turndown service. Wow.

"Deb, we're fast approaching fifty. The days of enjoying that kind of passion are long past for us."

She tosses her sweater over the back of her chair. "Maybe not."

"Really? The honeymoon doesn't last forever, you know." At least mine didn't.

The love-struck waitress comes to our table, and we place our order. I watch her as she walks away with a spring in her step. A tinge of jealousy pierces my heart. I remember those heady days of new love when Jerry would rather talk to me than watch football on television.

Debbie draws me back into conversation. "You've got to keep that spark. Otherwise what fun is it?"

"Yeah." I smile, even though my heart is sinking.

A look of concern crosses her face like a cloud obscuring the sun. "You and Jerry aren't having problems, are you?"

"Oh, goodness, no. We're just . . ." *Boring.*

The waitress returns with our tea. She arranges the china on the table, and the fragrant aroma of the fresh-brewing Lady Grey awakens my appetite.

I wrap my hand around the delicate, bone china teacup. "Things are fine between Jerry and me. And it's wonderful knowing I have someone I can always depend on." Despite the fact I can always count on *not* being surprised by a romantic gesture.

A mixture of pity and exasperation is reflected in Debbie's expression. "Really, Linda. You're talking as though you each have one foot in the grave."

We both fall silent for a moment and watch a young mother navigate a large stroller through the tiny restaurant. Yeah, the new mom thing was a cool phase, but I'm longing for what was before that. When it was just the two of us. The first year of our marriage, we went for walks after dinner almost every night and talked and dreamed about our future. I don't want to believe all our dreams are over. Or our romantic times together.

The waitress reappears and places our lunch before us.

Debbie puts her napkin on her lap. "Honey, if you want to keep it hot, you've got to stoke that fire."

I roll my eyes and take a bite of my cheddar cheese sandwich. The explosion of flavor when the coarsely grated sharp cheese mingles with the pungent chutney feeds my soul as much as my stomach.

She stabs the air with her spoon. "Hey, I know. Why don't you get your belly button pierced?"

I laugh at the idea. "Yeah, right. Wouldn't that be a little like putting a new spoiler on my old Taurus?"

Not a terrible suggestion but one a couple of decades removed from reality for me to pull off. And don't make me conjure up the mental image of a belly-button stud getting snagged on control-top panty hose.

Debbie places her ring-laden hands on the table and scoots

forward in her seat. "Remember when you got married? You thought Jerry was your hero, your Prince Charming."

"Yeah. He was." Jerry was the perfect cross between geek and jock—handsome enough to attract me and smart enough to keep my interest. "But that was before we had kids and a mortgage and when life wasn't moving at the speed of light."

Deb helps herself to a spoonful of soup and dabs the corner of her mouth with a napkin. "Get over it. Jerry is still your hero. His armor is just a little rusty."

I smile. She's right. But I wonder if I still have what it takes to put some sparkle in his Prince Charming suit.

● ● ●

I replay my conversation with Deb in my head all afternoon at work. As I'm straightening my desk to leave, the phone rings. I glance at my watch. It's 5:02. Technically, I don't have to answer it.

After four shrill rings, I accept fate. "Hello, Dream Photography. This is Linda. May I help you?"

"Linda, this is Angie Bullock."

It's Bridezilla. "What can I do for you?" As if I haven't jumped through enough hoops for this bride on steroids.

"I thought you were going to call me back before close of business today."

I mash my mechanical pencil down so hard on my notepad that I accidentally break off the lead while I listen to her whine. "Oh, dear. There's been a misunderstanding, Angie. I said when I got an answer on whether we can change the font on the invitation you liked, I would report back to you."

"I find it unacceptable to have to hound you for information, Linda. Aren't you supposed to be helping me?"

Now, am I crazy or is this woman just not getting it? "Of course I'm helping you. And I'll get that information to you as promised.

It's just that I have to receive it first." I amaze myself at how patient and pleasant I can sound when I really want to scream at this spoiled, selfish overgrown Barbie doll.

"Oh. Okay. Call me as soon as you have the information." Wedding princess Barbie's tone of voice changes from petulant to sweetly agreeable quicker than the Colorado weather.

"I sure will, Angie. You have a pleasant evening." Can't she bother her fiancé and leave me alone?

● ● ●

On the way home, I detour to the grocery store. Driving through the lot, I see a giant SUV exit the parking space closest to the door. I cruise in, park, and hustle toward the store in the dimming light of early evening. A display rack next to the carts holds flyers advertising a sale on chicken. Sounds good.

I beeline for the meat department, grab some Tyson breasts, race to produce, snag a bag of salad greens, and head to the checkout.

I hurry home and immediately spot what appears to be a blob of cream cheese on the family room floor. I wonder which one of my lovely children made this mess and just walked away. Why am I the only one who cares what the house looks like?

I grab a butter knife and some wet paper towels and set about cleaning up the caked-on mess. The house is empty, kids gone to various activities, leaving the kitchen a mess as usual. And Jerry isn't home yet.

All is quiet except for the hum of the refrigerator. Late afternoon sunlight falls on the pile of newspapers that clutter the coffee table, illuminating the cover story of the lifestyle section: "Love in Unusual Places."

And then it hits me again. After nearly twenty-five years, the sizzle has fizzled to a whiny hiss as the passion faded from my marriage. The last time Jerry surprised me was when I thought he was out of the house and I came upon him in the basement.

I want something more. The words to an old sixties song flow through my mind: *"Is that all there is?"* I, Linda Revere, want something more. Something like the bodice rippers displayed on the paperback book racks at the local library. Not that I ever read *those* kinds of stories. I want a husband who treats me like a queen in public and a most cherished hot mama behind closed doors. I want my car door opened, and I want flowers for no special reason. I want to feel that my value is far above rubies.

I want romance. *Ha.* Jerry doesn't even know the definition of the word. He's as romantic now as the day I married him, and he wasn't at all romantic when we married. The only time he ever held my hand in public was when I was pregnant and walking on an icy sidewalk.

My heart twists. I love Jer, but the thought of spending the rest of my life, decade after decade, without passion makes me want to lie down and cry.

4

Off with the suit, now smeared at the knee with cream cheese from hastily cleaning my new carpet. I throw on a pair of sweatpants and an old Steven Curtis Chapman T-shirt. *Hmm.* Not exactly the wardrobe of a romance heroine or a love goddess.

I gaze around my bedroom, a gloomy study in vanilla, with ivory walls, a faded bedspread, and nicked and worn twenty-plus-year-old furniture. The dresser is cluttered with credit card receipts, and the top of the chest of drawers holds an assortment of loose change and earrings. No romance here. *Mental note: redecorate bedroom.*

Yes, it is definitely time to mix things up. Make some changes around here. In my mind's eye I can see it now. Me, ten pounds lighter, wearing a flattering Ralph Lauren sheath dress and delicate little Cole Haan sandals as I wait expectantly for my family to come home for dinner. My hair is cut in a fresh style, and I have kickin' high- and lowlights streaking my perfectly coiffed tresses. My wrists are covered with bracelets that jangle a pleasant tune as I put the finishing touches on the dinner table. A perfect roast chicken fills the kitchen with a heavenly aroma, and I light two matching candles that grace my heirloom brass candlesticks in the center of the table.

So all I have to do is lose some weight, buy a new wardrobe, break out the cookbooks, get a new hairstyle, and find some sexy, jangling bracelets. Oh, and I better buy a tablecloth and some candles. *Another mental note: check to see if the treadmill in the basement is still in working order.*

Dinner tonight is an unpretentious affair as usual. Shake 'n Bake chicken, green spinach noodle knots, and a tossed salad. The chicken is baking, the water is ready to boil, and a tossed salad sits on the table waiting for my family. This is the time I usually set aside to check my e-mail and thumb through the snail mail. But fresh from my startling epiphany, I decide to sit in my favorite Victorian antique chair and ponder the reality of my life.

Before I reach my destination, the phone rings. I see from caller ID that it's Debbie. I snag the phone as I head to my chair and shoo the dog out of my seat. "Hi, Deb."

"I was just thinking about our conversation this afternoon."

"Oh?" I loop my arm around the top of the chair and absentmindedly glide my fingers over the grapes and leaves of the beautiful, ornate carved wood.

"Yeah. You seemed a little down. Are you okay?"

"Of course I am. My life is great. Nice home. Good church. Fabulous friends. Okay job. Good kids. Great marriage." If only I were satisfied.

I close my eyes and rest my head against the back of the chair. My heart feels full of love and emotion when I think of Jerry. The salt of the earth. My rock. My knight in rusted armor. But how much more wonderful can our marriage be? Weariness overtakes my limbs.

"Remember when you were first dating, how much you looked forward to seeing him every day?"

My heart skips a beat when I recall the intoxicating thrill of his anticipated arrival. "Yeah, I remember. Sometimes I would watch as he drove up the road to my apartment. The thought of being with him made my pulse race and my eyes sparkle."

"Well, how do you feel about Jerry now?"

A smile warms my face. "I love him with all my heart. Still, I want something more." I fall silent for a moment, wondering if it's too late for us to enjoy a little romance.

Deb's laugh brings me back to the moment. "You know, honey, maybe it's that you want something *still.*"

I recall the loving couple at the Chinese restaurant. Has Jerry ever stroked my arm in public? "I want my pulse to race and my eyes to sparkle again." And my skin to tingle at his touch. "I want to share those feelings with Jerry." There must be a way I can put that sparkle in his eyes again.

"Now you're talking. Put some pizzazz into that marriage of yours."

"Yeah, and just how do I do that?" Jerry will think I've watched one too many chick flicks if I tell him I want to turn back the clock, romantically speaking.

Debbie groans. "You've got to figure that out for yourself."

"Thanks for nothing. He's going to think the chemical cleanser I use to polish my jewelry has finally scrambled what sense I have left."

I hear my friend's husband clamor for dinner and know that she's got to take care of her family.

"Thanks for calling, Deb. Talk to you later." I push the End button and drop the receiver to my lap. My head spins as I try to sort out my emotions. I'm not sure what to do, but I know I better start out with baby steps.

Suddenly the clouds part, the sunbeams shine, and angels sing! Okay, maybe it's not *that* dramatic, but I decide to light the scented candle on the buffet in the foyer.

Wanting to get started on the new and improved me, I go upstairs to brush my hair and apply some lip gloss. I run my fingers from the nape of my neck midway up the back of my head to add some sassiness to my short hairstyle. For about four seconds I consider throwing on my new jeans, but how weird would that be? While finishing my primping, I hear the hum of the garage door opener announce that my love muffin is home from work. My heart beats a little faster as I hurry to greet him.

As I come down the stairs, I see Jerry. He's wearing his favorite faded denim shirt over navy pants. Jer's been blessed with a great metabolism. He rarely exercises, but his five-foot-ten-inch frame has only filled in as opposed to filling out. He's still—and always will be—quite a handsome man. His dark brown hair is slightly mussed, as if he just ran his hand through it.

He blows out the candle and smiles at me. "Where's Emma? She left a candle burning. What's she trying to do? Burn down the house?"

I stifle my sigh. Well, so much for fantasies of a fairy-tale affair. It seems my dreams for romance have been snuffed out right along with the flame of my lovely scented candle.

"She had a meeting at school," I say with a smile. "I lit the candle."

Is it my imagination, or did Jerry give me a double take?

"I thought it would be nice, Jer. Maybe add a little ambience to our evening. And the scent is so pretty." At this point I'm glad I didn't put a tablecloth on the kitchen table. I don't want to scare him witless.

He shakes his head and strolls to the dining room, where he lays his briefcase and extra books on the table that is used only a handful of times a year.

Jerry is a community college science teacher. He spent fifteen years in the world of synthetic chemistry before he decided to chuck it for what he considers a more gratifying career. The corporate rat race wore my poor honey down to a nub. I recall the days he would come home from work all worn-out and at the end of himself because of vicious office politics. He was genuinely happy with his choice to switch careers, which made me happy too.

I walk up to him with the intent of giving him a kiss that will curl his thinning hair. He sees me coming in for the kiss, leans down, and offers me a spot about an inch to the left of his lips, while he continues to flip through the mail I left on the table.

I pause before him with the coyest expression I can muster.

Probably sensing he's being watched, he lowers the bills and stares at me. "Dear? Is there something I can do for you?"

Well, there's a loaded question. A number of smart and playful responses run through my mind. Like, *How about a little one-on-one tutoring for your favorite student?* or *Kiss me, you wild and crazy guy.* Instead I shrug. What do I have to do to get this man's undivided attention? Meet him at the door decked out in plastic wrap?

"I love you, Jerry."

"Love ya too." He drifts past me to the kitchen. "Dinner smells good. When are we eating?"

Now, you've got to love a guy who sincerely thinks Shake 'n Bake chicken is delicious cuisine.

"Dinner should be done in about ten minutes. Emma's at cheerleading practice, and she said she might eat at Lyndsay's house. Why don't you go upstairs and get changed? Slip into something more comfortable."

Jerry gives me a questioning glance and leaves me alone in the kitchen to ponder my next move. So far my dynamic journey toward romance is on a bumpy road. But maybe a quiet dinner for two will jump-start our affair.

I decide on a bold step. I go to the cabinet and take out my little silver salt and pepper shakers, the ones shaped like tiny teapots. I polish them on the bottom of my T-shirt and arrange one at each end of the table. Wanting to go all out, I decide to relight the scented candle. Since Nick won't be coming home for dinner, I put it at his side of the table. That way Jerry won't be able to complain about a possible fire hazard.

I put some kibble in the dog's bowl and toss the spinach knots into the boiling water. A few minutes later I'm draining the noodles when Emma arrives home and Jerry comes downstairs for dinner.

I hear Emma drop her backpack in the foyer. I love my daughter, but her timing is not endearing her to me right now. I'm sure Anthony and Cleopatra never had to cancel a romantic evening on account of a chatty teenage girl coming on the scene.

Her cheeks are still glowing from the fresh air, and she carries with her the scent of a cool spring evening as she enters the kitchen. How lovely she is becoming. Emma takes after her father and is as smart as she is athletic. Her slender figure is the stereotype of the perfect cheerleader. She points to the lit candle. "Cool."

We all sit at the table, clasp hands, and bow our heads while Jerry blesses the food. Silently, I add a little prayer of my own. When the prayer is over, I give his hand a squeeze. He glances at me out of the corner of his eye. Now, even for a romance-challenged man like Jerry, there's no mistaking that something's up. My clues are dropping like lead balloons.

As we eat dinner, Emma chatters about the latest rumor from the world of high school cheerleading. "And the coach is thinking of training Jenny as a flier. Can you believe that? Last summer at camp, she wobbled every time we put her in a liberty. Really, Sara would be a much better choice. And she's *dying* to try. I think Coach Marci is just playing favorites. Everyone knows Jenny always kisses up to—"

"Don't gossip, Emma. It's not becoming."

In true teenage fashion, Emma rolls her eyes and stuffs a forkful of food in her mouth.

Oddly enough, my heart is pounding. I want Jerry to notice the little touches I've added to our dinner. I want him to look across the table at me, above the silver saltshaker shimmering with the reflected glow of the scented candle, and declare his love and his high regard for me, while our daughter yammers on about teenage girl politics.

I realize I'm staring at him, and I don't care. I'm observing the way his temple moves while he chews his chicken, admiring the hard line of his jaw, gazing at his beautiful, full lips. Oh, I love his mouth.

Suddenly Jerry swallows and looks into my eyes. "Are you all right?"

I take a sip of water to cool myself down. "Yes. I'm fine."

Wow. What a stupid answer. I want to say something romantic and clever. It strikes me that I need a plan. A twelve-step program to making your marriage the stuff of dreams—Linda's Adventurous Marriage Experiment, also known as LAME. Okay, maybe all is not lost. Actually, this man doesn't know what's about to hit him.

All I can say is my LAME plan had better work. If not, I might as well take up knitting to keep me warm and busy for the rest of my life.

I decide to sleep on the LAME plan. After taking an early shower, I grab some reading material and crawl into bed to pray about my next course of action. I am totally set. My bedside light burning, my Bible and a novel are spread beside me as I sit like a queen, leaning against my oversize reading pillow. I close my eyes and spend some time in prayer, before letting my mind wander to thoughts of romantic, sunset walks and quiet dinners for two.

I love my mattress. It's a spectacular pillow-top deluxe model, an extravagance I will never regret purchasing. The problem is that it's too comfortable. Since we bought it, I haven't been able to watch an entire movie in bed. Before the DVD is a third of the way through, I'm sawing logs. Jerry always has to tell me the ending in the morning.

Believe it or not—I fall asleep before designing my plan of attack.

My eyes pop open at 5:55 in the morning. Jer must have removed my books, pulled my reading pillow out from behind me, and turned out the light. His breathing is soft and even. Not wanting to disturb him, I quietly slip out of bed, slide my feet into my slippers, and grab my robe. Then I pick up my Bible and head downstairs.

The morning is beginning to dawn, and the soft light of a new day brightens the house. I sit with my coffee in my faithful Victorian chair, what Emma calls my prayer chair. A nice, hot cup of special blend sends wafts of fragrant steam into the air while I bow my head to begin my day's dialogue with my heavenly Father.

I fall silent for a moment, resting in the presence of my Lord before opening my Bible. My spirit blooms like a morning glory opening to the sun as the beautiful words of Psalms wash over me.

After a while, I hear the upstairs shower gush to life. I close my eyes. *Lord, I need Your wisdom to breathe life back into my marriage.*

I pause and wait for a word from God. I hear nothing but feel loving warmth as real as the morning sun that streams through the high windows above my chair.

As I'm putting my Bible on the side table, Emma yells, "Mom, can you make me some scrambled eggs? Please?"

I grab my coffee cup and walk into the kitchen. Some days I feel like the hired help around here.

By the time I have her breakfast on the table, Emma appears. She is dressed, and her hair is wrapped turban-style in a towel. Even before she is seated, she picks up her toast. She plops into her chair, takes a bite, and begins to tell me what's on her mind.

"I'll just die if I'm called on first to give my speech. I wish Mrs. Mason would assign us a day and time. My stomach goes into knots just wondering when it will be my turn." A frown creases her forehead. She turns her attention to her eggs and scoops up a forkful.

"You'll do fine, honey. Besides, it's good to have a little adrenaline pumping. It keeps you on your toes."

She sighs. I know I'm only frustrating her.

I take a different tactic. "Do you have assigned seats in that class?"

Emma shakes her head and grabs her orange juice.

"Sit right in the front of the room."

She stops in midsip. "Are you crazy? Why would I do that? I don't want to draw any attention to myself!"

I help myself to the other half of her rye toast. "Think about it. You say Mrs. Mason is known for picking the most unprepared student. If you were the most unprepared kid, where would you sit?"

Understanding dawns, and her eyes light up. "Thanks, Mom." Rising, she plants a kiss on my head and puts her dish on the counter before running upstairs to dry her hair.

I'm on a little mom high from thinking of such a good plan and actually having my daughter appreciate me. I pour a second cup of coffee and scoop my overcooked oatmeal from the pan into my cereal bowl.

As I'm finishing my breakfast, Nick meanders into the kitchen.

"What are you doing up so early? I thought your first class wasn't until ten thirty."

Nick lives at home while commuting to CU Denver.

"I'm meeting some guys for breakfast at the student union. We need to get together for a class project." He grabs the orange juice out of the fridge, pours himself a large glass, pulls out a chair, and joins me at the table. His hair is tousled, and there is a sheet wrinkle on his left cheek.

I may be prejudiced, but I think he's absolutely beautiful. His strawberry blond hair is just curly enough to add bounce to his hairstyle. The strong line of his jaw is exactly like Jerry's, and his clear complexion has a youthful ruddiness that is both innocent and handsome at the same time.

Emma pounds the steps as she descends the stairs.

"Emma-monster, get the paper for me. Please?" Nick winks at me, knowing that his sister dislikes his childhood nickname for her.

I hear her exaggerated groan, and then the front door slams behind her. A moment later she throws the plastic-wrapped paper to her brother. At least she's not throwing it at his head.

Emma arranges books in her backpack, then hoists it to her shoulder. Outside a horn honks. "That's Sara," she says. "Pray for me, Mom."

"You'll do fine. Love ya."

Nick drains his OJ, reads a few headlines, and goes upstairs for his shower.

By the time I clean the kitchen and pack my lunch, he's out the door too.

I go upstairs. Jerry is still sleeping. He's on his side and has moved to the center of the bed. On a whim, I crawl under the covers and cozy up to him. His eyes remain closed as his hand skims the flannel that covers my hip and comes to rest on my waist. I lean over and kiss his cheek. He gives me a pat on the bottom, stretches, and rolls out of bed.

"What's the hurry?"

He glances at our bedside clock. "You should have come up a little earlier, dear. I have a meeting before class."

Rats. It's not often both kids are out of the house this early. Maybe I should request that everyone post their weekly schedules.

And how horrible would it have been for Jerry to spend just a few minutes cuddling with me before we set out on our day? There was a time when we enjoyed even the briefest of stolen moments together.

I hear Jerry turn on the shower, and I reluctantly roll out of bed for the second time today. I make the bed and go to my closet to decide what to wear to work. The morning looks bleak.

Debbie's words come back to me: *"Honey, if you want to keep it hot, you've got to stoke the fire."*

Jerry usually fixes his breakfast while I'm showering and dressing. I decide to surprise him with his favorite breakfast. Maybe I can redeem the day.

I rush downstairs and brew a fresh pot of coffee and quickly make an egg sandwich. I slide the teak bed tray out from its spot between the refrigerator and the wall, then remove several years' worth of dust and grime from the once lovely, rarely used tray. I assemble his breakfast and hurry upstairs.

He's pulling his socks from the dresser when I arrive in our room. His expression moves from efficient determination to surprise to pure little-boy pleasure. "What's this, Linda?"

"Oh, I had a few extra minutes this morning, and I thought you might like a little breakfast," I say in what I hope sounds like a casual manner.

Jerry kisses my cheek and takes the tray from me. Like a child with a Cracker Jack toy, he struts to the bed and sits down. He sets the tray to the side and puts the paper napkin on his lap. Since he's already wearing his dress pants, I slip into the bathroom and grab a towel. As I place it on his lap, he grabs my hand, pulls me close, and gives me a sweet kiss on the lips.

My, my. My heart does a flip-flop. I think I like this. A burst of hormones surges through my system, and for a moment I feel like I'm twentysomething again. A totally spontaneous kiss—I can't remember the last time we shared one.

6

The drive in to work tries my patience as usual. The drawback to living in a growing community is that you come to truly understand the term *growing pains*. And I have the pleasure of living in Pine Grove, the fastest growing town in Douglas County, Colorado—one of the fastest growing counties in the country.

As I sit at the newest stoplight, I calculate the additional time it will take to get to work. After I pass through this light, I still have a ten-minute slow-and-go ride to the freeway. On top of that, I have to navigate the construction zone at my exit. The tension begins to travel up my spine like the progressive gears on a ten-speed bike. *Give me patience, Lord.*

Just as I move to turn on the radio, my cell phone rings. A glance at the screen tells me it's a call from Jerry. Suddenly my frustrations begin to melt away. The memory of our morning kiss sends sparks of excitement pinging around my stomach.

"Hi, Jer." My pulse accelerates in anticipation of sharing another special moment with him. My day is definitely picking up momentum.

"Linny, I can't find my tennis shoes."

Tennis shoes? That's not romantic. "What?"

"Where are the ones I usually cut the grass in? They're not in my closet."

My mind is still on the delicious kiss we shared forty minutes ago. Doesn't he want to thank me again for his breakfast surprise? "What?"

"I'm taking my class down to the pond today, and I need my tennis shoes."

I give myself a mental shake and sigh in slight frustration. Tennis shoes. Hmm. "Oh, Jer. Didn't you step in dog poop on Saturday when you were mowing the grass?"

"That's right. I left them in the garage. Thanks, hon."

Before I can say another word, he rings off.

A car horn blasts because I didn't move the nanosecond the light turned green. As soon as I navigate the intersection, the car behind me speeds up to pass. As she's cruising by me, the young woman beeps again and gives me an impolite gesture. This day is *definitely* not as promising as I once thought.

I turn on the radio and punch in one of the Christian stations. A favorite song of mine is playing, so I pump up the volume and sing along. Suddenly the air in my car feels lighter, and my poor attitude toward the day dissipates as my attention shifts to the voice of truth.

My exit looms ahead, and I slip into the right lane. Even the delay at the construction zone doesn't faze me, and I find myself wishing that my commute were a little longer today.

Although the sky is clear, the forecast threatens rain. If I don't bring my umbrella in, it will be pouring at quitting time. My hands are full with my purse, lunch box, umbrella, and briefcase. I imagine I look like the Mad Hatter dashing across the parking lot.

The door chime announces my arrival. Luke is at the end of the hall rearranging the portraits in the studio gallery. He glances at me and pointedly looks at his watch.

"Good morning, Luke," I call out with false enthusiasm.

"Morning." He turns back to studying the wall display.

I feel my face burn with embarrassment. I duck into the break room and swipe my card through the electronic time clock. It's

8:53. I realize that I'm not truly late, but my stomach is still in knots from the look of doom my boss just gave me. Why does he do that?

The staff at Dream Photography was optimistic a year ago when confirmed bachelor Luke Vidal *finally* tied the knot. We never dreamed he had it in him. And his wife is just about the sweetest woman ever. We all thought that she would be the catalyst to help Luke evolve into a decent human being. The jury's still out on that verdict, though. I stow my purse in my desk and power up my computer. Several sticky notes flutter around the edge of my monitor like hand-washed laundry hung out to dry. I remove them from left to right and begin to understand the attitude Luke is giving me.

Linda, ask me about this. VIP! is written in his chicken scratch on the bottom of a pink message sheet lying in the middle of my desk. The message is from Carol Ball—or as we refer to her here, Carol *Wrecking* Ball. Carol is one of our particularly needy clients, and it looks like she is demanding Luke call her with wardrobe suggestions for her yearly family portrait.

Her rambunctious family puts fear into our hearts every visit. One time her six-year-old twins poured a can of cola into the lobby toy box while they were waiting for their turn in the studio.

I grab my notebook and the message sheet and approach Luke. "What do you want me to do?" I ask, already knowing his response.

"Take care of her. Tell her I'm in a shoot, but I wanted to get back to her ASAP. Say I asked you to tell her that with the beautiful shade of her children's blond hair, dark tones would look stunning. Just make her happy. And don't give her a reason to call me again."

When Luke's taking pictures, he's the most charismatic man on the planet, able to coach perfect expressions from his clients. Without his camera he quickly becomes a middle-aged curmudgeon.

As a typical high-level creative type, Luke loves images and the endless possibilities he has to create gorgeous scenes. He reminds me of the wizard from Oz; he's the invisible genius behind the camera. Last Christmas I gave him a sign that says, "Nobody Gets in to See the Wizard. Not Nobody. Not No How." He's living up to that motto today.

He turns his attention to one of the portraits leaning against the wall, picks it up, and wanders down the hallway to decide where it should hang.

Knowing I'm dismissed, I head to the office again to tackle the more essential paperwork and check the sales schedule. I have four sales today, which doesn't leave me much time to complete all the tasks Luke assigned me.

Being the first image consultant to clock in, I claim the largest presentation room. After loading the sales images into my computer, I tread back to the front office for my plate of fresh cookies.

The next ninety minutes are spent in the company of Chad and Belinda Husser while they ooh and aah over the images of themselves and their new baby. The pictures are so captivating that they sell themselves. For all my complaining about Luke, I have to give him credit for the dramatic artistic photos he's so well-known for. An easy five hundred dollars later, I'm escorting my new friends to the door and wishing them adieu.

My next sale cancels, so I decide to call Carol Wrecking Ball. I punch in the number and wait.

After five rings a recorded message kicks in. "Hello. This is Dave, Carol, Clark, Cammy, and Corey." Each person shouts his own name. "We're not home right now," says one child. "But," continues a sibling, "if you leave your name and number . . ." Another voice continues, "We'll call you back." In unison, the family says good-bye.

Yuck. Even their answering machine is annoying. I leave a short message and hang up.

My growling stomach signals it's time for lunch. The weather is holding out, so I choose to enjoy some solitude and eat outside.

The professionally landscaped grounds surrounding the studio are spectacular. Each nook and cranny hosts a beautiful background designed to make gorgeous portraits. I slip unnoticed into the employee area. While I eat my tuna sandwich, I surreptitiously watch Luke finish up a shoot with a young family.

The two sons are posing together, and Luke is saying something to make them laugh. The mom and dad are standing off to the side. He puts his arm around his wife and whispers in her ear. She turns and makes eye contact, and they laugh. Something in their shared moment touches me. Luke finishes their session, and the parents walk inside, arm in arm.

I'm left with an unsettled feeling. All the fun moments Jerry and I shared in the past few days have been of my making. Contrived. I want it to be easy. I want give-and-take.

An idea begins to form. If I want to spur my marriage to new heights of satisfaction, then maybe I should let Jerry in on my desires. After all, he's half the equation.

I dial Jer's cell. After listening to his outgoing message, I take the plunge. "Hi, it's me. I was just thinking about you. I love you, Jerry. I feel kind of silly leaving you this message, but I think we need a little excitement in our lives. A little romance maybe. I'm really going to try, and I want you to try as well. Love ya." I pucker up and send a kiss down the line.

I disconnect the call and feel a sense of satisfaction. Let's see what happens next.

Everyone is already home by the time I get in from work. Jerry has water boiling and is heating pasta sauce for dinner. Emma looks up from setting the table and smiles, and Nick is at the counter slicing a loaf of French bread.

Something is not right. I'm usually the one who starts dinner and marshals the troops to help. This beautiful scene of domestic cooperation is quite unsettling. *Has someone replaced my family with pod people?*

Jerry gives me an endearing smile. "Everything's under control here, Linny. Why don't you change before we sit down?"

I stand in the middle of the kitchen like a deer caught in the headlights.

Jerry lays down the spoon he was using and turns from the stove to take my lunch box from my hands. He sets it on the counter and gives me a kiss on the forehead. Emma smiles at us. This is not the usual predinner scene in the Revere household.

In response, I raise my eyebrows and ask, "What's going on?"

Emma pipes up. "Come on, Mom. Can't we help around the house without the third degree?"

What planet have I landed on? I stare at her, shake my head, close one eye, and smirk. That's mom-speak for *You better let me know what's really going on.*

I turn and march upstairs, knowing full well that my daughter received my message loud and clear. If I know Emma, she'll be in my room within two minutes, spilling her guts.

I walk through my room and into the closet at the far end of the bathroom. I emerge wearing my favorite worn jeans and an old flannel shirt of Jerry's to find her sitting on my bed.

"Speak to me."

"I don't know what's going on. Dad came home and set us both to work."

"Why?"

She shrugs. "No special reason. He just said that we take advantage of you, and it's time to start pitching in more."

"Oh, okay." *Hmm.* I think there's something more happening. I decide to let her off the hook, especially since she's pretty much in the dark anyway.

Our family dinner is pleasant. By the time the last mouthful is eaten, Jerry jumps up and starts busing the table. Now I know something's going on.

I give him a questioning look. "Jer?"

He glances at the kids. "I think it's your turn to clear the table and do the dishes."

Nick and Emma exchange glances and reluctantly begin their chore. Interesting.

"It's not too cool this evening. Do you want to go for a walk, Linny?"

"Uh, sure." I need to find out what's going on.

We grab our jackets and exit the front door. The night sky is velvet blue with crisply twinkling stars and a thumbnail moon. We walk in silence for about half a block. The suspense is killing me.

"I guess you got my message, Jerry."

"Uh-huh. What's going on? Are you unhappy?"

I observe Jerry's pained expression and realize he's misunderstood. We stop and face each other, and I see a haunting look

of worry in his eyes. My heart skips a beat, and guilt weighs
me down for causing this wonderful man a moment of concern.
I grab his hand, go on tippy toes, and give him a quick kiss. "I
love you."

He surprises me by drawing me into an embrace. My Jerry?
Showing affection in public? Well, okay. A dark suburban street
isn't really all that public. Especially since we're the only ones out.

His face is so close to my head that his warm breath tickles my
ear. "Linda, I know there has to be something on your mind. You're
not happy about something, or you wouldn't have left that message
on my cell."

"I'm not unhappy."

He releases me and we continue to walk.

"I don't understand. What's the problem then?"

"There's no problem, per se. Remember when we were first married? The excitement of being together, making plans, having fun?"

"They were great times. But we've matured."

"Well, I want to feel that again. I want you to feel that way too.
When you think of us being together, I want your pulse to race and
your eyes to sparkle," I say, trying to make him understand.

"And what makes you think you don't do that for me now?"

My heart melts a little. "Oh, Jerry." He may not have a romantic bone in his body, but every now and then he comes up with a
winner.

He looks at me with hope in his warm, chocolate brown eyes.

We continue to wind our way through our quiet suburban neighborhood. Now that everyone has returned home from work, the
roads are empty of traffic. This walk reminds me of our first year
together. Just the two of us.

Jerry clears his throat, turns to me, and says, "Last week when I
was watching sports on television, I saw some ads for that program
Desperate Housewives. Have you been watching that show?"

"What? No!" For a smart guy, sometimes he can be pretty dense.

Does he view my quest for romance and passion as an act of desperation? "Can't we try to make our lives a little more interesting? We're not dead yet. I still want excitement, something to look forward to, some romance or mystery in my life."

He kicks a stone off the sidewalk and sighs. "I am what I am. I thought that was good enough for you."

"You're more than good enough. I love you."

"Yeah, but you're still not happy."

I'm more frustrated than I was the time I had to untangle Christmas lights. How can I make him understand that this isn't about being unhappy? *Argh.* The male ego is so fragile. This isn't about him; it's about us.

I get an idea. "It's like pie à la mode. A delicious piece of fresh pie is great, but add a little ice cream and it becomes fabulous. I love the fresh pie, but I'm wanting some ice cream now and then too."

Jerry is thoughtfully quiet, in his processing mode. After a few moments of silence he says, "I don't get it. What do you want me to do?"

At least he knows that I want some kind of change. "I want us to have nice moments. I want to delight in little surprises. I want to surprise you. I want to be preoccupied with thoughts of you, and I want you to think of me."

There now, I said it. It's all laid out. *Whew.* How much more elementary can I get? "Will you give it a shot?"

He smiles and shakes his head. "I don't know if this old dog can learn new tricks."

"Jerry?"

He puts his hand on the back of my neck and draws close to my ear. "You know I love you with every fiber of my being." He releases my neck and gives me a swat on the bottom.

Sheesh. I hope he doesn't think this is all about sex.

8

Well, it seems Jerry thought it was all about sex. Not that the earth didn't move last night. It was wonderful and meaningful and blah, blah, blah. All right, I know I sound a little callous. He is *so* thinking like a man! Which most of the time is a good thing.

The good news is that I was able to sleep in this morning. I have a late afternoon sales appointment, so I don't have to go into work until ten o'clock. The house is blissfully still. The living room clock tolls. I lie in bed and count eight bongs.

Time to get up. I roll out of bed and grab my robe. It's Thursday, so I go to the laundry room to start a load of wash. *Hmm.* The hamper is almost empty. *Where's my dirty laundry?*

Out of the corner of my eye, I see the window on my front-loading washer glazed over with condensation. What's this? Someone started the laundry? It had to be Jerry. This is not the work of either of my children.

Maybe starting the laundry is his way of being romantic. Okay, I know it doesn't sound like much, but this man hasn't had any training in the area, and he's entering an unknown zone. I put the wet load in the dryer and set the timer.

While I ponder this unusual situation, I go downstairs to start my day. I boil some water and make some tea. I pull a napkin from the holder on the counter and start to make my way to my prayer chair.

Whoa! What's this? A large sticky note hangs in the middle of the refrigerator door. It's in Jerry's handwriting. The note consists of only two words, written in all caps and underlined: *TAKE HEART*.

Wow. I'm all tingly inside. Pure joy rises from the soles of my feet to the top of my head. Jerry gets it! My heart kicks into double time. I wonder what romantic plan he has in store for me. I'm touched by the sweet simplicity of his note. I love this man. He knows me so well, and he knows this little message will mean so much to me. I can just imagine the look on his face as he wrote the note and put it in a spot where I couldn't miss it. I wish his face were right here with me now—I'd cover it with kisses.

I practically float into the living room and take my morning seat. I put the tea on the side table and raise my hands in praise as I thank my Lord for the wonderful man He has given me. I pray for my man, my marriage, my family. I read my Bible and pray some more. My heart squeezes with emotion. If that's all it took to shake things up, why didn't I do this sooner? I can't wait to tell Deb about this new development.

Oh, boy. Now I have to think of something sweet to do for Jer. I can't concentrate on an empty stomach, so while I daydream about him, I make myself a bowl of hot oatmeal. I bring the cereal and a fresh mug of tea to the table, then snatch the sugar off the counter and open the fridge for the carton of milk.

Good grief. What's that? A large plastic food-storage bag sits on the top shelf. It contains what appears to be a dark, moist piece of meat. I grab the mystery meat for further inspection. I turn the bag around and hold it up to my face. For a moment, my mind goes blank. *Oh no.* I know what this is.

It's a large, raw heart.

It's a large, raw heart that Jerry had intended to take to class. The note wasn't for me after all. It was for him.

Disappointment weighs down my spirit like heavy, spring snow on a young aspen tree. I replace the cold, repugnant heart and grab the milk.

The oatmeal tastes like chalk in my mouth. My tea tastes bitter in my distress. For a moment, I saw a glimmer of hope, a change of attitude. A simple, shining flash of anticipation, now squashed by a half pound of decaying organ meat.

Oh, Jerry. Why can't you be even a little bit romantic? I feel like such a fool. How naive of me to think those decades of behavior could change in a few days. It looks like I'm back to square one.

I go through the motions of getting ready for work, washing lettuce for my pathetic little salad and tossing rice crackers and an apple into my lunch box. *Sigh.* No enthusiasm here.

After a quick shower, I throw on my robe and stroll into my closet. My wardrobe choices are *so* uninspiring. Should I wear my green broomstick skirt with my tan sweater? the brown pants with the striped shirt? *Ugh.* I feel lost. It seems it will all come down to a question of hosiery. I dig in my dresser drawer until I find my new pair of black socks. I pull them on and pad to the closet again.

My day might be starting in the pits, but my feet feel fabulous. I choose the tan pants with a plain black sweater.

On my drive to work I call Debbie. After briefing her on the "take heart" debacle, what does my best friend say? She laughs. Actually, she laughs so hard I even hear a guffaw and a chortle.

"Thanks for the support," I interject between her fits of laughter.

"Don't be angry. Listen to yourself. It really is a funny story."

"Funny for you maybe."

She dissolves into another fit of laughter, and suddenly I'm beginning to feel less the victim.

When I arrive at work, the studio van is pulled up to the back door. Luke is directing people as they unload the next set of props from the van. On the patio sits our dismantled woodland fairy set. Every few weeks we shoot a new theme, complete with a realistic set and wardrobe. The freight engine that is Dream Photography keeps on chugging.

I step around a giant mushroom cap and a molded plastic tree trunk and enter the building. The phone is ringing, so I clock in and grab the receiver. "Dream Photography. This is Linda. May I help you?"

"Linda? Is that you?"

Isn't that what I just said? "Yes, this is Linda."

"Oh, good. This is Carol Ball returning your call."

Carol *Wrecking* Ball. First thing in the morning. I don't think I have enough caffeine in my system for this. I try to pump some enthusiasm into my voice. "Carol, good morning! Thanks for returning my call. Do you have any questions about the message I left you?"

"Well, it was a little vague. I still don't know how to dress my family for our portrait."

My stomach takes a swan dive to my feet. The message advising her on wardrobe was taken verbatim from one of the cheat sheets in our customer service binder. The instructions are elementary enough for anyone to understand. *Grrrgh.*

"Do you have a color theme in mind, Carol?" I smile as I talk into the phone; it's an old telemarketing trick that one of my friends told me about. It's supposed to make your voice sound pleasant. Hope it works because I just want to scream.

"Linda, if I knew what I wanted, I wouldn't be calling you." Carol pauses, and the sound of a deep sigh comes down the line. "I know he's usually busy, but . . ."

I hold my breath, anticipating the rest of her statement.

"Is Luke available?"

Yup. There it is. The question I was dreading. Why do I always get stuck with the high-maintenance clients? "Oh, I'm sorry, Carol. He's shooting a large group session, and he's still in the studio."

Heaven help me, I hate these white lies. What else am I supposed to say? *Luke told me in no uncertain terms that he does not want to speak with you.*

Silence reigns at the other end of the line. Seconds tick by.

Finally I think of an option. "If you have the time, why don't you stop by the studio and look through some of the sample albums. Maybe that will give you an idea."

I hear another deep sigh and imagine her pacing around the expensive elegance of her Cherry Hills Village home. If she doesn't get ahold of herself, she's going to hyperventilate.

"Oh, I guess I could make an appointment to come in. When are you available?"

"Well, you don't need an appointment to look through the studio samples. You can come anytime that's convenient for you."

She sighs again, and I can practically see her roll her eyes in exasperation. "Linda, if I'm coming *all* the way there, I want to be certain there will be *someone* to assist me." As she speaks, her voice gets higher and louder. And my confidence gets smaller and smaller.

"Let me check the schedule, Carol. May I put you on hold?"

"If you must," she snaps.

I step out to the lobby and take a seat behind the reception desk, flip open the sales schedule, and reach for the phone.

Before I can grab the receiver, Luke's voice barks from the intercom, "Linda? Are you there?"

I grab the receiver to prevent the clients in the lobby from hearing Luke at his worst. "Can I help you, Luke?"

"I can't find the business card with the pass code to the storage unit. And what's the combination to the lock?"

"It should be on the corkboard in the workroom." *Figure it out.*

"Yes, it should. But it's not there."

What am I? Your mother? I know he's annoyed with the situation, but it still doesn't help that I'm the one he's taking it out on. As usual. "It's okay. I have a photocopy in my files. I'll get it for you as soon as I finish helping a client."

The static of the intercom is silenced, and I know he's hung up. I move to poke the line-one button and freeze when I see it is not illuminated.

Oh no. I lost Carol!

My nimble fingers fly across the computer keyboard to access our database and get her phone number.

Just as I locate the information I need, a well-dressed business-man enters the studio. "My wife asked me to pick up some pictures."

I smile at his serious face. "I'll be right with you, sir."

Before I can do another thing, he tosses an invoice on the desk. "I'm double parked," he says with authority.

I sense it would be pointless to try to explain that he's number two in line for my assistance. I take the invoice to the storage room in search of his portraits. The name on the invoice is Grace Vecchio. I remember her. She was a delightful woman. How unfortunate that she's married to the impatient grouch in the lobby. I search the alphabetized files where finished orders are placed. There are no Vecchio portraits in the *V* slot.

My stomach turns sour. I rapidly search through the other files. When I get to *N*, I hit pay dirt. I sigh with frustration. How difficult is it to file the portraits correctly? Apparently I have a coworker who is alphabetically challenged.

Prints in hand, I rush back to the lobby and begin to open the gray portrait box so Mr. Double Parked can inspect his prints.

"I don't have time for this. If there's anything wrong, I'll have my wife call."

I barely have time to rebox the portraits before he grabs them and heads out the door without so much as a thank-you. Sometimes this job can be so thankless. Like right now.

Somewhere along the line, Barb, the receptionist, has slipped into the lobby and claimed her desk.

I inch around the back of her chair and close Carol Ball's file on Barb's computer so I can access it on mine. I'm about to go to my desk and give Carol a call when the door chime announces another client. *Oh, crumbs.* It's my ten o'clock sale.

"Hi, guys. I'll be right with you. I just need to turn on my projector." I leave the lobby, and as soon as I turn the corner in the hall, I step up my walk to a slow jog.

The next hour and a half are an anxiety-filled blur. My clients are not on the same page when it comes to ordering their portraits. I guess she is more interested in spending a small fortune than he is. I write up a mediocre sale and thank them for their time.

I barely have time to process their order when I'm informed that my eleven-thirty sale is waiting in the lobby. I load their images, haul the clients into the salesroom, and begin the sales process again. A dull headache is forming, as if I've been wearing a bicycle helmet two sizes too small. *Why isn't it lunchtime yet?*

The Griffins are a handsome couple. They sit on the love seat and hold hands through the slide show. Their sleeping baby lies bundled in an infant carrier at their feet. I can barely remember when life was so simple.

The pictures of Susan during her eighth month of pregnancy are an artistic marvel. She is the epitome of mother love in waiting. Her face absolutely radiates with expectation. The images of Susan and Gary are heartbreakingly gorgeous. The love they share and the desire they apparently have for their expected bundle of joy is awesome.

In one gorgeous image, Gary is standing behind Susan with his hands resting on her bulging tummy. They're both wearing blue jeans and white oxford shirts. Susan's shirt is unbuttoned at the bottom to expose her bare stomach. Her eyes are closed, and her head is tilted upward. Gary's eyes are closed too, and his cheek is resting on her head. The dramatic lighting makes their skin glow with an ivory luster that is a perfect contrast to the black velvet backdrop.

The slide show ends, and Susan wipes a tear away with the back of her hand.

"Wow. Your pictures are beautiful," I say with enthusiasm.

Gary smiles and passes a handkerchief to his wife. "Thank you. We waited a long time for our little Ashley."

Susan leans forward to look at me. "We've been married almost eleven years. And I had always thought I would never be a mother."

"Really," I say. "Lucky you."

"Yes," she says, "we are blessed."

As if on cue, baby Ashley begins to fuss. Susan reaches down to pick her up and continues, "For the longest time I didn't care to have children." She laughs. "Gary is the one who really wanted a baby. We decided to forgo birth control and see what happens."

"Well, this is what happened," I say as I move across the room to get a better look at the baby.

Susan unfolds the pink blanket that wraps Ashley, and I get a look at their beautiful daughter. Her little starfish hand is resting against her temple. Her long, soft blonde hair is styled in a curling Mohawk on the top of her head. She has a beautiful rosy complexion and a healthy-looking, plump body. My breath catches in my throat when I notice she is a Down syndrome child. Her dark blue eyes curiously search my face as I whisper her name.

I reach out and gently touch her tiny foot. *God bless you, little Ashley,* I pray silently.

"Shall we get down to business and start choosing your portraits?" I ask.

We start to go through the process, eliminating the images they aren't interested in. Finally, we are down to their ten favorites and begin to do the side-by-side comparison of similar poses.

"Look at us, Gary," Susan says while staring at an image of them gazing into each other's eyes. She turns to me. "Just before we came for our photo session, we found out Ashley has Down syndrome and a heart defect."

"Oh my."

"We were both devastated. I can't believe how happy we look, especially when I know how heartbroken we were at that moment."

Gary puts his arm around her. "It's amazing what four weeks will do."

"Yes," Susan agrees, "I can't imagine life without her. To us, she's perfect."

I fear I cannot speak around the lump that has formed in my throat. I bat my eyes to keep tears at bay, but unfortunately I'm not successful. I grab a tissue and pat my eyes. I'm sure they don't need a stranger blubbering about their situation. "I'm sorry."

They both smile at me as if this isn't the first time someone has reacted to their story with tears.

"What kept you going?" I ask. "How did you get through those first difficult days?"

"It was all God," Gary says with a smile. "I prayed for this child for years before she was conceived, and I know she is the answer to my prayers."

"She is our special gift," Susan adds.

We continue to work toward selecting their portrait package, and in the quiet of my heart I hear God speak to me about finding joy in all circumstances. I guess that would mean finding the joy within my marriage too.

9

It's another beautiful Colorado spring afternoon, so I decide to eat my lunch outside. Except for the squirrel that watches me from beneath the maple tree, I'm alone on the employee patio.

I pull my chair out of the shade, sit back, close my eyes, and tilt my face to the sun. Its gentle warmth has nearly lulled me to sleep when my cell phone chirps. I check the display. It's Emma. "Hi, Em. What's up?"

"Can I go to Sara's house tonight? I need to work on a history project." Before I can reply, she rushes on, "And can you drive us? Lyndsay's going too."

"Sorry, honey. I'm working until seven. Dad or Lyndsay's mom will have to take you."

I hear a dramatic sigh and imagine her pouty little face.

"Em, remember the discussion we had last week about—"

"Okay, okay. Gotta go. Bye, Mom."

I put my cell in my purse and stretch out my legs. My tummy's not full yet, so I grab a few of my rice crackers and begin to munch.

While I brush cracker tidbits off my pants, I remember the laundry Jerry started earlier. Maybe I *can* teach an old dog new tricks. I relax farther into the chair and dream of my honey. His gesture was so sweet. And surprising.

Oh no! I hope he *sorted* the laundry. What am I thinking? Does Jerry know about the practice of presorting laundry? I didn't even check the water temperature or the cycle he selected. The last load I did was towels. That means I had the washer set on hot water and the sturdy cycle. I hope he didn't wash any sweaters in that load. Was there anything red in the hamper? Could he have also washed Emma's new white cotton hoodie? Why didn't I check more carefully before I tossed the laundry into the dryer? If he ruined any of Emma's clothes, she's going to have a fit.

I feel a nudge in my spirit and know I'm letting my imagination get carried away. Relax. *Okay, Lord. Thank You for setting me straight.* I'll just enjoy Jerry's thoughtfulness.

I close my eyes and enjoy the solitude of the moment. It's too bad that most of the day's warmth is gone by late afternoon. I can't wait until I can sit on our patio at home in the evening with Jerry.

My mind wanders to a romantic summer evening I can share with Jer. Maybe I'll string white Christmas lights around some of the aspen trees that border the patio. I can picture it now—my garden blooming with lush beauty and the lights on the aspens glowing softly like little fairy beams twinkling around the perimeter of my flawlessly engineered setting.

The verdant lawn surrounding the patio will be freshly manicured, its scent competing with the heady aroma of summer blossoms. Thick candles on tall stands will flank a large potted bougainvillea plant, dripping with gorgeous coral petals. The table, decorated with a starched white tablecloth, will hold a vase of flowers, a small candelabra, a scrumptious appetizer, and two china goblets filled with a pale nectar and coated with condensation shimmering in the candlelight.

Music will drift on the evening breeze, something soft and from the seventies. Jerry and I will be relaxed and enjoying the moment. The kids will be out of the house, so we'll be alone with nothing to disturb our intimate moment.

It will be wonderful. But too far away. I don't want to wait that long. I have to devise a romantic moment to enjoy in the near future.

Still trying to brainstorm some romantic inspiration, I collect my belongings and return to work.

One of the best things about this job is that time passes quickly because I'm so busy. This afternoon is no exception. By the time I leave for the day, traffic has loosened up, so I'm flying down the highway.

A thought strikes me. The family's already had dinner. Maybe I can get Jer to join me while I eat leftovers. I'll clear off the dining room table and light some candles, make him a fresh cup of coffee, and the two of us can have some alone time. It's not exactly the corner table at Bistro Vendôme, but it's the best I can do right now.

This just might work. I can't wait to pull it together. Maybe we can even laugh over my "take heart" misunderstanding.

● ● ●

The family room is empty with the television still on when I come into the house. I hear footsteps on the basement stairs, and Jerry appears, carrying two fans.

"What's up, Jer?"

He moves to the front door and deposits the fans on the floor next to our ancient box fan. "Tammy called. She's having a crisis. Steve's out of town. She turned on the dishwasher and drove Emma and Lyndsay to a friend's house. When she returned, she walked into a first-floor flood. The unfortunate part is that their newly refinished basement is getting soaked too."

"Oh no," I groan. "Poor Tammy." It seems as though every time her husband goes out of town there's some sort of dilemma at the Wilson household. "Let me get changed, and I'll help you take the fans across the street."

Jerry shakes his head. "Don't worry about it. I can carry them all. I made BLTs for dinner; yours is in the fridge."

So much for a private dinner with my husband. Hold the candles. Hold the coffee. Hold the tender conversation.

I think about Tammy as I trudge upstairs and slip into my fleece pants and a long-sleeved T-shirt. I know what I can do. I devour my sandwich, standing in the kitchen while I rummage through my refrigerator and freezer. Fortunately everything I need is here. With my surprise in a brown paper sack, I head across the street.

I ring the bell and open the door. "Hello?"

"We're down here," Tammy yells above the hum of the fans.

Bunched-up bath towels are strewn about the kitchen floor. I put my paper sack on the table and go downstairs.

The carpet is pulled back from the corner of the room that sustained the most damage. Five fans circulate air, most aimed at Steve's pride and joy—his fifty-inch, wide-screen LCD HDTV.

In the midst of this chaos stands Tammy. Water stains darken the knees of her olive capris, her white shirt is damp and disheveled, and her shoulder-length hair tosses this way and that at the whim of the electric fans. One glance at her face and I know my friend is holding on to her composure by a thread. I walk up to her and pull her into an embrace.

That's all it takes for her to lose control. The tears start to flow with the force of Niagara. "I-I'm s-s-sorry," she stammers.

"Don't worry about it, Tam."

She draws a deep breath and struggles to contain her emotions. "It's just that every time Steve goes out of town s-something bad happens. Last time, the garage door broke with my car trapped inside. And then another time Lyndsay had an a-a-asthma attack, and I spent the night in the emergency room. Oh, Steve is going to die if the TV's ruined. We haven't even paid it off yet."

I glance at Jer out of the corner of my eye and see that he's uncomfortable with Tammy's waterworks, just as I knew he would be. I give him one of those thank-you-very-much looks for hanging in there. He's quite a guy.

It must have been enough to push him past his discomfort because he says, "Tammy, did you call your insurance agent?"

She wipes her tears with her fingers. "Oh no. I didn't call." Her face registers more alarm.

Jerry puts his hand up to stem her rising hysteria. "Point me in the right direction to find the number, and I'll take care of it for you."

Jerry. My rock. My knight in shining armor. Coming to the rescue again.

We all trudge upstairs, and Tammy hands Jer her worn telephone directory. He plucks the phone from the wall and goes into the living room to make the call.

"What's this?" Tammy asks when she notices the paper sack.

"Oh, I thought you could use a little pick-me-up." I empty the contents: a half gallon of French vanilla ice cream, chocolate syrup, and a can of whipped cream. "Ice cream sundae therapy," I explain.

Taking our seats at the kitchen table, we help ourselves to generous amounts of delicious fat and calories. So much for my desire to lose a few pounds. Sometimes you just need the comfort of, well, comfort food. After a few mouthfuls, I put my hand over Tammy's and pray that God will come into the situation, dry out the television, and provide an adequate insurance check to handle all the details.

"Th-thanks, Linda." Her voice quivers.

"I'm glad I can help."

I take stock of my friend, concerned that she's so shaken by her circumstances. "I think we need to count your blessings." I reach for the tissues that sit on the counter and hand the box to her. "This is not the worst thing that could happen."

She nods and blows her nose. "I know. I'm sorry for being such a baby."

"Stop apologizing. I know you would do the same for me." I

know that's true. When Nick got into a fender bender with my car, Tammy didn't think twice about driving me to the scene of the accident.

She puts an extra helping of whipped cream on her half-empty bowl of ice cream. A girl after my own heart.

"You know, Tam, sometimes I feel like my world is so small. I don't see anything but my own little circumstances. I forget how good I really have it—roof over my head; food on the table; beautiful, healthy family. We just have to remember our blessings."

She relaxes into her chair. "You're right. I know I'm blessed, but I get tunnel vision whenever I have to be the solo parent. I miss Steve terribly when he's gone."

"Well, concentrate on his homecoming. Do you guys do anything special when he comes back from one of his long trips?"

Tammy drops her chin and smiles, and I see a faint blush coloring her face.

I try to stifle a chuckle, but I'm not successful. "Oh, I didn't mean to get too personal."

"Oh, man. I guess I'm a little transparent," Tammy says. "I was just thinking of the kiss we share every time Steve returns."

"That good, huh?"

She sighs like a 1940s movie star. "Steve is the best kisser in the world. Then he hugs me tightly and tells me he loves me."

"Wow, that almost makes his trips bearable." I can only dream of such a romantic moment.

"Yeah, maybe you should send Jerry on the road every now and then, Lin."

We both laugh and enjoy our girlie moment together.

"Did I hear my name?" Jerry asks as he enters the room and hangs the receiver on its wall base.

Tammy hops up and gives him a quick hug. "I was just saying what lifesavers you both are. Steve will be grateful when I tell him what a help you've been."

Jerry smiles. "I'll leave you ladies to finish your ice cream while I go get Em and Lyndsay. Your insurance agent will call you in the morning, Tammy. See you at home, Lin."

We watch Jerry leave the house, and I can't help but wonder what it would be like not to have him home all the time.

"When is Steve back?" I ask.

"Tomorrow night." Tammy is suddenly lost in her own world. She grins again and confides, "I always light a scented candle the night Steve comes home."

"That's nice."

She gives me a pointed look. "In our bedroom."

"Oh!"

"I hope I haven't offended you, Linda."

I laugh. "Hardly. I *have* been married almost twenty-five years, you know." I smile, but somewhere in my heart I feel a void. In all our years, I never lit a scented candle in our bedroom. Jerry's always a little too cautious around candles. Maybe I should work on that.

I rinse out our sundae bowls while Tammy gathers the bath towels on the kitchen floor. She dumps them in her laundry room and walks me to the door.

We share a sisterly hug. "Thanks again, Linda."

"Sure. Call us anytime an appliance decides to malfunction."

Tammy laughs.

"Bye."

As I'm crossing the street, Jerry pulls up with the girls. Emma and Lyndsay exit the car and wave, then run across the street.

"They're going to check out the damage," he says. "Em says she'll be home in a minute."

Nick's working at the computer when we walk in. Jerry goes to his study, and I tell Nick about Tammy's flood.

I put away my ice cream, clean up the kitchen, and make my lunch for tomorrow. "Night, Nicky."

He makes a noncommittal grunt, and I go upstairs. A moment

later, Emma breezes in. She fills me in on the history project she and her girlfriends are doing and skips to her room for the night.

I'm alone with my thoughts, and I must admit I'm a little jealous of Tammy. I know Jerry loves me, but he hardly ever says it. Actually, I don't say it enough either. It's like pulling teeth to get an "I love you" from Jer. The most I can expect is a "love ya." And that's not the same thing.

I remove my makeup and get ready for bed. Before I slide under the sheets, I decide to follow an impulse.

I climb on my footstool to search the top shelf of my closet. *Aha.* There it is. I grasp the candle jar I got in an employee gift exchange last Christmas and place it on my dresser. I open my nightstand drawer and rummage around until I find an old book of matches. With a feeling of accomplishment, I fluff my pillow and grab the novel I'm reading.

About twenty minutes later, Jerry comes in and passes through the bedroom on his way to get ready for bed.

I'm lighting the candle when he reenters the room.

"What's this?"

I smile. "I love you, Jerry."

He glances at the candle. "What's going on?"

I step closer to him. "Tell me you love me."

He looks slightly puzzled and very pleased. I'm surprised when he reaches for my hand. "I love you, Linda."

10

One of the best things about Saturday is that it's cleaning day. My day to run our ancient, monstrous vacuum. Once that baby's humming, I can't hear anything else. It gives me an excuse to gather my thoughts, blissfully uninterrupted by my loving family.

I'm thrilled with the way my romance with Jerry seems to be shaping up. So what if my plan for a romantic dinner with Jerry was washed away with Tammy's flood? The night turned out to be quite interesting. Much, much more interesting than the quiet dinner I was planning. And I think Jerry's getting the idea of what I mean by trying to make our marriage more romantic.

While I push around my vacuum, which I fondly named Betty, I daydream about the wonderful surprise Jerry will have for me. After all, it's his turn.

Whoa. I guess I shouldn't let myself get too carried away, and it will probably be best if I take my expectations down a notch. This *is* Jerry I'm thinking about. Old reliable, never-has-been-romantic Jerry Revere.

On our first anniversary, Jerry came home from work and gave me a red rose. It was stunning in its simplicity and looked so elegant sitting in my crystal bud vase. I fully expected that on our second anniversary I would get two perfect roses, and for our third, three perfect roses. And on and on, getting an additional rose for each year of our marriage. But the reality of it is, we've been married for twenty-four years, and I still get one beautiful red rose to display in my lovely crystal bud vase each anniversary. Well, Jerry's consistent, if nothing else.

My thoughts are disturbed when Nick appears in front of me, holding out the phone. I shut down my vacuum.

"Mom! I've called you three times," he says with attitude.

"Well, excuse me. I couldn't hear," I say with what I hope is enough authority to make him consider his rude tone of voice.

He tosses his head and hands me the phone, then stalks away.

"Hello?"

Silence.

"Hello?"

Suddenly Nick returns, grabs the receiver, and pushes the button to take the call off mute.

Oh. "Hello?"

"Hi, Linda. It's Deb. Did I catch you at a bad time?"

"Not really. I'm just cleaning. What can I do for you?"

"I was wondering if I could borrow your panini maker tomorrow afternoon."

"Sure."

"Randy invited his girlfriend and another couple over to watch the hockey game. This is the first time my son's girlfriend is spending the afternoon with us."

I stifle a chuckle when I hear a tinge of nervousness in Deb's voice. "So are you cleaning your house too?"

"You better believe I am. We've been after him to bring Andrea over so we can get to know her better. Randy doesn't want us to make a big deal out of it, so I thought sandwiches would be casual enough, and panini would be fun. Anyway, the thought of another pizza party gives me indigestion."

"Okay. I'll bring it to church tomorrow."

We end our call, and I turn Betty on again. She roars to life with her usual gusto, and I continue to coax dog hair out of my living room carpet. Doing the cha-cha with Betty is a fabulous workout; it really makes me sweat.

Meanwhile, Jerry's busy rescreening our patio door. I see him going in and out of the garage, retrieving tools from the basement. This is part of his spring ritual. He's so organized and predictable. Gotta love him.

I move on to the dining room and pull all the chairs away from the table. I concentrate on the rhythmic motions of pushing Betty around and wonder if I should change hands to work out both arms. I'm in the cleaning zone and liking it when I feel a hand poke my back and turn to see Emma standing there. I flip the switch on Betty, and she shuts off with a moan.

"Dad wants you in the garage. I'll finish here."

I step into my ratty old tennis shoes that are waiting by the garage door and exit the house. Jerry is sitting in the car and motions me to join him. I open the door and take a seat.

He starts the engine. "Close the door."

I do as he asks and wonder if I'm supposed to be listening for a funny noise or something. To my surprise he puts the car in reverse and pulls into the street. "What are we doing?"

He glances at me with a self-satisfied expression. *Man, he's still so cute.* "Oh, I have a little surprise for you."

"Really?" I'm intrigued. What does he have up his sleeve?

We drive north on the highway through town. As morning slides into noon, a steady stream of cars passes through the business district. Jerry slows and takes a left turn at Main Street.

A moment later he pulls into the parking lot of TeaTime and shuts off the motor. "Well?" He faces me and smirks.

"Well, what? What are we doing here?"

"I'm taking my girl out to lunch at one of her favorite restaurants."

I'm almost too stunned to speak. A surprise lunch date is a very, very sweet idea. Unfortunately right now I look like Albert Einstein on a bad hair day and smell like ripe Limburger cheese. Can he be so dense?

"Jerry?" My voice is a bit too loud, and I've spoken his name in a less-than-loving manner.

He looks utterly baffled. How can he not get this?

"Look at me. Do I look like I'm groomed well enough to eat lunch in public? I'm sweaty and stinky, and I'm wearing cleaning clothes."

"I wanted to surprise you."

"Oh, you surprised me, all right. I am not going into a restaurant looking like this." My emotions are a tangle of surprise and irritation. This would have been such a nice treat if he had kidnapped me when I was in a presentable state.

I glance his way and see him staring at the steering wheel, disappointment etching his features. My heart plummets to the bottom of my empty stomach. I can be so selfish sometimes. "I'm sorry."

He shakes his head. We sit in silence. I wouldn't feel so bad if he would just say something, anything. It would be a relief if he lashed out, telling me I'm a self-centered idiot.

I release my seat belt and move as close to Jerry as our bucket seats will allow. I remember the young couple I spied in this very parking lot that day I had lunch with Deb. Inspiration strikes me. I lean closer, then give him the most passionate kiss I can conjure up.

At first Jerry is too stunned to react, but within seconds he relaxes and enjoys our moment. He flashes me his irresistible grin and says, "Are you premenstrual?"

I burst out laughing. "No, I'm not. I'm vain; that's all."

Jerry starts the car, pulls out of the lot, and crosses the street to a new burger joint in town. We enter the drive-through and place our order.

"Do I get points for trying?" he asks.

"Oh yeah. You sure do." I expect to head south toward our

house, but Jerry pulls off the road into an empty ball field and parks in the dirt lot. We exit the car in silence and take our seats at a weathered picnic table beneath a huge oak tree. The sun shining through the branches creates a beautiful, lacy screen that gently falls on our shoulders.

"Now this is more like it," I say.

We spread our lunch—two cheeseburgers, onion rings, and fries—out before us. I strip the paper wrappers from our straws and insert one in his cola and one in my chocolate shake.

We silently enjoy our picnic. The blue sky is dotted with a few high, puffy, white clouds. Birdsong combined with the hum of traffic provide background music.

Jerry is staring at the ball field. He's still such a handsome man, at least to me. He seems to sense me looking at him, and he glances my way and winks while he chews a mouthful of burger. He swallows and nods toward the bleachers. "Boy, we've spent many afternoons sitting there, haven't we, Lin?"

"Yeah. It seemed like forever, those days when we would follow the kids from one sporting event to another. I thought they would never end."

"They ended too quickly." He smiles his endearing smile, and I can see that he feels as nostalgic as I do for the days when our children were little.

We clear the garbage from the old picnic table and head back to the car.

"Thanks, Jerry."

He leans down so I can give him a kiss.

"There's nothing pressing at home. Do you want to go for a little walk?"

"Sure."

We stroll to the bicycle path that runs behind the park and eventually cuts behind our neighborhood. Jer talks about work, the faculty, and the students. I love listening to him describe his job. I love the way his mind works.

A thought strikes me. *Is this romantic?* I feel so happy to be enjoying this spring day with my husband, but is this the romance I've been looking for? There are no violins swelling sentimental music, and we aren't in a classy setting.

My heart is so full; could this be what I dreamed of?

11

As per our usual Sunday morning routine, I'm pacing the foyer, yelling to Emma to get a move on while Jerry sits in the car, occasionally beeping the horn. Nick smiles his I-guess-I'm-the-best-child smirk and heads out to his own car. For the life of me, I'll never understand why we can't all go to church in one vehicle.

I stop to examine myself in the foyer mirror. Not bad for an old chick. I glance at my watch. "Emma!"

• • •

We pull into the church parking lot with only a few minutes to spare. Once inside, Em takes off for the youth group Sunday school, and Jerry and I take our place in the forties-to-fifties class. We find a seat behind Debbie and Keith, and in greeting, I squeeze her shoulder.

"Hey, guys. Did you remember the panini maker?"

"Yes, of course." I smile. "You ready for company?"

Before we can continue to chat, the class is called to prayer and we begin our study. I open my Bible and settle in. We'll catch up later.

Between Sunday school and the service, Deb and I wander off in search of coffee while the boys go into the sanctuary to save our seats.

"You look great today," I say, taking in her gorgeous outfit straight out of the spring J. Jill catalog. "Especially nice."

She brushes an imaginary piece of lint off her blouse. "Thanks."

Debbie always looks good, but since I've known her, her wardrobe has been an indicator of her moods. The more precise she is in her fashion, the more nervous she actually is. Her freshly cut and colored hair and a new manicure reveal her anxiety about entertaining her son's steady girl.

Deb nods in the direction of Randy and his girlfriend. "Oh, there they are."

"Why are you so anxious?" As if my savvy friend has anything to worry about.

"Randy's really serious about Andrea. She seems pretty nice, but then we've only spoken to her in three-minute snatches."

Randy is a junior at the Colorado School of Mines, and Andrea goes to the community college. I guess you've got to figure there's something going on for him to drive home from Golden each weekend so they can be together.

"They're just so young," Deb says wistfully.

"Young for what?"

"Oh, Keith thinks Randy's found his girl."

"Really?" Now things are getting more interesting.

The bell that calls us to service chimes, and we hurry in to find our seats. I scoot past Jer and sit between him and Emma.

I lose myself in the praise music and sway and clap to the beat as I sing with all my heart. My family always makes me sit in the middle; otherwise I'll be bumping and jostling my unfortunate neighbor. It used to embarrass Em so much. It's mostly for her that I sit with my family buffer around me. If you can't be yourself in church, where can you?

The pastor moves to the lectern and begins his sermon. He's got me for the first five minutes, but then my mind begins to wander to our growing children and speculation about what comes next.

Of course you know your children will leave and marry. It's just that it always seemed so far down the road.

Before I realize it, we're moving down the aisle and out the sanctuary.

Jerry and Keith fall into conversation but are quickly interrupted by Deb. "We've got to get going. Let's move out to the parking lot so I can get the panini maker from Linda's car." Putting on her most determined face, she hikes her purse onto her shoulder and takes off. She's acting like a 260-pound blocker leading a running back to a touchdown as she moves our group through the throng of humanity in the large foyer of our church. *Yikes.*

I try to catch up to Deb, but she's moving double time through the parking lot. "Hey! What's the hurry?"

She glances over her shoulder at me and pauses long enough to look at her watch.

"Debbie?" I dig my keys out of the bottom of my lime green Prada knockoff. "Why are you freaking out?"

She tries to open the trunk, but I've only opened the passenger door. I toss my purse and Bible in the front seat and release the lock on the trunk. I'm seeing the closest thing to a glare as I've seen from Deb in a long time.

She looks at me, and I can see the stress on her face. "I'm sorry, Linda. I'm acting like a child, and I know it."

I reach out and rub her arm. "What gives?"

"Randy is so concerned I'll say something Andrea will misinterpret. You know how sometimes my sense of humor is too much an inside joke."

"He said that to you?" At this point I'm ready to throttle Randy, regardless of the fact that he's nearly twelve inches taller and eighty pounds heavier than me.

"Not in so many words."

The guys catch up to us. "Not in so many words, what?" Keith asks.

I fall silent, knowing better than to insert myself in this line of conversation.

Keith lifts the panini maker from the trunk. "What's wrong?"

Deb stares at her shoes. "You know, I'm a little anxious."

Keith raises his eyebrows. "That's putting it mildly." He turns to me. "Tell her she's got nothing to worry about."

I open my mouth to speak, but Keith continues, "Randy is nervous enough for all of us." He grins. "Me, I'm fine. After all, I'm practically perfect."

We laugh at Keith's self-assessment. Even Deb looks relieved. Keith closes the trunk, and the guys amble toward the Hinesleys' car.

Debbie hangs back with me. "I was talking to Marge last night . . ."

Oh, that's it. In over twenty-three years Keith's mother has never warmed up to Deb. Marge seems to enjoy putting it to her daughter-in-law. She has a real talent for saying just the right thing to make a bank vault feel insecure. And she always manages to deliver her jabs with a smile and a warm inflection.

I ran into her at the lawn-and-garden shop last week, and she said, "You look lovely, dear. I just love that little knockoff Prada *every* time you carry it."

How are you supposed to take a comment like that? Can I help it if I have only a handful of bags in my spring-to-summer repertoire? Was she being kind? Honestly, I think not.

"What did Marge say this time?"

Deb tilts her head and closes her eyes. "She hinted that Andrea might feel uncomfortable having dinner with us. Especially if we're having such a casual dinner on a Sunday afternoon." She smooths out an imaginary wrinkle in her blouse. "Now I'm worried Andrea's going to get the impression we don't think she's important enough for a big Sunday dinner."

"You're thinking too much. She's probably just as nervous as you are."

Deb appears lost in thought for a moment. "I probably should be roasting a chicken. Or barbecuing a steak."

"Deb—"

"Maybe it's not too late to pick something else up at the grocery store."

"Deb—"

"They're not coming to the house for another hour."

"Stop!" My urgent tone puts the brakes on her runaway monologue of thoughts. "You're going to have a nice dinner. Your son is falling in love with a Christian girl. You should be doing the dance of joy instead of the march of death."

Debbie seems to relax a bit. "I think Marge wanted an invite to dinner. I played dumb." She laughs and rolls her eyes. "I don't want to be a Marge to Randy's spouse."

"Good grief. Why would you think that could ever happen?"

"I don't know. Does anyone ever plan on something like that?"

Well, there's a good question. With Marge, maybe yes. "I should hope not. But I know you. And you always do the right thing."

"I try. I'll call you later and give you all the juicy details." Deb walks to her car and jokes with Jerry. She tells him to get lost and let Keith drive her home.

Jer comes toward our car smiling, and I see the young man I fell in love with in his grin.

We sit in the car and wait for Emma to show up. We don't bug her about coming to the car promptly after church because we want to encourage her to spend time with her Christian friends.

Nick waves as he cruises out of the lot. The sun has warmed the interior of the car to a toasty comfort. Jer cracks the window a bit, leans his head on the back of the seat, and closes his eyes.

"What were you and Keith discussing?"

"Wouldn't you like to know."

Uh, yeah. "That's the point of my question." Jerry likes to kid, and sometimes I'm just not in the mood for it.

"Keith's going to help me insulate the water pipes that run between the garage and family room wall. After that last cold snap, I was afraid they would freeze."

"I appreciate the thought. But why don't we just pay a professional to do it?" Jerry, sweetheart that he is, thinks more highly of himself in the home repair department than he should.

"It's not a big problem. Keith and I can do it in fifteen minutes."

Oy, I've heard that before. "So you're going to tear down the drywall in the garage?"

"That's the plan."

I pretend to concentrate on the group of teens that are exiting the building. But really I'm thinking about how much damage these two guys can do and whether it's important enough for me to take a stand in this issue. What's the worst that could happen? As far as worrying about aesthetics, it *is* only the garage. Besides, sometimes guys just like to do grimy, manly things. I decide that I can live with them tearing out the garage wall.

"When is this little job going to get done?" I ask.

"Two weeks from Saturday."

Two of the kids disengage from the group, and I see Randy and his girlfriend. I sit up and take notice. As they move away from their friends, Randy pulls her close and puts his arm around her. I could be wrong, but Andrea looks as nervous as Debbie did. Keith and Randy are going to have their hands full this afternoon.

I silently say a prayer for Deb and Andrea. I pray that God will knit their hearts together in love. They say a woman has two chances to have a wonderful mother-daughter relationship—once as the daughter and once as the mother. The same could be true about mothers- and daughters-in-law.

The church door crashes open, and out come my daughter and her friends. They play off each other like a group of puppies, laughing and jostling as they enjoy a lively discussion. When Em gets to the car, her face is colored with a sweet blush. She waves to some girls and climbs into the backseat.

All is right in my world. I don't have any worries about my children falling in love or breaking their hearts. At least not yet. And not for a while, I hope.

I nudge Jerry. "Wake up. We can drive home now."

Em buckles her seat belt. "Mom, did you see the guy in the navy sweater?"

Yikes.

12

"Good afternoon. Dream Photography. This is Linda. May I help you?"

"Yes, I would like to speak to Luke. This is Carol Ball."

My heart falls to my feet. I should have called her back after the disaster of last Thursday. On any good day, she's a difficult customer. Now that an entire weekend has passed, I have to face the fact that I've turned her into a force to be reckoned with.

I plaster a smile on my face, muster my courage, and try to think of a way to defuse the situation. "Hi, Carol. This is Linda. I—"

"I'm aware to whom I am speaking, but I need someone in authority."

A sweat breaks out on the back of my neck. Somehow I've got to calm Carol Wrecking Ball down before I lose my job.

Let's see how well I can eat dirt. "Carol, I apologize for not getting back to you on Thursday. I know it's no excuse, but things got extremely busy and I just lost track of my schedule. I'm—"

"No, there is no excuse. The customer service I receive from this company is abysmal. I would have been happy to speak with you four days ago but not any longer. I thought that was clear. I need to speak to Luke. *Now.*"

Wow. She must have plenty of practice speaking authoritatively; she does it so well.

"Let me check if he's available." I put the call on hold and pull myself to my feet. My stomach burns and bubbles like an erupting volcano, and my neck could be made of a dry, brittle, about-to-snap bamboo stalk. I go to the lobby and open the big black binder to access Luke's schedule for the day. I glance at my watch—10:50. Luke's ten o'clock shoot should just be wrapping up. I push the button to take Carol off hold. "He's finishing an appointment. Would you like me to have him give you a call?"

"No. I'll wait." Her voice is as cold as a Denver snowstorm and sounds as if it is dripping with the venom of revenge. She's a woman used to people kowtowing to her every whim.

I place the call on hold again and walk on shaking legs to where Luke's finishing his shoot. I hear him laughing and making small talk with a mom while she collects her children. I knock softly on the studio door.

After a moment, the door opens and Luke is standing there with a questioning look on his face.

"May I speak with you a moment?"

He steps aside and lets his client and her children exit. "Come in."

I enter the studio. This section of the large room is divided into two shooting bays. The left side of the area is stark white, with a white floor and back wall. The right side has a black background and black carpeting. The photographic light boxes that illuminate the space cast a gentle light. On any other day the ambience of the room is comforting and welcoming. But right now my stomach knots as though I'm about to step into an interrogation room.

My courage falters, and tears sting my eyes as I try to rein in my emotions. "Carol Ball is on the phone, and she wants to speak with you."

Luke blinks and jerks his head down to stare at the prop box on the floor. I can see the small vein in his neck begin to pop up as it does when he gets angry. "Can't you handle this?"

"She's angry with me. Her call was disconnected last week, and I forgot to call her back."

He shakes his head. "Oh, Linda. Do what you can to appease her. You know she's one of our best clients. She usually spends about four thousand dollars a year. Offer her a discount. Deal with it. If she still fusses, give her my private number." And then he simply brushes past me to his office.

I'm somewhat relieved that he didn't make a big stink out of the situation, but I still have to deal with Carol. I rush to my office and pick up the phone. "Carol, this is Linda. I'm terribly sorry, but Luke's not available. I was able to speak with him briefly, and he wants me to extend his most sincere apology."

"Well, I should think so."

"I take full responsibility for this problem. And—"

"Are you telling me he's not going to speak with me?" she says in her most imperial tone.

"Oh no. Not exactly. First I would like to offer you a complimentary session fee for your family portrait. He definitely wants to speak with you, but he had to go straight to a meeting. He asked me to give you his cell phone number so he can talk to you later."

"After being ignored and forgotten, *this* is all I get?"

My mind starts to work a mile a minute. This woman knows how to get blood from a stone. "I can also offer you a free eight-by-ten for your trouble."

"Fine. Thank you. What's Luke's number?"

I rattle it off and make an appointment for Carol to come in for her image consultation. With me. What a delight. I disconnect the call and search for a tissue. This confrontation has me in tears, and I need to pull myself together.

I only hope I can run to Luke's office before Carol calls and he answers it. I want to give him a heads-up, tell him the unfamiliar number is Carol's so he can let the call go to voice mail.

I sprint toward his office just as a family leaves one of our salesrooms. I'm forced to stop short so I don't step on the toddler zigzagging his way down the hall, much to the delight of Mom,

Grandma, and Grandpa. For a moment little Mr. Wonderful and I do an impromptu dance to see which way we'll go. No one notices my frustration, and they all think it's the most delightful thing they've seen this morning. Apparently they're still on their image-presentation high and think little Mr. Wonderful is the most precious child in the universe.

In the distance I hear the chirp of Luke's cell. Oh, holy mother of hope, I've got to make it to his office before he answers that call. I edge around their little prodigy, turn the corner, and nearly trip over the dad as he tries to navigate a huge and expensive stroller down the hall. Once again I do the two-step to maneuver around my obstacle, bang my hip on the marble side table that holds photo samples, and nearly fall into Luke's office just as he answers his cell.

"This is Luke."

Oh, please. Oh, please. Oh, please. My palms break out in a sweat as I eavesdrop on his conversation.

"Uh-huh. Yes. I see." Luke glances at me.

I turn my back and stand by the door in an effort to appear less obvious.

"Yes, I understand. . . . Okay, I'll have the bookkeeper look into this and get back to you within the next few days."

Oh, joy. He's not on the phone with Carol Wrecking Ball. I will my heart to slow its frantic drumbeat and take a deep breath.

"Linda?"

I ease my way into his office and perch on the edge of a chair. "I handled Carol. I gave her a free session and an eight-by-ten. But she still wants to speak with you. I gave her your cell number."

Luke shrugs. "Okay. Let me warn you though. I may have to throw you to the dogs to appease that woman."

Yeah, of course. That's Luke's usual modus operandi. He'll tell clients that I'm an inch away from termination due to my shoddy behavior. I've heard him do this to other employees. He comes out smelling Clorox fresh while the lowly worker bee gets swatted down like a worthless insect.

"Sure. I understand." *As if.* Could his king-size ego ever consider another person's feelings?

I slink out of his office and into the break room, where I grab my sack lunch, clock out, and flee the studio. Since I'm not in a social mood right now, I avoid the employee picnic table by the aspen grove and go straight to my car.

Inside, the dry heat is soothing, like a warm towel from a heated rack in the four-star hotels Jerry and I stay at on our anniversary weekend each year. I absorb the warmth for a while before I'm forced to open the window on the passenger side of the car.

The trees growing in the concrete islands of the parking lot are beginning to unfurl new spring leaves, and in the distance the drone of a lawn mower proclaims the advent of summer. Cars stop and go with the rhythm of the traffic light. For everyone else, this is an ordinary day. For me, it's another day with one more strike against me.

I truly try to do well at my job. I try to work as if for my Lord. But days like this make me feel like a failure. A failure at doing my job well and a failure at being a Christian. And the lies. All the white lies I tell for Luke. Sometimes I worry that they'll choke me like smoke and vapor from a toxic fire.

I dial Jer for a little comfort.

"Hello, you've reached Jerry Revere. I'm not able to answer the phone. Leave a message, and I'll get back to you as soon as I can."

I hang up without leaving a message. Just as well. Jer must be sick to death of me being so weepy and needy about my job. I sure am. But I wish just once he could be a bit more sympathetic about my emotional needs. It's always by the book for him—black or white, right or wrong. Jer thinks if you add two plus two, then four will undoubtedly be your answer. Too often for me the math doesn't work out. Life is simply not that tidy.

I concentrate on eating my salad and rice crackers. On a day like today a rich, gooey homemade chocolate brownie would surely hit the spot. Instead I polish an apple on my sleeve.

Out of the corner of my eye I see Traci approaching. I wish I could slide down beneath the seat. I *so* don't want to talk to anyone. Except Jerry, but that's not an option. I stare straight ahead and hope she gets the hint.

She doesn't. She smiles and taps on my window.

I do my best to look as though I was startled and lower my window.

"Whatcha doing out here?"

I stifle the urge to roll my eyes and hold up my lunch. "I wanted a little alone time."

Now Traci didn't just fall off the turnip truck. One look at my sorry countenance, and this woman knows something's up. She walks around to the passenger door, then dips her head to the window. "May I?"

Sheesh. What can I do? "Sure, help yourself. But be warned, I'm not in a good mood."

She settles herself into the passenger seat. "Yeah. I figured as much. What's going on?"

I give her the abbreviated version of the Carol Wrecking Ball failure, ending with the fact that I feel lower than low.

"I'm sorry, Linda. Luke always soothes the clients by tossing someone under the bus. It happens to all of us. It must be your turn."

I imagine I look like Wile E. Coyote, with tire tracks running up my back. "I'm not deliberately trying to mess up. He kisses his clients' feet while he tramples over us. I think it makes him feel good in some sick way to see us suffer for our mistakes."

Traci digs in her purse and pulls out some breath mints, offering the canister to me.

"No thank you."

She pops a tiny white tablet into her mouth. "Don't you sometimes wish you were a teenager again, and you could have a pity party with your friends and dish on how horrendous your life is? Remember how much fun it used to be to go to pajama parties and spend the night dissecting everyone else's faults?"

A wave of regret breaks over me. "I never went to a pajama party."

She cocks her head. "Are you kidding?"

"Dad worked nights, and Mother was chronically ill—couldn't be left alone."

Traci looks stricken. "That's a real shame. A real shame. I'm sorry." She squeezes my arm. Traci's a great gal. She tries to be a good friend. "Hey, let's get some of the other girls and go out to dinner soon. What do you think?"

"I'll check my schedule." That's as much as I can promise right now.

"Okay. I'll see what I can work out with Rose and Jill. I'll get back to you after I set it up." With that, she bounds out of my car and strolls into the studio.

I finish munching my crisp apple and say a silent prayer. *Oh, Lord, help me to have an attitude that would please You. Give me the thoughts You want me to have.*

After a moment, my mind wanders to contemplating Jerry. You know, it's my turn to bring on the heat. I love that he tried to surprise me with a lunch date at one of my favorite restaurants. It's especially touching because Jerry really isn't a tea-and-finger-sandwich kind of guy. He's more a ribs-and-baked-potato fellow.

I know. I'll plan a little dinner out to his favorite Pine Grove restaurant. The Gray Pony Inn is the perfect place. It's local, inexpensive, and has the best burgers for miles around. My day is looking brighter. Just thinking about Jer lights a spark deep within my tummy.

The lobby is full when I return, and I go straight to my next sale.

The little girl featured in the portraits is about four years old, with hair the color of a late autumn maple leaf—light brown and amber with natural gold highlights. Her big brown eyes are pools of innocence looking deep within your heart. She's dressed in a brown and cream dress and wears a gold locket. In several of the images, she clutches a small antique doll. This should be an easy sale. Who wouldn't want at least a sixteen-by-twenty portrait and several eight-by-tens and five-by-sevens of these adorable poses?

The presentation music ends. We compare similar images and narrow down the selection to the client's favorite six poses. This child is so stunning that I wouldn't be surprised if Luke chose one of her pictures to display in the lobby gallery. I mention this to my client, another tactic to increase the sale. Make her believe that she's not the only one who thinks her daughter is the most beautiful child in Denver.

I zero in on the close and unexpectedly feel as though I'm hitting a patch of quicksand. I'm slowly sinking, and I see my sales quota in trouble. Is this woman dissembling? Why does it seem as if she's only going through the motions to choose her photos? "What package would work best for you today?"

She stares down at the price sheet like she's cramming for finals. "I don't see any that will work for me."

I join her on the love seat with my own price list in hand. "Don't worry about that. We can always add on to a package."

"They're all too large. My husband will kill me if I spend this much."

Huh? Hello? Do you know where you are, woman? Clients are given a price list at their first introduction to Dream Photography, and Luke allows them to ask any questions about our processes during the photo session. For this lady to play dumb is pure manipulation. I know we have a fabulous reputation, but hopefully only the people who can afford our services and products become clients.

"Perhaps I can buy half a package."

Oh, you've got to be kidding. "Well, unfortunately we have a minimum purchase, and even half a package doesn't meet it."

We sit in uncomfortable silence for a while. She keeps staring at the price list as though she could change the figures by the sheer force of her will.

At our last store meeting, Luke was emphatic when he instructed us to stick to the price list. The days of massaging the packages are over. Period. He said we must have price integrity, no exceptions.

"I had a friend who only purchased four-by-fives of her son's session."

"I'm sure she did, but that must have been before our last price increase. We don't sell individual four-by-fives. It's not cost effective for the studio."

"Can you see what you can do for me?" She smiles pathetically.

I'm beginning to get stress pains in my neck again. "I wish I could. I really do. But I don't have the authority to break down packages."

Suddenly her posture becomes confrontational. "You certainly don't have a can-do attitude. Don't you know the client's always right?"

I clearly see that there won't be anything I can say that will appease her. "Will you excuse me? I'll go see if Luke's available to help us out." The minute I say the words, I know my quest is doomed to failure.

I stick my head in his office, where he is editing his previous shoots. "Luke?"

He glances at me with a vacant expression. I know he's focusing his attention elsewhere.

"My client can't afford a full package. Can I sell her some individual small portraits?"

Well, I have his attention now. "Were you not at our last meeting, Linda? We're sticking to our minimum requirements. Get her to buy a set of eight-by-tens." He turns back to his monitor and continues to view the pictures.

I suck in my breath and return to my salesroom. As clearly as I can, I try to explain her options.

She folds the price list and shoves it into her purse. "I have plenty of friends who come here to have their portraits taken. I've never heard of them having problems like this."

Yeah, that's probably because they come expecting to spend some serious cash. "I'm sorry. I wish I could do something for you."

She gets to her feet, pushes me aside, and walks out of the salesroom in tears.

I crumple to the love seat. I wish I could cry too.

I delete her image presentation from my computer and prepare for my next sale.

Fortunately my last client of the day is an oldie and a goody. She picks out a beautiful family package and chooses a twenty-four-by-thirty portrait with three eight-by-tens and two five-by-sevens. I'm even able to sell her an expensive frame and several sets of wallets. That's more like it.

I'm at my desk finishing my paperwork for the day when Luke's voice barks over the intercom on the phone. "Linda, come talk to me."

This is definitely not my day. I scamper down the hall.

Luke's sitting at his desk amid a sea of papers and folders. The disarray in his office is mind-numbing. He slouches in his chair, looking haggard, with circles under his eyes and his hair unkempt. On some days, his appearance resembles an age-progression illustration used in forensic studies. He starts out well-groomed, but by the end of the day his five o'clock shadow is saying eleven o'clock, his hair sticks up in random tufts across his head, and his bloodshot eyes dart around like he's a crazy man. This is one of those days.

"I just got off the phone with Rebecca Brassard. She's very unhappy." Luke sits back and folds his arms across his chest.

"She wanted to buy half a package. I told you that. I went back to her and explained that would be impossible."

"Well, now she's very upset."

I know it's unprofessional, but I begin to tear up. "What was I supposed to do?"

"I can't have you upsetting my clients like this. I don't think it's what you say so much as how you say it."

"I don't make your rules. I just try to enforce them."

"Well, here's another rule—don't tick off the customers. I was able to salvage the client. I sold her five four-by-fives." He waves his hand dismissively, and I race from the room.

My paperwork isn't finished, but forget it. I clock out and escape for the night.

13

Fortunately the remainder of my workweek passes uneventfully. I'm glad it's Friday, and I'm not on the schedule tomorrow. The Saturday rotation is a bummer, especially in the spring and summer.

The piped-in soundtrack to *Moulin Rouge* lodges in my brain, and I hum along while I pull the next day's client files from the cabinet in the front office. When my stack is complete, I put them in the bin labeled Sales. Rose will be all set for her first appointment in the morning.

I give my desk a cursory glance. My spiral notebook sits on top of a pile of manila folders, all stuff I'll have to deal with first thing Monday morning. I grab my lunch box and leave.

That easygoing, optimistic Friday feeling sinks into my bones. When I get into my car, I plug the earbud into my cell phone and dial Debbie. I can't believe we haven't talked all week. She called me on Tuesday, but I was out with Em and haven't had a chance to call her back.

After three rings, she answers. "Hi, Linda."

"Hey, Deb. Sorry I didn't get back to you sooner."

"Don't worry about it. How was your week?"

"That's a dangerous question. My life is good; my job pretty much stinks. My boss thinks I'm incompetent and lack finesse, I've got a to-do pile on my desk that threatens to swallow me whole, and only two clients hate my guts. Same old, same old."

Deb laughs at my exaggerated distress. She knows me well enough to let me whine.

"I've been dying to ask you—what happened at Sunday's dinner? How did it go with Andrea?"

She sighs dramatically. "I'm so happy. I think *I'm* falling in love with her."

"Really?"

"She's just about perfect for Randy. I love her sense of humor. And she's smart; she plans on transferring to CU Denver to get her BA. She's studying business."

"Oh, that's great."

"You should have seen Randy. He's so sweet to her. I'm very proud of him. But . . ."

"What?"

"They seem so in love."

"Is that a bad thing?"

"No, not bad. Scary. You know, because they're so young."

I can't help myself and laugh. "Come on. How old were we when we fell in love with our guys? Not much older, I can tell you that."

"Who can remember back that far? I felt old at twenty. Well, maybe not old but mature."

"That's probably how they feel."

In my mind's eye I picture Randy at eight, sweet tempered and lanky, wearing a big gap-toothed grin. He was such a neat little boy. And now he's almost all grown-up.

"Yeah, but *we* know how young they truly are. They've got so much life ahead of them and so many responsibilities with school. I just don't know how fast and how far their relationship is going to go."

"Unfortunately it's not up to you."

"I know. Keith tells me to let it go."

"What does he think about it?"

"You know Keith. Not much worries him. Besides, as he tells me, we trust Randy to make wise decisions. We did our best to raise him, and now it's time to step back and let him launch from the nest."

I'm glad for Deb. I guess that's the way life is supposed to go. You fall in love, get married, have babies, spend every waking moment caring and worrying about them, and nearly go broke paying for clothes, braces, sports, pets, video games, summer camp, and finally college tuition. And then you set them free in the world for someone else to enjoy.

"So how did dinner turn out?"

"Great. Thanks for the panini maker. I made Reuben paninis and potato salad. It was perfect. And best of all, Andrea was impressed. I'm so cutting edge in the culinary world, you know."

"I'm glad I could improve your image."

"Any plans for your weekend?"

"Right now I'm headed to Blockbuster for our Friday night video. Jer will make a bowl of popcorn, and if the kids are around, they'll join us. Quite honestly, I'm hoping Jer and I can be alone."

"Still adding sizzle to the old marriage?"

"We're not exactly sizzling yet, but I'm trying. And tomorrow we're going to dinner at the Gray Pony Inn. Well, three of us are going to dinner. Nick has plans to spend the weekend visiting friends who go to UNC." I merge into the right lane as I near the strip mall by my house. "Gotta go, Deb. I'm almost at Blockbuster."

I pull into the shopping center. The parking lot is a madhouse. It seems as though all of Pine Grove has decided to go to this video store for their weekend movie rental.

I practice my patience while I wait for a parking space and squeeze my Taurus between a Hummer and an Expedition. I cautiously open my door so I don't ding the steel monstrosity next to me. Some people are so ridiculous. A Hummer. Really? It's not like we're on the Serengeti and we need an all-terrain vehicle to chase down a herd of wildebeests as they gallop across the plains. *Hello. We live in civilization here, people.*

I enter the store and start perusing the DVDs. Jer requested *Troy*. It might be nice to see Brad Pitt and Orlando Bloom wearing tunics and showing off a little beefcake, but I think something with a little more romance is what's needed at my house. Maybe I'll choose a classic love story or a newer release. I finish walking the perimeter of the store and cruise the center aisles, ending up with two choices, *The Notebook* and *Ghost*. I figure my selections have a little something for both of us. After all, *The Notebook* features a macho off-to-war guy, and *Ghost* has the good guy/bad guy conflict for Jerry, while they both have a love story for me. Or should I say, for Jerry's encouragement. This is going to be perfect. I may even have to have a box of tissues on hand for the finale.

I maneuver out of the parking lot and enter my neighborhood. I'm surprised to be following Jerry's car down our street. He must have stopped to get a pizza for dinner. With our kids' schedules, you never know who will dine with us on Friday night. Sometimes it's no kids, and sometimes it's five kids.

Emma greets us at the garage door, and the sound of laughter bubbles from within my house. I see that she's set the paper plates and napkins on the kitchen table, and her friends Lyndsay and Hillary are helping themselves to some bottled soda.

Jerry delivers the pizza to the table, and we go upstairs to change. I put on my standby fleece pants, and Jer changes into his favorite worn jeans. By the time we come back down, half a pie is gone. The girls are engrossed in conversation about boys and cute clothes, and I see a new spark in Emma's bright eyes.

"What's the plan for tonight, girls?"

Lyndsay, who is nearly a fixture at our house, speaks up. "My mom says she'll drive us to Sara's house if you can pick us up later."

I look to Jerry for direction. He nods. "Sure, we can do that. What's happening at Sara's?"

The girls all dissolve in laughter.

Oh, this might not be good. Something's up. "Em?"

"We're just going to hang out. Maybe play some video games."

The girls erupt in laughter.

Now I know something's up. "Okay, what's going on?"

Emma, whose face is glowing red, fesses up. "Well, Sara's brother is going to be home with some of his friends."

I know that Sara has a twin brother, but I haven't heard much about him. "And?"

Hillary says, "His friend Ryan has a crush on Emma."

The girls start to giggle again.

I gaze at my daughter and realize the feeling is reciprocated. *Oy. Am I ready for this?* "Have we met Ryan?" I search my memory, and the various faces of pubescent boys parade before me like trailers before a feature film. Ryan doesn't register.

"He's a new guy at school. His family visited our church last Sunday."

Oh, now it's beginning to make sense. *The guy in the navy sweater.*

The girls finish inhaling their pizza and run upstairs to prepare for their big night. About twenty minutes later, they're primped and polished and heading out the door.

Jerry is reading his e-mail, and I clean up the kitchen. He signs off the computer and turns to me. "What videos did you get? Was *Troy* available?"

"Well . . ." I offer what I hope is a seductive and mysterious smile. Kind of like *Mona Lisa* meets *Venus on the Half Shell.*

If Jer notices, he doesn't give any indication. He launches himself out of the desk chair and starts to assemble the pans to make popcorn and melt the butter. "Okay, what did you get?"

I move over to the coffee table, grab the two DVDs, and hold them out like a treasured prize.

He reads the titles and gives a noncommittal shrug. Not exactly the enthusiasm I was hoping for, but I'll take what I can get. At least he isn't deserting me for a good book.

I decide to pop *The Notebook* into the DVD player, mostly because *Ghost* makes me cry so hard that I fear I may lose my romantic appeal. I push Play.

In a moment, Jer is on the couch next to me with his huge pop-corn bowl and a glass of cola.

We watch the first twenty minutes and begin to warm up to the romance when I have a brilliant idea. "Let's finish watching this in bed, Jer."

"Sure." He puts his bowl and empty glass in the kitchen and joins me upstairs. Since Jerry has to pick up the girls at eleven, he pulls on a pair of sweatpants, but I get in my nightgown. We set up our reading pillows, dim the lights, and get comfy.

Allie is so beautiful, and Noah is so handsome! If only her mother didn't keep them apart, then true love would prevail. If only her mother passed on the love letters. Oh, love letters—how romantic. I stifle a yawn and pull the blankets higher on my shoulders.

The sound of Jer getting out of bed and grabbing his keys off the dresser stirs my consciousness. *Rats.* I've fallen asleep. I've got to wake myself up by the time he gets back home. I want to . . . I pry my eyes open and see the sunlight filtering through our cellular shades. Oh, good grief. I slept all night. And I had such hopes for a little romance. A perfect night alone, just the two of us. I wanted to tell Jerry how the movie made me feel. I wanted to discuss the magic of written words of love. I wanted to talk about a love that could endure separation and loneliness. About how a woman wants a strong, romantic man to rock her world. And I had hoped that he would get the hint and say (*and do*) something to rock mine. *Phllbt!* And phooey. Another missed opportunity.

Little Belle starts to whine. I get up and head downstairs to start my day. The morning light always appeals to me, so I go around the house opening the shades.

Five minutes later Belle is fed, and I'm settling into my prayer chair with my Bible and a cup of tea. Disappointment dims the brightness of the new day. Sadness weighs my heart. I wanted to have a sweet, romantic moment with Jerry last night. Oh, well. As Scarlett would say, "There's always tomorrow" or some other kind of optimistic drivel.

I open my Bible to Song of Solomon, and my gaze falls on a line: *"Do not arouse or awaken love until it so desires."*

Maybe Jerry's not ready yet. Although one would think nearly twenty-five years of marriage would be fabulous preparation for romance. Or maybe I should do a little special preparation myself.

I sit in my chair a while longer, just thinking. When Emma gets up, she's delighted by my suggestion that we spend the morning at the mall. I promise Emma something for herself and enlist her help in finding me a new outfit. I'm stunned at how quickly she showers and dresses. We're out the door by nine forty-five, a small miracle.

● ● ●

Although there aren't many mall patrons at this early hour, Starbucks has a line out the door. We queue up and wait our turn for drinks and pastry. I pay the exorbitant price, and we take our breakfast to one of the tables in the dining area. My frothy cappuccino may not be the best thing for me, but the rich, creamy beverage satisfies my craving like nobody's business.

"Em? What happened last night? Did Sara's brother bring his friends over?"

She dips her head. I can barely read her face through the veil of bangs, but her hundred-watt smile tells me what I need to know. "Yeah." She takes a bite of her muffin.

Is this going to be like pulling teeth? "Was Ryan with them?"

"Uh-huh."

I follow her example and take a bite of my pastry. The amount of fat and calories I'm consuming is a little frightening. Some role model I am, sugar and caffeine for breakfast. I shudder to think of what Grandma would say.

Emma is so beautiful and innocent. And I'm determined to help her stay that way. I need to know what's going on with my daughter. "Tell me about Ryan."

She takes a timid sip of her hot beverage. "He's so mature and smart. He gets good grades." She taps her finger on the lid of her mocha.

It's obvious she has a crush on him. "Does he like you, Emma?"

"Mo-om."

Oh, my sweet girl. Are you guarding your heart? "Does he know you like him?"

Her face flushes. "I don't know."

"You weren't alone together, were you?"

She looks at me as though I asked her if the sky were green— a response that pleases me.

"Good. Remember what we talked about. Going slow. Getting to know a boy as a friend."

Emma glances around us. The food court is filling up.

I pat her hand. "Don't worry. I won't embarrass you."

We toss our empty paper cups and napkins into the trash and stroll through the mall. We have such a cool mall—or rather as their marketing department claims, a retail resort.

Emma leads me down the escalator. Her pace increases, and I see a spark of excitement in her eyes. I'm pleasantly surprised when she takes my hand. It's been so long since she's done that. She tugs me along and right through the door of our new Coach store. *I don't think so.*

The sales associate looks eager. This can't be good.

"Isn't this bag cool?" Em picks up a patchwork leather purse and strokes the side as though it's a genie's bottle.

"Yes, it's very nice." *And very expensive, I'm sure.* I flip over the price tag. *Wow, $198!* I try to act nonchalant as I look over the other bags in the store. After all, I don't want to make us look foolish by dragging her out. When what I deem a reasonable amount of browsing time has passed, I put my arm around her waist and direct her out to the walkway.

"What do you think?" she asks with an innocent optimism.

"It's lovely."

"That's what I want today, Mom."

I laugh at her naiveté. "Sorry, hon. When I said we'd get you a treat, I was thinking of something a fraction of that price. That's too much money to spend on one item. Besides, you love to change your bag to match your outfit. If you spent that much on one bag, you'd feel obligated to use it more often. And then it would wear out or you'd get bored with it." I hope she sees my logic.

She rolls her eyes, not swayed by my argument. "Didn't you see all the colors and patterns in that bag? It's versatile."

Hmm. It sounds like she learned a new vocabulary word. That's good. But still, I'm not convinced. "Why don't you save your money and buy it then."

She tosses her hair and slumps her shoulders. "What about for my birthday? I'll be turning sixteen."

I loop my arm through hers and give her that age-old answer of mothers everywhere, "I'll talk to your dad and think it over."

She starts a pout but is distracted by a shirt in the window of Express.

Twenty minutes later and one purchase down, we're walking the mall again. I go straight to Macy's, my old favorite. The minute we cross the threshold I see it. *Be still my heart.* On a display mannequin is one of the coolest outfits I've found in nearly thirty years—a filmy, green and tan broomstick skirt, topped with a gauzy tan tunic. *Wow!* An outfit straight from the seventies. There are even sequins randomly sewn into the bottom of the skirt.

"I used to have an outfit just like this when I was dating your dad."

Emma reaches for the skirt and examines the pattern. Her brow wrinkles in concentration, and she takes the tunic off the rack and holds it up.

Emma is my fashion consultant, a position she's held since she was in kindergarten and gave me her first piece of fashion advice. I was considering a pair of gold tennis shoes. Okay, at the time they were *in*—it was the nineties. She looked at me with shock in her eyes and said, "Sure, buy those shoes. Then everyone will know you're a dork." I kid you not—a fashionista at the age of five. Fortunately for me, her tact has improved with age. Oh, and I didn't buy the shoes.

"What do you think?" I ask Emma.

"This is cute, but you'll have to wear a camisole under this top."

"That's okay. I have one."

We go to the dressing room, and I try it on. I step out to view myself in the three-way mirror and feel as though I'm stepping back in time. If only my hair were long again. I love it. I turn around to view all sides. I'm sold.

I purchase my outfit, and we go into another store for Em to look for a denim skirt. I'm feeling generous after my shopping coup. While she paws through the rack, under my breath I start to sing along to the store music. "'Baby, come back. . . .'" Oh, goodness. It's a song from the seventies. I take that as a sign that I've made the right purchase. I can't wait for Jerry to see me tonight.

She finds the cutest little denim skirt I've seen in ages.

"I used to have one like that. In the seventies."

Emma rolls her eyes.

Poor thing, her mom is such a dork.

14

Em turns on the radio the moment I start the car and begins punching buttons. I try not to sigh and select another station. Oldies, of course. I enjoy the walk down memory lane with songs from my not-so-wild youth. As we're entering our town limits, the song "Downtown" comes on the radio, and I pump up the volume. I sing the words to the verses, and Em joins whenever the word *downtown* is belted out. We make quite a pair.

The song is nearly over when I pull into the little market near our house.

Emma raises her eyebrows.

"I need to drop off my prescription."

She's not too happy with the detour, so I make an effort to hurry through the throng of Saturday morning shoppers. My stomach is beginning to protest our scanty breakfast, and I know it's just a matter of minutes before Emma starts to beg for fast food. To head her off, I buy a small rotisserie chicken and pasta salad from the deli department.

• • •

Jerry's cutting the lawn when we arrive home. The air has the sweet fragrance of spring, and I open the kitchen window and set the table for lunch. By the time I'm pouring iced tea into glasses, Jer comes in through the garage. He looks irresistible, with his wind-tossed hair and old, faded jeans, as he steps out of his grass-stained tennis shoes and washes his hands at the kitchen sink.

"Are we still on for our date tonight?"

He stares at me with an innocent blank expression. "Date?"

"Dinner. At the Gray Pony Inn. Remember?"

I can see the pieces fall into place in his memory. "Oh yeah."

Not quite the enthusiasm I would hope for. *Is he forgetting our little talk so quickly?* He knows how important it is to me to spice up our life.

"Em! Nick! Lunch is on the table."

Jerry and I take our seats and within minutes are joined by our progeny. Nick looks half-asleep, and Emma comes to the table talking on the cordless phone. We all sit for a moment while Jerry gives her the look. She gets the hint and quickly ends her conversation.

I take my time chewing a mouthful of chicken before I throw out any obstacles to my big night. "Nick, are you still planning on going to UNC tonight?"

"Uh-huh. I'll probably leave for Greeley around four."

I glance at Emma. She's biting her lower lip. *What now?* "Em?"

She shifts nervously. "Would you be angry if I went to Lyndsay's house tonight instead of going to dinner with you?"

Be angry? Actually I'm thrilled. It will be like a real date with just Jerry and me. "Why, no, I—"

Jer puts down his fork. "Well, I'll be disappointed, Emma. I had planned on having dinner with both of my girls tonight."

Oh, I could just kick him!

Emma looks at her pasta salad, disappointment etching her features. "Sorry, Dad. I guess I could go to Lyndsay's after dinner."

Oh no. "I think we can let her go to her friend's house. Is there something special going on at Lyndsay's?" *I hope. I hope.*

"She's having a sleepover with a few other girls."

I nod my approval. "That sounds like fun, honey." I look to Jerry for his reaction.

He smiles. "That's okay, Em. Go and have fun."

Whew! Dodged that bullet. I can't wait for this evening. A date with my honey. And me wearing my new outfit from the seventies. Maybe I'll even splash on some fragrance.

We finish lunch, and I clean up the kitchen and put Emma in charge of vacuuming the downstairs. Jerry is finished with his Saturday chores, so he heads outside to the patio to sit in the chaise lounge and read a book.

Our shopping list hanging under the magnet on the fridge is a mess of scribbles. I retrieve it and start to rewrite the list according to the layout of the grocery store. "Anyone want anything from the store?" I quickly write down the items Nick and Emma request and stick my head out the door. "Jer? Want anything from Wal-Mart?"

He looks up with a bewildered expression, and I know I've interrupted him in a good part of his book. "What?"

"Wal-Mart. Want anything?"

"Razor blades, please." He escapes back into his fiction.

Okay, enjoy your peaceful afternoon, buster. Because tonight I hope to rock your world. My thoughts are so focused on romance that it doesn't even bother me that I have to do the grocery shopping, a task I have loathed for more than two decades.

● ● ●

Saturday afternoon has got to be the worst time to go grocery shopping. All the early bird eager beavers have come and gone, and you're left to rub elbows—or should I say shopping carts—with the less motivated shoppers. When I'm shopping, I want to get what I need and get out of the store. Hopefully in less than forty minutes.

As usual, the woman with the crying baby is following me through the store. I try to dash down a wide aisle to escape her, but my plan is thwarted by a young family deep in negotiation about what type of cookies they should choose from the end cap. Then I discover the candles on the bottom of my list are clear across the store. I put on my game face and tear through Wal-Mart like a triathlete nearing the finish line.

Finally my list is exhausted, and I approach the cash registers to jockey for position. Another grueling ten minutes in line and through the checkout and I'm free. I dodge the cars cruising through the parking lot, load up my Taurus, and head down the road.

One more stop and then I'm finished. I pull into the market by my house and sprint to the pharmacy department in the back. I wait my turn and pick up my thyroid medication.

By the time I pull into the garage, it's nearly three o'clock. My crew helps me unload the car and put away my purchases.

I'm moving to my own soundtrack, the seventies, visualizing my date. I want everything to be perfect. I rummage through my bathroom vanity to find just the right shade of nail polish. I think this evening calls for a fresh pedicure. I select three different shades of polish and line them up on the counter to decide which to wear. Chick Flick Cherry, Dancing in the Isles, and I'm Not Really a Waitress are some of my favorites. I love the names of OPI nail polish. I wish I could have a job making up exotic and whimsical names like that. Some of my creations would be something like Who Doesn't Love Chocolate? or Clinging in the Rain.

I trim the price tags off my new clothes. The tunic is a little wrinkled, so I fire up the iron and wait for it to heat. In the meantime, I wash off my makeup. I return to the ironing board and carefully press the creases out of the soft, gauzy fabric and put the garment on a hanger.

After a quick look in the bathroom vanity, I come up with some scented body wash and matching lotion. I love this fragrance, and what's even better, Jerry will love it too. The spicy smells of patchouli and jasmine tease my senses.

A moment later I'm luxuriating in a hot shower with my scented potions. I towel off, slather on some delicious scented lotion, and throw on an old sundress. I consider my nail polish options again and choose Dancing in the Isles. I leave my wet hair wrapped turban-style in my towel and head out to the patio for a quick pedicure.

Jerry's asleep in the lounge chair. The tinkle of our small water fountain is music to my ears until the AC unit on the side of the house fires up. Jer twitches at the interruption yet continues to nap.

I pull a chair into the shade and begin my primping. A layer of undercoat, a layer of polish, wait a moment, another layer of polish, and a layer of top coat. Beautiful. I extend my legs and admire my stylish toes. I only hope Jerry appreciates all my preparations for tonight's date.

Fearful that my hair will dry looking like Rod Stewart's, I rush upstairs to blow it out into something that resembles a style.

I'm applying fresh makeup when Jerry comes into the bathroom. He glances at the new skirt and top hanging on my closet door. I try to act nonchalant, as if my heart isn't beating like a teenager's on her first date. I have such hopes for our evening. Time alone, no distractions. Soft music, candlelight, delicious food, and one another.

"Do I need to shower?"

Jer's question brings me back to the moment. "Excuse me?"

"Do you want me to shower?"

Duh, yeah. "Well, you were doing some yard work. So, yes. Shower, please."

He shrugs and turns on the water.

While Jerry showers, I go to my closet and get changed. *Cool.* Someone might even mistake me for a sexy mama. Hopefully, it will be Jerry. I love my new tunic and skirt. I hop on my closet stool and snag my green Prada knockoff purse from the shelf. It will look perfect with one of the shades of green in the skirt. I'm standing in my closet trying to decide between gold sandals and black ones when I hear a knock at the bedroom door.

"Mom, I'm going over to Lyndsay's now."

I open the door, and Emma presses her lips together as she gives me the once-over. "Wow, you look beautiful."

I can hardly believe my ears. A compliment from my daughter. And a sincere one at that. "Thanks. What sandals do you think I should wear?" I hold up one of each.

Emma takes the sandals from me. Holding them at arm's length, she squints and cocks her head in her adorable, fashionista way. "Gold, definitely."

"Thanks, sweetie. Have fun at Lyndsay's."

She trots down the stairs without a care in the world. Life is good.

Oh, Jerry and I are going to have a perfect date.

15

While Jer finishes dressing, I feed Belle and quickly run upstairs with the candle I bought earlier. I hear him in his closet, whistling a jingle to a commercial for a local auto dealership.

You'll be whistling another tune when I'm finished with you tonight, sweetheart. I set the candle on my chest of drawers and drop a book of matches into the top drawer. I want to be all ready when the time is right.

I smell the fragrance of his Polo cologne before he is beside me. This man is simply delicious. He's wearing a pair of black jeans and a lightweight, blue Eddie Bauer pullover. He looks great.

"Ready?"

I make a deliberate effort to smile seductively. "Uh-huh."

He stares at me for a moment longer than usual, and I know he's figured out what I'm up to. We walk side by side down the stairs, and if I'm not imagining things, he just brushed his hand across my backside. I try to catch his eye, but he stares straight ahead, struggling as though he's trying to suppress a smile.

Oh, goody. He's playing along with me. Date night, here we come.

● ● ●

Jerry and I park around the corner from the Gray Pony Inn in the now-empty parking lot for Main Street Realty. The sun has nearly slipped below the spine of the Rocky Mountains, and the clouds above us are a splendor of pink and orange and gold.

As we enter the small steakhouse and pause at the hostess podium, the aromas of grilled beef and fries greet us. Within a moment, we're being led to a cozy booth. Perfect.

Our dinner date is wonderful. The restaurant isn't a romantic spot, but we're more than comfortable in its familiar Old West–style setting. The background noise of heels clacking over the rough plank wood floors and people enjoying their Saturday night dinner shelters us within our own little world.

I order my usual, the naked burger with blue cheese and fries. Jerry gets some beef fajitas. I share my fries with him, and he gives me a bite of his fajita. It kind of reminds me of sharing cake at our wedding reception—such an intimate gesture.

Despite the noises and the crowd surrounding us, we're alone together. Finally, we're focusing on us. I lean against the padded wooden seat and can't help but smile. It's as though we've traveled back in time when it was just the two of us. And I feel so cute and stylish in my new clothes. Our dinner conversation and his intense concentration on me warm the pit of my stomach. I feel so very loved, so cherished. My mind wanders to what might become of our evening. A quiet house, candlelight . . .

Jerry brushes his fingers over my hand. *Nice.* "A penny for your thoughts, Lin."

That just makes my grin wider. "I don't think you have enough pocket change to purchase the thoughts I'm having," I say with a come-on shrug.

He's beginning to look more interested. "Do you want to skip dessert?"

Oh no, bucko. I want to enjoy this moment a while longer. "Why don't we split a hot fudge brownie sundae?"

He smiles and nods.

A couple hundred calories later, we're on our way. During the drive home, Jer turns on the radio and we listen to the seventies station. *"How sweet it is to be loved by you. . . ."* *Yeah, sing it out, James baby.* This night is such a gift. Finally everything is going the way I've imagined it would. A perfect ten.

When we enter the house, I start for the kitchen to put away our leftovers, and Jerry goes into the study to check the answering machine. I'm nearly knocked over by Belle, who comes tearing down the stairs and breezes past me toward the kitchen. What's up with that crazy dog? Instead of going into the kitchen to beg as usual, she zips around the corner to the dining room, through the living room and foyer, and comes racing down the hall to the kitchen again. This time she heads for the back door and pounces on it with all her twentysomething pounds. She bounces off the door and looks up to me.

I hurry to let her out before there's an accident. "Jer, what's going on with the dog?"

"Oh, she may have been asleep on Emma's bed and was startled by the garage door opening."

I peer out into the darkness and see Belle's little white body bounding around the yard. Well, I'll let her run off some nervous energy and go upstairs to prepare for my assignation.

The light from the upstairs landing casts out the darkest shadows from my room. I forgo turning on the overhead light and walk toward my nightstand lamp. *Yikes!* Something underfoot crunches beneath my shoe. I switch on the light and look at the floor. Small pieces of amber-colored plastic are strewn about. What's this? As I begin to gather the shards, recognition hits me. *Oh no!* It's the container for my thyroid medication—the one I had filled earlier today. Belle must have chomped through the plastic bottle.

I drop on all fours and pull up my bedspread to peer beneath the bed. No pills. I stand and flip on the overhead light. I look around the floor and into the bathroom. No pills.

I hear Belle fly up the stairs. She runs a circle around me, frantically wagging her tail, and leaps onto the bed. That's when I notice her body trembling. I grab ahold of her and feel her heart pounding furiously. "Jerry!"

He must hear the panic in my voice because he races up the stairs. When he comes in, I'm wrestling to keep Belle from jumping off the bed.

"What's going on?"

"I think she ate all my thyroid pills. She's beyond hyper. Look at her."

I release the dog, and she nearly vaults into Jerry's arms as he approaches her. She's a swirl of constant motion. She rears up on her hind legs and tries to kiss him.

"How did she get the pills?"

"I put the bottle on the nightstand when I came home earlier, and—"

"Why did you do that? Why didn't you put them in the cabinet?" he demands. "You know she's gotten into stuff in the past."

Terrific. Play the blame game instead of helping solve the problem. Why does he have to put me on the other side of the issue? And it's not the first time he's prodded me with guilt.

Just then I hear a key in the front door dead bolt. Belle escapes Jerry's grip and runs down the stairs so quickly it sounds like she's tumbling. Jerry and I follow her to the top of the stairs.

"Hi, Bellie-boo," Emma croons.

Before Emma can pet her, Belle begins her frenzied race around the house again. Emma looks at us with a curious expression.

"Belle ate your mother's thyroid pills."

"What? What does that mean?"

My heart goes out to my daughter at the sight of her desperate expression. "It'll be okay, Em. I'll take her to the animal ER. Want to come?"

I hastily throw on a pair of sweats. As we're getting into the garage, I yell over my shoulder for Jerry to call ahead so they're ready for us. That's been our usual MO. Poor Belle has made more than one trip to the doggy ER. One time she ate half a pound of Brie, and another time she ate a bag of foil-wrapped chocolate candy.

Emma sits in the backseat with Belle, who is still a bundle of frantic energy, whining and smearing dog snot all over my window.

"What made you come home, honey?"

"I was just going to grab some CDs. Oh, I should call the girls. . . ." She pulls her cell phone out of her pocket, dials her friends, and explains the situation.

By the time she's finished with her conversation, we're at the animal ER. I'm relieved to see only a few other cars in the parking lot. I *really* don't want to spend too much time here tonight.

We walk into the lobby. The sound of dogs barking comes from the back room.

"This must be Belle." A thirtysomething woman wearing a medical smock decorated with puppies and kittens greets us. "I'm Laura."

"Yes, it's Belle. Here again."

Laura smiles and hands me a clipboard with a questionnaire and a pen attached to the board with a string.

We find a seat in an alcove, and I fill out the paperwork. When I'm finished, I take it to the service counter.

Laura leads us into an examination room; the strong antiseptic smell is overwhelming. She smiles. "Would you please put Belle on the scale?"

"Sure." Now, even under the best of circumstances, that's a difficult task with my curious dog. This evening it's nearly impossible. Belle feverishly sniffs around the room, probably seeing if any of her canine friends have been here.

Emma picks her up and places her on the scale. "Belle, sit!"

She stays on the scale but wiggles around and jumps on the wall with her front paws.

I give her lead a quick jerk to get her attention. The dog couldn't care less, so I place my hands around her neck. "Belle, please sit down."

She barely puts her derriere on the scale, all the while trying to lick my face. Her stubby tail hasn't stopped wagging, and I can feel her heart pounding like a drum.

Laura watches the scale's readout jump from seventeen pounds to twenty-six pounds. For a moment, when a dog in the waiting room barks, Belle is still.

"Aha." Laura scribbles in a chart. "We'll call it twenty-two pounds. You know, she's a little overweight."

I smile in response. We've been hearing that statement for years. And I blame Jerry. He's always sharing his snacks with the dog. About a year ago, Jer went on a diet. Both he and Belle lost weight.

Laura continues to assess Belle. She checks both ears, feels her torso, and finishes the exam by inserting a thermometer in my poor little dog. Belle's so sweet; she even accepts this indignity with her usual good temper.

As Laura leaves, she turns to back out of the room so Belle doesn't try to escape. "The doctor will be right with you."

Emma and I bide our time looking around the small examination room, reading posters on canine dental hygiene and heartworm danger. It looks like the veterinary community loves graphic, disgusting posters. Perhaps they think the best course of action is to scare pet owners enough to motivate them toward responsibility.

Within a few minutes, there's a knock on the door, and a middle-aged man enters the room. "Hello. I'm Dr. Carey." Without waiting for a reply, he begins to study the file he carried in. "According to the phone call we got before you arrived, it seems Belle got into some medication. Is that right?"

"Uh, yeah. It was a new prescription for my thyroid pills."

I could be mistaken, but it looks like his eyebrows just spiked. As if I need any more guilt in this situation. "It was an accident," I add.

"What type of pills are they?"

"Armour Thyroid."

"Hmm."

Well, that doesn't sound good.

Dr. Carey lifts Belle onto the exam table. "Okay, little lady. Let's see what's going on with you."

Em and I stand on either side of the table to prevent Belle from leaping off.

The doctor listens to her heart and stomach with his stethoscope while she wags and wiggles. His expression is too grim for a guy who modeled his career after the good Dr. Doolittle. "I think we should keep Belle here overnight. She's definitely going to need an apomorphine emetic and some ToxiBan therapy among other things. I—"

I hold up my hand. "In plain English please, Doctor."

His face finally warms with a grin. "Sorry, we're a little busy here. I don't mean to be abrupt. What we'll do for Belle is give her a morphine derivative to make her vomit; perhaps some of the pills aren't yet digested. Then we'll administer activated charcoal to absorb the toxins. I also want to give her some pepsin for her stomach. In addition, we'll monitor her blood pressure, get her on an EKG, and give her fluids as necessary. Does that sound like a plan?"

"Sure, whatever you need to do."

"Alrighty, then. I'll take her on back. Laura will meet you in the lobby with the paperwork you need to sign."

I unhook Belle's lead and try to keep her still while the doctor slips a temporary leash on her. Em and I both pet her and kiss the top of her head. The doctor walks her out the back door. Without Belle's frantic antics, the room seems eerily still. We troop out to the lobby.

There is more action out here now. A dad and his preteen daughter sit with a cat carrier between them on the floor. Inside the carrier, the cat hisses and moans at the same time. A young man paces the floor with a large black puppy in his arms. He's holding a blood-soaked towel around the puppy's front paw. The young woman with them is perched on a chair, shouting questions to him as she fills in the paperwork.

Laura's behind the service counter, organizing papers and working on a computer. She glances at us. "I'll get back to you folks as soon as I can."

I see the writing on the wall and settle into a chair in the alcove. Em plops down beside me and picks up a scrapbook on the nearby table. We thumb through the pages together. It's a collection of thank-you cards sent to the clinic by grateful pet owners. Some come with photographs of the former patients.

"Mrs. Revere?"

I look up to see Laura motion me over. She has paperwork spread out on the counter and quickly runs through an explanation of everything they want to do to my dog overnight. I sign and initial and surrender my Visa card number. Among other things, I've given them permission to extend treatment for procedures that could run as high as twelve hundred dollars. Jerry's going to flip.

"Thank you, Laura. You'll call if there's any change in Belle, won't you?"

"Of course. And our phone number's on this sheet." She circles the number with a red Sharpie. "You can call anytime you want."

I drape my arm across Emma's shoulders, and we walk to our car. The warmth of the day has dissipated, and the night has turned chilly. While I'm fumbling in my purse searching for my keys, Laura calls my name.

"Mrs. Revere, Dr. Carey thought it might be a good idea for you and your daughter to say good-bye to Belle before you leave."

We start to return to the clinic, and the look on Laura's face brings home a horrible thought. *Say good-bye to Belle.* As if this might be the last time we see her.

Another attendant is in the lobby holding Belle's lead while my crazy dog attempts to befriend everyone in sight. She's such a sweet girl. *Lord, don't let my dog die.*

I squat in front of her, and she hops on her hind legs to slobber me with kisses. I bury my face in her neck and breathe in her doggy fragrance. "See you in the morning, Belle. Be a good girl."

Emma scoops the dog in her arms and rocks back and forth for a moment, kissing the top of her head. "Nighty-night, Bellie."

Laura stands off to the side, watching our farewells. As the attendant leads Belle away, Laura escorts us to the door. "You see, the problem is that there's no medical literature on counteracting a natural thyroid medication. If you took Synthyroid, we'd know for sure what to do."

Emma stops dead in her tracks.

I grab her hand, and we leave the building in tears.

16

Emma is sobbing before we get to the car.

I put my arm around her and draw her into an embrace. "It'll be okay."

"I'm not a baby, Mom. I can put two and two together."

"This isn't the time to panic. Let's see how Belle is in the morning."

Emma tries to suck it up, but I know it's difficult. I feel like crying too.

My daughter puts the radio on, and we drive home without conversation, allowing the sound of random music to fill the space between us.

I can only imagine her thoughts, and while I'm concerned for Belle too, I can't help but regret the night of romance Jerry and I would have shared. I long to connect with him, and I don't just mean on a physical basis. I want to understand what his dreams are and talk about a promising future. Just like we did years ago— before children and mortgages and car insurance bills and college tuition. Back when everything and anything seemed possible as long as we had each other.

When we arrive home, Jerry's watching the late news. Although he's always been a stoic man, you can see the concern etched on his face. He cocks his head and glances toward the door, and I know he's looking for Belle. I hope he doesn't load more guilt on my disheartened shoulders.

"We had to leave her overnight for treatment."

Emma brushes past me. "Daddy . . ." She rushes into Jerry's arms, and her sobs start anew.

Jer holds her tightly. "Don't worry. We did the right thing by taking her to the ER. They'll take good care of her." He glances up and looks at me. Am I reading blame into that glance? Where's my white knight? The one who's supposed to make everything better?

She draws in a deep breath and goes to the kitchen for a tissue. The clock chimes ten thirty.

"What are you going to do, Emma? Are you going back over to Lyndsay's?"

She shakes her head. "I think I'm too upset. I want to stay home in case the doctor calls."

I'm not surprised by her answer.

"Mom, do you want to sleep in the extra bed in my room tonight? That way if the phone rings, it won't wake Daddy up." She looks like a lost little girl. We've had Belle since Em was six years old, and to say she loves her dog is an understatement.

"Uh, sure. Let's get some sheets and make the bed up."

As I rummage through the linen closet, I reflect on my evening. It started with such promise. Now I'm going to spend the night down the hall from my sweetheart, waiting for the vet to call with grim news about my pet.

Date night is definitely a bust.

I'm more weary than I thought because as soon as I slide under the covers, I feel sleep beckon. For a moment, I think I hear Belle's collar tags jingle, but then I realize it's Emma removing her jewelry.

She busies herself in her room—hanging her jacket in her closet, slipping into her nightgown, throwing an extra comforter over her bed. She shuts off the light and settles in her bed. "Mom?"

"Hmm?"

"Are you asleep?"

"Nearly . . ."

"Is Belle dying?" Her voice catches in her throat as she speaks the unthinkable.

"Only God knows, Em. We just have to put her in His hands and pray for the best."

She's silent for a moment, thinking I don't know what. I hope she's strong enough to face facts if Belle doesn't make it.

"Honey, you know what a tough dog she is."

"It's just that I don't need *this* happening now too."

Excuse me? All of a sudden, I'm wide-awake. I turn over to face her in the darkness. "What else is going on?"

She sighs and lets her breath come out with a shuddering moan. "I think I'm going to fail history this term."

"Emma! What's going on? You usually do so well."

"It's Miss Boothe. She hates me."

"Why do you say that? What have your test scores and home-work grades been?"

"We've only had one quiz, and I didn't do well—a 68 percent. Most of the assignments have been group projects. Except the other girls in my group got Bs, and she gave me a C."

"What?" This is highly unusual; Emma's always been a good student.

"I told you. That creep hates me."

"I'm sure there's been a misunderstanding, and don't call your teacher names."

"Why do you have to side with her?" Emma's voice grows higher in pitch and volume. "Why can't you just believe me?"

"I do believe you. I'll call school on Monday, and we'll make an appointment to speak with Miss Boothe. It doesn't make any sense that four girls in a group project would get different grades."

"She's the worst teacher in the school, Mom. She's evil."

"Don't worry. We'll figure this out. Do you think you can do any extra assignments to bring up your grade?"

She takes a moment to blow her nose. "I doubt it."

"Well, we'll see."

We fall silent for a while, and as I lay still and listen to the night sounds of my house, I hear Emma tossing and turning. "Em?"

"Yeah?"

"Anything else on your mind?"

"Mmm."

Although I can only make out her outline in the dark room, I see her shrug. "What's going on?"

"It's Ryan."

The name sounds vaguely familiar. *Oh, I remember now. The new boy in school.* "What about Ryan?"

"I really like him." She makes that pronouncement as though it's a curse.

"Well, that's good, isn't it?"

"Sometimes he acts like he likes me too. And then sometimes he acts as though I'm annoying him."

"You don't need that in your life. If I were you, I'd cool it a little."

"I want to be his friend."

"It sounds to me like you want to be his girlfriend. And he may not feel the same way."

"I don't want to talk anymore." With that, she rolls over and faces the wall.

I know I've been dismissed, but I can't let the conversation end there. "You'll be happier if you put some distance between you and him. If you're both looking for different things in a relationship, neither of you will be happy if things continue as they are. Besides, you don't want to look like you're chasing him."

"I'm not chasing him, Mom. Don't say that!"

"Okay, okay. We'll talk more tomorrow."

I hear her sigh deeply again, and then her breathing slows, and I realize she's dropped off to sleep. Lucky her. I feel as though I'll be awake for hours. I fluff my pillow and adjust my covers.

Occasionally a car cruises down our street, a lonely sound so late in the evening. I wonder about Belle. Should I call the ER? I sit up and strain my neck to view the digital clock radio on the dresser. It's not quite midnight. This is going to be a long night.

Emma begins to snore. She's making a soft purring sound. Even asleep, she's so very feminine.

An idea strikes me. I get out of bed and pad down the hall to my room. Jerry's sound asleep, the volume of his snores the opposite of Emma's. I turn down my side of the bed and climb under the covers. He's lying on his side with his back to me. I curl up beside him and rest my arm around his waist. His warmth soothes my weary body. A yawn swallows me in its desire, and I allow myself to succumb to its irresistible suggestion.

Just as I am falling asleep, I hear the phone ring. I roll over and reach for the handset when I realize it's in Emma's room. I race down the hallway and enter her room as she's answering.

"Hello?" She sounds breathless as she pulls herself from the depths of slumber. "Oh no. She's still at the ER. . . . They kept her for the night. . . ." She looks in my direction. "I don't know. Here's Mom." She hands the phone to me and falls back on her pillow.

I exit her room and go downstairs so I won't further disturb her. "Hi, Nick. How did you hear about Belle?"

"Em called while you were still at the ER. What's going on?"

I bring him up to date on Belle's prognosis, promise to call if there's any news, and disconnect the call. For a guy who claims indifference toward the dog, it seems like he loves her an awful lot.

I wander around the house, checking to see that the doors are locked and the oven's been turned off. Old habits from other restless nights. After a moment, I climb the stairs to Emma's room and go to bed.

"Where were you?" she asks.

Not wanting Emma to know I deserted her in her night of distress, I tell a fib. "I forgot to take my hormone pill, and I had just gone into my room to get it when the phone rang."

"Oh, I thought you went back to your bed."

"Night, Em."

She falls asleep again quickly, like only the young can do, and I'm left to sift through my thoughts.

17

The delicious aroma of fried bacon mixed with the distinctive smell of freshly brewed coffee awakens me. I peek over at Emma. She's still sleeping, her mouth slightly open and her arm slung over her head. I close her door as I leave the room and follow the mouth-watering scents downstairs.

Jerry's reading the paper with a mug of coffee on the table in front of him.

I kiss the top of his head and pour some coffee too. "Has the ER called?"

He lays down the paper. "I called them when I got up. It looks like Belle will be fine."

The stress of worry evaporates from my shoulders like snow on warm pavement. *Thank You, God.* Now I just have to be concerned about how much this little fiasco will cost us.

"You know, Jer, when we admitted her into the clinic, I signed an agreement saying they could provide treatment up to the amount of twelve hundred dollars." I pause to let that information sink in.

He doesn't look pleased. He takes a sip of coffee and spills some of the dark beverage when he carelessly sets down the mug. "Are you kidding me? Don't you think you should have called so we could discuss it?"

I pull out a chair and sit across from him. If he was so concerned, he could have gone with us to the ER. "You have to consider the money is for more than keeping the dog well. It's also to ensure the mental well-being of your family. Em and Nick would be heart-broken if Belle died this way. Me too. For the rest of our lives, I would be the one to blame for our pet's death. Besides, you love Belle too."

He screws up his face. I realize he's not happy about it, but he knows it couldn't be helped.

I walk to the counter and open the canister of biscotti and, after a moment's consideration, select a chocolate-coated one. I'm so relieved that Belle's going to recover. "What time did they say Belle could come home?"

"She's good to go. I guess we can pick her up after church."

"What? Let's get her now. I don't want to wait." We're both star-tled by Emma's plea, unaware that she came downstairs.

I settle at the table and let her and Jerry battle it out.

"Daddy, she's been through so much. Can't we let her come home and take it easy? She probably didn't sleep at all last night."

This has upset Emma more than I realized. She's been calling Jerry Daddy since we discovered Belle was in trouble—despite the fact she's called him Dad for over two years now, evidence of her growing maturity. Her sleep-tossed hair has the appearance of a halo, backlit by the bright morning sun. She pulls her robe tighter around her torso, and believe it or not, she looks as if she's going to start crying again. This is more than my sleep-deprived mind can handle.

Jerry obviously feels the same. He lifts his hands in surrender. "Okay, okay. We'll get the dog as soon as we finish breakfast."

She surprises both of us by giving him a big hug.

Jerry makes us all fried eggs and toast. Emma's the first one fin-ished eating and rushes upstairs to dress. I put the dishes in the sink and unplug the coffeemaker.

Within twenty minutes, Em and I are on our way to the ER.

When we arrive, we're their only customers. In the daylight, the

ER looks welcoming—a happy place where no little dogs die of accidental poisoning and cats really do have nine lives. Sunlight streams through the east-facing windows and warms the medical establishment beyond the sterile, efficient clinic we experienced last night. Or maybe I'm so relieved I didn't kill the family pet that anything would look good to me now.

The attendant on duty gives us the rundown on all the procedures done on Belle and slides the bill across the counter.

Yikes—$659! I sign the credit slip and say good-bye to the new laptop I was dreaming of buying.

The door to the clinic opens, and a young man comes out with Belle on a plastic lead. She's thrilled to see us, although she looks quite pathetic. Her right foreleg has been shaved and is wrapped in a bandage, and her two front paws are shaved as well.

Emma clasps her hands. "Oh, look at you, Belle."

"It was from the IV and other procedures," the tall young man explains. "If you have your own lead, I'll take this one off and you can go."

If only I were that organized. Belle's leather lead is at home, hanging on the pantry doorknob. "Uh, we don't have her lead."

Emma is on her knees hugging Belle, but her eyes are fixed on the boy holding the lead. And his eyes are locked onto her as well. *Interesting.*

"May we put her in the car and bring your lead right back in?" I ask.

I get no response.

Hello? Am I speaking to myself? "Excuse me."

Veterinary Boy looks startled at my interruption. "I beg your pardon?" His face colors a darling crimson.

I repeat my request, and he seems eager to be helpful. I grab the discharge papers, the invoice, and my receipt and follow Em to the car.

She deposits Belle in the backseat. "I'll run back in with the lead, Mom."

I start the car and wait. And wait. And wait. I glance at the digital readout on the dashboard. It's been six minutes since Emma went inside. I consider my options. I could honk the horn or go in and get her, but that would be the start of an argument. For the sake of my sanity, I sit tight.

A moment later I see Veterinary Boy escort Emma to the front of the lobby and open the glass door.

She comes to the car glowing, and I know it's not because her pet is out of the woods, medically speaking. She hops in the backseat and immediately turns her attention to Belle. "I think she's lost weight."

Belle wiggles onto her lap and smears more dog snot on the window she missed smearing last night. *Great.*

"Who's the boy, Em?"

"What?" Her face is the picture of innocence.

Nice try. I give her a deliberate glance in the rearview mirror.

"Oh, he's from school. A junior. Isn't he cute?" Before I can answer, she rushes on. "His name's David."

"Oh."

"He plays basketball." She falls silent, perhaps thinking about David. I guess this means we won't be agonizing over Ryan anymore. *Hallelujah.*

● ● ●

I pull the car into the garage, and we allow the overhead door to close before we let Belle out of the car. Jerry must have heard the garage door because the door to the house opens. Belle leaps from the car and makes a beeline for him, all happy and excited to be home.

I'm glad to see the kitchen's been cleaned up. Belle runs to the back door and immediately scratches to go out. A moment later, she comes in and curls up in the middle of the family room sectional couch. Within seconds, she's asleep.

I settle down at the kitchen table to read the Sunday paper, and Emma's installed herself on the computer. Out of the corner of my eye I see her composing an e-mail. I wonder if she's writing about Veterinary Boy to her girlfriends.

I hear a muffled yelp from the couch. Belle's having a dream.

Emma leans over the back of the sectional and puts her hand on the dog's back. "Bellie, wake up. It's okay."

Belle opens her eyes. She glances at all of us and buries her snout under her paw. Poor thing. She looks exhausted.

We all resume our activities. I continue to sort through the paper. When I come to the television guide, I toss it to Jer, which again wakes Belle with a start.

"Mom, can't you let her sleep? She's pooped."

"I'm sorry." I shuffle the papers into a neat stack and go into the living room. I open my Bible in Psalms, my favorite book, and I read through some familiar passages.

After a while, I put the Bible on the side table and close my eyes. *Thank You, Lord, for giving the doctors the wisdom to help Belle.* I can't imagine what this morning would be like if things had gone differently.

The sound of something banging on the stairs disturbs me, and I open my eyes to see Emma carrying Belle's nighttime cage. She puts it in the dining room.

"Belle—cage!"

My obedient dog hops from the couch and walks to her cage with her tail wagging. She curls up within the confines of her personal space, and Emma covers her with her tattered, old flannel blanket. Belle opens and closes her mouth, the tip of her pink tongue briefly appearing between her doggy lips in what we've come to interpret as her way of saying thank you.

"Oh, look. She just wants to sleep in peace." Emma tucks the blanket around the dog's small form and leaves the cage door open. I can see Belle saying thank you once again.

Em grabs a pillow from the living room couch and lies down in a sunny spot on the floor by Belle's cage.

I briefly consider stretching out on the couch and luxuriating in the powerful Colorado sun too. But I know I'll fall asleep the minute I close my eyes and experience the comforting, baking heat of high-altitude sunshine. Instead I decide to spend some time with Jerry.

The family room television is tuned to a Sunday morning political talk show, and Jerry's nodded off too. So much for thoughts of togetherness or romance. Or not. Just because he's sleeping doesn't mean I can't make some plans. I log on to the computer and start surfing the Web for the perfect anniversary getaway. After all, our twenty-fifth is only a few weeks away. I'm sure he'll appreciate some suggestions.

Oh, so many possibilities—San Francisco, Cozumel, New York City . . .

18

I'm not ready for the weekend to be over, but here I am, good little soldier, driving to work. I'm beginning to wonder if I should look for a new job. This one's wearing me down. It's always something with Luke. I doubt that man has had a good day since the last millennium. I pray for him regularly. The only thing that could change his sour outlook on life is almighty God.

The studio's quiet when I arrive. I'm the first one here. I punch in my security code to disarm the alarm, run my time card through the clock, and turn on the stereo system.

I'm powering up my computer when Luke comes in. I want to catch him to ask about a client's reorder request.

I hop from my desk and follow him into the hall. "Luke? Did you see the note I left on your desk on Friday? The Samsons want to know what the reorder fee will be on the portrait that has sun damage."

He turns around and glares at me. "Do we *not* tell clients *not* to hang their portraits in direct sunlight?"

Duh. Am I the one who ruined their pictures? "I'm sure they were told. But they're asking about the guarantee on their portraits."

"Linda, give me ten minutes. Please," he blurts while waving his arm to keep me at bay.

Perfect. Another week begun. I walk back down the hall to my office. If it weren't for the girls I work with and the money I make, this job would have little to offer.

Traci breezes in next, springtime personified, wearing a floral skirt, a light green sweater, and the cutest little flamingo-colored denim jacket. "Hey, Linda." She slides her time card through the clock in a swift, determined manner.

I greet her and return to my desk, looking through my daily calendar to organize the next eight hours. I feel the weight of Traci's gaze and raise my eyes to meet her inquiring look. She lifts her eyebrows and inclines her head. I can't help but laugh; her comical affectation breaks the spell of gloom Luke cast over the studio.

"Ay caramba," I say. "It's Luke. He's already blowing me off, and I haven't even been here ten minutes."

Traci comes up behind me and squeezes my shoulders. "Take a deep breath and let it go, woman. He'll bury himself in his studio, and we'll enjoy our day. Hang a note on his corkboard and put it back on him."

I nod in agreement. She's right. I don't know why I let Luke get to me so much.

Traci smiles. "Hey, don't make plans for Friday night."

"What's going on?"

"My brother-in-law gave me some great coupons for Abacus—yum! And I think we're due for a dinner with the chicks. I already spoke with Jill yesterday, and I hope everyone else can make it."

"Oh, that sounds good. I'll check with Jer and let you know."

About every other month, the girls from the studio go out to dinner together. We call it dinner with the chicks. We laugh together like teenagers, and it's always therapeutic to vent to one another.

Besides, Abacus is one of my favorite Chinese restaurants. My thoughts turn to Governor's chicken, satay beef, and crab-and-cream-cheese wontons as I shuffle through a stack of sample images, sorting them according to session type.

Within twenty minutes, the remainder of the staff trickles in, and the studio's up to full steam, with clients coming in for photo shoots and sales appointments and the phone ringing off the hook as usual. I love it when the rhythm of the day kicks in. It puts a spring in my step to feel that I'm plowing through whatever needs to be dealt with.

This is my morning to catch up on marketing deadlines. We have to send out postcards or flyers six weeks prior to a particular children's special-themed portrait session. I choose some images for Luke to approve and hope I can get them back from the printer quickly enough to start organizing the bulk mail campaign.

I'm distracted from my work by the sound of a familiar laugh. I walk out to the lobby and see Sharon Wells and her adorable little boys sitting there. We all have favorite clients, and Sharon is mine. She was one of my first sales when I came on board. She was happy to part with her money in exchange for the beautiful portraits she cherishes.

Jack's eyes light up, and he comes running to me. It doesn't hurt that I always give him a sucker on his way out. I'd be happy to think he likes me, but I know it's the treat he's after.

I squat for a hug from the towheaded boy, lifting him in my arms, then turn to his mother. "Hi, Sharon. What can I do for you?"

She smiles as she stands and lifts Joey to her hip. "We'd like to pick up the portraits of the boys. I know they're not due till Wednesday, but could you please check on their progress?"

"Sure thing." I put Jack down next to the toy box and head to the workroom.

The back of the studio is like another world. While the lobby is elegant, with high-end furnishings, classic rock tunes softly playing in the background, and the smell of freshly baked cookies wafting through the air, the workroom is pure, hot organized chaos. Due to the number of computers and amount of photo equipment, the temperature is always about fifteen degrees higher. Colored rope lights coil below the ceiling tiles, and the air pumps with the sound of loud music—the genre depending on whoever stacks the CD player. All manner of Happy Meal toys and Beanie Babies hang from strings tied to the maze of rope lights. A cheesy disco ball, lit with a red spotlight, rotates where it is suspended in the center of the ceiling. I just love it back here.

Jill's busy framing a large portrait, oblivious to the rest of the world as she unashamedly belts out a chorus to the song throbbing through the air. The fact that she's slightly off-key only adds to her quirky appeal.

I have to say her name twice before she lays aside her screwdriver, giving me her attention.

"Wells. Sharon Wells. Her order's not due until Wednesday, but do you think you could put it together for me?"

Jill bops across the room and drops to her knees before the large plastic tub that holds the orders waiting to be processed. She flips through a few files before she finds the one she's looking for. She holds up the bundle of plastic-wrapped portraits. "Give me ten minutes."

"Thanks. I'll be back in a minute to help you." I leave our little version of Disney World and walk through the building to my office. I access Sharon's order in our software and print out an invoice.

The lobby's become busier since I left, and I have to step over some crawling babies on the way to my client.

"There's a balance due, Sharon. Shall we take care of that while you wait? Jill will have your order put together in a few minutes."

She forks over her American Express card, and I run it through the credit card machine. Another $450 to add to the till today. Not bad. She signs on the dotted line, and I return to the workroom to help Jill put the order together.

Five minutes later, I carry the portraits to our checkout station and start to line them up on the marble counter for Sharon's approval. The images are incredible. It's amazing how someone like Luke, who seemingly has no heart, can create such gorgeous pictures. The boys look like angels, but there is a picture of Sharon and the boys together that is just perfect. The last image to be scrutinized is a framed sixteen-by-twenty portrait of Sharon alone.

"Oh, Sharon. This is beautiful; you're beautiful."

She laughs self-consciously. "I think whoever did the artwork on this one was very kind."

"Oh, not at all." And that's the truth. Sharon's one of those gorgeous ladies that even other women can't help but stare at.

The image is stunning. She's wearing a scoop-neck black blouse with a long, full sapphire skirt and is sitting on a gray velvet couch, turned toward a window. The natural sunlight plays off her auburn hair and defines the contours of her profile. One hand rests on her lap, where she gently holds a single rosebud. The other is held behind her head, as though she is about to fluff up the back of her hair. The casual, candid feel of the image evokes an intimacy that is almost embarrassing to behold.

"This is for John. It's his birthday present."

"He's going to love this. It's fabulous." I repackage her portraits in boxes and large bags and help her out to her car.

The rest of the day evaporates in the Monday-back-to-work blur. Luke's left a note for me on my board with a reasonable price for the Samsons' sun-damaged portrait reorder. That was easier than I thought.

When I have a break, I call the high school to try to reach Emma's history teacher, Miss Boothe. After being put on hold twice, I'm transferred to her voice mail. I leave a message asking her to call so we can set up an appointment and hang up. *Aarrgh!* I'll be so glad when Em's finished with high school.

My thoughts keep returning to Sharon's portrait, and there's something bothering me. I can't quite put my finger on it. Throughout the afternoon and the drive home, I keep feeling as if there's something I'm trying to recall.

When I arrive home and enter the family room, I finally remember. I stop and stare at the portrait I gave Jerry for Valentine's Day. He loved it so much he hung it right up. The frame and matting perfectly match the decor of the room, and the spot where it's displayed catches the eye of anyone who walks by. It's just the subject matter that has me concerned.

When I presented it to him, Jer rolled his eyes—the box, embossed with the Dream Photography logo, gave the gift away. He knew it was a portrait. I can still see his face as he lifted the lid from the fifteen-by-fifteen box and peeled aside the tissue paper. My heart warms at the remembrance of the look of delight when he first laid eyes on the picture.

I was inspired in January when we assembled our Valentine Angel set. It's one of the more popular children's sessions. And we have the most adorable little angel dresses, complete with lovely gold wings and golden harps to complete the image. Jerry's eyes drank in the beautiful rich tones of burgundy, deep green, and gold that were in the background—all his favorite colors.

Before you get carried away—no, I did not dress up as an angel nor did Emma. The subject of our beautiful portrait is Belle. Yup, I gave my husband a portrait of our dog for Valentine's Day.

And therein lies my problem. What sane, reasonably intelligent, mature woman would choose a gift like that? No wonder our marriage is lacking in romance. *Sheesh. I'm so lame.*

19

My dismal realization took the wind out of my sails, but I'm determined to get back on course. Throughout the week I concentrate
on trying to make special moments in the snatches of time Jerry
and I are alone together. Believe me, with two active kids in the
house, it's no easy task. This discovery leads me to decide that, for
the sake of my children's spouses, Jer and I should be more open
about displaying the way we cherish one another. And it's cool to
think that someday my future son- and daughter-in-law may thank
me for raising such wonderful spouses for them.

On Tuesday, I got out of bed early to make breakfast for Jerry.
My ideal breakfast would consist of oatmeal and a piece of fruit,
but Jerry would typically prefer eating Belle's kibble to my oatmeal.

He was thrilled when I called him to the kitchen for a hot breakfast. I made blueberry pancakes, sausage, and coffee. Fortunately,
his happiness offset the dismay of being awakened too early by the
sound of me using the shower and ironing my skirt prior to my
stint in the kitchen. I never said I was perfect.

Last night I took some scissors, red construction paper, and a
felt-tipped marker and made my honey a little love note. I even
cut it out in the shape of a heart and made it a coupon for a free
massage. I hid it in his lunch box this morning before I left for
work. All day I imagined the look on his face when he discovered
my note. I can't wait to see him to get his reaction.

My musing is interrupted by the ringing telephone. As usual, Emma's on it within four seconds. She glances at the caller ID, makes a face, and passes the phone to me.

"Hello?"

"Mrs. Revere? This is Alice Boothe, Emma's history teacher."

"Thanks for calling me back, Miss Boothe. I was wondering if we could set up a meeting to discuss Emma's progress."

"Parent-teacher conferences are in a week and a half. How's that?"

I can't decide whether this woman is bored or annoyed. "Well, I have some concerns, and I don't know if they should be put off until then."

"I am not putting you off, ma'am."

Okay, I guess she's more annoyed than bored. Fortunately, during the four years Nick was in high school, I learned the politically correct way to speak with teachers with whom you had an issue. I thought I had done well—saying I wanted to discuss Em's progress rather than her problem and saying I had concerns rather than I flat out want to know why my daughter's grade on a group project is less than the other students'.

"I wasn't suggesting you were putting me off, Miss Boothe— only that I think we should discuss this matter before it becomes a problem."

"And what matter would that be?"

I really don't want to get into this over the phone. I ignore her question and ask, "When might be a good time to meet?"

I hear her flipping through papers, and then, "It's already Thursday. I'm available after school Monday. Will that work for you?"

"Yes, that will be fine. Around three o'clock?"

She agrees and quickly ends the call.

Super. Monday is going to be interesting. Now, if only I can remember to get off from work early.

My thoughts return to Jer and the construction paper heart I slipped into his lunch box this morning. I feel a smile start in my heart and travel to my face. Just thinking about him stirs my senses.

The hum and rattle of our old garage door opening announces his arrival, and I rush to meet him at the side foyer. I shared my surprise with Emma, so she's playing it cool in the family room, pretending not to eavesdrop.

When Jer comes through the door, I have to jostle with Belle for space to greet him.

"Hello, girl." He blocks Belle's path to the garage with his brief-case so she won't run out.

Uh, what about the loving wife?

He must have read my thoughts because he flashes me his usual perfect grin and winks. This man still gives me butterflies.

I follow him to the closet, where he hangs his jacket. "So, I guess you got my note."

"Uh-huh."

Something about his smile tells me there's more to this story. "What?"

"Lin, did you remember when I told you they found a new Span-ish teacher to replace the guy who fell and broke his hip?"

I shrug. *So what?*

"And do you further remember that some of the faculty members planned on eating together in the lounge today to welcome her to the college?"

"So?"

"Well, it was a beautiful day, and one of the guys decided to open the window at lunch." He pauses once more and smiles.

Now I'm getting butterflies in my stomach again but not because I've had a hormone burst. I'm not sure I like where this is going.

"Just as I opened my lunch box a breeze came in through the window. . . ." He hesitates for effect.

I could just kill him. "And what?"

"Your little red heart note came fluttering off the top of my sandwich and landed at the feet of Kelli Vadney."

"Who's Kelli Vadney?"

"The new Spanish teacher."

I hear Emma giggle from the family room. *Great.* "Well, didn't she hand it back to you?"

"In a way. Rich Slattery was sitting next to her and offered to take it so she wouldn't have to get up."

Well, that sounds okay.

"Only instead of walking the note across the room . . ." He begins to laugh, and Emma's chuckles become a full belly laugh too.

"Jer!"

"Rich passes it on to the person next to him, who passes it on to the person on her right, who passes it on to the head of my department, who hands it to me."

Oh, I could just die. I know it's a humorous situation, but I feel the sting of tears in my eyes. I begin to back up, thinking of where I can run and hide.

But before I can make my escape, Jerry catches me in an embrace. "It's okay, Lin. Everyone thought it was pretty cute."

"Yeah, cute. Does everyone think it's cute that you're married to an idiot?"

Emma joins us in the hall, still laughing.

I glare at her. *Traitor.*

"Mom, lighten up."

"Oh, that's easy for you to say. You don't have to socialize with those people. I'll never be able to hold up my head at the faculty barbecue this summer."

Jerry leaves an arm around my shoulders and leads me into the kitchen. "To tell the truth, I think they were jealous of me." He looks very pleased when he says this, and I'm beginning to believe him.

Emma sets the table and goes upstairs. The salad spinner is sitting in the sink, where it was abandoned when Jer got home. I wash some lettuce, and Jerry goes into the dining room with his briefcase. The clasps of his attaché case snap open, and the sound of papers shuffling consumes the next few moments. I wonder what the faculty at the college really thinks of me. *Oy.* A red construction paper heart. How junior high can I get?

My hands are getting chilled from rinsing tomatoes and cucumbers for the salad. When I shut off the water and turn to grab the hand towel, I'm startled to find Jerry standing a few feet away, staring at me.

"Yes?" I ask.

He shifts from one foot to the other and grins, one arm behind his back and his index finger resting against his bottom lip, as though he wants to say something but is editing his thoughts.

I feel the heat from a slow flush travel up my throat. I honestly have no clue what this man is thinking, other than perhaps he married a ninny.

Jerry removes his finger from his lip and hands me the terry cloth towel. Our eyes are locked—something that hasn't occurred in eons. The moment is beginning to seem strangely intimate. A magnetic pull draws me farther into the depths of his dark brown eyes. *Ah, I could stay like this forever.*

An abrupt ring of the telephone brings me back down to earth. But before I can move to pick up the handset, Em yells down that she's got it.

I realize that I'm standing there, dripping water on the floor, gazing into my husband's eyes like a love-struck teenager. In an instant of self-consciousness, I begin to dry my hands.

"Lin."

Our eyes meet again. He takes his hand from behind his back and holds out a plain, white envelope. I toss the towel on the counter and take his offering. He smiles a self-satisfied grin, hands in his pockets, and watches while I carefully lift the flap and slide out the card.

The front of the card has a picture of an ice cream sandwich. I flip it open. The inscription reads, "I love you inside and out." Beneath that, in nearly illegible handwriting, he's scribbled his name.

A lump forms in my throat. This is the first time Jer's ever given me a card that wasn't for a birthday, anniversary, or Valentine's Day. Before I realize it, my eyes fill up. I bat my eyes to maintain my composure but not before an errant teardrop slides down my face.

Jer picks up the towel and gently touches a corner to my cheek. *Oh.*

He pulls me into an embrace and tenderly holds me. I close my eyes to memorize the moment. *Is this my Jerry?*

"Thanks for the homemade card."

I look into his smiling face, go on tiptoe, and give him a soft kiss. "You're welcome."

"When can I collect on my massage?" Jerry raises one eyebrow, changing his expression from a sweet smile to a contrived lecherous grin.

"Hmm. I bet we could work on that—" I pause and mimic his expression—"a little later tonight."

Twenty minutes later, Nick arrives home, and we sit down to dinner. Not surprisingly, Emma is thrilled to recount the embarrassing details of my homemade card. "And then the card was passed on to everyone in the room before Dad's boss handed it to him."

Nick closes his eyes, presses his lips together, and gives a small shake of his head, as if to say, "Oh, Mom. What have you done now?"

"Hey," Jerry says, "I can't remember the last time someone took the time to make me a card." He reaches over and squeezes my arm. "Someday you should be so lucky, Son."

I smile in agreement. Yeah, I hope someday both of my children will be as lucky as we are.

"Mom," Emma says sweetly, "don't forget you were going to look over my history essay tonight."

"We'll get to it as soon as we finish the dishes. Nick, give us a hand."

Jerry brings his dish over to the sink and escapes to his study. He always spends time after dinner going over his lessons and checking assignments.

After the dishes are done, I throw a load of towels into the dryer and go straighten up our room. I stack my to-be-read pile of books on the floor by my night table, grab some earrings off the top of my dresser, and put them away in my jewelry box. The fragrance of my scented candle that sits on the dresser reminds me of our upcoming intimacy, and I double-check to make sure the matches are within reach. My heart soars when I think of how far our romantic adventure has come in just a few short weeks.

"Mom!"

Oh, crumbs. Emma's essay. I forgot about that. "I'll be right down!"

The next forty minutes are spent discussing the European Middle Ages and arguing over the finer points of grammar with my stubborn daughter. By the time we're finished, I'm exhausted.

I put together some leftovers for lunch and arrange them in our lunch boxes. For a fleeting moment I consider putting another note into Jer's lunch box but discard the idea because I don't have a good follow-up in mind.

The clock chimes eight times. I head upstairs again to fold the laundry and choose my wardrobe for the morning. All the while I'm thinking of Jerry. I can't wait to be alone with him behind a locked door, with the room aglow from the flame of my scented candle.

To pass the time, I read a couple pages of a novel that Deb

loaned me. It's about a wisecracking, middle-aged woman trying to get her life back in order after her leg's been amputated.
Myrna seems like one tough, capable chick, but as I read farther
into the story, I see her tender, aching heart. I wonder if all
women feel a lack of some sort at different points in their lives.
Although I do believe that episode is coming to an end for me.
Thank You, Lord.

I imagine what our lives will be like when the kids are out of the
house. I know it won't be as soon as I previously thought. Jerry's
making noises about bribing Emma with a car if she'll stay home
and commute to college like her brother does. But the day will
come when our children are launched from the nest, and it will be
sweet. Just my husband and me. Dinner for two nightly. I loved it
when it was only the two of us, with little responsibility.

I'm brought back to the present when I hear Nick teasing Em
in his big-brother way. He's not really malicious. It's just how he
shows her attention. To tell the truth, I think Emma enjoys their
banter.

I set a bookmark in Myrna's tale and go into the bathroom to
shower. Ten minutes later, I pull on my nightgown and toss my
robe over my shoulders.

I'm feeling rejuvenated and desirable. I can't wait to get my hands
on Jerry, to knead out the tension of the day and let him know
what he means to me. I have an irresistible urge to kiss his shoulder—an urge that I will satisfy shortly.

I rouse Belle off the couch downstairs and escort her to the back
door. The air carries the ripe scent of springtime. A soft breeze stirs
the pine trees, and shadows play across the yard. From a distance,
I hear the cry of a lone coyote. I'm glad our backyard is fenced in.
We don't need another incident with our dog. Not tonight.

On my way upstairs, I grab the card Jer gave me so I can put it
on our dresser. This night is turning out perfect.

Jerry passes through our room, gives me his best smile, and gets ready for bed. When he returns, I'm pleasantly surprised to see him light our candle.

I fold aside the covers, and he joins me in bed. . . .

I wonder if there is a word that would accurately describe how I feel. *Satisfied* is too inadequate. Jerry has slipped into sleep and for once breathes quietly. I inch closer to his side of the bed and rest my head near his to breathe in his scent. I can't resist the desire to touch his soft, curling hair.

A low chuckle proves that he's not asleep yet. "Linny? Can I help you?"

"Sorry. I'll let you sleep."

We roll over in tandem, and he lays his arm across my waist.

"Jerry?"

"Hmm?"

"Thanks for the card."

"You're welcome."

"I really loved it."

"Good. Kelli said it might be a nice idea."

Hello? For once in my life I'm speechless. The new Spanish teacher is giving my husband romance advice? *Not good, Jer.*

After a restless night's sleep punctuated with bizarre dreams of a faceless woman tutoring my husband in the art of romance, I awaken with a headache. At least it's Friday. I know there's a boat-load of projects in my to-do bin at work, but I roll over and dive into dreamland once more. Besides, this is my day to go in to work late.

My headache continues through the day, and I work on auto-pilot. Not my best efforts, but some days you just need to skate through. Because I have the late sale of the day, I'll be the last to arrive at Abacus tonight to meet my coworkers for our bimonthly edition of dinner with the chicks. I'm looking forward to letting my hair down and relaxing with the girls. I think we'll all be there except for Pam. She rarely socializes with the rest of us.

I turn on my cell phone and dial home. After five rings, the answering machine kicks in. I listen to the outgoing message and clear my throat. "Hi, it's me. I'm on my way to the restaurant. I guess you're driving through somewhere getting your dinner too. I expect to be home by nine."

I disconnect the call and am surprised when a feeling of relief washes over me. Because I went in to work on the delayed schedule today, I slept in and didn't talk to Jerry this morning. When I heard him getting ready to leave, I lay still with my eyes closed until I knew I was alone in the room. He was actually whistling downstairs before he left. *How clueless can he be?* It wasn't until after I heard the garage door open and close that I got out of bed.

During my lunch break, I toyed with the idea of calling Jer, but the irritation was still too great to gloss over. There will be plenty of time to have *that* discussion over the weekend.

I'm so peeved that a stranger advised my husband to buy me a card. I wonder if she helped him pick it out. I can almost imagine them together in the bookstore at the student union, laughing and chatting while they perused the card racks, but I really don't want to go there. How old is this woman? And what does she look like? Is she married?

Yeah, Jerry has a lot of questions to answer later.

Despite leaving work so late, the rush-hour traffic continues to tie up the highways. I glance at my watch. It's nearly 6:50. I'm already five minutes late, and my stomach is protesting the scanty lunch I ate hours ago.

The thought of crab-and-cream-cheese wontons has me salivating as I turn into the parking lot of the upscale Chinese restaurant. An SUV pulls out of what seems to be the last space in the lot. I breathe a sigh of relief and hurry to stake my claim. Before I exit my car, I flip down the visor and give my face the once-over. This late in the day, any effort to spruce myself up would pretty much be futile. I toss my cell phone into my purse, shove my hair behind my ears, and climb out of my Taurus.

The delicious fragrance of fresh Asian food teases my senses as I push through the double doors and enter the restaurant. The aroma lures me through the large foyer toward the ornate podium.

Mr. Tang, the owner of Abacus, recognizes me and inclines his head in greeting. "Ms. Revere, how nice to see you." His sparkling eyes nearly disappear in the smile that overtakes his weathered, old face.

"Hi, Mr. Tang. I'm meeting some friends tonight."

He nods and gestures toward the back corner of the room. "May I lead you over?"

I spot the familiar faces of my friends. "No, thank you. I'll be fine."

As I move toward the gals, something doesn't seem right. What are they wearing? I don't recall what they had on earlier, but I know they've changed. *What on earth?* They're all wearing what looks like brand-new flannel pajamas.

Traci springs from her chair. "Surprise!"

The rest of the girls erupt into giggles. I'm laughing too but more from embarrassed confusion than pleasure. Rose calls my name, and when I glance her way, the flash from her camera momentarily blinds me. *Thanks.* Sometimes hanging out with photographers can be a royal pain.

"Uh, what's going on?"

Jill, who's laughing too hard to speak, pats the empty chair next to her.

I feel like I've entered an episode of *The Twilight Zone.* I hang my purse over the back of the chair and cautiously ease myself down between Jill and Barb. The urge to run for the door to escape these crazy ladies flashes through my mind. Half the restaurant is staring at us, including Mr. Tang, who stands in the aisle clasping his hands. "Can someone please tell me what's happening?"

"Surprise," Traci echoes. She reaches under the table and pulls out two gift-wrapped boxes.

Now I'm totally confused. "It's not my birthday."

"No, it's not," Rose says.

Traci, who looks so pleased she could pop, claps and says, "Girlfriend, this is your long-overdue pajama party!"

What? By now the patrons sitting near us are laughing too.

And as if she hasn't already been speaking loudly enough to wake the dead, Traci announces to those sitting around us, "This poor girl never went to a pajama party when she was growing up."

Etiquette for a situation like this was never covered by Emily

Post, and I'm at a loss for how to respond, other than the natural blush I feel creeping across my face.

One of the beautifully wrapped boxes is thrust into my hands. "Open it, Linda."

I carefully tug the lavender tulle ribbon from the corner of the box covered in bright, paisley paper. My hands tremble as I slide my index finger under the seam to release the tape.

The box opens to reveal pale pink tissue paper sealed with a sticker in the shape of a silver star. I tear through the tissue and find a pair of bright pink and black flannel pajamas covered with images of old rotary telephones. The second box, wrapped in matching paper, holds a pair of neon pink fuzzy slippers. "Guys, thanks."

Jill is on her feet, grabbing my arm. "Come on. I'll go to the ladies' room with you while you get changed."

"What?" Apparently I'm a little more modest than my friends. This doesn't sound like a great idea to me.

"Go on," Barb coaxes.

"It's the rules, Lin. We're all in our pj's."

Traci stands and does a little pirouette to show off her nightwear designed with gray snowflakes on a cobalt blue background. Could she be any more conspicuous?

Oh, whatever. It won't kill me. And I've never heard of anyone dying of embarrassment.

A moment later I'm hurrying back to my table as quickly as I can shuffle in the two-sizes-too-large fuzzy slip-ons. I'm sure my face is colored the same shade as my bright pink pajamas.

Traci is pulling apart a steaming crab-and-cream-cheese won-ton when I return. She dips her appetizer in duck sauce and pops it into her mouth. While she chews, she holds her hand over her lips and says, "I've been planning this ever since that day we spoke while you were in your car in the parking lot at work. It broke my heart that you never went to a pajama party."

I shake my head in wonder. "I can't believe you guys. Thanks."

It's awesome to know I have friends who care enough about me to embarrass themselves for my sake.

"Okay," Rose says, "let's talk about boys."

Everyone but me starts to laugh. I suck in my breath when I remember Jerry and his love tutor. My anxious thoughts destroy the carefree moment like a thunderstorm on a wedding day.

"What's wrong?" Jill's face creases with concern.

The happy party comes to a halt while I look from one dear face to another. I smile and shake my head. "Oh, it's nothing much. I was just thinking about Jer."

"Well, what's he done?" Traci asks with her usual candor.

I launch into an explanation of the paper heart I gave Jerry, complete with the embarrassing way it was delivered to him via his coworkers and department head.

My friends all laugh. Jill clutches her heart. "That's about the sweetest thing I've heard in a long time. So what's the problem?"

"While I was preparing dinner, Jer surprised me with a greeting card."

"Do tell!"

"I was stunned. He's only ever given me cards on my birthday, our anniversary, or Valentine's Day."

Moisture coats the fringes of Barb's eyelashes. She pulls out a tissue and carefully blots her face.

"And the bad part?" Traci asks.

I raise my eyebrows and continue, "The card was sweet. An ice cream sandwich was on the front, and the sentiment inside said, 'I love you inside and out.'"

"What's wrong with that?" Traci asks.

I cross my arms over my chest to deliver my punch line. "Kelli Vadney picked it out."

"Who? What?" Their confusion and indignation mirror my emotions from the previous night.

"That was my reaction exactly." I feel justified with my escalating irritation with my husband. "She's a new Spanish teacher at the community college."

Rose looks as though she's trying to connect the dots, grasping to understand the situation. "Why would she do that?"

I give Rose a pointed look. "Why indeed? That's exactly what I want to know."

"Furthermore," Jill adds, "why would Jerry want her help?"

We all fall silent, pondering the answer to my dilemma, and take a break to dig in to the food that's been placed before us. My friends have ordered a delicious feast—steaming cups of egg drop soup; sesame chicken in a spicy sweet-and-sour sauce; fragrant ginger beef with chunks of big, juicy mushrooms; crispy lemon chicken with a pungent citrus sauce; vegetable lo mein with thick, greasy noodles; and a serving of beef fried rice. *Forget the calories, full steam ahead.*

"Okay, Linda. Let's figure this out," Traci says as she twists a few strands of lo mein around her fork.

"Well," Jill interjects, "maybe Jerry asked her for help."

Traci makes a face. "Puh-lease. What man would ask anyone for help? Especially a woman. And one he doesn't know well."

The expression on Jill's face shifts for a moment, and then she tries to replace it with a mask of indifference. Bless her heart. She's never been able to hide her feelings.

Not one to miss a beat, Traci asks, "Jill, what are you thinking?"

She blushes and gestures with her hand to wave away the question.

"Spit it out, girl."

She lowers her gaze. "I'm sorry. I guess I must have a suspicious nature."

Jill used to be married to a cheating, lying, sneaky, low-down bum of a man. I guess it's only natural that her thoughts would go in that direction.

"We've all met Jerry. I doubt there's any hanky-panky going on," Rose says.

"Yeah, I'm sure that's not the case," I say emphatically. *At least I hope so.*

Barb takes another helping of sesame chicken. "Don't be putting stupid ideas in Linda's head."

Amen. I glance around at my friends. What a sorry pajama party this is turning out to be.

As if she read my thoughts, Traci changes the subject. "Hey, did anyone notice that Luke's been grooming himself more carefully lately?"

"Yeah," Jill says, "what's up with that? Yesterday I think I actually smelled cologne coming from his office."

Rose leaned forward. "And I haven't seen him wear his ratty old brown sweater in weeks. I wonder what this means."

Barb smiles like the cat that swallowed the canary. "I think maybe our old grump's new wife is whipping him into shape."

We enjoy the rest of our dinner, and I try not to think about Jerry anymore. By the time we're walking out of the restaurant, I've even forgotten that I'm wearing pajamas. What a sight we must be—five women, some pushing middle age, striding through the parking lot in brightly colored discount-store pajamas and big, fuzzy slippers.

During my drive home, I can't help but let my thoughts wander back to Jer and his new friend. Why would he let a strange woman pick out my card? I wonder who saw them together. The slow burn that started in the restaurant has built up to a bonfire as the ache in my heart returns. *Oh, whatever shall I do?*

21

Belle greets me at the back door. Of course she's only happy to see me for the dog biscuit she knows I'll toss her way.

"Hello?"

No one answers.

My footsteps echo across the tile floor into the kitchen. I nearly step on the dog as she runs excited circles around me on the way to the pantry. "Jer? Emma?"

"I'm upstairs, dear."

I go upstairs, all the while silently praying that my temper won't get the better of me. I glance down the hall. Emma's bedroom door is open, and the light is off. She must be out with friends. And Nick's car isn't in the driveway.

When I enter our bedroom, Jer's lying on the bed watching television. He flashes me his endearing grin. Only tonight it's not working.

"Guess what?" he says. "We're home alone." He lifts his right eyebrow in what I usually consider one of his more precious expressions. He hops up and comes toward me. As he leans in for the kiss, I turn my head so it lands midway between my lips and my ear.

"What on earth are you wearing?"

"I think it's pretty obvious. I'm wearing pajamas." My statement and the tone of voice it's delivered in stop him cold.

"What's wrong?"

He's totally clueless. He looks like he just got off the Tilt-A-Whirl at our town's summer festival—as though he's slightly ill and a little off-balance.

I mutter the four words I know he hates to hear: "We need to talk."

"But we're home alone," Jerry repeats. His countenance fades from anticipated pleasure to guarded concern. I'm certain he had other plans in mind for our evening. A serious little heart-to-heart is probably the last thing he wants.

My prayers must be working, because as I peer into his face, my heart softens a bit with the realization that he doesn't have a hint as to how irritated I am with him. "Jer, I was so thrilled and touched by the card you gave me last night."

He perks up and startles me by catching me in a quick embrace. "I owed you a nice card after the one you made me." He bends down and tries to kiss me.

I back away. *As if, buster.*

I'm certain if he were blindsided by a two-by-four he couldn't look any more bewildered.

I shake my head and sit on the edge of the bed. I may as well spit it out. "I can't believe you had another woman pick out my card. Why would you do that?"

"Well—"

"And why would a stranger agree to do something like that?"

"She—"

"As if *she* would know anything about me or what kind of card I'd like!"

"Lin, I—"

"How many people saw you together picking out *my* card?" The fury in my heart threatens to choke me if I don't get an answer soon.

Jerry steps toward me, his expression clouded with anger. "Linda! Let me speak."

He rarely raises his voice to me. I'm shocked into silence and sit there glaring at him while he stands over me with his hands on his hips. I see the little vein in his forehead twitch the same way it does when he's disappointed with one of our children.

"I don't know what you're talking about," he says.

I open my mouth to speak, but he silences me by holding up his hand. "What woman are you talking about?"

"The new Spanish teacher. Kelli some-face-or-other." Suddenly I'm feeling less righteous in my anger.

"Vadney. Her name's Kelli Vadney, and where did you get the idea she helped me choose your card?"

"From you, Jer. You said it last night."

"What?" The look of anger on his face turns to confusion.

"Last night. After . . . well, before we fell asleep. You said Kelli thought the card would be a good idea."

"And from that sentence, you thought she helped me pick out your card?"

"Uh, yeah."

Jerry closes his eyes and slowly shakes his head. "Well, you're wrong."

"I am?" A stab of guilt pierces my heart when I realize my assumptions may be incorrect.

He runs his hand through his hair and takes a seat beside me. For a moment we sit silently.

Finally Jer releases a loud sigh. "I picked out your card by myself."

"Oh?"

"Yeah."

"No offense intended, but buying a greeting card seems to be something out of character for you. Unless it's my birthday or something."

"Rich Slattery suggested I buy you roses. I thought that was a little overkill, so I thought to get you a card myself."

A painful knot settles over my heart. What have I done? The first time Jerry does something sweet and spontaneous, I turn into a raging lunatic. "I'm so sorry."

"Hmm."

I think I'd feel better if he were angry instead of disappointed. "You told me Kelli said it would be a nice idea."

"Well, yeah, she did. But that doesn't mean she helped me find it. She didn't even see it. Kelli was still sitting in the lounge when Rich and I had our discussion. That's all. I'm not an idiot, Linda. I can pick out a greeting card."

Oh, I'm such a dope. I've turned a puddle into the ocean. "I'm sorry, Jer. Really, I am." My thoughts have scattered like dandelion seeds in the wind. I know I should say something deeply apologetic and loving, but I'm coming up blank. I swallow hard to fight back the tears that threaten to surface. *Oh, man. Don't let me cry. How feeble would that be?* I stare at my hands and fight to maintain composure.

The bed shifts as Jerry turns toward my night table. He plucks a tissue from the box and offers it to me.

My self-control fails, and the tears start to flow.

Jerry stands, and on his way into our bathroom, he snatches the card from our dresser. A moment later, I hear the vanity door shut, and I know he's thrown the card in the garbage. He leaves the room without a word.

I fall back onto my pillow and let my tears flow. How could things have gone so horribly wrong? How will I make this up to him?

I don't know how long I lie in bed weeping. After a while, I get up to wash my face. *Ugh.* I couldn't look worse. My face is covered with blotches, and my eyes are swollen and red rimmed. A cool washcloth is not going to cut it. What I need is a major facial. I run the brush through my hair and sit on the edge of the tub. Somehow I have to make this right. I rummage through the trash, find the card, and place it on my dresser again.

When I'm about to go downstairs to grovel for Jerry's forgiveness, the phone rings. I answer it on the second ring and hear Jerry's baritone voice answer. It's Em. She needs a ride home.

I hang up the phone and go to the top of the stairs. "Jer? Do you want me to ride with you to get Emma?"

"Whatever."

Could be better, but beggars can't be choosers. I dash on a little mascara and some fresh lipstick and follow Jerry into the garage.

He puts his right hand on the stick shift between our seats to put the car in reverse.

Before he goes into gear, I place my hand on his. "I feel terrible. Please forgive me."

Jerry looks down at our stacked hands. He frees his thumb and strokes my pinkie. "I'm sorry I got so angry."

"So you forgive me for being such a jerk?"

He smiles his teasing grin. "Don't I always?"

His familiar banter helps return our relationship to normal. I lean over, and we meet in a sweet kiss.

We drive through town, listening to Paul McCartney and Wings. To tell the truth, I'm exhausted from my tantrum. We drive without conversation, content to have righted our relationship.

Jerry hands me the scrap of paper with the directions, and together we search for the correct address. After navigating the maze of roads, we reach the right house. I punch in my daughter's cell number, and in a moment she comes running out.

Emma waves to her friend as she climbs into the backseat. "Guess what?" She smells like popcorn, and the excitement she brings to our confined space is palpable.

Before we can speak, she launches into a monologue. "While we were watching our movie tonight, Hillary's brother came home with some friends. And guess who was with them?"

I open my mouth to speak. "Wa—"

"It was David! David Watkins."

Jerry and I speak in unison, "Who?"

She sighs loudly, as if we are the densest parents in the world.

I turn to look at her and see her roll her eyes in frustration.

She pulls on a strand of hair. "Mom, you remember. He works at the animal ER."

Oh, Veterinary Boy. It's all coming back to me. We fill Jerry in on the crush du jour.

"And he asked me out on a date for next Friday." She starts chattering on about how nice he is and how cool he dresses. "Not ultra trendy, which is *so* overtrying. You know, like someone who looks like a walking Abercrombie ad. Bleh!"

She rattles on about the movie she watched, what she might wear next Friday, and her hopes that we'll make a trip to the mall this week.

Emma leans forward and pinches the sleeve of my flannel pajama top between her fingers. "What are you wearing?"

"Oh, let me tell you about my evening. . . ."

Two hours later, I lie in bed and listen to the night sounds. Belle whimpers out a bark while she dreams, Jerry snores, the heat kicks on, and the wind stirs the chimes on the patio.

I stretch and flip over my pillow. In the soft darkness of the room, I see the card Jer gave me sitting next to the scented candle. All's right with my world again.

22

How can it be that weekends fly by so quickly while the workweek drags on and on? The morning sun falls across the kitchen table, where I'm finishing reading the Sunday paper. I take my final swig of coffee, stack the papers to put in the recycling bin, and hurry upstairs to get ready for church.

When I come back downstairs, Jerry's in the garage waiting for Emma and me to join him. I race into the living room and grab my Bible off the side table, where I left it yesterday.

I pause at the bottom of the stairs and yell to my son, "Nick, we're leaving for church. See you there."

"Okay."

I cruise through the kitchen to make sure I've turned off the coffeepot and follow Em out the door.

There's something quite comforting in some forms of routine. Especially when it's worshiping with your family on Sunday mornings. We all meet up in the narthex after our Sunday school classes and take our usual spot in the sanctuary. Deb and Keith slip in behind us. Jerry reaches over the seat and greets Keith with a handshake.

Deb leans forward. "Linda, can you meet me for lunch Tuesday?"

I'm not so dense that I miss the sideways glance Keith directs at his wife—that exchange of information given in a look the way only long-married couples can pull off.

163

Deb winks at him and asks me, "What time is your lunch break?"

"I think I can leave the studio around one. Where shall we meet?"

We finalize our plans, and I can't help but think Deb's got something juicy to share. I can't wait to find out what's going on.

The music begins, and we stand to start worship. The power of the words and heartrending melody transports me to a place where there's only myself and my Lord. My heart feels both as light as air and as though it's being pulled by an intense magnetic force toward the power of Almighty. I lose myself in the awesome majesty of God and sing with abandon. The music ends much too quickly. I sit down and fumble in my purse for a tissue to dry my eyes.

The pastor is preaching from the book of First Samuel. I'm sure today's message is for me: "What to do when you are where you aren't going to stay." I'm beginning to think that I won't be staying at Dream Photography forever, not unless Luke gets a major attitude adjustment and a heart transplant. I concentrate on the sermon, scribbling notes in my composition book and starring the points that strike my fancy.

When the service ends, I feel spiritually energized. We walk out of church with our friends.

"Look. There're the kids." Deb points across the parking lot to where Randy and Andrea are getting into his car.

We say our good-byes and head our separate ways.

The rest of the day passes in that lazy Sunday way. I do a few loads of laundry, and Jerry thrills me by making a spaghetti-and-meatball dinner. We watch an early movie with Emma and Nick, and thus ends another weekend.

● ● ●

I think the ringing phone may drive me crazy today. If only I could hold on to the peace I feel at church a little longer than twenty-four hours. *I'm such a flawed vessel, Lord.*

"Dream Photography, this is Linda. May I help you?"

I flip through the sales schedule while I listen to a client's litany of activities that consume her time. *Really, I don't care. Get to the point, woman.* "So, ma'am, what day *will* work for you?"

I finish scheduling her in and call Rose to take over for me at the front desk. I glance at the wall clock that hangs in my office. If I leave now and take the toll road, I'll make it to the high school in time for my meeting with Emma's history teacher. I grab my purse and lunch box, run my card through the time clock, and race out of the studio before anyone else demands my attention.

This is my lucky day. I make it to the highway in record time and set my cruise control.

Twenty-eight minutes later, I pull into the school parking lot. I see Em sitting on the bench outside the main door. Together we walk up the stairs and through the double doors.

The school smells like potato chips and sweaty socks. Some things never change. Gum wrappers and wadded-up papers randomly litter the hall that is lined with dreary, gray lockers. I follow Em's lead through the labyrinth of hallways to the history department. We knock on the door.

"Come in."

Emma wipes her palms on her jeans and pushes open the door.

Alice Boothe sits at a desk to the right of the room in front of a smudged window. Her features are obscured by the glow of sunshine that pours in from behind her.

"Hello, Miss Boothe. I'm Linda Revere. We met during the parent orientation in August."

"Yes, please take a seat."

Help my attitude, Lord. I'm already annoyed at her lack of etiquette. No *Hello, how are you? Nice to see you.* No smile or look of welcome.

I sit across from her, and Em takes the seat to my left. I smile, although this woman seems to resent our presence.

Miss Boothe looks about my age. Her brown hair is shot through with coarse gray streaks and has a definite lack of style, falling in straggly lines just above her shoulders. Pink blush accents her pale complexion when peach tones would clearly flatter her appearance much more. Her lips are coated with cheap, chalky pink lipstick, and the pale blue blouse she's wearing could be fifteen years old.

Now I know I sound a little snobby, but part of my job description is image consultant. I advise people on how best to groom and attire themselves to optimize their appearance. Miss Boothe definitely needs to bring her wardrobe and grooming habits into the twenty-first century. Hasn't she ever watched *What Not to Wear*?

"Well?" she says.

Oy. This is going to be difficult. I take a deep breath and plunge in. "Emma is concerned that her grade is below what she believes it should be."

"Really? Emma?"

"Uh, yes. The other girls in my group project all got Bs, and you gave me a C."

"That's because I believe you *earned* your C."

Sheesh. I don't like this woman. I clear my throat and sit on the edge of my seat. "I thought that participants in group projects all got the same grade."

"No, they don't." Miss Boothe gives us a dispassionate look.

"Could you please explain why that is?"

"Clearly some students work harder and do better work than others."

"And you've determined that Emma is not one of those students?"

"Apparently."

Okay, now I'm really ticked. "Are you aware that Emma gets As and Bs in all her other classes?"

"Actually, no. But then her other classes are none of my concern."

Does this woman have ice water running through her veins? How can she have such a negative opinion of my little angel? I try another tactic. "Well, how can she improve her grade? May she do an extra-credit assignment?"

"No. I don't operate my classroom like that. A student needs to do consistently good work to earn a good grade."

I feel my jaw begin to clench. If it were forty years ago and we were on the playground, I'd throw sand in her face. "Miss Boothe, I hosted the girls from the group project in my home while they did some of the work. I know that Emma contributed as much as anyone else."

"I don't mean to sound callous, Mrs. Revere, but that's not my experience with this group."

"How many groups are in this class?"

She gives me a curious look. "There are six groups."

Aha! "And how can you be sure Emma's not contributing as much when you have to divide your attention among so many students?"

"Are you questioning my ability to monitor my students? If you would like, you may take this matter up with the assistant principal."

I wonder if, like the Grinch, her heart is two sizes too small. "Perhaps I will."

Miss Boothe nods at me, as if to say "bring it on." This is clearly not going the way I had hoped. Maybe Emma was right when she accused Miss Boothe of hating her.

I glance at my daughter, and she looks scared to death. "Miss Boothe, what assurances do I have that you'll treat Emma fairly through the rest of the term?"

"I treat all my students fairly."

Meeks. This is beginning to turn into a spitting match. And I really don't want to play. "I will be monitoring Emma's homework and assignments to make sure she does her best. I hope you recognize her efforts."

The history teacher regards me coolly. I feel a trickle of sweat worm its way down my back. Finally she rises to signal this appointment is over.

I extend my hand. "It's been nice to see you again."

She grasps my hand in a cold, hard squeeze. "Likewise."

Emma and I escape the bleak office with relief.

Em looks ill. "See, Mom. I told you she hates me."

"I don't know what her problem is. But I guarantee I will keep a close eye on your progress, and I will go to the assistant principal if I feel she doesn't give you fair credit."

There, mama bear has said her piece. But I'm not sure my little cub is buying it. I put my arm around her waist and draw her close to me. "This is one teacher from one class, Em. You'll move on, and in the big scheme of things, this will be a tiny blip on your radar screen. Promise."

That entire meeting took less than ten minutes. As we step outside the school, the warmth of the sunshine feels like nourishment to my soul.

Inspiration strikes me on the drive home, and we stop at the coffee shop just south of our neighborhood for a little treat. Em orders a chilled caramel coffee, and I get a low-fat, decaf, extra-wet cappuccino. Liquid heaven.

I can't wait to get Jerry alone, so I can unload about this obnoxious teacher.

23

I leave for work early on Tuesday but not before giving Emma a pep talk about behaving beyond reproach in history class.

The morning clouds resting on the mountains glow in anticipation of a beautiful day. I turn the corner and drive toward Pine Grove Road. The traffic light at the intersection turns from red to green. I punch the accelerator. If I floor it, I may be able to make the light. My poor old Taurus accepts the challenge and climbs the slight incline with gusto. *Great. I've got it. Just another two hundred yards.*

Rats! The light turns amber. I let up on the gas and slam the brakes. That was disappointing. At least I'm first in line to go through the intersection. I take advantage of the delay and try to bring down my adrenaline by applying some hand lotion.

The light turns green, and I cruise. Just as I'm about to slide into the left-hand lane, a red SUV speeds up and cuts me off. I hope it's not going to be one of *those* mornings.

My cell phone rings. I slip my hands-free device into my ear and answer the call. It's Jerry.

"Didn't you see that Jeep's directional?"

Huh? "What? Where are you?"

His laughter floats down the line. "I'm two cars behind you. What's up? Are you distracted this morning?"

"Excuse me? There's nothing wrong with my driving." I flip on my turn signal. Pine Grove Road is three lanes. Sometimes the right lane moves the fastest.

"Watch that white car, Linda."

I realize I'm clenching my jaw. "I see it."

I glance in my rearview mirror. A car's pulled in front of Jerry. *Good.* We navigate the busy road in silence.

"How fast are you driving?"

I glance at my speedometer. "I'm only going two miles above the limit."

He sighs. "Do you think that's wise?"

"Don't worry. I'm a good driver, Jerry."

I can hear him tune through his radio stations. I love my husband dearly, but he's driving me nuts. It's bad enough he's a backseat driver when he's a passenger in my car, but to be critiquing my driving while he trails me is crazy.

I switch lanes. Maybe he'll lose track of me.

"What are you doing now?"

"Jerry!"

"Do you always drive like this when I'm not with you?"

"Drive like what? I've never gotten a ticket, you know."

"Well, there's always a first time."

I silently fume as we make our way north. Two miles above the speed limit is perfectly acceptable. At least for me. Jerry's sense of right and wrong can sometimes be a little overwhelming.

"Linda?"

"Yes?"

"You know traffic sometimes snarls around that curve coming up. Do you think you should slow down?"

He's annoying me so badly I think I should keep my thoughts to myself.

"Hello? Are you there, Lin?"

The light before me turns amber. "Yeah, I'm here." *But not for long.* I put the pedal to the metal and streak under the traffic light. "Catch ya later, Jer."

As usual, chaos reigns at Dream Photography. I barely get into the building when I'm bombarded with the fires I have to somehow extinguish, and Luke's in a particularly foul mood. I wonder if he's having trouble adjusting to married life, and there's trouble in paradise. Traci comes in smiling. Thank goodness for her.

Under the weight of the demands on my time, the morning flies by. I'm thrilled to clock out for my noon break because I'm meeting Deb for lunch.

I drive half a mile to a newer strip mall. I'm surprised to see her SUV already waiting in the parking lot. I enjoy the embrace of the warm spring sun on my face as I dodge lunchtime drivers racing for the last available parking spaces.

My best friend is sitting on the bench by the hostess station when I enter the restaurant. "Here she is," Deb announces to the young girl standing behind the podium.

The hostess leads us to a booth and distributes the menus. She needn't have bothered. Deb and I meet here for lunch so often we both know the menu by heart.

Deb's glowing, and I know she has some good news to share. She reaches across the table and grabs my hand.

My gaze is forced from the overly familiar menu to Deb's face. "What?"

"I have exciting news!" She clasps her hands over her heart. "Randy asked Andrea to marry him—and she accepted." Tears well up in her eyes.

I rise from my side of the booth and we embrace. "Congratulations. I'm so happy for you and for Randy. Was this the cause of that twinkle in your eye on Sunday?"

Deb smiles. "Keith and I thought it was coming. Randy's been acting really cute and has been asking us questions about our marriage. I've prayed for my children's spouses since they were babies. It looks like God truly answered my prayers."

For a moment, we both sit there, smiling, tears glistening in our eyes.

"I can't believe it. It seems like just yesterday Randy was a baby. Have they set a date?"

"They're thinking of July—if they can make the arrangements."

"Wow. So fast."

"Well, they're deeply in love." Deb pauses as though considering her next words. "They are wonderful, Christian kids. They've been praying about their relationship and their future. We know they're struggling to do the right thing."

I must look confused because Deb shakes her head at me. "They're struggling to remain pure. They say that without a doubt they know God has designed them for each other."

Oh. I didn't consider that.

"Keith and I have given them our blessing."

"How are they going to continue college?"

"Randy's almost finished. Andrea's going to transfer to CU Boulder, and they'll get an apartment between both colleges."

"Can they afford that?"

"Keith wants to finish paying for Randy's education, and it looks like Andrea's getting a pretty good scholarship. They're planning on working for a campus ministry, so that will be their income. We think they can make it."

"Wow."

The waiter comes over, and we place our order.

Deb fills me in on the arrangements they're trying to make. ". . . that way we can save money on the reception. Andrea's parents are . . ." She goes on and on.

I try to follow the conversation, but I'm lost in memories of Randy as a toddler, a schoolboy, a high school athlete, and finally a young college man. I'm privileged to have watched him mature. I can't believe I'll soon be witnessing his wedding.

"Yowsa!" The thought that strikes me is a sobering consideration.

"What's wrong?"

"Deb, I just realized that this wedding will be the first one I'll be attending as an *old* person."

"What are you talking about?"

"Well, at first I was younger than the brides and grooms, then they were my friends and cousins, and now I'm going to be in that other group. Friends of the parents—aka the old people!"

"Oh, Linda. Only you would think like that."

"Yeah, only me and all the other old people. And I thought only your own kids made you feel old. Wait till I get my hands on that son of yours."

We enjoy our juicy hamburgers and chat about the wedding. My heart is warmed when I see pure delight radiating from Deb's eyes.

"Hey, have you started looking for a photographer?"

Deb laughs. "I was hoping you'd give me a hand with that."

"Oh, Dream Photography does beautiful weddings. I'll get some brochures on our different packages for you."

● ● ●

I arrive back at work fifteen minutes past my allotted break time. Hopefully, no one notices.

I hear footsteps echo on the hardwood floor in the hallway. A moment later, Luke walks into the front office. "Well, it's about time." He glares at me with one hand on his hip and the other holding a pile of fax paper.

I ignore his comment. "What can I do for you?"

"The new frame company has messed up the order. The billing's off. Fix it." He drops his problems on my desk and leaves.

Somewhere between my desk and the reception area, Luke

seems to have gone through a major transformation because I can hear him charming the clients and laughing as though he's the sweetest man on earth, without a care in the world. *Bleh.* I can just imagine how the corners of his mouth softened from his perpetual backroom scowl and eased into a sugary-sweet, toothy grin. I don't think his smiles ever make it to his eyes. Or his heart.

I organize the mess of crumpled fax pages. I'm unable to focus my concentration on the figures and frame codes before me. But even Luke and his foul disposition can't get me down today. My best friend's son is getting married. Life marches on.

I think back to my wedding day and can't believe it was almost twenty-five years ago. So much life has unfolded since then. I remember my hopes and dreams and the love I had for Jer. I feel a flame of desire in the pit of my stomach and realize how much I still love that man. But just for a little while, I would like to again experience that newness of love and the excitement it brings. With Jerry.

The canned sound of the "Hallelujah" chorus reverberates from my purse. I retrieve my phone and flip it open. It's a text message from Emma.

RU there?

Hi.

Too nice to be inside.

She's so much faster at texting than I am. I've seen her fingers fly over those digits with amazing speed. I fumble to respond more quickly. **Amen. Randy's getting married.**

Good 4 him. To Emma, Randy is more like a beloved cousin than a friend of the family.

I sigh and continue to punch in the code to further communicate with my daughter. Since we're not face-to-face, I take the opportunity to bring up a subject I know she'll fight me on. **Check out summer school. History.**

#*#*

I knew she wouldn't be happy with that request. I text her back. **Humor me.**

I'm bringing up my grade.

Check it out.

I stare at the blank digital readout and assume she's through with this conversation. I put my phone on vibrate and place it on the side of my desk.

A moment later, Traci strides into my office and tosses a chocolate kiss on my desk.

"Thanks. As if I need that."

She laughs and gives me a wink. "It's chocolate, woman. The most important food group."

"Yeah, well, I don't know if I should pop it in my mouth or just apply it directly to my hips."

She shakes her head, grabs her next sales file, and leaves the room.

I open one of the drawers in the tall file cabinet. My fingers walk through the cardboard dividers until I find the folder that holds our contract with the new framer. I toss it on my desk, and just as I'm about to get back to business, my phone vibrates.

Another message from Em. **I was having a great day till u brought me down.**

Sigh. **Sorry, sweetheart.** Sometimes we just have to do what we have to do. I concentrate on my reply. **Get the info.**

A moment later she responds. **K.**

Whew. That was easier than I thought. I place the phone aside and grab a ruler to go through the contract line by line.

My phone buzzes again, and the vibrations start to dance it off the desk. I snatch it up and glance at the screen.

This class is boring.

What? Oh, that little stinker. I didn't know she was in a class. I assumed she was in the cafeteria eating her lunch. **What class?**

History.

I could just kill her! **Turn your phone off!**

24

Great-grandma's crystal rattles with a vengeance in the china cabinet. Makes me wish I bought that extra insurance coverage when we switched agents.

If Emma slams one more door in this house, I'll scream. Jerry and I decided to ground her through the weekend since she was text messaging me during her history class—which means she had to reschedule her date with Veterinary Boy. The way she's carrying on, you'd think we were planning on locking her up for the next three years.

I feel sorry for Jer. But I'm deserting him tonight because I promised Tammy that I'd go to her home shopping party. Not that I'm even sure what she's selling. I think it's either candles or cookware. As if I need any more stuff.

The clock chimes, sending peals of somber notes throughout the house. I grab my purse and slip into my shoes. "Jerry, it's seven o'clock. I'm heading to Tammy's."

I hear him say something that I assume is an acknowledgment.

I scoot out the door and cross the road. Cars line the driveway and are parked up and down the street. How many people did she invite?

I let myself into Tammy's house. Classical music is playing softly in the background, competing with the chatter of female voices. The house smells divine—a cross between aromatic appetizers and spicy candles. One look around and I'm convinced that I've come for a candle party. I'm sure I can find one or two candles that will tickle my fancy.

"There you are." Tammy motions me down the hall and toward the back of the house, where she has goodies set out on her kitchen island.

"Hi. Sorry I'm late."

"No problem." She links her arm through mine. "Let me introduce you to a few people."

We're heading toward the living room when I spot the back of a head covered in shoulder-length brown hair with natural gray peppered through it. *That lady seems eerily familiar. Where do I know her from?* The woman is wearing a black blouse, punctuated with dandruff specks on the shoulders.

When Tammy and I arrive in the living room, at least fifteen pairs of the eyes shift to us.

The mystery woman turns her head. I feel my heart fall to my stomach. It's Alice Boothe, Emma's dreadful history teacher. *What's she doing in my neighborhood?*

Miss Boothe obviously feels the same way about me because her polite little smile freezes on her face, and she suddenly finds her appetizer much more interesting than greeting me.

As if that will deter me from acting appropriately in a social situation. My mother didn't raise any social misfits. "Why, Miss Boothe. Nice to see you."

She glances toward me, pops a spinach-cheese quiche in her mouth, and nods in dismissal.

Just as well. *I really didn't want to talk to you either.* I let Tammy introduce me to some of the gals she works with, then escape to the kitchen to get some food.

Tammy's an amazing hostess. The array of choices is perfect; both sweet and savory foods entice my taste buds. I fill my paper cocktail plate, pour a cup of punch, and return to the living room.

The party leader is certainly not lacking in energy. She's actually got a little too much. After all, it's just candles. Nevertheless, I get caught in her enthusiasm and end up spending sixty-eight dollars on various candles and candleholders. I don't think Jerry will mind. He likes my new candle fixation. Besides, who can resist a lilac-scented bedroom?

The partygoers who drove to the festivities disperse and leave my street in peace, while I linger to help Tammy reclaim her house. I'm taking a bag of garbage out to the garage as the candle hostess departs.

Tammy closes the door and allows her thank-goodness-everyone's-gone sigh to escape her lungs. "Thanks, Linda."

"No problem. So how do you know Alice Boothe?"

"Who?"

"Uh . . . your guest? The one who sat in the green armchair."

"Oh, that lady. She's a friend of our new neighbor from down the street."

"Really? She seems so nice. What's she doing with a friend like Miss Boothe?"

Tammy lifts her eyebrows. "Be nice."

Ouch. I'm getting too snarky as I approach middle age. "Sorry. But didn't she seem a little . . . unusual. Sort of sour?"

Tammy slowly shakes her head. "I didn't get to speak with her that much. She seemed okay to me. Maybe a little shy."

I guess it's time for me to zip it. Besides getting disapproval from Tammy, I feel that familiar God-tug at my heart. *Sorry, Lord. I'll try to be nice to Miss Boothe. Really, I will.*

"Mom? Is it safe to come downstairs?" Tammy's daughter Lyndsay poses at the top of the stairs.

"Sure, honey. I was going to offer Linda a cup of hot tea. Want one?"

Lyndsay scrambles down the stairs. "I just want to raid the left-over quiche if you have any."

Tammy puts a kettle on the stove and opens one of the cabinet doors. "What kind would you like?" She gestures to the shelves lined with at least ten different types of tea.

"Wow. What a selection."

Lyndsay laughs. "Mom got carried away last fall when we took a tour of the Celestial Seasonings factory in Boulder while Grandma was visiting."

"Apparently."

I select some Lady Grey and plop the bag into one of the mugs on the counter.

Tammy chooses peppermint, pours the boiling water into our mugs, then opens another cabinet. "This is my supersecret stash," she says with a touch of mystery in her voice as she pushes aside a box of rice. She proudly produces a box of organic chocolate truffles.

"Oh, now you're talking." I help myself to a paper plate and place two more on the table.

Lyndsay pulls up a chair and joins us for our snack.

"So, Lyndsay, what's new?"

She shrugs. Typical teenager.

I take a bite of my truffle and nearly drown in the rich, creamy flavor that hijacks my senses. I try to engage Lyndsay again. "How's school?"

"Okay . . ." A small frown creases her forehead. "Mrs. Revere, Emma really tries in history. I don't know why she's not getting good grades."

Hmm. I see how it is. She's sticking up for her friend. It's an admirable quality, but this time poor Em got caught with her hand in the cookie jar. "Well, maybe she'd do better if she stayed off her phone during class."

Lyndsay's good sense overcomes her loyalty to Em, and she allows a smile to play at the corners of her mouth. "Yeah, that could help."

I know I said I'd try to be good, but I just can't let it go. I take a sip of my steaming brew and ask Lyndsay, "Did you come downstairs to say hello to Miss Boothe tonight?"

She blinks in disbelief and drops her jaw in surprise. "What? She was in my house? Mom? You invited her?" She turns and glares at Tammy as if she were a traitor in our midst.

I'm beginning to feel a little remorseful for mentioning it. My palms start to sweat, a reaction I've had to feelings of guilt since I was four years old. "I'm sorry, Tammy. Lyndsay, I didn't need to tell you that."

Tammy stares at me with a mixture of irritation and regret. "Our new neighbor brought her along. I thought she seemed nice enough."

"Mom?" Lyndsay stares at her mother, holding her quiche suspended in front of her face.

Tammy levels a piercing stare at both of us. "Excuse me, but can't we show a little kindness?"

Lyndsay drops her quiche on her plate and wipes her palms on a napkin. "Mom, do you know what that woman did?"

I explain the situation to Tammy, aided by Lyndsay's editorial comments along the way.

Tammy frowns. "There must be some kind of misunderstanding."

"Well, that's the understatement of the century."

Tammy helps herself to another truffle. "I'm sorry for Emma's trouble. I hope she can end the semester on a good note."

"Yeah, it better end well. We're keeping a close eye on Emma and the work she's doing. I just worry about Miss Boothe."

"She's a horror, Mom. We're lucky I'm not having problems too."

"Let's keep it that way, kiddo. I certainly hope that you treat your teacher with respect."

Lyndsay's face flushes crimson. "Yes, I do." She wraps her mini quiche in a napkin and flees the room.

Interesting. If Tammy also thinks her daughter's reaction is a bit overboard, she's not letting on. Maybe I'm reading too much into it. It's probably just a case of teenage sensitivity.

"She seemed like a lonely woman to me, Linda. I could be wrong, but I think we should give her the benefit of the doubt."

"Come on. I've seen the girls working together on projects. I know Emma's doing as much as the rest of the group. I don't know what Miss Boothe has against Emma, and I don't intend to let her get away with gouging her grade."

"At least you've spoken to Miss Boothe. Maybe things will begin to improve."

I'm not terribly optimistic about that, but I'm not going to further argue the point. "I'm sorry for unloading about this. And for bringing Lyndsay into it."

Tammy shakes her head dismissively. "Don't worry about it. I'm not perfect either."

I retrieve my purse, say good night, and stroll across the street.

When I get home, I hear the sound of pots clanging. "Nick? What are you cooking?"

My oldest child gives me a disarming grin, so similar to his father's. "I had a craving for some shrimp and linguini with garlic sauce. Want some?"

"Thanks, but no thanks. Isn't it a little late for such a heavy snack?"

"No worries, Mom. I'm going to be up for hours, working on an assignment."

I pick up a few glasses and a small plate that are sitting on the table and load the dishwasher. "How's it been around here tonight?"

Nick stifles a chuckle. "Let's just say you're lucky you weren't here."

"How awful was it?"

"Emma's in rare form. I'm sure Dad will fill you in, poor guy."

Ouch. I trudge upstairs and find Jerry reading an autobiography, his reading glasses perched on the end of his nose.

"It's about time you got home."

I sit on the side of the bed. My poor sweetheart looks drained. "That bad, huh?"

Jerry lays his book aside. "It was pretty much what I expected. Emma's peeved that she had to cancel her date with this new guy—Don? Or Doug?"

"David."

"Whatever. She's afraid he won't reschedule their date because we're—and I quote—'weird parents.'"

"I'm sorry I left you alone tonight to deal with her tantrum."

Jerry smiles. "That's okay. I was up for the challenge. She just needed to know who's the boss around here."

"Poor Em. And she's stuck with us."

Jer tosses his reading glasses on the night table. His face warms with a self-satisfied grin.

His mysterious affectation has piqued my interest. "What?"

"Wouldn't you like to know?"

A little playful, are we? "Wouldn't you like to tell me?"

"Okay, I can tell you part of my secret." Grinning, he sits back and crosses his arms. He loves these dramatic pauses.

I try to wait him out, but I'm unsuccessful. "Jerry?"

"I made some plans tonight."

Oh, goody. "What kind of plans?"

"Anniversary plans."

"What? Where are we going?" *Punta Cana? Turquoise water; cool, fruity drinks; and hot, steamy nights!*

He stretches out his arms, laces his fingers, and puts his hands behind his head. "That's the secret." He looks so satisfied, sitting there with his Cheshire cat grin.

"Oh, come on. Tell me." *Please, oh, please, New York City, Niagara Falls?*

"Then it wouldn't be a surprise."

I scoot closer to him on the bed. "I bet I could make you tell me."

"Do you now?"

"Uh-huh."

"Well, bring it on."

25

"Mom, Dad wants you to move your car."

I don't know why Jerry can't move my car himself. It's not as if what I'm doing is any less important than his plans. I shut off Betty and push my vacuum to the side of the room.

Jerry's and Keith's voices filter into the house from the garage, where they're preparing to demolish the drywall to insulate the pipes running up to the second floor.

I retrieve my keys from my purse and join the men. "Hi, Keith."

As I'm walking past him toward my car, he captures me in a brotherly hug. "Hey, Linny. Want to help?"

Yeah, as if. "I'll leave all that fun to you guys."

I move my car out to the street, saying a quick prayer that all goes well with their little project. They've got enough tools here to build a small shed. As I breeze past them toward the house, the sound of a hammer pounding through the garage wall nearly launches me off the ground. I spin around with my hand on my heart. "Thanks a lot. That sounded like a gunshot."

They both smile as though my discomfort is their badge of honor.

"We had to make a hole to use the saw."

"Whatever. I'm going to finish my cleaning." Unfortunately, I've never been accused of having a poker face—they might have seen me roll my eyes as I turned around.

Yeah, they saw me, and their laughter follows me as I reenter the house. I'm about to resume my cleaning, but the buzzer on the clothes dryer begins to play my tune. Like one of Pavlov's dogs, I immediately trot up the stairs to the laundry room.

On my way, I pass Emma. The deep freeze that radiates from her stony countenance could cool hell. She brushes past me as though we're strangers on the street. Unfortunately, I don't take it as well as Jerry. I'm a little ticked off that she feels entitled to pull her attitude.

Well, two can play the cold-shoulder game, at least for a while. I act like I don't have a care in the world and we're on normal terms. I manipulate the dry clothes into the laundry basket and put the load of towels into the dryer. Maturing is a slow process, but just once I'd like to be able to fast-forward through Emma's difficult times.

I skip back downstairs to resume my chores. With a click, I power Betty up again, and I'm grateful that the roar of her ancient motor nearly blocks out the electric whine from the tools in the garage. I should go on the Internet someday and figure out how many calories vacuuming burns an hour. Betty and I have been aerobic partners for almost twenty-one years, since we bought this monstrosity after a slick salesman gave us one amazing product demo in the comfort of our tiny first apartment.

Betty and I do the cha-cha throughout the downstairs while I daydream about where Jerry might take me for our anniversary weekend. Could air travel be involved? *Maybe San Francisco or the Mexican Riviera? Oh, wouldn't that be cool?*

As I'm about to begin cleaning the stairs, Jerry opens the garage door and yells in, "Linda, what's for lunch?"

You've got to be kidding. I'm supposed to stop what I'm doing and cater a lunch for the construction crew? And according to the trio of male voices drifting in, the crew now includes Nick. Weekend lunches at our house have been self-serve for the past few years. So why does Jerry want to be waited on now?

I put a lid on my slow simmer and walk to the garage. Large pieces of drywall are stacked in a small pile, and the fine, white chalk dust coats everything within six feet of the wall—including Jerry's car and our bicycles. I wonder who's going to be responsible for cleaning it up. The three guys shoot me goofy smiles. It takes all the self-control I can muster up not to shake my head in wonder.

Jerry's staring at me with an expectant expression. As much as I would like to remind him that preparing his lunch sounds like a personal problem to me, I wouldn't embarrass him in front of Keith.

"Are cold cuts okay?"

"Sure, thanks."

Well, good. If he had requested anything more, I might have gone for the jugular. I go to the kitchen and with one efficient motion grab cold cuts, condiments, and vegetables out of the fridge. After slicing some tomatoes and onions and washing the lettuce, I arrange the vegetables and cold cuts on a platter. I dump half a loaf of bread onto a tray, grab a pitcher of iced tea from the fridge, and place it all on the kitchen table with a handful of paper plates.

I nudge Belle aside and open the garage door. "Lunch is on the table."

They file in and take turns washing up at the kitchen sink. Jerry motions me toward the dining room, and I walk in and wait for him to join me.

"Lin, you didn't *make* the sandwiches?"

I fist my hands and rest them on my hips. "Excuse me?" I hope the look on my face precludes me having to say anything more.

He must get my message because he raises his hands, palms facing me, as if in surrender. "Okay, sorry." He smiles and pulls me into an embrace.

"Tone down the testosterone, pal. Maybe I shouldn't let you play demolition man anymore."

I move to step back, but he continues to hold me. I tilt my head to look into his face. His suggestive smile captivates me. *Wow.* The hormonal surge would knock me off my feet if I weren't being held so tightly. Maybe I'll let him play demolition man again if I get to spend time with this appealing fellow.

As though he can read my mind, he leans down, kisses my earlobe, gives me a squeeze, and joins the boys in the kitchen. Kevin Costner couldn't have pulled off that move any better. *Amazing.*

I stumble into the living room and into the waiting arms of Grandma's Victorian chair. My heart dances within my chest in a way I haven't experienced in decades. Now I know how Dr. Frankenstein must have felt, taking delight in the creature he created.

Before I can further evaluate the situation, the phone rings. I hop to answer it so the guys can enjoy their lunch. My presence seems to go unnoticed as I grab the receiver off the kitchen wall and return to the front of the house. "Hello?"

"Hey, Lin. House still standing?"

Deb makes me laugh. "So far, so good. And they seem to be enjoying their work." Some of them almost a little too much, but I'm not complaining anymore.

"I need to talk to Keith, hon."

"Sure."

I stroll back to the kitchen. "Your sweetie," I say as I pass off the phone to Keith.

He smiles and leaves the room.

I snag a CD lying on the counter and go into the dining room to put it away in the case next to the audio system. While I'm kneeling on the floor, Keith comes in and takes a seat in the adjacent living room.

"Oh, come on, babe." He absentmindedly taps his fingers on his leg while he listens to his wife.

I begin to put away some of the CDs Em left scattered around. I should have her do it, but I don't want to kill my good mood right now by having to speak to my ice princess.

"Deb, remember what I said. . . ." The tone of Keith's voice changes from pleasant and cajoling to something else. Something I've never heard from him.

The hairs on the back of my arms rise, and I wish I could stop up my ears. But if I get up and leave the room, Keith will know I've overheard him. Could I somehow slink away unnoticed?

"Definitely not. No! Forget about it."

I've never heard Keith talk to Deb like that. Almost as if she were a naughty child. I scrunch down farther. Maybe this way I'll be less conspicuous.

He jumps to his feet. "You know what my answer is. And don't cross me on this, Deborah."

Oh no. Now it sounds as though he's talking to a dog. *Why do I have to overhear this conversation?*

Any semblance of love is absent from his voice. "I've already apologized once. I don't need to do it again. And I don't need to share our problems with a stranger." Keith's fingers grip the phone tightly while his usually pleasant countenance becomes a mask of anger. "You listen to me. . . ."

He stalks from the living room to the foyer, and I make my escape to the kitchen. The sting of a strong flush travels up from my neck. If Jer ever spoke to me like that, I'd just die.

I busy myself making a sandwich and hope no one notices my flaming face. Jerry and Nick are engrossed in conversation, their chatter a balm to my taut nerves.

Keith's voice becomes louder as he strolls into the kitchen. "Okay, honey. We'll talk later." He smiles and places the receiver in the cradle. Without missing a beat, he takes his seat and joins in the boys' conversation.

I couldn't be more shocked if he sprouted horns and a tail. Is that man for real? One minute he's talking to his wife like she's dirt and the next he's being sugarplum sweet.

That dog. I glance at him, and he seems oblivious to me. He has no clue that I overheard his conversation.

The men finish their lunch and retreat to the garage but not before Jer tosses out the paper plates. My guy's a gem.

My mind is buzzing when I turn on my vacuum and begin to clean the stairs with a vengeance. How dare Keith claim to love Deb and speak to her that way! Is he always this two-faced? Should I speak with her about it?

Would she be mortified if I knew?

26

A finch serenades the world from the pine tree outside our bedroom window. I could complain about the early wake-up call, but I remember all too well the treeless prairie we moved to ten years ago. Now that the neighborhood landscaping is mature, we have birds and bunnies galore.

Jerry snores on. Birds or no birds, that man can snooze. I reach out and toy with a strand of his hair. From now on I won't balk at his playing handyman. The garage wall is in order again, pipes sufficiently insulated to prevent any further worries about a burst during one of Colorado's cold snaps. He was so proud of his accomplishment; his usual work is often more cerebral than physical. He shifts position, and I slide out of bed. Let him sleep.

I go downstairs to start my day. Belle trots to the kitchen and can barely contain herself while I unlock the back door.

I peek out the front window. The *Rocky Mountain News* lies in the middle of the driveway, snug in its blue plastic sleeve. A glance up and down the sleepy street convinces me I'm probably the only one awake at this early hour. The dead bolt on the front door thumps as it's released from its cradle. I pull the belt tighter on my robe and hustle to the drive to fetch the newspaper. My moves are as swift as a relay racer's, the newspaper my baton. As I'm about to leap onto the porch, I hear a high-pitched whistle followed by masculine laughter.

"Morning, neighbor." Bill from across the way waves as he steps from his door to retrieve his paper.

Rats. Jer's always saying I should get dressed before I go outside. Now Bill has that mental image of me racing, unkempt, for the morning paper. I hope I don't hear about this at the next neighborhood get-together.

Belle's scratching furiously at the back door when I enter the kitchen. I feed her, brew a pot of coffee, and sit down to enjoy catching up on the news.

I skim the paper, but comprehension is weak at best. All I can think about is the way Jerry swept me off my feet with a mere glance yesterday. What a man. That's the guy I fell in love with so many years ago. Where has he been, and why did it take so long for him to reappear? I should plan a romantic surprise of some sort for him.

My bubble of happiness is tempered by the memory of Keith's conversation with Deb. She's never let on that their marriage is anything but bliss. Come to think of it, she's often bragging about the state of her union. Where does the truth lie? I rack my brain to recall any hints of trouble. Did she ever drop any clues I was too dense to see? Does he speak to her like that often? I've seen Keith's temper flare, but that was always about an issue with the kids. How could she always seem so satisfied if she goes home at night to that?

"Mom?" Emma's standing next to me as though waiting for a response.

"What? Did you say something?" I'm stunned that she's speaking to me. "I didn't hear you come in."

She flops into the chair across from me. "Yeah, I asked when can I have my cell phone back."

I hate this part of parenthood. If only it could be all ice cream and amusement parks. "I didn't like taking your phone away. Dad and I are trying to get you to think more than five minutes ahead.

How could you possibly learn anything in class if you're busy text messaging?"

"You don't need to chew me out again. I just asked a simple question."

"Sorry. But do you understand what we're trying to teach you?"

"Duh, yeah. Do we have to go over it again?"

I narrow my eyes and try to choose my words carefully before I open my mouth. She's right about going over the same point again, but her attitude leaves much to be desired. "First, lose the attitude. Second, you lost your phone privileges for the weekend. It's only Sunday morning."

She tosses her head back so far I'm surprised it doesn't dislocate and roll across the floor.

In spite of her temporary teen-induced insanity, I love her to pieces. "If you feel like you want to chat, I'm always available," I say with a smile.

She cuts her gaze at me and flattens her mouth, but I can see a hint of a smile tug at her lips.

I push the issue. "How about a game of Scrabble this afternoon?"

Her stomach growls like a bear, and we both laugh.

"Cereal?"

She smiles and nods.

I retrieve the bowls. She snatches a few boxes of cereal from the pantry and pours herself a heaping bowlful of Cheerios. "I'm sorry. Really."

Oh, my sweet girl. I reach across and put my hand on her baby-soft one. "I know. I only hope it's not too late to redeem your grade."

"It's only history, Mom, not rocket science."

"True, but you still need to study and do your assignments."

A look of discomfort crosses her face. "I do my assignments. I just don't get proper credit for them."

"I plan on checking every assignment you hand in and rechecking after it's graded. Maybe if we keep an eye on the situation, things will get better."

Emma grunts in dismissal and returns her attention to her soggy breakfast.

• • •

We follow the script of our usual Sunday morning routine, but somehow we fall behind schedule. At church Emma displays the first real smile I've seen in days and skips off to join her friends.

Jer and I slip into our Sunday school class late and take a seat in the rear of the room. From my vantage point, I watch Deb and Keith. His arm casually rests across the back of her chair. The teacher says something funny, and they glance at each another and laugh. It looks like their relationship always has—happy. Their marriage always seemed rock solid until yesterday, when I got a glimpse into their private reality, and seeds of doubt fell into the fertile soil of my imagination.

Class dismisses, and I haul Jer out of the room and into the hall. I'm not ready to speak with Deb and Keith yet.

"Lin?" Jerry studies me as though he suspects something's up.

I try to sound natural. "I want to have a quick cup of tea."

We meander to the beverage station, and I take my time choosing a brew.

The crowd swells as people pour from classrooms. "Hey, aren't they the missionaries?" I ask.

"Who?"

"The missionaries from Brazil."

Before Jer can stop me, I flag them down. They're thrilled to give us a report of their work, and within minutes there's a small group listening to their adventures.

By the time we join the service, our usual seats are taken. I'm relieved we can't sit near Deb and Keith.

We slip into a pew toward the back, and I sink into my seat. Pins and needles dance along my scalp as guilt plunges its cold tentacles, jagged and painful, into my consciousness. I'm a lousy friend.

Jer smiles at me, and for a moment, I consider discussing the situation with him. But how do I tell him one of his best friends is a louse? Knowing Jerry, he'd be uncomfortable facing embarrassing details about Deb and Keith's marriage. And he might accuse me of gossiping.

Worship music begins, and I lose myself in the wonder of the Almighty. The rest of the world fades while I allow Him to search my soul. *Oh, Father, if only I could quiet myself during the week to spend more time like this with You. Help me to be the friend Deb needs.*

After the service ends, we join the humanity flowing from the sanctuary. Jerry gets a cup of coffee, and I search the crowd for Deb. I press down my rising anxiety and tell myself that I need to be close to my friend. I spot her standing alone while Keith is talking with a couple of men. Hiking my purse on my shoulder, I cross the room and give her a hug.

She freezes for a moment, then returns my affection. "Oh, Linda. You startled me."

"Good morning," I say a little too brightly. I look deeply into her face to see if there's trouble brewing in her sparkling green eyes.

As if she finds my behavior odd, her smile dims. "What's up?"

Should I let on that I overheard Keith? "Uh, I was wondering—"

"Linda." Keith is at my elbow, giving me a big smile.

"Hi, Keith." I'm usually not one to be found speechless, but I don't have anything to say to this man. Not after what I heard yesterday.

A broad smile splits his disgustingly handsome face. "Am I interrupting?"

"No, not at all." *Did I say that too quickly?*

Deb looks at me as if I have my blouse on backward.

I pull myself together. "I was just about to tell Deb what a wonderful job you did on my garage wall." *Liar, liar. My pants are on fire.*

"Well, thanks. It's always fun to do a little demolition." His grin is self-satisfied, the creep. Keith seems unaware of my discomfort. He scans the room as if he's looking for someone more interesting to talk to. I've dropped off his radar screen.

Whew. I lucked out on that one. Men can be so dense. He continues to glance about the room and finally sees Jerry, gives my arm a squeeze, winks at Deb, and walks over to join Jerry. The dog. *Yeah, act all lovey-dovey, fella.*

"What's new?" I ask. Maybe it would be better if she initiated the conversation.

Deb stares at her shoes. "Not much."

I glance down too. "Nice shoes."

"I bought them last night. I was a little restless and made a quick trip to the mall."

I take in her appearance. Nearly perfect as usual. "Restless?"

Deb opens her mouth to speak, but as if a veil falls, she closes up. An awkward silence stretches between us.

I put my hand on her arm. "Deb?"

She shakes her head and forces a brittle smile on her face. "Sorry, Linda. I've been distracted lately."

"Distracted? How so?"

Out of the corner of my eye, I see Jer and Keith walking toward us.

Deb smoothes another imaginary wrinkle from her skirt. How can she not know she looks perfect? "Hey, Jer."

"Your husband could be a master plumber. You should see our garage."

She laughs. "I'd call him more of a hobbyist."

Keith grins and puts his hand on the small of Deb's back. "We've got to run, hon."

Deb and I make eye contact.

"Call me later, Deb."

She smiles and allows herself to be escorted from the building. Is it my imagination or is there an air of sorrow hanging over her head?

Ah. Peace and quiet—such an unusual condition for Dream Photography. I rejoice every year when the weather allows Luke and the associate photographers to take advantage of the incredible scenery in the portrait backyard and conduct their outdoor shoots. The only clients in the building are tucked behind doors, enjoying their image presentations, and I'm left alone to catch up on paperwork. Even the telephone is mercifully silent.

The staccato clatter of high-heeled shoes on the tile floor warns me my solitude is about to be disturbed. I knew it was too good to last.

"Hey, Linda." Pam nods to me and busies herself looking through client files.

"Hi, Pam."

I hate to admit it, but I'm uncomfortable around her. She's been a salesperson with Dream Photography for about six months. In all that time, we've had only a handful of conversations. We're a tight-knit group, but she always declines our invitations to lunches or dinner.

She turns soulful brown eyes in my direction. "Have you seen the Wyckoff file?"

I know she's speaking to me, but I'm distracted by her outfit. She's wearing skintight black yoga pants under a flaring aqua miniskirt. On top of that she has three layers of thin, gauzy shirts—

white, aqua, and pink. The pièce de résistance is about a pound of vintage costume jewelry. While bizarre, it works for her. I wouldn't even know where to shop for such things. "Pardon?"

"Wyckoff. They're finally coming in to view the images taken two months ago."

"Oh yeah. Sorry. We have a new file for overdue orders. It's in the bottom drawer."

She shuts the top file and bends down to continue her search. She claims her file, rams the drawer shut with her foot, and leaves the office without another word.

I continue to sort through invoices to put them with their corresponding receipts. My desk is stacked with piles of paper when Barb, the receptionist, pokes her head in.

She sports her perpetual smile. "Your appointment's here."

My brain whirs, trying to recall my schedule. "What? I'm not on the schedule for an image presentation."

She shakes her head. "No, not an image presentation. A session consultation."

I must look dull witted because she continues to explain, speaking slowly and enunciating her words. "Carol Ball. She's here to discuss their family session next week with Luke."

"Oh, crumbs!" I forgot about her. My stomach flips, and my glands kick into perspiration overproduction. She's probably the only woman on the planet who can put me into a panic.

I snag a file of family portraits from my desk drawer and frantically thumb through them for the samples I know she'll want to see. I'm putting them in a file folder with some brochures on wardrobe suggestions when Barb returns.

"I think you better get a move on. She looks impatient."

I grimace. "She was born that way."

I take a calming breath—probably a waste of time—wipe my grimy palms on my skirt, and follow Barb to what feels like the Inquisition.

When I enter the lobby, Carol Ball is pacing. *Pacing.* No wonder she's so thin. She most likely doesn't stop moving from dawn until dusk. Her wardrobe screams couture, and she's wearing tens of thousands of dollars' worth of gold and jewels. Her handbag alone is probably worth the GDP of a developing nation.

She looks at me with cold, hostile eyes. "It's about time. The reason people set appointments is to keep to a schedule."

I plaster a smile on my stunned face. *Eat dirt; get this over with; grovel.* "Good afternoon, Carol. Nice to see you again."

I extend my hand, but she grunts and fingers her necklace. *Am I not even good enough for her to acknowledge?*

I make the mistake of glancing at my watch, knowing her eyes are blazing at me.

Carol clears her throat as though she were an imperial Royal Highness about to address a serf. "If you care to know, our appointment was for 2:30. It is now 2:36."

"I'm very sorry. Shall we get down to business?" *Eat dirt; get this over with; grovel.*

She stares down her nose at me. "Please."

"Fine. Let's go to the conference room, then."

She grabs her purse and a garment bag that was laid over the back of a chair. *Sheesh.* Talk about coming prepared. I begin to lead her down the hall.

"Uh, Linda?"

I turn to face her, and she's rooted to the floor, holding out the garment bag. *Are you kidding? Am I now her beast of burden?*

She twitches her head and barely stifles a sigh. "Do you mind?"

"Uh, no. Not at all." *Eat dirt; get this over with; grovel.*

We proceed to the conference room, and I can't help but feel like a court jester leading the way in a parade. I hope nobody sees me.

I lay the bag on the huge walnut table, and Carol pushes me aside to unzip the luggage and distribute various garments the length of the table. I hate to say it, but I'm impressed with her choices.

She points a meticulously manicured talon at a blue and gray shirt. "I think I'm leaning toward that theme, but I like this as well." She gestures to a cream and brown sweater.

My fingers itch to touch the gorgeous fabrics, but I'm afraid she'd slap my hand. "Well, you are having your portrait taken in our natural grass area, aren't you?"

"Yes, I believe that's what Luke recommended." Carol appears thoughtful. "That was his advice, wasn't it?"

Her tone of voice makes me nervous. "I think it was."

She looks as though she's just caught a whiff of last week's fish. "You think so? Would you mind verifying that?"

"Uh, yeah. I'll be right back." *Eat dirt; get this over with; grovel.*

I hustle to the lobby and access her file in our software. I'm relieved I was right. I scurry to the conference room. "Yes, your appointment is for that area of our portrait garden. It's a beautiful part—large trees, natural grasses. You'll love it." I hope to win her over with my enthusiasm. "You know, that cream and brown would look incredible in that setting."

"Don't you offer your clients water anymore?"

Yikes. I forgot. "Yes, I'll be right back." I gather my composure and ease myself from the room. Once I'm two steps from the door, I kick into high gear and power walk to the refrigerator in the workroom.

Jill's at the counter, wearing what she calls her *frapron*, her framing apron. She places a twenty-four-by-thirty-inch portrait into an elaborate frame and glances at me. "Whoa. What's wrong?"

I don't have time to explain. "Carol Ball." I pull open the fridge and snag a water bottle.

A peal of laughter escapes from deep within. "Take a breath. It'll be okay."

I nod and rush back to the conference room. *Yeah, okay for you. You don't have to deal with Carol Wrecking Ball.*

When I return, Carol's already opened my file and has pictures scattered across the table. Her claws rhythmically tap the table. She glances up and puts out a hand to accept the bottle. "This looks very promising," she says as she stabs one of the portraits with her long nail.

Uh, thank you? Hello? Am I an invisible servant? "This is one of Luke's favorite outdoor settings. Especially for large families."

She puts her water bottle down on one of the portraits.

Grrrr. I produce a coaster from the credenza and place her drink on it.

"Oh, sorry."

"No problem." *Eat dirt; get this over with. I can grovel.*

Once again, I amaze myself with my patience and guide Carol to choose the cream and brown theme. "Really, Carol. Neutral earth tones will look fabulous for your portrait. I think you'll be pleased."

"For what I pay for your services here, I'd better be."

I smile. What can I say?

She stuffs her garments back into their bag with an air of indifference. "Oh, I want to reorder some large prints from last year's portrait session. Can you help me with that?"

Inwardly, I groan. "Sure. Let me run to the back room and get your file."

Carol sits down in a gesture of dismissal.

I rush to find her file. I'm able to locate it without a hitch. The sooner we get this done, the sooner she can leave.

Twenty minutes and eight hundred dollars later, I escort her to the door. Not once did she threaten to call Luke. What I accomplished was nothing less than an amazing feat of diplomacy. Luke can put that in his pipe and smoke it.

The large candy bar I spied in the back room calls out to me, and I go accept my chocolate therapy. My weary self falls into a seat at the break table, and the rich dark chocolate soothes my battered spirit. My eyes close in delight as the thick, sweet flavor numbs the wounds inflicted by that rude woman.

"Linda?" Barb's voice calls over the intercom, followed by a laugh.

I'm jolted back to reality. "Yes?"

"Carol Ball's on the phone for you. Line two."

Oh. Heavens no. What does she want? I grab the receiver and stab the button to take her call off hold. "This is Linda."

"One more thing." Carol doesn't even bother to identify herself. Does she think she's our only client or our most important one?

"Yes, Carol?"

"Because of the past difficulties, I fully expect you will rush that portrait order *and* deliver it to my house."

Will it never end? "Sure. That won't be a problem. I'll call you when they're ready. Have a nice day." *You filthy animal.*

28

I couldn't be happier to clean off my desk and clock out. I eye the digital readout on my monitor—4:55. Yes. I can hang on for five more minutes.

"Linda!"

Oh, rats. "I'm in the front office, Luke." *Eeww.* I can smell him before he enters the room. "Was it hot out there today?"

He ignores my question. "That large postal envelope that was on my desk—did you put it out for the mailman?"

"No."

"It needs to get to Cleveland by Thursday. Now it's going to be late, and we'll have to pay a penalty."

I'm sure there's a method to his madness, but I don't have a clue what he's yammering about. "Cleveland?"

His face is flushed, either from a day in the sun or because he's about to lose control. "You should have put it out with the mail."

"You never mentioned it to me." *And I'm not a mind reader.*

Luke runs his hand through his sweaty, stinky hair. "I'm sure you saw it there."

Of course, nothing's ever his fault. "I'll drive to the post office on my way home." I hope he takes the hint that I'm about to leave.

He sucks in a breath and retreats to his office.

I put my computer to sleep and sling my purse over my shoulder, then grab my lunch box and start toward Luke's lair. My appearance shouldn't leave any doubt in his mind that I'm outta here.

He's already on his cell phone, and he raises a finger to delay me.

I move his backpack aside and take a seat in one of the chairs opposite his desk.

"Yes, yes. I'll call you back . . . ," Luke says. "Mmm-hmm." A moment later he's off the phone. He turns his gaze on me. "Carol Ball left a message on my cell."

Groan. A group of jolly gnomes starts doing a conga dance through my intestines. "What did she say?"

He crosses his arms and grins.

Spill your guts, man.

"She said that she's very prepared for her family session, and you did a great job helping her."

Knock me over with a feather. "Are you kidding? She was a bear."

He stands and hands me the envelope. "Thanks for driving this through. And thanks for handling Carol. Good job."

I pick my jaw up off the floor. "You're welcome."

Luke smiles and waves me off.

I escape before he recovers from his heat-induced personality disorder and reverts to his usual surly self.

Belle greets me at the door, dancing and curling her upper doggy lip in a smile. We waltz into the kitchen together for her treat. I'm surprised to find Emma at the sink, washing lettuce for a salad. "Hi, Em."

"Did you notice I set the table?"

"Yeah, what's up?" Did she get caught text messaging in class again?

"Can't I just do something nice without you thinking I'm up to something?"

"Sorry. I thought—"

"You wouldn't say anything like that to Nick . . . your favorite."

"Emma, don't say that. You know it's not true. Thanks for pitching in. I'm sorry if you misunderstood me."

She stares at me for a moment, dries her hands, and marches from the room. When is she going to emerge from the dark tunnel of adolescence and be a human being again?

I put my lunch box on the counter and toss some food into Belle's bowl.

I wish Jer were home. I go upstairs and change into my capri sweatpants and a T-shirt.

As I'm descending the stairs, Jerry comes through the door. He smiles as he enters the dining room to dispose of his briefcase. I follow him, my sweet human tranquilizer.

There's a box on the table I hadn't seen before. "What's this?" I burrow through tissue paper to find the candles I ordered at Tammy's party. *Cool.*

"I walked over to Lyndsay's to get it. Her mom left a message today." I look up to find Emma standing in the doorway, smiling like an angel. This girl cycles through moods faster than Belle chases after a trespassing bunny.

We enjoy a pleasant dinner. No sibling sniping, no lessons to teach our maturing children, no disagreements of any type. When both kids volunteer to clear the table and put away leftovers, I think I've died and gone to heaven.

Have I stumbled into a parallel universe? First Luke was complimentary; now my children are falling into line like perfect little Stepford kids. *What next?*

"Lin, I have a surprise," Jerry calls from the living room.

Oh, good heavens. Will Jerry be waiting for me with a bouquet of roses? Will he be holding a beautiful blue Tiffany jewelry box cradling my long-desired tennis bracelet?

My soapy hands drip dishwater across the kitchen floor before I grab a towel. I bet this will be good.

When I arrive in the living room, Jerry is preoccupied with sifting through the contents of a Home Depot bag. Maybe he stopped there after he went to the jewelry store.

"Jer?"

He smiles as he looks at me. "I stopped to buy some batteries on my way home, and I saw this. . . ." He fumbles through his large bag. "I thought you'd like it, so I bought a few packages." He holds out a large, thin rectangular item packaged in a see-through plastic shell. It's silver.

Curiosity drives me, and I take a step closer and accept the article. "What is it?"

"Disposable grill covers." Jerry looks as though he just handed me a million dollars. What could he possibly be thinking?

"For?"

"You put them on top of the grill before you cook your meat."

"And I would be interested in them because?"

The expression on his face shifts from delight to confusion. He's confused? *Hello? Where're the diamonds? and roses?* He could have at least picked up potted roses for the garden.

Jerry clears his throat. "It makes it easier to keep the grill clean."

I look down at the shiny aluminum liners. The weight of his gaze transmits the importance of my reaction. Is this a test? or a hint? Is he taking me to Hawaii for our anniversary and we'll enjoy a luau on the beach? "Uh, neat."

He gestures with his hand. "If we use these, the grill will stay clean, and there will be less work."

"Okay. But you usually tend to the grill. Not my job."

He throws his head back and laughs. "You're right." He takes the package from my hand and exits the room chuckling. "I'll keep them in the garage."

I'm left alone, too disillusioned to speak. Thank goodness Grandma's chair is at my elbow. I fall into the upholstered lap of comfort that has held generations of my family and ponder what just happened.

Apparently my expectations are too high. I guess I let that sexy-hug-and-earlobe-kiss thing from a few days ago cloud my vision. I don't want to have cross words about this. His motives were probably pure, although grossly misguided.

The garage door slams, and Jerry breezes in again. "What are you doing?"

I smile to disguise my disappointment. "Thinking."

"Anything I should know about?"

My mind's a blank. "Uh, yeah." I give him a bland grin.

"Well?"

Yeah, well what? "I was thinking about our anniversary."

His face warms with a delicious grin. "Do you still want to get some information out of me?"

Man, this guy's cute. He walks toward me and runs his index finger along my jaw. He's still got those moves.

"Well, you need to tell me what to pack. Or you could just tell me where we're going." I cross my legs and shrug. Two can play this game.

Jerry sits on the couch. "Okay, pack a dress."

I uncross my legs and lean forward. "Just tell me. What have you planned?"

He affects an air of superiority. "I thought we decided last year that you would plan the even years, and I would plan the odd ones. Twenty-five—odd year. My treat."

I narrow my eyes. Sometimes I think he likes keeping secrets just a little too much. "All right, bucko. But this better be good."

Jer slowly nods. "Oh, no problem. It will be good."

I move next to him on the couch. "How about a little hint?"

"I guess that won't hurt. Think sophisticated."

"Like New York City? London? Honolulu? San Francisco?"

He stands. "Yeah, I guess you could say something like that."

Nick walks in. "Mom, telephone." He hands me the receiver. "I think it's Deb."

Jerry pats my shoulder and leaves the room.

"Hi, Deb."

"Are you alone? Can you talk?"

"What's wrong?"

Her reply is a muffled sob.

29

Every bone in my body aches as I attempt to rouse myself from a restless night's sleep. I stayed up way too late talking to Deb and tossed and turned for half the night.

Deb's words echo in my mind: *"Please don't speak of this to anyone. Especially Jerry."* That's something I would never do. Poor Deb. At least my husband desires *only* me.

The thought of Keith turns my stomach. I don't know if I can ever look at him with friendship again, although that's what Deb's begged me to do. Nothing could have surprised me more than when she aired their dirty little secret—a burden she's carried for most of their marriage. And she still finds it in her to make excuses for him. "It's not as if he's cheating on me," she said.

Oh, Deb. But he is. When she told me that he confesses to her his attraction for other women, I thought I'd puke. Doesn't he remember Jimmy Carter's lusting-in-his-heart confession?

And then after he discloses his fantasies about some woman like the personal trainer at Fitness 21 or the teller at the bank he visits, what does he do? He showers Debbie with flowers or chocolate or a designer handbag. He takes her out to a romantic restaurant and begs her forgiveness.

Humph. I think it's more like he continues with his fantasies, except he uses Debbie in place of the tart he's currently lusting after. How can she look past that?

And to think I was always jealous of their romantic marriage. What a joke. What a sham. What a tragedy for my sweet friend.

Memories of bad dreams cling to my between-worlds consciousness. Deb and I were outside, and the sky was dark and brooding, as though a storm was just about to break. Deb tried to yell something to me, but the fierce winds carried her voice away. I couldn't understand what she was saying. Then I dreamed I was being poked in my breast by something sharp. I can't recall more of that nightmare, but it must have been frightening because it woke me with a start.

The aroma of freshly brewed coffee sifts into our room and coaxes me from the warm bed. Despite my four pitiful hours of sleep, I throw on my robe and descend to the kitchen.

"Morning, Mom." Emma practically sings her greeting.

What's with that? Since last night she's been all sweetness and light. "Hi, honey."

Jerry raises one brow. I'm sure his curiosity is piqued about my long conversation with Deb last night. I stretch a sad smile on my face and shake my head. He gets the hint and pours coffee into my tall latte mug.

I measure out my oatmeal and water and set the pot on the stove while Jerry dishes up scrambled eggs.

Em scoots her chair toward the table. "Guess what?" Her eyes are shining, and her fresh-scrubbed face is glowing. What I'd give for such a simple life.

Before either of us can venture a guess, she rushes on. "David invited me to a party this Saturday."

"Oh?"

"I can go; can't I?"

Jerry puts down his coffee mug. "Who?"

I jump in to run interference. "He works at the animal ER."

Jerry looks like he's still not sold. "Have we met this guy?"

"Oh, Dad, don't go acting Dark Ages on me. You would have met him last weekend, if I wasn't grounded."

I give Emma a playful wink. "Don't worry, Jerry. I plan on calling the veterinary clinic and getting a reference."

Jerry smiles at me. "What do we know about him?" You've got to love papa bear, looking out for his cub.

"We met him the night Belle was at the ER. He seems nice."

Jerry accepts my assurances with a shrug. "Who's having the party?"

Emma twists her paper napkin. "A guy named Jared. You probably don't know him, but David says we can call Jared's parents."

"You better believe we will. And I'd like David to come over for a little visit so Dad can get to know him."

Her sweet young face colors a peach blush. "Mom!"

Nick joins us, flexing his arms in a stretch. "What's this? My little Emma-monster has a new boyfriend?"

"Shut up."

A sigh forces itself from my lungs, and I frown. "We don't say that in this house, missy." I turn to my troublemaking son. "Knock it off."

Our family breakfast is subdued. I'm too weary to converse, Emma's pouting, Jer's reading the paper, and Nick knows better than to push the issue.

● ● ●

Some days it's wonderful to go to work, and this is one of them. I drop my worries at the threshold of Dream Photography and embrace the chaos within. Deb and her troubles will still be waiting for me at five o'clock. Until then, I'm all about portrait photography. There's enough drama here to keep me preoccupied all day anyway.

My morning appointments go well. My first sale keeps me

laughing throughout the image presentation with the clients' self-deprecating humor. Their two college kids put me in stitches with the running commentary on their photos. I am grateful for the box of tissues on the table in the salesroom, not because we are weeping tears of joy but because we all laugh till we cry. Not only are they delightful to spend time with, but they purchase a sizable order. I hope I run into them when they come back for their order.

The last sale of the morning is as smooth as an iced grande cappuccino on a warm spring day.

I eat my solitary lunch outside on the picnic table with the company of a good book. On the other side of the hedge that cuts through the portrait garden, Luke's laughing as he arranges a family on our rock outcropping. Off to my right, Thomas, another photographer, instructs his clients on how to pose.

When I return inside for my afternoon shift, the front lobby is busier than usual. It seems all our clients decided to pick up finished portraits on their lunch break. "Who may I help?"

A pleasant-looking woman gives me her attention. "Hi, Linda. I'm here to pick up my order. It should have been completed yesterday."

Crumbs. Who is this woman? Think; think; think. "I'd be happy to check for you, uh, Diane." *Whew. That was close.* Our clients love it when we remember them by name.

She smiles. "It's Janet. Janet Springer."

I tried. "I'll be right back, Janet."

I'm able to put my hands on her order without a problem and bring them to the counter for inspection. While Janet is scrutinizing the prints, the phone rings. Barb is busy talking to another client, so I answer. "Dream Photography. This is Linda. May I help you?"

A familiar voice comes over the phone. "Mom?"

"What's wrong, Em?"

"Can I go home? I don't feel good."

"How so?"

She moans softly. "Headache, stomachache."

I flip open the sales schedule. My afternoon's booked. "Let me see if I can switch appointments with Traci so I can get away from here. Maybe I—"

"That's okay. I called Nick. He can pick me up. I just need you to speak to the secretary to excuse me."

"All right. I'll call you between my sessions this afternoon. Put her on."

The scary school secretary comes on the line, and I give my permission for Em to leave school. I'm sure she does her job well, but she's so stern and humorless she frightens me. I haven't had the pleasure of meeting her in person, but I've had to speak on the phone with her several times over the past few years. I always feel that I'm talking to that nasty nurse in *One Flew Over the Cuckoo's Nest*.

I help Janet rebox her order and spend the next forty minutes assisting other clients.

When I have a moment, I give Em a call at home. The phone rings and rings, and just as I'm about to hang up, she answers.

"Hi, honey. Are you feeling any better?"

"No, not really."

"Oh, you sound congested now. Have you taken anything?"

"Yeah. I don't want to talk, Mom. I'll see you later."

I'm surprised when she hangs up on me. Usually Emma's such a baby, she wants to dwell on every little ache and pain.

The rest of the afternoon is spent doing two image presentations. I love a job that keeps me hopping. I leave work with a spring in my step, until I recall Deb and her situation. My heart feels heavy beneath my ribs. I want to honor her requests, so I won't call her tonight. *Please, Lord, be very close to Deb while she goes though this situation.*

• • •

At home, Nick taps out an assignment on the computer, and the drone of the television comes from upstairs. I climb the stairs to Emma's room.

The door's been left ajar. I knock softly, then enter. Em is sitting propped up by pillows watching television, and Belle is snuggled against her leg. My daughter looks awful. Her eyes are red-rimmed, and her nose looks irritated. Discarded tissues are tossed in a pile on the floor.

I sit on the bed beside her and place my hand on her warm forehead. "Oh, Em."

To my surprise, she starts to cry.

"Don't worry. We'll figure out what's wrong and get you fixed up. Is your stomach upset?"

She hiccups a sob. "Not really."

I glance at the plastic bottle on her night table. "Do you need another Tylenol?"

She nods and grabs for another tissue.

"Let me make you some broth. Want the ice bag for your headache?"

"Please."

I heat some chicken broth. As I'm about to bring it upstairs, the phone rings. Caller ID tells me it's Tammy. "Hey, Tammy."

"Did you notice that Emma picked up your candle order?"

"Yeah, I haven't had a chance to sample any yet. Em came home from school sick today. I'm just about to go upstairs and take care of her."

"Sick? What's wrong?"

"It's probably a virus. She's got a headache and is congested."

"So she doesn't have diarrhea?"

"No, not that I know of. Why do you ask?"

"She and Lyndsay were hanging around here yesterday afternoon when Alice Boothe stopped by to pick up her candles. Apparently she's pretty sick too."

Now, I don't have a soft spot in my heart for that woman, but I'm sorry to hear she's not well. "Hmm. Must be something going around school."

"Maybe. I called Alice to tell her the rest of her order came by UPS today. She said she's got diarrhea so bad that she's thinking of going to the emergency room if it doesn't stop."

"I hope we don't get sick."

"Me too. Lyndsay doesn't seem sick, but she's not acting like herself."

"Keep an eye on her."

We end our conversation and I assemble the broth, some ginger ale, and saltine crackers on a wooden tray. I hoist my remedies and go back upstairs. As I walk down the hall, I hear Emma speaking softly. The one-sided conversation means she's on her cell phone. Something in her tone stops me in the hallway.

"I know. Yeah, as if I'll say anything. . . . I feel terrible too. What were we thinking? I've been crying all afternoon. . . . If they find out, we'll be in really big trouble."

Excuse me? I round the corner into her room so fast, the broth sloshes over the bowl's rim.

The look on Emma's face tells me she knows I overheard her conversation. She unceremoniously disconnects her call and drops the phone on the bed. Her stricken face contorts, and the tears begin to flow.

A cement block lodges in the pit of my stomach. "Oh, what have you done?"

30

Emma covers her face and sobs with abandon. Strands of light brown hair fall forward, veiling her shoulders, and a keening wail wells up from within her.

Anxiety locks my joints. I stand and observe the situation as though it's nothing more than a movie or a remnant of a bad dream. Emma looks like a stranger trapped in the grip of grief. What could cause a young girl so much anguish? Her cries are miles removed from my reality. We don't have such big issues in this house.

Fear urges me to run from this problem, but I walk to the dresser and put down the tray. Standing above my weeping girl, I know the words she'll speak could change our lives.

I long to stroke her hair, but that response will break the spell of absurdity, and I will have to acknowledge that this miserable girl is my daughter, and the torment she carries will soon become mine as well. The oppressive weight of her burden pains my heart, and alarm dries my mouth. Somehow I find the strength to step into my destiny and sit on the edge of the bed. "Emma?"

She casts herself into my arms. "Oh, Mommy. I'm a terrible person."

Movement catches my eye, and I turn my head to see Nick standing in the doorway. His usual calm demeanor is transformed into something I've never seen before. But then, grief like this has never visited my family. Goose bumps rise on my arms.

I gently cradle her in an embrace. "Shhh, baby. It can't be that bad."

"But it is. I could go to jail."

Her declaration sucks the air from my lungs, and a frosty glaze coats my heart like the brittle ice that encases our aspen trees after a cold October storm.

I feel a hand on my shoulder and look up to find Nick standing above me. My tears flow as I sit holding my daughter while my son quietly anchors our trio of grief.

Nick clears his throat, and his voice trembles. "Should I call Dad?"

I nod, and he leaves the room. I fumble for the tissue box and share it with Emma. "Tell me what's wrong."

She shudders, trying to stop the flow of tears, and reaches for her glass of water. She holds it for a moment before taking a sip. "Lyndsay and I did something terrible yesterday."

Yesterday? Emma was in a wonderful mood yesterday. I recall walking through the door to find her smiling while she made our dinner salad after she had set the table. She even got my candles from Tammy's house. And this morning she was pleasant. Were those happy faces an affectation to hide something sinister? *Who is this child?*

"Tell me."

She pours out her pitiful story slowly, as if even she can't believe the tale. Nick has returned to the doorway, blessedly silent.

My world feels less safe; evil has insinuated itself into our lives through a thoughtless adolescent prank.

"We have to call Lyndsay's parents. They need to know what you girls did."

I hear the garage door slam and Jerry running up the stairs. When he comes into the room, the air feels lighter, as though the oppression crushing my heart is just a bit relieved.

He pulls out her desk chair and sinks into it.

She begins to weep again, but it's time to fess up. "Tell your father what you just told me."

Her eyes plead. "Mom?"

I hold her hand. "Emma, you have to face what you've done. We'll help you."

She turns melancholy eyes to Jerry. "Yesterday when I was at Lyndsay's house, Miss Boothe was there picking up her candles too. She and Mrs. Wilson were sitting in the living room, and Mrs. Wilson asked Lyndsay to make them some tea. Mrs. Wilson wanted some Earl Grey, and Miss Boothe asked if they had any decaf tea. Lyndsay said, 'Yeah, we'll find something.' And then when we were going through the cabinet, she found an old box of tea."

Emma's eyes fill again, and she begins to cry. With a broken voice, she continues. "It was the tea Lyndsay's father used when he was constipated after his knee surgery last year."

Jerry shakes his head. "What did you do? That's like medicine. You can't give someone medicine without their knowledge, especially when you don't know their health history."

Her weeping begins anew. "I know. And she liked it so much that we cut off the tag and gave her an extra tea bag to go. Then I heard this morning that Miss Boothe was sick and wasn't in school. Lyndsay called her mom, and she told Lyndsay how sick Miss Boothe was. There's a zero drug tolerance at school. We could be arrested and kicked out of school. And . . ." She buries her head in her hands, and regretful sobs rack her small frame.

Jerry scrubs his face and runs his hands through his hair. "Linda, call Tammy and Steve and have them come over with Lyndsay." He stands. "Emma, wash your face."

When I join him downstairs, he's going through our business card stash. "What are you looking for?"

He thumbs through the cards without looking up. "Didn't we have a card from the lawyer who joined the church last year?"

"Do you think it's that serious, Jer?"

His eyes lock on mine. Beneath his strong veneer, I see a heart breaking. *Where will this journey take us?*

I reach for the phone, call Tammy, and quickly tell her the story Emma related to us. I feel like a rat, but I'm secretly grateful that the scheme was their daughter's idea.

Tammy's voice goes flat, as though the joy in her heart has been deflated like a failed soufflé.

Within minutes the doorbell rings. When I open the door, Lyndsay is crying, holding her mother's arm. Tammy's eyes are like those of a wounded animal's, and Steve's face is gray, as if the color has gone out of his world.

The grim party joins us in the living room. Belle prances around our guests, wondering why nobody is playing with her. Nick grabs her by the collar and leaves the room. A few seconds later, I hear the powder room door close. Nick returns and sits, his hands clasped while he watches our drama unfold.

We all sit in silence for a moment. Shall I serve cookies? I'm ignorant of the etiquette required when your daughter poisons someone.

Jerry breaks the silence. "Would you like something to drink? Coffee, water?"

I jump to my feet, ashamed that I didn't try to make our friends more comfortable in this hideous situation. "Sorry. What can I get you?"

Tammy stares at the floor. "Water will be fine. Thanks."

Emma comes down the stairs. She looks smaller than she did this morning, as though her guilt is eating at her from the inside out.

"Em, please get us all some water."

She nods and walks to the kitchen.

Lyndsay follows. "I'll help her."

Steve's eyes flash in her direction. "Make sure you don't put anything in *our* drinks."

His daughter freezes for a moment and continues to the kitchen. When she gets there, we hear her cries.

Please, Lord, help us all.

Jerry shifts to face our friends. "If need be, I know a lawyer who may be able to help us."

Steve shakes his head. "A lawyer? We don't need a lawyer."

Jerry faces him. "We don't know how far Miss Boothe will take this. We need to be prepared for—"

Steve holds up his hand. "Stop right there. As far as we know, the only people aware of the cause of that lady's illness are under this roof."

Are you kidding? I stare incredulously at a man I thought I knew. "What are you saying?"

The girls return with our water and hand them out. Lyndsay sits across from her mom, and Emma stands behind Jerry's chair.

Steve gestures toward the girls. "Look at them. Don't you think they realize what they did was wrong? I can tell you, my daughter won't taste freedom for some time. I don't see any reason not to let this end right here."

I stare at Jerry, imploring him to handle this. To somehow make this nightmare disappear.

Stress paints his face. He folds his arms and clears his throat. "We need to tell Miss Boothe what's happened. This involves her health. Not to inform her would be unethical."

Steve leaps to his feet. "That's a load of—"

Tammy stands and puts her hand on his arm. "Steve."

He glares at her.

My heart hammers within my chest. *Could Steve be right? Should we let this ugly problem blow over our heads? Is Jerry making the situation worse?*

Jerry continues, "I wish this predicament would just disappear. But it can't. What the girls did was wrong. For us to gloss over it would be wrong as well."

Steve sits and shakes his head.

"I'm going to call her. Now." Jerry looks at Tammy. "Do you have her number?"

She wrings her hands. "It's at home." She stands and heads to the door.

"Tammy!" Steve's face contorts in anger. "Sit down."

She turns to him. "No. I know you want to protect Lyndsay, but it's not in our hands." She glances at Jerry before leaving the house.

We sit in strained silence. The clock chimes, and I hear Belle scratching to get out of the powder room.

Jerry moves next to Steve. "We'll all get through this somehow. But not your way. You're a good man. You know I'm right."

Every muscle in my body tenses. For all I know, Steve could be contemplating taking a swing at Jerry. I clench my fists and glance at Nick. He's sitting on the edge of his chair. Perhaps he harbors the same fear.

Steve exhales loudly, and his head falls forward. Jerry puts an arm around him, and Steve's weeping daughter joins him on the couch.

My taut nerves leap at the sound of the door opening as Tammy comes back inside. She stops dead in the foyer and stares at the scene before her, seemingly without comprehension. Does she also feel as if she's stepped into a parallel universe? I stand and hold out my hand. She drops a piece of paper in my palm and approaches her family.

Jerry rises, allowing Tammy to take his seat. He motions for our family to leave the room.

The four of us stand in the kitchen. Emma's softly weeping. Jer's shoulders slump slightly while he lifts the receiver from the wall to call Miss Boothe. I pull out a chair; my legs feel like wilted spinach. Nick places his hands on Emma's shoulders, reminiscent of something Jerry would do. He's so like his dad, bless his heart.

The Wilson family joins us. We silently watch Jerry while he dials the phone number. If tension were a storm, the room would be consumed by threatening, pitch-black clouds about to thunder and boom like the wrath of God.

"Hello, Miss Boothe? My name is Jerry Revere, and my daughter, Emma, is in your history class. . . . Excuse me. May I speak with Miss Boothe? . . . No, this can't wait. . . . Yes, I've heard she isn't well today. I'm sorry, but I need—"

The voice coming through the telephone sounds like the *waaa-waaa* voice of adults from the Charlie Brown movies. The whole situation is beyond the pale of reality.

"Oh, I'm very sorry to hear that," Jerry says. "Please tell her she's in my prayers. . . . Uh, also alert her doctors that her illness may have been caused by some laxative tea she inadvertently drank. . . . Yes . . . uh, yes."

He replaces the receiver. My heart falls to my feet; he's wearing his bad-news face. He runs his hand through his hair. *Oh no. This can't be good.*

"That was her niece on the phone. She's there to drive Miss Boothe to the hospital. She called her aunt on her cell phone while she was running errands, and Miss Boothe's voice was slurred. Since she was in the neighborhood, she used the key Miss Boothe gave her to let herself in the house. She found her aunt sitting in a recliner. Her face and mouth were swollen, and she was wheezing."

Emma slumps into a chair and begins to cry harder. "She's going to die, and I'll go to prison for life!"

I throw my arms around her shoulders. "Don't say that. She'll be okay."

Lyndsay's face is the color of oatmeal, silent tears coursing down her cheeks. Her shoulders heave slightly, her eyes open like saucers, and she runs to the powder room.

Tammy follows on her heels. The door opens, allowing us to hear Lyndsay's retching.

We're all startled when Steve's fist crashes to the counter. The lid on the sugar bowl jumps. His face is crimson. "Look at this can of worms you opened."

Nick steps forward. My brave young man. I appreciate his support, but Steve could snap him like a dry spaghetti noodle.

Jerry stands his ground. His face is set like flint. "Bullies don't scare me."

The two men stare at one another like male elk about to tangle antlers. In the screaming quiet, my ears ring. What's going to happen next?

31

"Steve!" Tammy looks as though she's ready to go head-to-head with her irate husband.

We remain frozen in some insane tableau, like entertainment for an invisible audience. The bitter scent of anxiety hangs heavy in the air.

Tammy breaks our bizarre spell by striding across the floor. "Enough!" She jerks Steve's arm, as if to bring him back to sanity.

He remains rigid, still staring at Jerry.

She moves in front of him and grabs the front of his shirt. "Steve!"

He blinks and looks down at her and then at the rest of us. Without saying a word, he takes a seat at the table.

We all heave a collective sigh and catch the breaths we were holding.

"I think we need to go to the hospital," Tammy says.

Jerry nods. "Let's go."

The Wilsons cross the street to their house. By the time we're pulling out of our garage, their taillights are turning the corner at the end of the street.

I glance at my watch. Only seven o'clock?

The ride to the hospital takes ten minutes, and we find a place to park without a problem. I'm surprised my legs have the strength to walk to the ER. Jer and I flank Emma, giving her our support. Nick's long-legged stride slows to keep pace with us.

The antiseptic hospital smell assails us as we enter the medical center. At the end of the long room, we see Tammy talking to a nurse. She hands over a cardboard box of tea.

The seven of us sit in the waiting area, everyone too weary to speak.

A woman in her late twenties approaches us. "I'm Robin Allen, Alice Boothe's niece. Did I speak with one of you earlier?"

Jerry rises and extends his hand. "Jerry Revere. I'm sorry to have to meet you under these circumstances."

Robin judges us with a glance. "And what exactly are the circumstances?"

Steve stands. "We don't have to speak to her."

Again with the confrontational attitude? Now he's getting my hackles up. "Hello, Robin. I'm Linda Revere. Have you heard how Miss Boothe is doing?"

"No. She's still being evaluated."

I force a smile. I don't want to scare her. "I'm very sorry for this trouble."

"Mrs. Revere, I'm Alice's next of kin. I think you should tell me what's going on. How do you know her problems are caused by laxative tea?"

Steve steps forward. "We don't know that for sure."

Could somebody please shut this man up? I gesture to a group of chairs on the other side of the room. "Can we have a seat?" I glare at Steve. I think he gets my message because he sinks into his seat.

The three of us women sit in the corner, Tammy and I on one side, Robin on the other. I don't even know where to start.

Tammy clasps her hands. "I'm afraid our daughters thought it would be funny to give Alice a cup of laxative tea."

"Funny? My aunt is gasping for breath. Is that funny?"

I shake my head. "Certainly not. I can't tell you how sorry we are."

Robin follows my gaze to the other side of the room, where the girls are holding hands, trying to contain their emotions. She sighs. "I can see we're all upset. I'd like to—"

"Ms. Allen?" A young man in scrubs approaches. It looks as if he's been out of medical school for about ten minutes.

Robin springs from her seat. "Yes?" She walks toward the doctor, who puts his hand on her elbow and steers her away from us.

Tammy and I trudge back to our group. A tension headache grips me down to my shoulders. I slip my hand in Jerry's and my arm around Emma. *Help us through this valley, Lord.*

We all watch while Robin Allen disappears behind a glass door with Dr. Doogie Howser.

Jerry scoots his chair toward the center of our group. "We need to pray."

Boy, do we. I feel stress flow from my shoulders, and we put our heads together and beseech God. To my surprise, even Steve prays, asking forgiveness for his actions and attitude.

The tension in the room has decreased by several degrees after we pray, and we sit and wait for news of Alice Boothe.

My myopia lifts, and I begin to notice the other occupants in the room. Two young parents anxiously try to soothe a crying toddler. An old man sits, holding a cane between his knees, staring at the floor. We're not the only ones with troubles tonight.

The sound of footsteps draws my attention. We all stand when Robin Allen reaches our area. I hope it's not my imagination, and she really is less upset.

"Aunt Alice seems much better."

The relief we feel is visible, as though the shackles that gripped our hearts have been loosened.

She continues, "Apparently, she's allergic to senna, which is a major ingredient in that tea. The first cup she had yesterday gave her the diarrhea. Ironically, today when she wasn't feeling well, she gave herself another cup of that tea and started to go into anaphylactic shock. Thank goodness that's when I stopped in. Right now she's being given an antidote and some fluids to help with her dehydration. I'll be able to take her home within the hour."

Jerry approaches her. "I can't tell you how happy we are to hear that. If it's possible, I would like to speak with Miss Boothe."

Robin shakes her head. "No. I told her you were all out here. She asks that you leave. She doesn't want to see any of you."

Tammy's hand clutches her heart. "Please, Ms. Allen. We would truly like to apologize."

"I'm afraid that is out of the question. She cried when she heard her illness was caused by malicious behavior. Aunt Alice is very upset that someone would purposefully try to harm her."

Lyndsay touches Robin's arm. "I didn't mean to hurt her."

Robin Allen gives her a stone-cold stare. After a moment she says, "Oh, really. Exactly what *did* you intend?"

Lyndsay shrinks away from the woman. "She was so mean to Emma. We just wanted to get her back a little."

Emma wipes tears with the back of her hand. "I'd give anything for this to never have happened."

Robin glares at us. "Sure. But it did."

Jerry shifts from one foot to another. "May I call her at home?"

"I don't know. Why don't you give me your number, and if she wants to speak with you, she'll call."

Jerry reaches in his wallet and pulls out a business card. He hastily scrawls our home phone number on the back and hands to it her. "Again, I'm very sorry about this situation."

Robin thrusts the card in her pocket and turns from us. She strides a few feet away and pivots around. "I think this *situation* is called assault. My advice to Aunt Alice is to file charges against your vicious children. If you don't hear from us tonight, I'm sure you'll be hearing from the police tomorrow."

32

Emma's knees buckle. If Nick hadn't been next to her, she would have fallen to the floor. Both girls start to wail again. We usher them out of the hospital before any more attention is focused on us.

We stand as an awkward group, huddled together on the sidewalk.

Jerry shakes Steve's hand. "I'll call our lawyer when we get home."

Tammy gives me a hug. "We'll talk."

The drive home is as somber as any I've ever experienced with my family. We're usually a happy, fun-loving group. How did we get to the place where one of us may become a convict? I wish I could close my eyes and wake up from this horrid dream. I feel as if I'm walking through a nightmare, about to slip off the side of a steep mountain.

We silently troop into the gloomy house. Belle runs to greet us, and Nick pours kibble into her bowl. My stomach turns. I couldn't eat if you pried my jaws open and poured food down my throat.

My son puts his hands in his pockets and looks at me. "What's for dinner?"

Jerry, Emma, and I halfheartedly pick at turkey sandwiches. Nick, on the other hand, eats a large sandwich, some potato chips, and a pickle. I didn't have the energy or the desire to make anything more to eat.

Jerry left a message for the lawyer and put his business card on the refrigerator underneath the magnet from the animal ER. I can't help but notice it hanging there, accenting the desperate mood of our evening. I'm sure Peter McCormack is a great lawyer, but I never wanted to find out through personal experience.

No one discusses the incident at the emergency room, although Jerry prays for Alice Boothe during our blessing. The thought of that woman—sad and ill and feeling victimized—haunts me. I can barely imagine her exhibiting any emotion, but to know she was weeping at the hospital tonight pierces my heart.

Despite the fact that Miss Boothe and I didn't hit it off when we met to discuss Emma's grades, Tammy always claimed Miss Boothe was a good woman. Now she has the fate of my family in her hands. That realization chills my blood. I don't think the school district could become involved, but the law . . . well, that's another matter.

Everyone helps me clean up the dinner table. When the last crumb is wiped away, I go into the basement to walk off my anxiety on our treadmill. I turn on the television and sweat through a few senseless sitcoms.

My home is like a haunted house when I emerge from my exercise session. The only light is in the kitchen, and when I go upstairs, I find Belle lying at the top of the stairs. Everyone else is hiding behind their closed bedroom doors.

Belle cocks her head and wags her tail, which I take as an invitation to join her. I sit on the top step and stroke behind her ear. "How's my good girl?" She leans into my caress. I put my arm around her little neck and bury my face in her fur. Her sweet, uncomplicated warmth melts some of the fear in my heart.

I drag myself to my feet and push open our bedroom door. Belle rises and follows me into the room. Jerry is lying on the bed, staring at the wall with his novel resting on his abdomen. He looks at me and makes an attempt to smile.

A few moments later when I head for the shower and glance at Jerry, he's still staring at the wall, petting Belle as she rests beside him.

Our desperately awaited phone call from Alice Boothe never comes. With an air of defeat, I go to bed. Will the police call us in the morning or just show up at the door, handcuffs ready for my daughter?

Every creak and groan of the house is amplified in my terrified heart. I fear another sleepless night, but blessedly, I drift off quickly.

I awaken in a sweat, dreaming of Emma wearing an orange prison jumpsuit, her hands and feet shackled as she's led down a long, dark hallway. My heart beats so fiercely beneath my ribs that I'm afraid it will wake Jer. *How can this be happening?*

I slip out of bed and walk down the hall to Em's room. The door's ajar, so I push it open and gaze at my sleeping daughter. I'm surprised to find a nightlight plugged into her wall. I can only imagine how terrified she must be. Even in slumber, her features are not at rest. A slight furrow mars her forehead. I whisper a prayer as I stand over her bed.

The night air is cool on my arms, and I return to my warm bed. I move as close to Jerry as I can without waking him and allow my fatigued body to surrender to sleep once again.

When I awake, I'm alone in bed. Although I had no trouble falling asleep, I found myself tossing and turning throughout the night. I slide my hand over Jerry's side of the bed. The sheets are cool; he must have gotten up some time ago. The bedside clock registers 6:11. I throw back the covers and drag myself from the rumpled sheets.

I usually love being downstairs in the early morning. Sunshine splashes through the high window in the living room, causing the shadows of night to recede for another day. I wish the sunshine could penetrate the shadows of my heart. Soon I'll learn the fate of my thoughtless daughter. If only I could have gotten her to think beyond the present moment, to think on the consequences of her actions.

Jer sits in my rocking chair, a Bible resting open on his knees. To my surprise, Emma's joined him, lying on the couch with an afghan pulled up to her shoulders.

I sit in Grandma's Victorian chair and clutch a pillow to my chest. "How long have you guys been up?"

Jerry glances at the clock. "Too long. I already need a nap." He closes his Bible and places it on the end table. "I think I got up around 4:50."

"Em?"

Her eyes are puffy and her skin looks blotchy, as though she's been crying again. "Five thirty."

So what do we all do now? Sit and stare at one another? "How long do you think we'll have to wait?"

Jerry just shakes his head.

I'm sitting with strangers. My husband usually has all the answers, and my daughter is a sweet, harmless girl. *Who are these people?*

If I have to sit here on this watch for long, I'll lose my mind. "I'll brew some coffee."

My head feels full and clunky, like it's stuffed with leftover turkey gravy that's coagulated into the shape of the storage container. *Please, Lord, give us the strength to face whatever comes our way this morning.*

Jerry's coffee drips while I put the teakettle on the stove to boil. I sit at the kitchen table listening to the waking sounds of my neighborhood. I'm jealous of the people in the cars that cruise down my street—I'm fairly certain they're not worried about spending the morning in juvenile hall.

The screaming kettle brings me back to the moment, and I hurry to stifle its insistent whistle. I measure some strawberry green tea into my infuser, dropping it into my little teapot and filling the container with water.

Three minutes later, I'm sharing the brew between two mugs. I grab the half-and-half from the fridge, put a splash into Jerry's coffee, set all three mugs on my tray, and rejoin my family in the living room.

I set the tray on the coffee table, right next to the silent telephone receiver.

The clock chimes six thirty. Do I want time to move quickly so I know Emma's fate, or do I want it to move slowly like thick body lotion when you're trying to coax that last drop out of the bottle? The suspense is killing me, and I hope the reality of what happens won't push me over the edge.

At 6:50, Nick stumbles downstairs. "Any news?"

Jerry glances at him. "Nothing yet."

Nick sits with us for a few moments, shrugs, and goes into the kitchen. I hear him get a bowl from the cabinet and pour his cereal. His appetite amazes me; it always has. It never occurred to me to offer to make breakfast for Jer and Emma, and right now I couldn't swallow solid food for the life of me.

The sound of a thunk draws our attention to the front of the house. We turn to see the newspaper deliveryman slowing at each driveway to deliver his wares. I half expect to open the daily paper and find the headline "Local High School Girls Poison Hated Teacher" on the front page. How will we move past this? And the people at church. What will they think of us?

The telephone rings. I feel an electric current run up my spine. We all sit up and stare at the receiver. Nick rushes into the living room.

At the third ring, Jerry picks it up and peers at the caller ID readout. "It's Miss Boothe."

Emma jumps to her feet, her hands clasped to her chest.

"Hello. This is Jerry Revere." He listens, his expression unreadable. "Miss Boothe," he says gently, "please let me offer our sincere apology. I'm heartbroken this happened to you. . . ." He presses his lips together. "Yes, I agree. It was a terrible thing to do. . . . May I put Emma on the phone?"

Emma's head snaps up, and she mouths "No" and begins to back away. Nick grips her arms, and I see him give her a brief squeeze. Jerry stands, reaches out, and draws her to him. I join them, and together we loosely embrace Emma.

She accepts the phone as if it were dollar-store cosmetics. "Miss Boothe," she sobs out, "please, please forgive me. I've never been more sorry. I didn't mean to hurt you. You can flunk me if you want."

I pass her a tissue.

"Yes, ma'am. I feel terrible. I wish I could undo the past two days. . . ." She falls silent while her teacher's voice squeaks into her ear, and she weeps softly while she listens to the woman she poisoned. Finally she holds out the phone to Jerry.

He leaves one arm around Emma and takes the phone. "This is Jerry Revere. . . ."

I'm dying to hear what Miss Boothe has to say.

"Yes, I understand. Please let me know what you decide. . . . Later today will be fine. Call anytime you like." Jerry disconnects the call and falls into the chair. "She hasn't decided what to do. She's going to rest and call us later. All we can do now is wait and pray."

Oh, what I wouldn't give for the days when my biggest problem was organizing carpools to my kids' sporting events.

Nick races off to college, trying to beat the morning rush on I-25. Jerry decides he'll stay home with Emma, and I should go to work.

I don't remember packing my lunch or getting dressed, but I find myself standing at the door to the garage. "Call me if there's any news. Bye."

Emma flies to my arms, hugging me tightly like she used to when she was in preschool and didn't want me to leave her. I grip her slim form securely. I feel the same way. When we release from our embrace, I hurry out the door before she can see my weepy eyes.

As I drive to Dream Photography, I pray today will be so busy that I won't have time to catch my breath, let alone worry about Emma.

I sit staring at my computer monitor. Am I tired or stunned? After a moment, I pull out my to-do file and start to plod through it.

"Linda?"

I look up. Jill's staring at me, eyebrows raised.

"Yes?"

"What's wrong?"

Oh no. Can she tell? "What do you mean?"

"I called your name three times before you answered."

I force a smile. Nothing could feel more artificial. "Sorry. Just concentrating. What did you want?"

She has a pleasant glint in her eye. "Good news. The lab rushed Carol Ball's order, and I finished framing the last portrait."

As if I really care about that. "Oh, good. Thanks. Uh, let's see if we can find someone to deliver them to her house." I don't trust myself behind the wheel right now, not to mention what I might say to Carol Wrecking Ball in my present state of mind.

I stroll to the front desk and page through the sales schedule. Thank goodness Rose had a cancellation today.

I track her down in the workroom. "Rose? Can you deliver some portraits?"

She puts the cap on the marker she was using. "Sure. I'd be happy to run an errand. When will they be ready?"

I hold up my index finger and walk to my office and dial Carol. She answers on the first ring, as though she was sitting there waiting for my call.

"Hi, Carol. This is Linda from Dream Photography. I've got good news."

"Yes?"

I see the ice queen is still in deep freeze. "Uh, your portraits are ready and—"

"I thought we'd agreed they would be delivered to me."

I grind my teeth and try to breathe so I don't climb through the phone and choke the life out of this witch. "That's correct. Rose will be happy to bring them to your house. She's—"

"When are you planning on sending her? I have an appointment this afternoon, and I can't miss it."

Give me patience, Lord. "She's ready to leave now. She can be at your house in twenty minutes. Will that work?"

"Perfect. I'll be looking for her."

Jill and I encase the portraits in bubble wrap and help Rose put them in the studio van. She waves as she drives off.

A pang of guilt passes through my conscience. She's like a lamb to the slaughter, poor dear. But better her than me . . . especially today.

I escape to the comfort of my desk. I wish it were in a cubicle; I need walls today. I fall back into the rhythm of my work until Luke interrupts.

"Linda, would you do me a favor and tell Pam that she shouldn't be chewing gum while she does an image presentation?"

What can I say? "I'll take care of it."

He smiles and leaves the office.

I go to the lobby desk and look at the sales schedule again. Pam should be out of her sale within ten minutes. Barb is busy on the phone. I write a note asking her to send Pam to see me and put it on the bottom of her monitor. She nods, and I return to the quiet of the office once again.

Mercifully, I have plenty of paperwork to keep me tied to my desk. I welcome my task and lose myself in details.

Moments later I'm distracted by the sound of a cow chewing her cud. Oh, wait. That's Pam smacking her gum. No wonder Luke was concerned.

Today she has a chiffon scarf tied around her head like a bandanna. Where does she get these ideas?

"Barb said you wanted to see me."

I gesture to the empty chair. "Yeah, do you have a moment?"

Pam folds herself into the chair and continues to chew away.

"It's come to my attention that you've been chewing gum during your sales today. I wanted to give you a heads-up. That kind of thing drives Luke nuts." I stop and assess her reaction.

"Whatever. Thanks for the advice." Pam rips a sheet off the message pad, spits her gum in the paper, and banks the crumpled mess off the wall into the trash can. "Two points!" She laughs at her joke and heads for the door.

"Uh, thanks, Pam."

The phone's been ringing off the hook today. For a moment, I debate if I should answer it or put my line on mute. It could be Jer. I lunge to get it. "Dream Photography. This is Linda. May I help you?"

The line is fuzzy, like a cell phone connection. "Linda?"

Car horns and the rumble of tires on pavement come through the line. "Rose? Are you stuck in traffic?"

The sound of an emergency vehicle siren blocks out her response. "I didn't hear you. Can you say that again?"

"—an accident."

"What? There was an accident?"

"Yes. I was in an accident."

My head begins to throb. "Are you hurt?"

"Yeah, my arm's killing me. I'm going to the hospital."

If I didn't ask her to do me this favor, she'd be okay. "Do you want me to meet you there?"

"No, I called my husband. Look, I have to go. Let Luke know that the van's smacked up and it's being towed away. And of course the portraits are inside."

"Don't worry about that, Rose. Have your husband call the studio to let us know how you are."

I exit the side door to our portrait garden and scan the landscape. Luke's on the far side by the koi pond. I sit on the picnic bench and wait for him. He finishes his session and walks toward me.

"Bad news. Rose was in an accident in the van."

He winces. "Is she all right?"

"She's hurt her arm. An ambulance took her to the emergency room."

"And the van?"

"I don't know. It's been towed away."

"Track it down and give me a report." Luke turns and goes into the building.

My cotton-stuffed head is going to explode. First things first. I better call Carol and tell her what's happened. The phone rings and rings. I swallow to prepare to leave her a message when she answers the phone.

"Carol, this is Linda. I've got some bad news."

"To whom am I speaking?"

Oy. "Linda from Dream Photography."

"You're not the only Linda in the world, you know—"

I think she could possibly be the single person on the planet who I dislike so intensely. "Excuse me!"

"Are you raising your voice to me?"

You betcha. "The woman driving the portraits to your house was in an accident on the way there."

"Oh, dear."

Hmm, could she be human? I take down my aggression a notch. "Yes, I just spoke with—"

"So are you telling me I won't get my portraits delivered today?"

What? If only my head had a pressure valve so I could release some steam before I blow. "Mrs. Ball! One of our employees is in the hospital because she was doing you the favor of delivering your portraits. Free of charge. I'm sorry for the inconvenience this apparently has caused you. When I have more information, I'll give you a call."

I slam the receiver down with enough force to shatter steel. Unfortunately, it doesn't break. I'm so angry that I'm seeing spots before my eyes.

I look up to see Jill and Luke staring at me as though I've completely lost my mind. Perhaps I have.

Luke looks confused. "Did you just hang up on Carol Ball?"

"Yes, and I'm not sorry. She's a st—"

Barb sticks her head in the office. "Linda, Jerry's on the phone."

I press my lips together and try to compose myself. It's no use. Tears begin to flow as I lift the receiver.

34

Jerry's deep, desperate sigh comes through the phone. "Linda, can you leave the studio and come home?"

"Did you hear from Miss Boothe?"

His answer is almost drowned out by Emma's sobs. "No, her lawyer called. Miss Boothe is pressing charges."

I stifle the sob in my own throat. "I'll be right home."

"What's going on?" Luke asks.

"Family troubles." I push through the crowd that's assembled in the office and run from the building.

"Linda!" Jill has followed me out of the studio and is standing on the sidewalk, waiting for a car to pass.

I raise my arm to wave her off and keep on walking. I don't want to speak to anyone but my family. When I reach my car, I struggle to find my keys in the bottom of my purse.

She's upon me faster than a bunny in my spring garden. "Linda?"

I look in her eyes and see how despondent I must appear. Jill's expression is so grave. "What's wrong?"

I'd prefer to make her go away, but manners override emotion. "Emma. She's gotten herself in trouble."

Jill's mouth opens in a perfect O. She blinks about five times and says, "I'm sorry. Is there anything I can do? Has she been to a doctor?"

I've no idea what she's talking about. I shake my head and escape into the stifling heat of my car. The engine starts with a roar, and Jill jumps away from my vehicle just in time for me to drive off.

Because I can't find a tissue, I'm forced to wipe away my tears with the fast-food napkin I had stowed in my glove compartment. The road blurs before me, and I pray the Lord will bring me home safely. When I get on the highway, I put my car on cruise control. If not for that, I would probably drive ninety miles an hour to get home to my daughter.

The "Hallelujah" chorus chirps from my purse. I fumble in my bag until I grasp my cell phone. The call's from Dream Photography. I hit the No button and toss the phone on the front seat.

Scenery whizzes by as I race home. On the seat next to me, the phone vibrates, telling me I have voice mail. I really love Jill, but can't she get the message and leave me alone?

The traffic light on Pine Grove Road stops me. I plug my hands-free headset into the phone and punch the button to retrieve my message.

"Linda, this is Jill. I know you're upset and don't want to talk to anyone right now. But I want you to know that however bad this feels, it will pass, and you and Jerry will help your daughter deal with this situation."

A long sigh comes through the connection, as if Jill were uncertain if she should continue. "I never told you this before, but my older sister got into trouble too. It seemed like the world was coming to an end for a while, but now we can't imagine life without my sweet little nephew. Take heart, Lin. This will all be a bad memory someday and you'll move on." The call ends.

Oh, for goodness' sake. She thinks Emma's pregnant. I almost wish that were the case. At least then she wouldn't have a criminal record following her for the rest of her life—or the possibility of spending time in juvenile hall.

When I arrive home, the house is still. Jerry's on the phone in the kitchen, intently listening and taking notes on a yellow legal pad, and Emma's sitting on the living room couch, clutching a stuffed bear to her chest. Nick sits at the kitchen table, tapping a business card on the table.

I rush into the living room and stand over my shell-shocked daughter. She remains silent and takes hold of my hand. *Give me the strength to go through this, Lord. Protect Emma. Please.*

I look up, startled to see Jer standing next to us. "What?"

He sighs and takes a seat in my rocking chair. Oh, how weary he looks. "We had quite an afternoon."

"What happened?"

Jer looks at Emma. I follow his gaze and see her weeping.

"Sit down, Lin." His expression is grim. "A police officer came by this afternoon to investigate the charges."

My fists are balled so tightly that my nails are boring holes in my palms. "And?"

"Emma confessed to the incident."

How did it come to this? Mr. Black and White has us all marching to the beat of his drum. Couldn't we have waited a day to see how Miss Boothe was doing? Did we really have to fess right up and run off to the hospital? My breath huffs out in a rush. I didn't realize I was holding it in.

Jer gestures for me to sit.

Good thing. I feel as if I could collapse on the floor. "What do we do next?"

"I just got off the phone with Peter McCormack. He says it may be a week before charges are filed." He flips through his notes. "There will probably be a preliminary hearing within a few weeks."

I can't believe I'm hearing this, and I don't understand it one whit. "And?"

Jer tosses his notes on the side table. "That hearing will be to determine if there's enough evidence to go to trial. And—"

I see a glimmer of hope and snatch it. "So it may not go to trial?"

He shakes his head. "An admission of guilt will automatically send it to trial."

Emma wiggles to the edge of the seat. "What do I do in the meanwhile?"

Jerry turns to her. "Peter says we live our lives and hope for the best."

She springs up. "I can't go to history class with Miss Boothe!"

Panic rises in her eyes and I reach for her hand. "Oh no, we'll get you into another class. I'll call the school now and set up a time with your guidance counselor in the morning."

While making the appointment, I'm surprised how ambiguously I can speak. I'm sure the school secretary is scratching her head over our conversation.

Later I toss some salmon on the grill for dinner. I'm beginning to understand how people lose weight during stressful situations. If food weren't necessary to sustain life, I wouldn't bother to eat.

Nick works online, completing a homework assignment. I finish cleaning the kitchen and go upstairs. Emma's sprawled on her bed, surrounded by books. It looks like a typical night, but I don't know how many more of those we'll enjoy. Jerry's watching sports on television in our room. I toss my big pillow on the bed and grab the novel I was reading.

For the next few blessed hours, life is calm. I pick out tomorrow's clothes, put Belle outside for her last potty break of the day, tuck her in her kennel, and lock up the house. Stress still holds my head in a vise, so I decide to take a hot shower.

By the time I get into bed, Jer's already snoring. I sink into my pillow, but the way my mind is racing, I may never fall asleep.

I fluff up my pillow and begin my nightly prayers. I pray for my family, the same as I do every other night. Except tonight, I pray for mercy and grace for Emma. My weary body is pulled toward slumber like rain flowing down my roof. I can't resist, and I don't want to. My last prayer is for a brighter day tomorrow.

The sudden intake of my breath drags me from sleep. My hand flies to my right breast. I can't believe I've had that same awful dream—being stabbed in my breast by a sharp object. It's the same one I had the night after Deb confided in me about her marriage.

A sheen of perspiration coats my face. *Let me rest so I will have the energy to face another day tomorrow.*

I roll to my side. There it is again. *Oh, that hurt.*

Jerry sits up. "What's wrong?"

My exhausted brain cycles through what just happened. In a split second, I decide to keep it to myself. "Sorry. Just a bad dream. Go back to sleep, dear."

Every fiber of my body vibrates with fear. *What is that pain?* I gently roll onto my back. My terrified heart beats in time with every piercing throb from deep inside my breast. I will my breathing to slow and try to relax my taut muscles with a cleansing breath. I search the shadows while I silently count the pulsing, burning pain . . . *seven, eight, nine.* A deep sigh flows from my lungs when the pain finally releases its nauseating hold on me. I grab a tissue and wipe the sweat from my eyes.

I'm not surprised to taste a salty tear slide into my mouth. What more could possibly happen?

35

The gentle morning sun filters through the bedroom shades, announcing the start of a new day. I roll over and turn my thoughts toward heaven. Today I need to rest in the everlasting arms for a few moments before I enter into my living nightmare.

Hey—no pain in my breast. Hallelujah. Maybe it was a fluke. Perhaps the Lord knows I can only handle so much.

When I get downstairs, I dial work and wait for the outgoing message to end. "This is Linda. I have personal business to take care of this morning. I'll be in as soon as I can." I imagine they'll give me a little slack after yesterday's meltdown.

On the surface, breakfast seems normal. We all munch on cereal and juice, with coffee for Jerry and Nick and tea for Emma and me. My flavor of choice this morning is Enchanted Forest. If only it were a magic potion that would whisk us to a fairy-tale land where we could ride unicorns all day and nap beneath the rainbow. But instead, we eat breakfast, share the newspaper, and pretend there isn't an elephant in the middle of the room.

Emma and I are first out the door. I don't know who dreads going to school more, her or me. When we enter the counseling office, my stomach has those crazy gnomes doing the conga again, and my hands are drenched with sweat.

We sign in and take a seat on the aqua pleather sofa. I know the school district needs to be careful about spending money, but please—either buy real leather or a nice upholstered piece of furniture, not this tacky plastic junk. At least I'm wearing a long skirt, and I don't have to worry about peeling my legs from its suction grip when we're finally allowed our five minutes with the counselor.

"Mom?" Em's standing above me.

"Hmm?"

"Let's go. We've been called."

Yikes. My brain is pure mush. We're ushered down a dimly lit hall in the office suite and into a room the size of a large closet. I take a seat in an industrial folding chair, and Emma sits in the corner next to an out-of-control spider plant.

A thirtysomething woman holding a manila file breezes in and extends her hand. "Good morning. I'm Karen Murphy." Under other circumstances, it would be a pleasure to meet her. She looks like a doll.

I shake her hand and hope she's not grossed out by the damp sponge hanging off the end of my wrist. "Hi. I'm Linda Revere, and this is—"

She gives a conspiratorial wink. "Oh, I know Emma."

Really? I don't think so. I don't even know her anymore.

The fresh-faced woman looks from Emma to me, her long brown hair bouncing with the energy in her movement as she sits behind her desk. "What can I do for you ladies this morning?"

"An uncomfortable situation between Emma and Miss Boothe, her history teacher, has occurred, so we need to move her to a different history class."

Ms. Murphy knits her eyebrows. "Well, a change like this can't be made at random. It will involve shuffling Emma's schedule, and then we'll need to speak with Miss Boothe about it. Perhaps you can iron out your difficulties?"

Beside me, Em drops her chin, crosses her legs, and bounces her foot up and down.

I feel as hopeless as she seems. I take a deep breath and sit up straighter. "Unfortunately, that won't be possible. What has occurred was off school property and isn't anyone's business but ours and Miss Boothe's. And I'm fairly certain that she would think this is the best course of action."

Ms. Murphy presses her lips together in concentration, and charming dimples populate her rosy cheeks. "I'm not sure I can pull this off without a little bit of time to manipulate Emma's schedule."

I don't really believe that. Or maybe I'm just not in the mood to be put off. "If that's the case, I'd like to have Emma dismissed from history class until we can change her schedule."

Apparently the woman reads the determination in my voice and nods as though she knows there's no way around our request. She takes a piece of paper out of a drawer and writes a short note.

She stands and hands the hall pass to Emma. "Come down to the counseling office during history class, and we'll work it out."

Whew. That was easier than I thought it would be. "Thank you very much, Ms. Murphy. I appreciate your time."

The bell rings, saving us from further conversation. We exit the tiny office, and my daughter and I hug.

"I'll be praying for you, Emma. See you later."

She gives me a kiss on the cheek and disappears in the swarm of kids that flow down the hallway.

I stand and watch, though I can't see her anymore. My feet are as heavy as if I'm wearing fifty-pound swimming fins while I fight my way upstream to the freedom of the front door.

● ● ●

The studio's in full swing when I arrive. Barb catches my eye and lifts her index finger while she continues her telephone conversation.

I clock in, escape to the office, and fall into my chair. When I see the extension light on the phone dim, I drag myself out to the lobby. "Barb?"

She passes the sales schedule to me. "Rose isn't feeling up to coming to work. Can you cover her sales today?"

"Sure. How is she?"

Barb shakes her head. "She broke her arm, poor dear."

More guilt. "Oh no."

The telephone rings, and Barb turns her attention from me.

I glance over the schedule and walk back to my desk. We're jam-packed today. I'm thrilled. If ever I need to be locked away in a dark room, today is the day.

I load the client's files into my computer and assemble a plate of cookies and water bottles on the coffee table in my image presentation room. My first sale is one of our special edition children's sessions. The images pop up on my monitor.

The star of our show this morning is an adorable little girl about four years old. Leah's long brown hair hangs loosely over her shoulders, and she's encased in a mermaid costume. In the first image, she's poised inside a giant oyster shell, holding a colossal pearl. I select the music to accompany the slide show and wait for Leah and her mother to arrive.

I'm not at my desk for three minutes before Jill comes into the office. *Does she have radar?* Without a word, she gives me a hug. I squeeze her back. I know she only wants the best for me.

She moves a step away. "You don't have to say a thing; just know that I'm here if you want to speak with someone."

Tears spring to my eyes. "Oh, Jill." I grab a tissue from the desk and blot my eyes. "Sorry. Please understand that I can't talk about this right now."

She pats my arm. "Hold on to your hat, girl. You'll get through this."

If only she knew. "Thanks."

The studio door chimes, and I rush out to greet my client. Leah is a delight. She and her mom are enthralled with the photos. And I don't know if it's because of my state of mind or not, but even I get a little teary eyed looking at this beautiful child become the Little Mermaid.

Midway through the sales session, Leah turns to me and says, "Aren't I beautiful?"

"Oh, sweetheart, you're gorgeous."

It's a joy to see how the girls get so involved in their fantasies when they dress in our elaborate costumes and enter the set. Leah really did become the Little Mermaid, if only for forty minutes.

She snuggles closer to her mother. "Daddy will be so happy."

I keep my chuckle to myself. Daddy will love the images, but the bill he's going to get could choke a horse.

"Now," I say to Leah's mom, "didn't you say this picture would go in Leah's bedroom? Let's look at a twenty-four-by-thirty. . . ."

One more sale, and my morning's done. I check the schedule. *Oh no.* It's Jessica Kent. Six months ago when she and her ignorant husband came in, I nearly lost both my patience and my job. Jessica and Brennan were on the phone with Luke before they even left the parking lot. While they were in the image presentation room, they complained about everything under the sun, and when they got Luke's voice mail, they let loose about me.

I get fresh cookies and cold water bottles. I don't want them to find any fault in my service today.

The Kents don't return my smile when they come into the image presentation room. I'm sure they were expecting to see Rose instead. Well, I'm not thrilled to be shut in a small room with them either.

Brennan Kent sprawls out on the love seat as though he's in his family room, half lying across the small couch with his right leg on the arm of the furniture. Jessica, acting as though she just ate a bad hot dog, takes the upholstered chair. Fortunately they left their squawking kids with someone else.

The last time they were here, their snotty son repeatedly peeked out of the room to harass passing clients, then slammed the door hard enough to make the frames on the wall vibrate. How I would have loved to sit that little fellow down and given him what-for. But, no. I followed company policy, and since the kid wasn't destroying anything, I kept my lips zipped. Oh, and while junior was annoying everyone else in sight, Brennan and Jessica completely ignored his shenanigans.

We all pretend to tolerate one another and get on with the show. Today they're viewing images of their daughter at her one-year session.

I turn on the charm and tell them the truth. "These images are gorgeous."

"Hmm." The bum can't even bother to turn my way when he responds. I'd love to throw a wad of paper at the back of his greasy head.

The first thing they want to do is choose the four pictures to be matted and framed together. The series is of their daughter in bloomers sitting on the floor behind a big birthday cake. In the first photo she's smiling as she looks at the pastry. The next three images show the progression of her diving into the cake, ending up with a very messy little girl, covered in frosting. What's not to love?

Brennan points his index finger. "Put those two side by side."

"Uh, number twenty-seven and thirty?"

"No. That one."

Sheesh. He's just as obnoxious as the last time we worked together. "I'm sorry. Could you please tell me by number?"

He sits up and jerks his head my way, glowering. "Twenty-seven and twenty-nine."

Could he be any ruder? I highlight the images and display them on the screen.

The breath is sucked out of my lungs as a burning sword pierces my right breast. I stifle the urge to cup my pain-filled flesh. Perspiration oozes from my pores, and I can feel a bead of sweat rise on my upper lip.

Jessica's curt voice cuts into my fog. "Excuse me."

I breathe slowly, trying to get on top of the pain. "I'm sorry. What did you say?"

Her lips pucker as she spits out her words. "Is it too much to ask you to pay attention?"

All I can do is bat my eyes at this witch. I'm going to explode—both from anger at these ignorant people and from the pain in my breast.

"Would you please excuse me?" I bolt for the door.

As I'm running toward the workroom, I can hear their angry voices demanding assistance. Well, it won't be from me.

Jill's putting orders into boxes when I come in. "What's going on?"

I don't slow my pace as I dash toward the restroom. "Get someone to finish the Kents' sale."

I lock the door and sit on the commode to catch my breath. After a moment, I tug on the toilet paper for tissue to dry my eyes and blow my nose.

Oh, Father. Help me.

36

"Linda? Linda!" Jill pounds on the powder room door. Noise rises behind her, a chaotic chorus of muffled voices.

Jill responds to the questions being shot at her. "I don't know. She ran through here like the devil was chasing her and locked herself inside."

I hear my coworkers speculate on my bizarre behavior, asking questions and offering theories.

Luke's voice booms above the others. "Traci? Can you please finish Linda's sale?"

Despite the hubbub on the other side of the door, I can only clutch my arms around myself and wait out the pain. I wish I'd had the presence of mind to run out of the building instead of inside the bathroom. I feel like an animal caged at the zoo.

The torment dissipates from my breast, and I become myself again. Now, how can I gracefully extract myself from this situation?

A knock, more gentle than the previous, sounds. "Lin? Can I come in?"

I rise and blow my nose. "Okay, Jill. Just a minute."

I glance in the mirror. *Ugh.* I look like yesterday's trash. My mascara is streaked beneath my eyes, and my red nose looks twice its size. There's not much I can do about this damage. I swallow my pride and release the lock.

Jill steps in, then closes the door behind her. She opens her arms, and I gratefully accept her comfort. When she releases me, she looks through a cabinet and finds a container of wet wipes. She pulls a sheet from the tub and gently dabs at my face. "Oh, honey, it will be all right."

"It's not Emma."

She gives me a blank stare, and I explain. "I've got a problem. A pain. In my breast."

Her face is a study in sympathy. "Oh no."

"I want to leave. I'm going to call my doctor. Do you think it's—?"

Jill puts an arm around my shoulders. "You do whatever you need to do. I'll explain to Luke." She gives me another hug. "Call me later." She steps out into the workroom and ushers everyone back to their workstations.

I escape the powder room and rush to the office. I don't bother to shut down my computer. I grab my purse and clock out.

The noon sun hurts my weary eyes. I stumble to my car and sit with the AC blasting at my face. After a moment, I grasp my cell phone and dial my doctor's number, cruise the automated phone system, and get a nurse on the phone. Fortunately, she's familiar with me and must sense my rising desperation.

"Let me put you on hold for a minute, Linda. Okay?"

"Sure."

Out of the corner of my eye, I see a few of my coworkers standing on the sidewalk in front of the studio, looking my way. I close my eyes and lean my head on the back of the seat.

"Linda, I just spoke to Dr. Parrish, and she thinks she can squeeze you in today. She had a cancellation, and if you can get here within fifteen minutes, she'll be able to see you."

My body goes weak with relief. "Thank you very much. I'm on my way."

On the drive to Pine Grove my cell phone chirps. It's Jerry.

Heaven help me, I don't have the energy or desire to speak to any-one. I let the call go to voice mail.

The waiting room at my doctor's office is half full. I check in with the receptionist, surrender my insurance card, and take a seat. To pass the time, I page through a two-year-old copy of *Better Homes and Gardens*.

"Ms. Revere?"

I follow a young nurse to an exam room, where she directs me to take a seat.

"So, what's going on?"

I give her the rundown on my breast pain. She nods and scrib-bles in my file. "Okay, I'll check your vitals."

The competent young woman takes my blood pressure and adds that information to my record. She seems all business and barely looks me in the face. Is this because dying women make her ner-vous? She slips out of the room, her spotless tennis shoes padding her footsteps.

I strip to the waist, put on a robe, and sit alone, waiting for Dr. Parrish. My cell phone rings again. Jerry. I turn it off.

A soft knock precedes Anne Parrish. She's been my doctor for nearly eight years now, and I couldn't be more pleased. She's always been outside the mold of the usual busy doctor, taking time to listen to me and making me feel as though we're in a partnership to maintain my health.

Her soft smile reassures me. She's carrying my file and flips it open. "Let's see. It looks like you've had a bit of a scare."

I can only nod.

She continues, "Lie back and let me take a look."

I concentrate on the pattern in the tiled ceiling while she does a manual breast exam.

"Well, I don't feel anything. But even a small tumor can cause discomfort."

My mouth has gone dry. "Tumor?"

She smiles and lays a hand on my shoulder. "In the medical sense, that means any kind of growth—not necessarily cancer. It could be as simple as a cyst. But we need to figure out exactly what it is."

My heart sinks. It's not as if this is really new information, but to hear it put into words is beyond belief.

Dr. Parrish adds, "You might want to try restricting caffeine."

Caffeine? As in the tea and coffee I love and the chocolate I crave? "And?"

She takes a seat across from the exam table I'm perched on. "I'm going to send you to the Sally Jobe Breast Center for an ultrasound."

A lump the size of Pikes Peak forms in my throat. "Oh."

She reaches out and puts her hand on my knee. "I've had the nurse check, and the next available appointment is Monday. Shall I have her schedule you?"

I nod.

"Linda, don't panic. Let's get more information and go from there. Okay?"

I nod again.

She writes out a prescription to take to the breast center, hands it to me, and closes the manila file. "The doctor at Sally Jobe will give you a report as soon as they determine the cause of your pain."

Like a bobble-head doll, I continue to nod and watch her walk out of the office.

37

I'm surprised not to find Nick's car parked in front of the house. He's usually home by four thirty. The garage door opens, and I slip my Taurus inside. The dim bulb from the opener lights my way to the door.

The house is silent. Even little Belle is tucked away somewhere. "Hello? Emma?"

She doesn't respond, but I hear the sound of canned laughter coming from the television in her room.

The stairs creak beneath my feet as I climb the risers. When I get to the landing, I pause. Shall I change into leisure clothes or greet my daughter?

I stand like a statue at the top of the stairs. The act of making a simple decision is more than I can handle. If only I could crumple into a ball and let someone else take care of my life.

Instinct overcomes selfishness. I push my hair behind my ears and trod down the hall to Emma's room. An old sitcom plays on the TV that sits on her dresser. Emma is leaning against her pillow with Belle at her side. They're both sleeping. I aim the remote and turn off the noise.

Downstairs I sit in the familiar embrace of Grandma's chair and cup my breast—my newest enemy. I toss my right arm over my head and let it rest on the top of the chair. Visualizing the breast self-examination diagram that hangs in Dr. Parrish's office, I slowly begin to massage my breast. Nothing. I feel no bumps, no mass, and no tumor.

As I'm finishing my task, the phone rings. I hurry to answer it so it doesn't wake Em. A glance at the handset tells me it's Jer. "Hello?"

"Where have you been?" His voice is edged with anger.

"Oh, I—"

"I called you at the studio, and Jill said you left work sick."

"Yeah, I—"

"And then you didn't answer your cell, and—"

Jerry silences his tirade when I begin to cry. "Honey? . . . Lin? What's wrong? Is it Emma?"

I pull myself together as best I can. "No. It's me."

"What?"

"I've been having a pain. In my breast. Today it got so bad I called Dr. Parrish, and she squeezed me into her schedule."

"What did she say?"

I take a deep breath to regain my composure. "Right now she thinks it might be a tumor of some sort."

"Cancer?"

"I go for an ultrasound Monday. We'll know more then." I pause for a response but only hear silence. "Jer?"

"I'm turning on our street right now. I'll see you in a minute."

I shift my gaze to the window and see his dark blue SUV cruise down the street. My eyes pool with tears.

When Jerry comes into the room, I leap toward him. He accepts me into his arms and holds me tightly. His warmth takes the edge off my anxiety. Jerry moves us both toward the love seat and pulls me onto his lap. Tears silently flow down my cheeks, and he wipes them away with his fingers, cradling me with his arm.

"We'll get through this, Lin. We'll get through this."

Oh, how I want to believe him.

The key in the dead bolt announces that Nick's home from

school. He comes through the door and stops dead at the sight of us. His face blanches. "Emma?"

Jerry shakes his head. "No, buddy. She's okay. Your mom might be sick."

Nick drops into the chair facing us. "Sick?"

"She might have a tumor in her breast. But we don't know if it's cancer. It could just be something benign."

Emma's tiny voice squeaks out my name. "Mommy?"

We all turn to see her standing at the bottom of the stairs. She rushes into the room and falls on her knees in front of us, throwing her arms around my waist. Her face contorts with emotion, and she breaks into sobs. Her torment adds to my own, and I weep with her. I wiggle off Jerry's lap to be able to put my arm around Emma.

Nick stands and moves the footstool next to the love seat, sits down, and wraps his arms around his sister and me. Jerry shifts to stretch his arm to reach around our son. We huddle, gaining strength from our love.

Jerry clears his throat. "Dear Lord, . . ."

His prayer washes over me like a balm. I close my eyes and feel as though I'm being bathed with warm sunshine and fresh air. I am impressed with the idea that the fragrance of life is filling my senses, and I'm warmed to my core, somehow believing that no matter what the consequence, it will be okay.

Jerry finishes his prayer, and my mother's heart sings when Nick picks up where he left off. How blessed I am. Before he says amen, Em joins in and prays for me. When our prayer time is finished, we dry our eyes and release from our huddle.

Jerry pats my knee and stands. "Okay, this is how it's going to be. Until we get a definite answer from the doctor, we're going to pray that Mom will be well. You know, she's not the first woman to go through something like this." His glance holds mine for a moment longer than usual. *What's he really thinking?*

I muster a confident smile, push myself up from the cushions, and straighten my shirt. The clock chimes the hour. "Let's make dinner. How about burgers?"

We all pitch in together. I take the ground beef out of the refrigerator, Jerry turns on the barbecue grill, Emma sets the table, and Nick washes lettuce. I don't think we've ever worked as a unit like this before. I impress this moment on my heart and promise myself to never forget the power of family.

Jerry comes in from the patio. "How's school going, Em?"

She shrugs. "Okay, I guess."

"Did you get a new history class?"

Emma nods and makes a face as though she just tasted cold brussels sprouts.

"What does that mean?"

"I feel like the class freak. And so does Lyndsay—her mom switched her to another history class."

"Why?"

"Who starts a new class in midsemester? Everybody wants to know why we changed classes, and I think Mr. Flynn is afraid of me."

I put the raw burger patties on a plate. "Oh, don't say that. Why would he be afraid of you?"

She shifts her gaze to the floor. "Well, look what I did to my last history teacher."

Oh, my girl. If only I could wipe away her guilt like I do the smeared fingerprints on my pantry door. "Sweetheart, don't say that. We know that you really didn't mean to hurt her."

Emma sits at the table and puts her head in her hands. We all watch her desperate actions. Her shoulders move in silent sobs.

Jerry picks up the burgers and walks to the door. "Enough of that. You made a mistake and we're moving on. Each day puts this more in the past. God knows how this will shake out. We'll just have to trust in Him." He slides open the screen and goes out to the patio.

She plucks a napkin from the holder on the center of the table and makes an effort to pull herself together.

I'm not so sure I agree with Jer's tough-love strategy. I want to sit and hold my daughter, rock her in my arms, and promise her a happy ending. But unfortunately, I don't know if that will be the case.

We try to make conversation at dinner, but the air is too heavy to discuss what's really on our minds. After a few minutes of silent dining, Nick and Jerry start talking about baseball and the Colorado Rockies.

As if I care. I push my salad around my plate, occasionally stabbing a piece of cheese or lettuce, hoping Jerry doesn't notice my lack of appetite. Emma looks miserable.

The pain returns. I close my eyes and try to breathe.

"Lin?"

I look at Jerry. "Pain. Not too bad. It'll pass."

Conversation is suspended. How awkward. I wave my hand. "It's over," I lie.

The boys continue where they left off, talking about what game they want to go to Coors Field to see.

I shift my attention to Emma. She's as interested in food as I am. How did we get to this place? A shudder of irritation grips my stomach. I glance at my family. They're unaware of my little tremor—like a small earthquake you only know about because it's mentioned on the evening news. My thought is irrational, but I can't help but recall Steve's words the night the laxative tea episode unfolded: *"As far as we know, the only people aware of the cause of that lady's illness are under this roof."* Could he have been right? Should we have kept our daughters' involvement to ourselves? I feel my emotions become more removed from Jerry, like the bishop on a chessboard—sliding diagonally farther away. When did he stop being my knight in shining armor?

"Linda?"

I come back to the moment and see my family staring at me. "What?"

Jerry sighs. "I asked you what time your appointment is on Monday."

"Uh, it's at three thirty."

Jerry pushes away from the table. "Okay, I'll call you kids as soon as we know something."

Nick and Em scramble to clear the table. I begin to rise, but Jer puts a hand on my shoulder. "We'll take care of this, dear. Why don't you go relax?"

So much for Jerry's act-normal routine. Being freed from evening chores couldn't be farther from normal. I refill my glass of water, grab the phone from the wall, and go to my favorite seat in the living room.

I punch in the familiar number. "Hi, Deb. It's me. Can you talk?"

38

"Well, hello, stranger. What's up?" Debbie's voice sounds so cheer-ful, so normal. Has she glossed over her issue with her husband already? Is it possible to move on knowing the man you love is lusting after almost every female in sight? What was the bribe this time? Designer shoes?

"What's new with you? How are things with Keith?"

She laughs. I can't tell if it's sincere or if she's trying to throw me off track. "Oh, we're just crazy busy around here. I'm helping Randy and Andrea make wedding plans. It's so exciting."

Okay, I'll play along. I don't want to ruin my friendship with a dear friend because her husband's a jerk. "Tell me about it."

She launches into an explanation about the reception venues they've been visiting, the colors Andrea's choosing for the bridal party, and the premarital counseling the happy couple is attending. On and on and on. I grunt at the appropriate times, and Debbie continues her monologue.

She pauses in midsentence. "Lin?"

"Huh?"

"What's wrong?"

Bless her heart, she's zeroed in on me. "Oh, Deb, I hardly know where to begin."

"What's going on?"

"You know I trust you, but you have to promise not to tell a soul. If Jer knew what I was saying, he'd have a heart attack."

"Honey, you can rely on me."

I fill her in on Emma's incident. Some of the bricks I've been carrying around on my shoulders evaporate. "Thanks. We're acting as if things are ordinary around here, but I need to talk things through to cope with this problem."

"I'm sure you do. Don't worry. I'll be praying for Emma and the whole situation."

I kick off my shoes. "There's more."

"Go on."

I launch into the story of my possible tumor, and by the end of my speech, I'm teary eyed.

"Oh, Linda. Why didn't you call me?"

I snuffle before I speak. "The past few days have been such a nightmare. I can barely put one foot in front of the other. I've had all I can do just to go through the motions."

"Do you want me to go to the breast center with you?"

"Thanks, but Jer's going."

"Okay. Call me. I mean it."

Her stern voice makes me laugh. "I will. Thanks for listening."

We end the call. Almost immediately the phone rings. I scan the digital screen. It's Jill. *Sheesh*. I told her I'd call. "Hi, Jill."

"How are you?"

I sigh deeply. It's beginning to be a drag, going over the dismal facts again and again. "I really don't know much, except that I might have a tumor of some kind."

"Oh no." Her voice is choked with emotion.

I'm blessed with loving friends. "We're not panicking yet. On Monday I go for an ultrasound. It could just be a cyst. And that's where we're pinning our hopes."

"Okay, I can go with that. Are you coming into work tomorrow? Or should I find someone to fill in for you?"

Work. I haven't even thought of that. "Uh, yeah. I'll be there bright and early."

• • •

I awake, pleasantly surprised to have slept through the night. No nightmares, no pain. Maybe it was only a cyst, and it's resolved itself.

Jerry's still deep in slumber, so I grab my robe off the foot of the bed and quietly close our bedroom door. I hear Belle's collar tags jingling downstairs. Didn't she get put away last night? I hope she hasn't messed in the house. I hurry downstairs and am caught off guard to find Emma in the kitchen, filling the teakettle. "What are you doing up so early?"

She opens the cabinet and rummages for the tea canister, speaking without turning around. "Couldn't sleep."

My poor girl. Life is beating her down. "Want some oatmeal?"

"Nah."

"How about scrambled eggs?"

She carefully measures the loose tea and drops the infuser into the pot. "I'm not really hungry."

"Maybe some toast?"

She glares at me. "I'm not an idiot. If I was hungry, I'd eat."

"Watch your attitude."

Emma ambles over to the computer and goes online. I can only imagine the amount of tension coiled inside her. Her fingers pound the keyboard with a startling intensity, and her forehead is furrowed in concentration. She navigates from one site to another at lightning speed. "Mom, I want to be homeschooled."

"You can't run away from your problems. Besides, won't you miss your friends? And what about cheerleading?"

She swivels around in the chair. "Forget cheerleading."

"What? You love that."

Her chin trembles. "I'm going to be kicked off the squad anyway."

"Why do you say that?"

"If you can't stay on the team with poor grades, do you think they'll keep me with a criminal record?"

My enemy—pain—returns. And not at a worse time. I try to ignore the flaming arrow boring into my flesh and grip the kitchen counter. The kettle on the stove screams, giving me a reprieve from our conversation. I busy myself brewing some caffeine-free peppermint tea. Again, I count out the pulsing pain . . . *four, five, six.* As quickly as it attacked me, it dissipates. My heartbeat slows to normal, and I carry the pot and two mugs to the table.

"Em, nothing's going to happen until we hear from the DA."

For a moment she stares at me, a look of defeat pulling down her beautiful features. I wonder if we should take her to counseling. She blinks, breaking some weird spell cast between us, and turns back to the computer.

I put milk in my tea and retreat to my prayer chair. I beseech my Lord for my daughter and my health, but my prayers feel as if they're going no farther than the ceiling. I take a sip of tea and open my Bible. I flip through and stop where a scrap of paper was folded into the pages. I read the handwritten note where I long ago rewrote a Scripture verse into a personalized prayer: *"For You have not given me a spirit of fear but of power and love and a sound mind."*

Thanks for the reminder, Lord. I was never one to play Bible roulette, but that's something I can cling to today.

The kitchen is deserted when I go to eat my cereal. After I've scraped the last cornflake from my bowl, I rise to clear the table and reach for Emma's mug. It still has three-quarters of a cup of cold tea.

Never in a million years did I think my family would be facing an ordeal like this. If only Lyndsay never thought of giving Miss Boothe that tea. If only Emma talked Lyndsay out of serving the tea. If only she didn't go to Lyndsay's house that afternoon. If only Miss Boothe didn't want to press charges. I wonder if we should have listened to Steve's advice.

I feel like a traitor to my husband, but I've begun having the same thought over and over again. We could have remained silent, and Emma wouldn't be suffering this agony. How will this change the direction of her life? of all our lives?

39

My coworkers go out of their way to be nice to me. Makes me
wonder what they would do if they knew all our troubles. Take
up a collection and help us secure the services of the best criminal
attorney in Denver?

My schedule is light this morning—two consultations on how
to prepare for portrait sessions and a sale for a business headshot.
Ironically, my headshot sale is with a local attorney. How I wish I
could confide my problems and have him give me a magic answer.

He's a no-nonsense type of guy, and his image presentation takes
only about thirty minutes. We fly though his images, deleting all
but four, spend about five minutes discussing the merits of his three
favorites, and settle on two poses to be put on a CD for him.

Soon I'm out of the salesroom. I clock out and decide to enjoy
a little solitude on the employee patio. The sun embraces me with
a sweet kiss, and I make myself comfortable on the chaise lounge.
I hear a photo session being conducted in the distance and tune out
the sounds of laughter and voices.

My peace is disturbed when I hear the rush of a match being
struck and smell the acrid scent of sulfur mixed with cigarette
smoke. I sit up and look behind me. Pam smiles and takes a deep
pull on her cigarette.

I wonder how much longer she'll be working here. She doesn't exactly fit into the Dream Photography mold. Most of the employees project a tailored and professional appearance. Not only is Pam's wardrobe unusual, she also applies her foundation so pale that she often looks ghostly. Combine that with her jet-black hair and vividly painted fingernails, and on days like today you get an Elvira look-alike.

I've begun to realize that her makeup application and her hairstyle are a barometer of her mood. The more angst she seems to have on a particular day, the less she looks like a natural woman and the more she looks like a caricature of a woman.

Today her long, brittle black mane is pulled into a low ponytail with the hair on the crown of her head teased to extreme. She looks as if she grew an inch and a half overnight.

"Linda." She nods in greeting.

"Hi, Pam. How are you today?"

Her heavily penciled eyebrows, drawn with an exaggerated arch, give her an artificial scowl. She tilts her head and exhales. "I can't complain. Well, not too much, anyway," she says with an air of indifference. To distance herself from the nicotine cloud encasing her, she waves her hand over her forehead.

As usual, I'm not sure how to respond to Pam. Some days she acts as though she wants a friend, and other days she keeps her distance. Rumor is, Pam doesn't have a good home life. Her children are unruly, and her marriage may be in trouble. I'm sorry for her, but don't we all have problems?

The last thing I want to talk about is my situation. "What's going on?"

She stares at me through her Cleopatra eyes and quickly looks down, as though there were something infinitely more interesting at her feet.

I point to the vacant chair. "Come sit in the sun with me. It feels great."

She tosses her cigarettes and lighter on the table and drags her chair alongside mine. I've left my comfort zone, and I'm traveling in uncharted waters. What do I have to say to Pam?

She stretches out one long, emaciated arm and admires her blue manicured nails. Staring straight ahead, she says, "I hope I don't break a nail when I strangle my husband later."

A nervous giggle escapes my mouth. Surely she's kidding.

We sit in uncomfortable silence for a few moments. I'm certainly not going to talk about my personal life to her. "Do you have a flower garden, Pam?"

She takes a long, slow drag on her cigarette and exhales with her head turned away from me. "Yes. I love to get out of the house and into the dirt." Her face warms to a slow smile, and I know she has just invited me into her world.

Better than having her involved in my issues. "Really? Tell me about it."

She stubs her cigarette out on a patio brick and tosses the butt into an empty flowerpot. So much for the ecofriendly gardener.

She closes her eyes, lost somewhere in her mind. Finally she speaks. "My garden is my life in the summer. I got my Master Gardener certificate last September. Something always blooms in my garden, from spring until fall."

Now I'm intrigued. I didn't see that coming. *Pam, a Master Gardener?* I always plant a few petunias, but that's about it. I can hardly imagine those perfectly manicured hands digging in the soil.

"I've already planned how I'm going to lay out my garden this year," she continues. "I'm going to have one section devoted to different varieties of daylilies."

Suddenly, the sullen and quiet Pam begins to bloom before my eyes; pardon the pun. She rambles on, extolling the virtues of different seed companies and hardy, pest-resistant plants. I'm beginning to feel a little off center. My preconceived views of her are beginning to crumble.

She blushes faintly. "I'd be happy to help you with your gardening this summer, Linda."

Am I the company charity project? I'm not sure I like this. "Oh, I don't do that much gardening. A few petunias along my front sidewalk and a hanging basket or two in the backyard are enough for me."

When Pam looks at me, I can practically see the veil fall between us. She appears to get smaller, as if her heart were folding in on itself. I feel awful. Somehow I've just made a huge mistake. Maybe her kind offer wasn't about me at all.

I pray to be a light in the world, but right now it looks like I've extinguished Pam's inner light.

She glances at her watch. "My break's over."

Before I can make amends, she's on her feet and grabbing her cigarettes off the table.

"Pam, maybe this year I should think about expanding my garden," I say to her retreating form.

She shrugs and disappears into the studio.

Oh, I'm such a jerk. Would it really be so terrible to have let Pam give me gardening tips? The gnomes in the conga line kick up their heels and dance through my stomach.

A moment later the studio door opens. I glance up, hoping it's Pam, but instead I see Barb pantomime that I have a phone call.

Going into the building is like walking into a cave. I pause while I wait for my eyes to make out the shapes of the tables before I move farther into the workroom. Heaven forbid we should turn on one of the fluorescent lights; the imaging artists would have a fit. They don't like any glare on their monitors while they perform their digital magic.

I inch my way around one of the workstations and punch the button to take the caller off hold. "This is Linda," I say in what I hope is a cheerful voice.

I make quick work of dealing with a frame supplier and end the call.

I'm just about to go find Pam and somehow try to make it up to her when Luke steps into the workroom doorway. He points at his wristwatch, then jerks his head toward the lobby and stalks off. Apparently my next sales appointment has arrived.

The afternoon grinds on. I spend an excruciating ninety minutes with a high school senior and her mom while they obsess over every detail of each photo. The wind is blowing her hair too much in one; another makes her nose look too big; one shot shows her twisted shirt, and in another image the clasp on her necklace is in the front. They have the uncanny talent of finding fault with every picture that sails across the screen. Okay, I'll give them the necklace clasp, and we can remove that digitally, but really, why didn't Mom notice the other things when they were doing the shoot?

I have a few moments before my next appointment, so I slip into the office. A fax is churning out of the machine.

It's from the frame supplier. They're back-ordered on one of our favorite frames. We're already behind deadline on several files, and now it will take another two weeks to get our backlogged orders out the door.

Luke is going to freak out. He's not exactly the kind of guy who takes small setbacks in stride. I glance at my watch and decide I can catch him between shoots. Better that he knows about the snafu sooner rather than later.

As I head to Luke's office, I breathe a prayer of gratitude for no breast pain.

As usual, Luke's office door is ajar. Between shoots he edits the previous session, eliminating the images that don't meet his standards. He prefers that we don't interrupt him, forcing us to wait for him to turn his attention toward us. Knowing that, I quietly slip into his office and prepare to practice my patience.

The sight that greets me is so surprising that I can't help myself, and I let out a huge gasp.

40

Two pairs of eyes stare at me with astonishment. I've never seen Luke blush before, and his face looks like it's going to explode. Pam steps out of his embrace and stumbles over the trash can that sits alongside his desk. The clash of metal as the trash can meets the wooden floor echoes through the room.

I back up to make a hasty retreat. "E-excuse me," I stammer. I'm dizzy from the air that has been sucked out of my lungs. My head buzzes with a million angry bees, and the conga line in my intestines just started dancing faster. I stagger from the room and charge toward the front of the studio.

"Linda."

I turn when Thomas, a photographer who's been with the company for a little over a month, calls my name. I stop in the hall, waiting for him to catch up with me.

He arrives breathless, which isn't unusual for him. Thomas is always in a crisis or between crises or inventing his next crisis. *You've got nothing on me, fella.*

"I can't find the prop box for a nautical scene," he whines. "I thought it—" He grabs my hand. "Are you okay? You don't look well."

"I think I ate a bad sandwich for lunch. I'll be all right." I try to smile to reassure him that my lie is authentic, but my face feels as if I've left a peel-off mask on for too long, and my cheeks refuse to cooperate with my charade.

"Let's get you into a chair." Thomas is really a sweet, gentle man, and his concern is very touching.

"Thanks, but I'm okay. Did you look in the seasonal storage closet?"

He smacks his head with his palm. "Duh. Thanks. I've got to get back to my clients."

I continue toward the front of the building and duck into the office. I fall into my chair and grab the bottle of water on my desk.

I'm not sure what I interrupted in Luke's office, but I wish with all my heart that I didn't see what I'm not sure I saw. *Like I need this in my day.*

My mind races to all sorts of unsuitable conclusions. *Maybe that's why Pam's marriage is rumored to be on the rocks. And what about Luke's marriage? His wife is one of the sweetest women I've ever met.*

"Linda."

How am I going to act around Luke and Pam now?

"Linda!"

I look up. "Oh. What?"

Barb is standing over me with a puzzled expression. "Your next appointment is here. Are you okay?"

"Yeah. I'm just dandy."

I greet my clients with a wooden smile and lead them to the sales-room. All through the slide show, I think of the sleazy scene between Luke and Pam. I'm barely able to concentrate on the sale, and even a brief episode of breast pain barely registers. We conclude business, and I escort them to the lobby and bid them a pleasant evening.

A pleasant evening. Ha. All I know is I don't want to run into either Luke or Pam tonight. How am I ever going to stand to be around them again? I want to slap his arrogant face and yank her chemically damaged hair out by the roots.

I sit at my desk and rush through my paperwork. With a sigh, I gather my belongings and escape the building.

The parking lot is emptying, signaling the end of the workday. I double-time it to my car. With one well-practiced movement, I take my seat and swing my armful of purse, lunch box, and thermal coffee mug onto the passenger side seat. While the AC kicks in, I put on the glasses I need to drive, turn on my cell phone, and push the button to activate the voice recognition directory.

After the high-pitched tone, I say, "Home."

An electronic voice prompts me. "Say a name."

Sigh. "Home."

"Say a name."

I hate technology. "Home!"

"Did you say Deb?"

"No!"

"Say a name."

I have a death grip on the stupid phone, and I wish I could just pitch it out the window. Instead, I rein in my emotions and speak as calmly as I can. "Home."

"Did you say dial?"

"No!"

"Word match unsuccessful. Exiting voice recognizer."

I look down at the display to manually scroll through my directory. It's all a blur. Sometimes it really stinks to get old. I can't see anything up close with these silly glasses. I tilt my chin down to peer over the rim of the glasses and hope that I don't run my car into a light pole before I exit the lot.

The phone at home rings; no one answers. I disconnect and take a stab at my voice recognition again.

The tone chimes, and I say, "Jerry."

"Calling Jerry."

Oh, right. Now you're being agreeable.

He answers on the third ring. "Oh, Jerry. I've had the worst day."

"Are you in pain?"

"Actually, not much. Where are you?"

"Kevin called. Their dog finally had the pups a couple of days ago. Em and I are going over to check them out. What's wrong?"

"Ugh. I don't want to talk too much about it if Em can hear. I think Luke and Pam are having an affair. I caught them in each other's arms in Luke's office today."

Jerry lets out a low whistle, and I can hear Emma in the background asking if I'm okay. He reassures her everything's fine and turns his attention back to me. "Do you want to meet us and see the puppies? take your mind off things?"

"No thanks. I have a splitting headache. I just want to go home."

• • •

The house is blessedly peaceful. Belle greets me with her tail wagging. I let her outside and draw in a deep breath of fresh air. The sweet fragrance of soil and spring grass reminds me of my conversation with Pam this afternoon. Which reminds me of walking in on Luke and Pam, which makes me feel ill.

I forgo the tea I crave in favor of juice and toss a few pieces of bread in the toaster for my dinner. A few minutes later I take a seat at the table and spread my toast with almond butter and raspberry jam. A feeling of loneliness quietly drifts over me like a winter breeze.

I dial Debbie.

"Hi, Lin. Feeling all right?"

I toss a crumb to Belle. "I think the pain is diminishing. At least I hope so." I release a deep breath through my teeth.

"Well, what's wrong then?"

My words tumble out in a rush. "I saw something I shouldn't have seen today."

"What are you talking about?"

The whole sorry story pours out, from my awkward lunch conversation with Pam to me walking in on her and Luke. It feels great to unload this terrible secret to my best friend. "What do you think I should do, Deb?"

"Wow. I don't know. I really don't know."

We continue to talk about the implications the affair will have on my work environment.

During our conversation, Jerry and Emma arrive home. She strides through the living room, talking on her cell phone, and Jerry forages around the kitchen for a snack.

"I've gotta go, Deb. Jerry and Emma just came home. I'll talk to you soon."

I walk over to Jerry, longing for my husband to put his arms around me. The world may tumble down, I may have breast cancer, and everything can go topsy-turvy, but I still have my sweet, loving, wonderful husband to count on.

Jerry's leaning with his back against the counter, eating an apple and staring out the window.

I put my arms around him and cozy up to his chest. But . . . he doesn't reciprocate. It's like hugging a piece of plywood. I gaze into his eyes and see in his expression a mixture of pity and disgust.

I shake my head. "What?"

He grasps my shoulders and puts some distance between us. "What are you doing?"

My confusion morphs into anger. "I'm trying to get a hug from my husband. Trying to get some comfort after the stinking day I've had."

His jaw is rigid, and he crosses his arms over his chest. "Why are you gossiping to Deb? What possible good can it do the situation to spread this rumor around?"

"Rumor? It's not a rumor, Jerry. I *saw* them together. Remember? Nobody *told* me about their affair. I walked into Luke's office and saw them embracing. It just makes me sick. They're both married.

Why are you taking their side? Can't you see how upsetting this is for me?"

"Whatever they're doing or have done is their business, Linda. Not yours."

I keep my voice low so Em doesn't hear. My heart is whirring like a ceiling fan, and the little hairs on the back of my neck are standing at attention. "Well, I was dragged into their sordid affair when they left Luke's office door open. This isn't something I wanted to see or know about. Why are you attacking me?"

Jerry glances out the window again, and I can see him make an effort to bring down the tension a few notches. When he shifts his gaze to me, I see a softness in his expression as though his heart is once again open for business. He gently rubs my cheek with the back of his knuckles. "I'm sorry, Lin. I know we've been put through the grinder lately, and this is a difficult situation. But you're making it worse by talking about it with Debbie. Can't you see how this is wrong?"

I'm temporarily at a loss for words. I don't see how sharing my dilemma with my best friend is such a crime.

"I'm not the one having an affair." I narrow my eyes and take a step toward him. "All I know is that I saw two people, *who are each married to someone else*, sharing a passionate embrace. This isn't a soap opera I'm talking about; it's my life. And right now, I'm going to take a long, hot shower."

With that pronouncement, I march upstairs and shut the bedroom door with more force than necessary. I pace across the floor to my dresser, where several earrings and necklaces I've worn the past few days lay in a heap. I sort through the mess, untangling beaded necklaces and pairing earrings. I need at least a little order and predictability in my life right now. I thread my arm through the necklaces, place the earrings in my palm, and stride to my jewelry armoire to carefully put my ornaments where they belong.

I continue with my little cleaning spree, straightening the books on my nightstand and beginning to sort through the magazines that have accumulated by my side of the bed. I look up from my spot on the floor when I hear the bedroom door open.

Jerry comes in, a few sheets of paper in his hands. "I've done a little research on the Internet. There are more options for breast cancer than I realized. Local and regional treatments, systemic treatments, even alternative and holistic therapies. And as far as surgery is concerned . . ."

I stare at him. His mouth is moving, and I know he's spouting off more data on breast cancer. Blah, blah, blah. His lecture voice drones on and on. He finishes his little speech and holds out the sheets he's printed from the computer.

I take the information from him while still sitting on the floor. I nod, too weary to answer verbally. Jerry dusts off his hands as if he's satisfied with his work and leaves the room.

When I look down, the pages are swimming in my vision, so I swipe at the tears spilling down my cheeks. Does he think he's being helpful? The last thing I want to see right now are diagrams of breast reconstruction.

I move to the bathroom to unwind my coiled emotions in a hot shower. I don't know whether I'm more angry or disappointed with Jerry.

As I'm disrobing, the phone rings. It's a call from Tammy and Steve's house, probably Lyndsay calling for Emma. I answer it the same moment Jerry does.

"It's Steve. I'm glad I've got both of you on the phone."

Great. He's about the last person I want to speak with. Jerry mumbles a greeting.

Steve's voice booms in my ear. "Well, I'm not going to take this business lying down. There's got to be something we can do to convince this woman to drop the charges."

"Our lawyer advised us to stay away from her," Jerry says. "I don't want to make the problem any worse than it is."

"I don't think it could get any worse. The way I look at it, if we—"

This is more than I can deal with. I drop the receiver onto its base. Besides, I might just take Steve's side in this argument, and that would only add to the anxiety on this side of the street. I wish that sweet feeling of oneness that Jer and I used to have would return.

There's nothing more appealing right now than a hot shower. The pelting spray soothes my aching shoulders. I give myself another breast exam and feel nothing out of the ordinary.

I turn off the water, and the sound of Jerry's voice filters upstairs. I grab the phone and push the Talk button. They're still at it. I disconnect and reach for my lotion and begin to slather my legs.

As I bend down, I'm ravaged with pain. I allow my knees to buckle, and I slide down the wall to the floor. My world is consumed by the fiery skewer that pierces my breast. I bury my face in my towel and weep.

The pain subsides. I stand and pull my nightgown on and continue with the mundane tasks of my nighttime rituals. What else can I do? Brush. Floss. Take my evening pills.

The family room television is blaring, and Jerry and Emma are getting a laugh from a sitcom. I fall into bed and surrender to the comfort of a good book.

41

Belle's whining rouses me from slumber. A glance at the clock shows 6:30 a.m. I silently get out of bed, pull on some sweats, and grab my walking shoes.

I wish I could say I enjoyed a restful weekend. But that's not the case. Despite the fact that I've not had much physical pain, my psyche is wounded every time I think of the gruesome research Jerry shared with me. I can't stop thinking about my upcoming appointment today and what I'll find out.

The sweet light of morning welcomes my little dog as she trots out to the yard. I dial the studio, and my cheerful voice greets me on the answering machine.

After the beep, I speak. "This is Linda. I just wanted to remind you that I won't be coming to work today. See you tomorrow. Bye."

I replace the handset in the cradle and stare out the window at the treetops swaying in the breeze. I can't stop thinking of what's ahead for Emma. The preliminary hearing has been set for tomorrow. Jerry and I debated whether or not we should keep her home for the day. Our presence isn't required; the matter will be between our attorney and the district attorney. In the end, we decided being in school would keep her mind occupied. Besides, we already know the outcome won't be good.

I pull a bowl from the cabinet and begin to mash the overripe bananas that sit on the counter. I gather flour and other ingredients and mix a batch of muffins.

By the time I'm taking them from the oven, Emma appears. "Yum. Smells good. Can I have one?"

Well, this is a good sign. "Sure, help yourself."

While I turn my attention to cleaning up my mess, Emma serves herself breakfast. "Why are you dressed in sweats, Mom?"

I answer without turning around, rinsing my bowl and utensils and loading them into the dishwasher. "I'm going for an early walk."

"Don't you have to go to the breast center today?"

I'm trying to put that out of my mind, thank you very much. "Not until three thirty."

She lingers over breakfast and reluctantly goes upstairs to get ready for school.

I pour another glass of juice and get comfortable in my Victorian chair. *Oh, Lord, I'm putting myself in Your hands today. I don't know what else to do.* I reach to the side table and grab my small gray devotional book. I flip through the well-worn pages, soaking up the courage I know I'll need.

I'm still in the living room when Jerry comes downstairs. "Morning."

He comes toward me, and I stand. "Morning, dear."

We fit into each other's arms like the two parts of the whole we always used to be. Jerry rests his head on mine and holds me tightly. He prays over me, and I close my eyes and lean into his chest. I'm transported from a moment of fear and doubt into a safe place of light and peace.

Jerry kisses my forehead, and together we walk to the kitchen, where he pours a cup of coffee. I put two muffins on his plate and join him at the table. We try to make everyday conversation. It's a strain. *Doesn't he know enough to tell me that no matter what, it will be okay? Doesn't he care that I may be scared witless?*

"I'll be home to pick you up at three o'clock, Linda."

Words lodge in my throat, so I just nod. Why couldn't he have called in sick today? Even if we just sat in silence together it would be better than me rattling around the house alone.

"Call me today if you need to speak with someone."

He looks so grim that despite my disappointment, I force a smile. "I'll be fine, honey." Even I don't believe my false declaration. *Of course I need someone today. I need you, Jer. Why can't you extend yourself to me? Especially today?* Is he purposefully distancing himself from me?

He drains his coffee and goes upstairs to finish getting ready for work.

I put the cool muffins in a canister and load our mugs and plates in the dishwasher. Footsteps on the stairs tell me he's ready to leave. He comes toward me while I'm wiping the counter. His breath warms the back of my neck, and his lips nibble on my ear.

"I love you, Jer."

"Love ya too."

I watch him leave through the garage door. A second later I hear the hum of the electric door close after his car exits the garage.

"Mom?" Emma walks in, her backpack slung over her shoulder and her eyes wide. "Can I go with you this afternoon?"

I stroke her thick hair. "It's best if you stay home. Nick will be with you."

Maintaining her composure looks like a struggle. "But, Mom—"

"Shhh, Em. You'd just be sitting in a waiting room. We'll call home as soon as we get the results."

Her shrug says she regretfully accepts my answer. She warms my heart with a hug and a kiss. We linger longer than usual in our embrace, until a car horn toots, sending Emma out the door to catch her ride to school.

I take a seat and watch the car disappear down the street. *Oh, Emma. What tragic flaw in your immature brain allowed you to commit that awful act? So much heartache could have been avoided, but you allowed this scenario to unfold. Why?*

I heave myself up, stack the newspaper, and put a note on the table to let Nick know there are fresh muffins for breakfast.

The bright morning light stabs my eyes as I head out the door for my walk. Belle tugs on her lead, hurrying us both down the street while I fumble in my jacket pocket for sunglasses. All the normal, ordinariness of the day reaches out to me. An occasional car passes, neighbors retrieve their morning paper from their driveways, and a dog barks in the distance.

It seems incredible that somehow I could have a killer within my body. *What will this enemy do to me? How might it affect my appearance? Will Jer still find me desirable if . . . ?*

We walk a block to the trailhead leading from our neighborhood to the Cherry Creek path. Within minutes I'm transported from a busy suburban subdivision to the peace of the Colorado prairie. A gossamer cloud floats on the horizon next to the rising hulk of Pikes Peak. Tall prairie grasses bow to a gentle breeze and roll like waves on the ocean over the halcyon landscape.

How will this day end? I've been steeling myself for the expected onslaught of daily pain, but my enemy has yet to visit me this morning.

Emma looked so small and lost when she left for school. Oh, how her world's been turned upside down. If only I had the power to set everything back in order. If only I could shield her from the consequences of her thoughtless actions. If only we could run away to another place where we didn't have to face all these issues. If only she hadn't created such a big problem.

An alert prairie dog sees Belle coming and slaps the earth with his tail, signaling the threat of danger to his community. The fuzzy little bodies of his homeboys dive into their holes in the ground.

If only someone could have signaled the threat that my daughter's actions would be to our family. *Sigh*. The *if only*s are never far from my thoughts. And the biggest of them weighs heavily on my heart and continues to come to the forefront of my thoughts. If only we listened to Steve and kept silent about Miss Boothe's tea. I'm sure the doctors would have been able to treat her without our confession. At least then Emma would have one less heartache to deal with. I truly know that I can deal with my health issues, whatever they may be, much easier than watching Emma implode a little day by day. Every night she looks more diminished. I fear that within the time it takes to resolve her problems, she'll nearly be invisible.

The path leads south and runs alongside the creek. Last season's snowmelt rushes by. As I round a corner, a flock of red-winged blackbirds take flight. I pause to watch them sail through the sky and marvel at the intense orange patch within the jet-black feathers. A few horses munch on the tall grass by the fence that separates their land from the trail. Their large, peaceful eyes gaze at me with wonder.

Yeah, well, you guys aren't the only ones wondering about life right now. I live every day in wonder. Wondering if I'll survive this year. Wondering if Emma will.

Oh, Jer. Why do you always have to do the right thing? I pray that Emma won't grow to hate him for deciding to make her awful confession public. Will she be able to get into college with an assault charge on her record? And what kind of teacher reference will offset that black mark? My poor baby. Her life's ruined.

42

The day crawls by. I go home to an empty house and begin to pick up, sorting loose papers, doing laundry, and cleaning bathrooms. Anything to keep myself busy. Belle follows me from room to room while I lightly sweep my possessions with a feather duster. Lingering over each Precious Moments figurine, I'm nearly brought to tears recalling the events each statue signifies. So much of my life can be summed up by the clutter that I've surrounded myself with.

Okay, girl, suck it up. I toss a seventies CD into the player and sing along to my old favorites. The beat of the music captures me, and my steps pick up. The feather duster becomes my instrument; I'm moving to the tunes vibrating within my walls. I dust the buffet in the foyer and run the feathers along the array of portraits hanging above it, swirling on the faces of the pictures and gliding across the tops of the frames. As I turn to move on to the living room, I'm startled by a loud clatter. I whirl around and see Emma's last school portrait on the tile floor, the frame broken and the glass shattered. *Oh, what have I done?*

Tears spring to my eyes. I lunge for Belle and lock her in the powder room while I sweep up the shards of glass that surround Emma's smiling face. Will I ever see that worry-free grin again?

I know one thing: if we hadn't confessed Emma's crime that night, she'd probably be wearing that smile today. I've always found comfort in Jerry's ability to make the right choices. But lately I've been seeing gray areas while he can only focus on black and white. My heart chills with the thought that forms in my mind: *Could this be Jerry's fault?*

I've trusted him forever, but now I see the mistake he's made. He's destroyed the happiness in our home. He's the cause of Emma's shattered world. He's the cause for my broken heart. In over twenty-four years of marriage to Jerry, I've run the gamut of emotions in dealing with him. But the one I'm feeling now is foreign to our relationship.

I'm beginning to feel as though we're no longer a unit. Not the two sides to the one heart I always thought we were. Jerry insisted on going to the hospital the night Miss Boothe got sick, but where is he now? Where is he for his wife? And where is he in the midst of Emma's troubles? Whose side is he on? Somewhere along the line we've disengaged from one another. Harsh emotions toward him form in my heart. Resentment. Disappointment. How did our lives unravel so?

My self-admission leaves me stunned. The clock chimes two. Jerry will be home in an hour to get me. I'd rather go to the breast center alone than with him.

Later I paw through my closet. *What's appropriate attire for going to find out if you have breast cancer?* A giggle rises from my throat. How crazy am I? I'll be wearing my pants and an examination robe. I slip into my most comfy jeans and a plain blue T-shirt.

I'm sitting in the living room when Jerry rushes through the door. "I'm going to put on a pair of jeans, dear. I'll be downstairs in a minute."

I nod and continue to stare out the window. I'm surprised to realize I've been pain free the entire day. I hope it lasts.

The drive on I-25 is without traffic, and before we know it, we arrive at the Sally Jobe Breast Center. If Jerry realizes I'm quiet, he doesn't say a word. Perhaps he thinks I'm nervous. Which I am. Really, my problem is that I'm totally freaking out. Why is he so nonchalant? I could use a little mindless chatter right now. Or better yet, he could tell me it will all be fine.

We walk through the parking lot and find the center's suite without trouble. I sign in and fill out my insurance information. The waiting room is nearly filled to capacity and is overwhelmingly feminine. Even the walls are pale pink. Jerry and I claim the last two adjacent chairs in the large room. I'm pleasantly surprised to find that the magazines are current.

I thumb through a copy of *Denver Woman* magazine and stop at an article reviewing a local restaurant. The food sounds delicious. Did I eat lunch?

Jerry is paging through *Reader's Digest*. He must sense me looking at him. He closes the magazine around his index finger, raises his eyebrows, and smiles.

I give a small shake of my head and turn back to my magazine. He follows suit. *Good.* I really don't want to speak with him. In my current state of mind, who knows what I'll say.

Out of my peripheral vision I see Jerry wearing his concentrating face. I used to think that was such a cute expression. Now I begrudge his ability to focus on something so mundane while our world is falling apart.

I shift my gaze across the room. Everyone here has a partner—a husband, a mother, a girlfriend. I guess this is just the kind of place you don't go alone. Unfortunately that's just how I feel. Alone and isolated.

Jerry gives my arm a slight shake.

"What?"

"They're calling your name, Lin."

A technician props the door open with her hip, smiling at me as though I'm some sort of dim-witted emotional wreck. And I'm not. *Or am I?*

I hop up. "Sorry."

Jerry stands with me. "Shall I come too?"

"No, that's okay. Stay here."

The woman leads me through a maze of hallways and brings me to a large room with four curtained dressing rooms against one wall. I'm instructed to strip to the waist, put on a robe, and wait in one of the chairs until I'm called. I do as I'm told and take a seat. *Oh, goody—another waiting room.*

Three other women sit in the bland, upholstered chairs. One pages though a magazine, a look of boredom etching her petite features. Another attends to a fussy baby in a car seat by her feet, trying to distract the child with a rattle. The third gal, in her midthirties, looks as nervous as a termite at an exterminator convention.

Poor thing. I catch her eye. "Hi."

She nods, gives a quick, false smile, then returns to the open book on her lap.

Well, I tried. We wait in silence, and one by one, they are called out of the room.

Finally it's my turn. I follow a perky technician down another hall and into a dimly lit room.

She gestures toward the machine sitting in the middle of the room. "We'll start with a mammogram."

I know the drill, so I slip one arm out of the robe and allow her to position my breast on the plate. The technician couldn't be nicer. She even apologizes for what she calls "the discomfort."

Discomfort? The exam goes okay until the diagonal squeeze. *Yowsa!* I blink back the tears.

She apologizes and tells me that it'll be over in a second, which is hogwash. I know this part will be over soon. But is it the beginning of something else?

The machine releases its steel gums, and we go through the same procedure for my other breast. When that's over, I shrug into the exam robe again, smushed and humiliated and scared to death.

The sweet technician leads me back to the previous room and

tells me I'll be called in for an ultrasound in a few minutes. My former waiting room–mates are gone, replaced by another set of anxious-looking women. I get as comfortable as possible and leaf through a gardening magazine.

Within twenty minutes, I'm the only one left. The electric clock on the wall hums. It's really annoying. I've gone through almost every magazine, so I count the tiles on the floor and the rings holding the curtains on the dressing area.

A woman in scrubs sticks her head through the door. "Linda?"

I toss the magazine aside and stand. "That's me."

"Hi. I'm Candice. I'll be doing your ultrasound."

The dim lighting is calm and peaceful in the ultrasound suite. Candice has me lie on a cushioned exam table and positions me with pillows. She squirts warm gel on my breast and pushes the ultrasound wand around. She pauses every once in a while to push buttons and make notations on a keyboard. Occasionally the wand burrows into me like a tick on a human host. Not the most comfortable feeling in the world. I glance at her monitor. I can't imagine how anyone can make sense of those shapes and shadows.

Candice puts the wand aside and hands me a small terry cloth towel. "You can clean yourself up and go back to get dressed. The doctor will review your information and give you a report."

Back to the waiting room again? By now I'm familiar enough with the tricky corridors and find my way to the dressing/waiting room.

At least I feel more in control now that I'm fully dressed. There's no one else in the room. I retrieve the *5280* magazine I read earlier and turn to an article about Denver's hottest neighborhoods. The clock hums along. I'd like to take the batteries out. I hear some of the staff say their good nights. Is it that late?

To pass the time, I arrange the magazines, tiling them across the table like napkins at a baby shower. When I'm finished with that, I walk down the hall to the door that leads to the lobby and crack it open. Besides Jerry, there are only two other people out there. They're all sitting in different areas of the room, as if they're islands of the same archipelago, each lost within their own minds.

Jerry looks worried. That's not a face he's let me see the past few days. My heart thaws a little in spite of my anger toward him.

I take a deep breath and return to my waiting area. For a change, I sit on the other side of the room.

Before I can get comfortable, Candice appears in the doorway. "I'll show you to Dr. Law's office."

When I enter the office, a young woman sitting behind the desk smiles at me. "Hi, I'm Betsy Law." She gestures to the chairs opposite her desk.

I ease myself into a red leather chair and fold my hands.

Dr. Law shifts through papers.

Come on now. Let me have it.

She looks up and pushes a strand of long brown hair behind her hair. *How old is this girl? She looks like a college student.* "Good news, Linda. It's nothing serious."

Tension drains from my body. I breathe a quick prayer of thanks and scoot back farther into the seat, making myself taller. "So?"

Young Dr. Law smiles and picks up a pen. She draws a small circle, the size of a spring pea, on one of the papers in front of her and slides it across the desk. "You have a few cysts about this size, something that's not uncommon in a woman your age."

"Cysts? That's what's been causing the pain?"

"Yeah. Do you drink much coffee or tea? Caffeine can cause cysts to enlarge."

"Yes, I drink both tea and coffee, but I haven't had any caffeine in the past few days."

"Well, perhaps you might consider cutting down a bit."

"What else should I do? Will you need to aspirate them?"

She shakes her head. "Not if they're this small."

That's a relief. "I haven't had any pain today except during the mammogram."

"You know, since you haven't had any caffeine lately, the cyst may have shrunk, and the pain may have resolved itself." Dr. Law stacks the papers and shoves them into a file. It looks as though I'm being dismissed.

I stand and offer my hand. "Thank you."

The energy in the office suite is subdued. Most of the staff has left for the day. Jerry's the only one left in the waiting room. He's slumped in the chair, looking alone and forlorn. But there he is, hanging in for me, despite what the news will be. Despite how abrupt and cool I've been to him. Against my will, tears spring to my eyes.

When Jerry sees me, his expression falls; then he launches from his seat and is across the room in three long-legged strides. He opens his arms. "Dear?"

I smile and allow him to pull me into an embrace. "It's okay, Jer. Just some cysts."

"Praise God! What needs to be done?"

He releases me, and I move to his abandoned chair to retrieve my purse. "Nothing."

"What about the pain?"

Jerry opens the door for me, and we exit the suite. "Except for the mammogram, I haven't had any pain today. The one that was bothering me may have shrunk. Cutting down on caffeine should take care of the problem."

Fresh spring air greets us as we walk through the parking lot. I can see relief spelled across Jerry's face. Much to my surprise, he grabs my hand. Such a gesture would have meant the world to me a few months ago. But now it seems too little too late.

The romance I longed for now feels absurd. Never in a million years would I have thought Jerry would have been so indifferent while I went through this trial. It makes me feel sad to realize that maybe he's not the man I thought he was. And the way he's dealing with Emma's problems is just as troubling. The desire for a love affair is shallow and pointless in light of the challenges that I've had to face recently. My heart feels as if it's being torn to shreds. And it pains me to think that Jerry could have been our shield in the Miss Boothe episode, but instead he served Emma up on a silver platter.

He aims his key chain and unlocks the door. "Let's call the kids."

I climb into the passenger seat while Jer pulls out his cell phone. He's thrilled to give the children the good news. I lean back in the seat and close my eyes. Jerry must assume I'm too weary for conversation. He begins to whistle—a sure sign that his mood is light. I'm willing to let him believe anything he wants, just as long as I don't have to speak with him.

43

On our way home, we stop at Abacus for some Chinese takeout. Jerry is more relaxed than I've seen in weeks. He goes overboard, ordering more food than the four of us will ever be able to finish.

While we wait for our dinner to be prepared, we sit in the overstuffed banquette bench alongside the wall. Jerry looks around, watching the action. For all my relief at not having to worry about fighting deadly cancer cells, I can't muster much enthusiasm for life. I'm out of the woods, but my daughter is still caught in the thorny brambles of a treacherous forest.

I focus my attention on the scuff mark on my left shoe, trying to keep Jerry out of my world. It's a temporary fix to a bigger problem, but at this point it's all I can think to do.

"Revere?" the young man at the counter calls and holds out the paper sack with our dinner.

Jerry scoops up the bag and deposits a few bills in the tip jar. He must really be in a good mood. He never tips for takeout.

The sweet fragrance of Asian food fills the car and stirs my appetite. I sit holding the heavy bag and stare at the familiar landscape flying by my window. All I want is to be home with my kids.

Emma greets us at the door and nearly knocks the breath out of me with her ferocious hug. I wrap my arms around her to return the sentiment. Her hair smells delightful, like the oatmeal-and-honey conditioner she loves so much. I release my grip and run my hand down her back. I'm startled at how prominent her ribs feel. How much weight has she lost in the past few weeks?

Nick is standing beside us with his adorable grin lighting the room. As we walk toward the kitchen, he drapes his arm across my shoulders and gives me a brief squeeze. How nice. Even the table is set.

If only we didn't have Emma's problems hanging like a shroud over our heads, this could be a true celebration.

Before we begin our meal, Jerry blesses our food and thanks God for my good diagnosis. Everyone digs into the array of cardboard and Styrofoam containers with gusto. My mood dips slightly. Doesn't Jerry think Emma's troubles warrant a prayer too?

Nick dips a crab-and-cream-cheese wonton into duck sauce and holds the appetizer over his plate. "Mom, you have a couple of messages on the answering machine." He pops the dripping wonton into his mouth and speaks around the food. "From Debbie and Jill."

"I'll call them after dinner."

Conversation stalls. The only sound in the kitchen is the clatter of silverware on ceramic plates. Ever since Emma poisoned her teacher and we found out that charges were being filed, we've ceased to be able to have normal dinner conversation. Our family no longer functions like the unit it used to be. Could all this have been avoided? My resentment toward Jerry rises, and my hot-and-sour soup turns bitter in my mouth. If it wasn't for my children sitting at the table with me, I'd get up and leave the room.

Jerry must sense the awkwardness. He clears his throat. "How are classes this semester, Nick?"

Isn't that a question a stranger asks to be polite? If Nick thinks it's heavy-handed, he doesn't let on. "Not bad."

Jerry tries again. "When is your next cheerleading competition, Em?"

Her gaze slowly lifts from her bowl of egg drop soup to her father's face. "Sometime next month."

The ringing telephone saves us from more uncomfortable conversation.

Em springs to answer it. Some things never change. She politely asks the caller to hold the line and passes the phone to Jerry.

I'm relieved I don't have to maintain dinner conversation with my husband. We all listen to his one-sided chitchat and finish eating.

While I bring our dishes to the sink, Nick closes the take-out boxes and finds room for them in the refrigerator.

I'm exhausted, but before I head upstairs to the comfort of my bed, I pull my cell phone from my purse and call Jill. While the phone rings, I walk to the living room and settle on the love seat, lying on the cushions with my legs dangling over the arm. "Hi, it's me. Thanks for the call."

Her voice sounds tentative, not knowing my diagnosis. "Well, what did they find out?"

"It's okay. Just cysts."

"Oh, Linda, that's wonderful news." I hear the relief in her voice. "Will you be at work tomorrow?"

"Yeah. What's the word on Rose?"

"She's doing better. Pain pills and rest are what she's focusing on. We expect her back to work in another day."

I wonder if there's been any news or scandal about Luke and Pam. How do I work this into the conversation? "What happened there today?"

Jill chuckles. "Same old, same old. Your friend Carol Ball called wondering about her portraits. I guess we've got to figure a way to get them delivered. Are you game for that?" She laughs as she makes the suggestion, knowing that's probably the last thing I want to do.

"I'll be happy to drive them to her house." At least that will get me out of the studio for a while until I can figure out how to act around Luke and Pam.

"Really? I thought you'd beg for someone else to run that errand."

"No, it's okay. I don't mind."

We finish our conversation, and I navigate through my voice recognition and call Debbie. She answers on the second ring.

"Good news, Deb. I only have cysts."

"Oh, thank God. I've been praying for you all afternoon."

A lump rises in my throat. "Thanks, hon."

"Your family must be relieved."

"Yeah, one less worry for the Revere family."

"Everything else will work out too."

I appreciate her optimism, but I'm not buying it. "We hope so." I don't have the energy to play this game. "You know, I'm awfully tired. It must be the emotion of the day. I'm going to let you go and head up to bed."

After we say good-bye, I turn off my cell phone and drop it in my purse. Emma's doing homework at the kitchen table when I go in to load glasses into the dishwasher. Her eyes follow me. I give her a wink and see the gratitude on her face, knowing that I'm not going to die and leave her motherless in this terrifying world. On my way out of the room, I stroke her shoulder and plant a kiss on her head.

I take an extra hot, extra long shower and wrap myself in a towel. Canned laughter comes from the television in our bedroom. I take my time applying body lotion and combing out my hair.

Jerry pulls back the covers for me when I enter the bedroom.

Not tonight, pal. "Night, Jer."

"How are you feeling?"

"Tired." I roll over to face the side of the bed and pull the sheets up around my shoulders.

44

I take my time getting ready for work. It's dishonest, but I deliberately make myself late. This way I'm sure Luke will be in a photo shoot and Pam will be in her sales session.

The lobby is hopping when I walk through the door. I squeeze between clients and stroll to the workroom to collect Carol Ball's portraits.

"There she is!" Traci puts down the file she's holding and gives me a hug. "I heard your good news."

I nod and smile. "Hey, I need to load Carol Ball's prints in my car to deliver them. Can you give me a hand?"

Traci cocks her head. "Are you kidding me? *You're* taking the portraits to Carol?"

I press my lips together and force out a smile. "Believe it or not, I am."

We retrieve the flatbed dolly and carefully place the bubble-wrapped portraits on the platform. Traci pushes our cargo, and I place a hand on the top portrait to balance the load as we navigate through the parking lot to my car.

What's the buzz concerning Luke and Pam? "So, what have I missed while I was out?"

Traci shrugs. "Nothing much."

By now someone must surely know about the boss's indiscretion. Maybe Jill does. I'll ask her when I get back.

Traci helps me load the portraits into my backseat, and I'm on my way. I've succeeded in escaping the building without running into either of those two lousy cheaters.

The rush-hour traffic has dissipated. I zip up to the tony Cherry Hills Village neighborhood that is home to the Ball family. It's hard to believe I'm so close to Denver. The hustle and bustle of the metropolitan area fades away the farther I wind through the old-money suburban community. I double-check my Google map directions and make a right-hand turn.

Holy cow! The private lane I'm on winds between tall oak trees and frames an enormous Tuscan-style villa—the kind of house people like me only see in the pages of big glossy magazines. It must be fifteen thousand square feet if it's an inch. I lift my foot from the accelerator to give me more time to take it all in.

The facade of the building is natural stone, aged to perfection and looking for all the world like the home of European royalty. I park near the grand entrance and stare openmouthed at the mansion in front of me. A curtain moves in the front room and prompts me to step from my car. After all, I don't want the police called to investigate the woman in the old Ford Taurus—a vehicle that couldn't be more out of place in this neighborhood.

The silence of the area speaks volumes. This is one of those special places designed for only the very wealthy to enjoy. The soft music of a cascading fountain accents the morning calm. Silver and orange koi fish sparkle in the sun as they swim in the basin of the ornate water feature.

I march up the stone steps and ring the doorbell. *Westminster chimes. What else?*

While I wait for the imposing oak door to be answered, my gaze falls to the side of the estate. I can't believe my eyes; it's a small vineyard. No wonder Carol has attitude. She *lives* attitude.

I'm just about to ring the bell again when the door swings open. An old woman, not even half the size of the huge door, regards me with detached curiosity. Her voice is thick with an Eastern European accent and an air of annoyance. "May I help you?"

"I'm Linda from Dream Photography. I'm delivering some portraits."

She steps back and sweeps her arm toward a two-story foyer larger than my family room. I can't help myself and gape at the grandeur displayed before me. The floor is tiled with an intricate design, using three different shades of marble. A round, glass-topped table graces the middle of the floor, upon which stands a colossal floral arrangement. Behind the table is a massive fireplace, its mantel rising to the ceiling. *A fireplace in the foyer? Can you say pretentious?*

The Ice Matron looks me up and down as if to decide whether I'm telling the truth. "Where are the portraits?"

I gesture. "The car."

"Wait. I'll see if you should bring them in the back door."

The back door? What is this, Upstairs, Downstairs? *It's the twenty-first century for crying out loud.*

The clickety-clack of her heels fades as she walks into the depths of the home.

I take advantage of the opportunity and tiptoe to the edge of the foyer. The room diagonally to the right is a formal living room. The floor is burnished hardwood covered with an Oriental carpet that probably costs more than what I owe on my mortgage. Carol's furniture is plush and inviting, upholstered in elegant blue and yellow fabric. The coffee table actually holds coffee-table books and what looks like an expensive sculpture. At home, mine is littered with the *TV Guide* and last night's popcorn bowl.

This house even smells richer than mine.

The sound of approaching voices interrupts my snooping, and I hustle back to the center of the foyer. Shoe leather slaps the marble tile floor, and I see the silhouette of a woman striding toward me. Tall, emaciated, and determined. It could be no one else but Carol Ball.

My heart jumps into overdrive, and my palms begin to do that damp sponge thing again. Man, no one puts me into a panic like this woman.

"Linda? Is that you?"

Sheesh. Has she been out in her vineyard this morning? Is she suffering from heatstroke? "Good morning, Carol."

She joins me and looks around expectantly. "Where are they?"

There is obviously a communication problem in this household. "In my car."

Carol stares down her nose as if I'm a door-to-door magazine salesperson. "Don't you think you should bring them in?"

She makes me so nervous. My tongue is suddenly too big for my mouth. "This door?"

Carol rolls her eyes. "Yes."

Okay, I'm not an idiot. "I was told to wait in case you wanted them delivered in the back door."

She tosses a scathing look over her shoulder at the Ice Matron and lets out an exasperated sigh. "Why would I want you to do that?"

My scalp is beginning to itch. "I don't know. That woman said I—"

Her upheld hand silences me. "Just bring them in here, please."

I drop my purse on the table and hurry outside. At least she said please. That may be a first for our relationship.

I open the back door of my car and gently maneuver the largest portrait out of the vehicle. By the time I haul them all inside the house, I'm drenched with perspiration. I survey the neat stack of portraits and wonder what to do next.

"Hello? Carol?" My voice echoes in the cavernous foyer. I aim my ear toward the center of the house and listen. There's no response.

I try again. "Hello?" I'd really just like to escape this house and get back to work. "Excuse me?" Maybe I should just leave. Should I walk through the house to find that old woman? I dig in my purse for my keys.

"Miss Linda."

I'm startled to find the Ice Matron standing five feet from me. My blush rises up my neck to my hairline. Even Carol's housekeeper makes me nervous. I'm such a jellyfish. "I've brought all the portraits in. I guess I'll be on my way."

"Mrs. Ball would like you to join her for coffee in the library." She turns and strides with stiff dignity down the hall.

I couldn't be more surprised. With my open jaw and my aura of stress, I bet I resemble that painting of *The Scream*.

The housekeeper stops in her tracks and turns. "Well? Are you coming?"

"Uh, yeah." I trot after her. Neither she nor Carol is used to being ignored.

We walk to the east side of the house and into a room that belongs in Buckingham Palace. Carol is seated in a leather chair opposite an upholstered love seat that sits before an enormous fireplace. I nearly lose my balance on the carpet as I move toward her. It's like walking on a giant marshmallow. How much did this carpet pad upgrade cost?

I take my seat and drop my purse by my feet. Carol's sitting with her ankles crossed. I do the same. How awkward. This affected pose is not comfortable. I uncross my ankles and surreptitiously wiggle into a more relaxed position on the couch.

She clears her throat. "Thank you for delivering my portraits."

Despite my throbbing temples, I smile. "You're welcome."

While we exchange pleasantries, the Ice Matron returns with a tray of coffee cups, sugar, and cream. She places it on the coffee table and silently departs.

Carol smiles, an expression I've seldom seen on this woman. To tell the truth, it's a little frightening. *A side effect of too much Botox?* "Please help yourself." Her invitation sounds like a command.

I pick up one of the beautiful cups, resisting the powerful urge to look at the bottom to see the manufacturer's label. It's probably fine china or porcelain. The brew smells delicious, not like the super-market sawdust Jerry brews each morning. I begin to help myself to some cream and pause with the creamer midair. I recall Dr. Parrish's advice. "Regular or decaf?"

Her face goes blank. "Marina?"

We sit in uncomfortable silence until the Ice Matron comes pad-ding into the room. She puts a small plate of cookies in front of us.

Carol reaches for one of the delicacies. "Marina, is this decaf?"

"Yes, ma'am. Decaf."

Carol beams her weird smile. "Excellent. Now where were we?"

Honey, I feel as if I've landed on another planet. I smile and shake my head. *This is your game, lady.*

"Oh, I was just about to ask you if you've made your summer plans yet."

Are you kidding me? "Uh, not really. We've talked about going to the mountains for a few days. How about you?" *What is this about?*

She tilts her head as if my question were ridiculous. "We always travel to our place on Martha's Vineyard for a few weeks in the beginning of the summer and then spend a week on Grand Cay-man in August. I guess you could say we're island people." She giggles.

Okay, we've determined you take fabulous vacations and mine stink. What shall we discuss next? "What can I do for you, Carol?"

Her head snaps up.

I immediately regret my brash question. I'm not used to this coffee-and-vacation-talk game. "I'm sorry." I glance at my watch. "I appreciate your hospitality, but I really must get back to work."

She places her cup on the coffee table. "Well, there may be some-thing you can help me with."

Okay, bottom line it. What do you want? "I'd love to help you. What can I do?"

Carol leans back into the huge leather chair. "A dear friend of mine, my college roommate actually, has a daughter who just finished her junior year of college. She's very interested in photography, and I was hoping you could help her secure a summer internship at your studio."

Now I see. Our internships are legendary in the industry. Her friend must know Carol is a client and hopes she can make the necessary arrangements. "We get applications for our program starting in February for the summer apprenticeship. The candidate may even have been selected already. I'm not sure I can help you."

Carol picks up the plate of cookies and holds it out to me. "I'm sure there must be something you can do. I know you're the office manager at Dream Photography."

I accept one of the sweet pastries. "Has she applied for a position yet?"

Carol waves her hand as if the thought of going through proper procedures is too common for her and her kind. "You're a mother. Wouldn't you want someone to help your daughter achieve her dreams?"

If only you knew. "It may be out of my hands—"

"Nonsense." A chill hangs on the edge of her word. "The last time I spoke with Luke, I gave you a glowing recommendation. Didn't he tell you?"

"Actually, he—"

"I would hate to have to tell him you didn't represent his company well while you were in my home." She sits forward and narrows her eyes.

The last thing I need is more problems with Luke, that letch. I take the path of least resistance. "What's her name? I'll see what I can do."

As if by magic, Carol produces a business-size envelope from a drawer in the side table and holds it out. *Is this woman good or what? Does she always get her own way?*

I accept the heavy ivory stationery and take a peek inside. The top page is a cover letter accompanied by a transcript, resume, and our downloaded application form. "This looks impressive. I'll make sure Luke gets it today."

She rewards me with a smile. "I knew I could count on you."

Count on me? Intimidate me is more like it. "I'm happy to help." I return her smile and keep the charade up.

Carol's voice takes on a silky quality, and she leans toward me in a conspiratorial manner. "If there's ever *anything* I can do for you, just ask."

Hmm. Said the spider to the fly.

45

Back at the studio, Jill's sitting at the reception desk, scowling. "Don't you turn your cell phone on anymore?"

Panic makes my heart gallop. "Did my husband call?" *Could something have happened to Emma?*

"No." She squints and tilts her head, regarding me with curiosity. "I was just wondering what was taking you so long. We need to take these brochures to bulk mail." She gestures to the stacks of USPS mail baskets that lean against the wall. "Since you're not on the sales schedule today, Luke suggested you go to the post office."

Oh, joy. "Can I take someone with me?" I'm not going to haul seven thousand brochures by myself.

"Traci's next appointment canceled, so she's available."

I maneuver the loaner van the insurance company provided out of the parking lot and aim for the post office. Nice ride—leather seats, tinted windows. It'll be a drag when our old van is repaired and returned.

Traci is chatty, relieved that her photo session with three-year-old triplets was canceled.

When she stops to catch her breath, I interrupt. "I feel like I've been out of the office more than in lately. Anything going on that I should know about?"

She cracks up. "As if I would know. I'm stuck in the studio snapping pictures most of the time."

That sounds right, but if Luke and Pam are having an affair, maybe they're good at keeping it under wraps.

Traci snaps her fingers. "Oh yeah. There is some news."

I'm all ears, but I make an attempt to sound casual. "What?"

"Luke's going to be out of town for the rest of the week. Leaving tomorrow. He's a last-minute speaker for a state PPA conference somewhere. I think he's filling in for someone who had to cancel."

We pull into the post office, load our dolly, and traipse into the bulk mail department. We're the only customers here. *Hallelujah.* There are times when it takes *forever* to get through this ordeal. We pull the dolly to the counter and wait for Cecilia, the quirky postal worker, to finish her telephone conversation.

I can't help but hear her one-sided conversation. "Cremated remains?" She pulls a flower-topped pen out of a bucket loaded with dried beans and scribbles furiously. "Country of destination? . . . The People's Republic of China?"

Yeah, and I thought my job was crazy at times.

Cecilia holds up her index finger. This is so entertaining that I don't mind the wait. A minute later she hangs up the phone and turns to me. "Bar-coded?"

By now she really should know me by sight, and we've never bar-coded our bulk mail. "No."

The phone rings. Cecilia glances at it as though it's a pile of stinky garbage and looks at me. "How many pieces?"

I pull the postal form from my purse. "We have 7,643."

She takes the form and gives it a cursory glance. "Sorted by zip?"

I used to be a patient woman, but now I want to throttle this little bureaucrat. "Yes, sorted by zip."

Cecilia grabs a handful of brochures, counts out a few, and puts them on the scale. "Do you have more than two hundred of each zip?"

Hello? Over seven thousand brochures. "Yes, I surely do."

The public address system in the building crackles to life. The tinny announcement interrupts our business. "Would someone in bulk mail acceptance please volunteer to help Jordan?"

Cecilia lifts her index finger again and turns to the telephone. She punches in an extension and scowls. "Hello, this is Cecilia in bulk mail. I have too many customers to leave the counter." She hangs up and returns to her task.

Traci pokes me in the back. She's barely able to keep a straight face. I just want to finish our business and be on our way. We negotiate the details of the mailing, and I fill in the check signed by Luke.

"Thanks, Cecilia. We'll see you in a couple of weeks."

She waves us off as she schleps the bins into the bowels of the U.S. Post Office.

I walk to the side of the room and snatch some replacement mail bins. Traci joins me, and we load ourselves up with the plastic containers.

As we're leaving the building, Cecilia gets on the phone again. "This is Cecilia from bulk mail. I've done a little research, and I think you ought to send your remains by FedEx. . . ."

● ● ●

When I get home, Emma's in the kitchen making tea. Her shoulders are rounded, and she shuffles across the floor with as much energy as a slug. She pours a mug and hands it to me. If it's possible, my heart shatters even more. I've never seen such a broken girl.

I put the mug on the table and gather her in my arms. "Oh, baby, we'll get through this."

She nods and sits. "Criminal mischief, that's what it's called, you know."

Yeah, unfortunately I know. "Let's pray for the best outcome, sweetheart."

She takes a deep breath and sucks it up, just as her father recommended. We begin our game of pretend. Pretend it will be okay. Pretend it's just another afternoon.

46

I don't know whether to be relieved or disappointed that I didn't run into Luke before he left town. Pam darts around the building as she always does, in her own little world, apart from the rest of the staff. Since our botched conversation and my stumbling into her *affaire d'amour* with Luke, she's kept her distance from me. And I can hardly confront her with the details of her tryst—besides, I need my job. Who knows how much our legal fees will cost?

I'm mulling over the dismal aspects of my life, pulling sales files for tomorrow when I realize that my LAME plan of romance has been seriously derailed. Romance walked out of my life the day my daughter committed criminal mischief. And to think that next week will be our twenty-fifth anniversary. I guess Jerry will want to celebrate, maybe go out to the Gray Pony for dinner. The last time we ate there, things were really heating up in our marriage, and then Belle OD'd on my thyroid medication. Perhaps we should choose a different restaurant. But I don't want to stray too far from Pine Grove. I'm always fearful that Emma will have a meltdown and I won't be at hand to rescue her. I hope Jerry's canceled our plans early enough to get our credit card refunded.

Jill rounds the corner of the office and stops short so she won't run into the open filing drawer. "Pulling Friday's files?"

I continue to work my way through the alphabet, searching

for the Sinclair file. "Yeah, I wanted to get a jump on tomorrow's workload."

She stares at me as if I've just proposed we tell some of our clients what we really think about them. "Why do you care about tomorrow's workload? You won't be here."

Now it's my turn to give her a strange look. "Yes, I will."

"Jerry cleared it with Luke for you to leave early for your anniversary weekend."

Knowing he did that thaws some of the chill from my heart. "Maybe so, but things have changed since then. We can't go out of town."

"Because of Emma?"

"It's just not a good time for us right now."

Jill's kind, and she doesn't press me. She retrieves her purse from her locker and leaves for the day.

I continue to pull files. Not a good time for us—what an understatement. Not only is Emma facing the possibility of spending time in juvenile hall, but I've betrayed my marriage vows by turning my heart and my body away from my husband.

I know Emma's ultimately responsible for her actions, but I think Jerry's responsible for the huge price she'll have to pay. More and more I'm discovering that Jerry's not the man I thought he was. I used to think he was my hero, my knight, the guy who always did the right thing. Now all I can think about are the many ways he's disappointed me.

Why does he think he's the harbinger of all the right choices? And he never fails to insert his opinion, whether it's solicited or not. Just thinking about how he nagged me as I drove to work while he followed in another vehicle gives me a migraine. And the way Mr. High-and-Mighty declared that sharing my concerns about my sleazy boss with Deb made me a gossip makes me want to scream. Not only that, but Jerry missed the boat when I was going through my breast cancer scare. He could have supported me with love and tenderness, but all I got were dismal facts and diagrams. It was as if he stepped away from me when I needed him most.

I feel as if I've been sucker punched when all these somber truths pile up. My heart fractures even more when I realize that these disappointments have cooled my affections for him and shut off the spring of love that had flowed so freely in our relationship. Of all the valleys we've endured, I think this is the one that might lead us down a path we never thought we'd go. And Lord help me, but I've even entertained the *d* word in my musings. I always thought my bones would rest alongside Jerry's in side-by-side cemetery plots. Now I can barely force myself to lie next to him in bed.

I go through the motions of pretending we're a happy family for Emma's sake, but my brain won't let me stop considering the fact that life as I've known it may cease to exist. And if I can't count on Jerry to help me through these difficult situations, why are we even together?

● ● ●

The table's set for dinner when I arrive home. Ever since Em's troubles, she's been trying to be the perfect child. How ironic. I'd give anything for that defiant, selfish girl I had a few weeks ago.

On the surface, our family looks as it always has. We assemble for dinner but make conversation about things that don't matter. The heart of our family is broken, and I don't know if I can mend it. I eat tasteless chicken and green beans and push mashed potatoes around my plate.

"Mom?"

I look up and smile at Emma. "Sorry. I wasn't listening."

She grins at me with such sweetness it makes me want to cry. "What time are you and Daddy leaving tomorrow?"

I put my hand on her arm. "Oh, honey, we're not going away."

Jerry puts down his fork. "Excuse me?"

I look at him. How can he possibly think we'd go away to celebrate our marriage when our family is in crisis? "This isn't the time to go away."

"It certainly is. It's our twenty-fifth anniversary. The only one we'll have."

Right now I wonder if we'll make it to our twenty-sixth. I shake my head. The last thing I want to do is have a disagreement in front of the kids.

Nick pipes up, "Go. Have fun. Relax. Emma-monster and I will be fine."

"Yeah, Mom. Nick's going to take me to the movies tomorrow night, and on Saturday I'm going shopping with him to make sure he doesn't buy any dorky clothes."

They both look so happy, so carefree. But I'm not eager to celebrate my marriage. "Oh no. Maybe in a few months Dad and I will get away. But—"

Jerry gazes at me with determination in his eyes. "We're going. It's arranged."

As if. What is he? A cave man who's going to throw me over his shoulder and take me away? I shake my head.

Conversation begins about the movie the kids are going to see. *Fine.* I'll just wait until I'm alone with Jerry to put the kibosh on this ridiculous plan to go out of town.

When I go upstairs after cleaning the kitchen, a suitcase sits in the middle of my bedroom floor. I stare, dumbfounded. Even on his most clueless days, he's never been this dense.

Jerry comes out of his closet with clothes draped over his arm. "Better get packing."

An eerie calm falls over me. I stand my ground. "Jerry. No."

He comes to a halt. "It's our twenty-fifth anniversary. We're going away for a celebration."

I don't hide my annoyance and slam the door shut. "A celebration? In a few days we're going to learn our daughter's fate. I'm not in the mood for a celebration."

He looks like I'm straining his patience. "In a few days we learn the results of the preliminary hearing. Emma's pleaded guilty. This will go to trial. We know all this."

A cloud of anger consumes my brain, and I can barely think straight. "And you're okay with that?"

"Keep your voice down, Lin. The kids will hear."

I fold my arms across my chest and sit on the edge of the bed.

Jerry puts his khakis in the suitcase. "Of course I'm not okay with it. Unfortunately it's out of our hands and in—"

I stab a finger toward him. "Thanks to you."

He snaps his mouth shut and stares at the floor.

I let my anger have full rein. "If only we hadn't pushed her into a confession, then Emma would be happy and safe."

Jerry lifts his head, and his eyes, bright with unshed tears, meet mine. "I didn't bring this trouble into our lives. Emma did. But the only—"

"You compounded the problem. You brought this trouble into our home—"

He lifts a hand to silence me. "So what you're saying is that when trouble comes we should teach our children to do the easy thing? What about all the times we taught them to do the right thing?"

My brain feels as though it's going to shatter. At least that way it will match my fractured heart. "Look what you've done! I—"

The door vibrates with a heavy knock from the hallway. Jerry opens it. Emma stands outside the room, tears freely rolling down her face.

I rush to hold her. "I'm sorry. I didn't mean to upset you." I toss a chilly glance toward Jerry and think of my unspoken words: *I hate you.* I quiver at what almost came out of my mouth.

Jerry is beside us in a moment and wraps his arms around the two of us. "Emma, Emma. It's in God's hands. Whatever happens, we can trust Him."

We stand there for a minute, and I feel Emma's spine stiffen. She steps away from our embrace and gives us a watery smile. "I know, Dad."

I pluck a tissue from the dispenser on my night table and hand it to her. She mops her face and blows her nose. "Please go away for the weekend. I don't want to ruin your anniversary."

Jerry gives Emma a hug. "It's okay. It will all be okay."

A moment later she leaves the room, and I'm alone with my husband. We've always been one unit, but now the chasm that divides us seems irreparable.

Jerry leads me to the bed. I sit. He runs his hand through his hair and plops next to me. I scoot away a tiny bit. "Linda, I know we've all been under a lot of pressure lately, especially you. This is one of those walking-through-the-valley situations. With God's help, we'll get through it."

I keep my mouth shut because what would come out would not be nice. Not at all. I'm thinking words I've never said.

He rests his hand on mine. I try to move from under his touch, but he doesn't let go.

I spit my words out. "Do you think you can impose yourself on me, Jerry?"

His face reddens as if he were slapped, but his hand remains firm. "Our lives are upside-down, but it won't stay this way forever. If we remain united and put our trust in God, this trial will pass."

I look him in the eye. "Do you know how much I hate—?"

Before I can finish my sentence, he puts a finger to my lips. Gently. "I love you with every ounce of energy within me. You love me. I know you do. We've hit a bump in the road. Don't let this destroy our family."

I leap to my feet. "A bump in the road?"

Jerry rises and puts his hands on my arms. "What's happened to your faith? Or is it just a Sunday thing?"

I'm stunned. *Is he right? Has my faith been just a Sunday thing?* No, it's real. I have encountered God. I have known the supernatural. I'm caught in the center of a vortex, and I'm being sucked into a watery grave. My legs feel as weak as two licorice sticks. I bury my face in my hands and weep. I feel sturdy arms surround me, and I'm rocked like a child.

"Shhh. It's going to be okay, Lin. Shhh."

He allows me to cry through the moment. When my tears are spent, an emptiness fills my heart.

Jerry sits me back down. "This is what we're going to do. We're going to trust God and Nick to watch over Emma this weekend, and we're going to pamper ourselves and come home in a few days refreshed and prepared to deal with whatever comes our way."

I nod, not because I believe he's right but because I lack the energy to do anything else. "What do I need to pack?"

47

I need some of that cream that sucks up the bags under my eyes. I tossed and turned most of the night. Before I had shut the light off, I gave Jerry a look that told him he'd better not try to wander to my side of the bed. He must have gotten the message because he rolled over and within five minutes was peacefully snoring away as if he didn't have a care in the world.

We see the kids off to school and hit the road by nine on Friday. For all I care, we could spend the weekend at the local Holiday Inn. We travel north on Pine Grove Road and get into the lane to merge onto E-470. Jerry looks amused. He's probably dying for me to bug him about where we're going. We sail past the first entrance ramp and get on heading west. *Good.* At least we're not going to the airport. This way I'll be only a few hours away from Emma should she need me. I expect Jerry knows me well enough to figure out I don't want too much distance between my daughter and me right now.

I bet we're going to a B and B in Denver. Or maybe to Colorado Springs. For years I've wanted to stay at The Broadmoor. As we approach I-25, Jerry's driving in the middle lane, but we don't veer right to get on the ramps going north or south. We stay on 470.

The mountains? He's taking me to the mountains for our anniversary? Don't get me wrong. The Colorado Rockies are some of God's best work, and we've gone to several resorts with the kids, but it's not what I would have thought of for a special anniversary celebration. But then, this is Jerry. You'd think by now I'd have learned to keep my expectations low when it comes to romance. Not that it really matters anymore.

"Uh, Jer, I thought you said to think sophisticated when you gave me that hint about where we are going. Have you since changed plans?"

He stares straight ahead and grins. "Nope."

Apparently, sophisticated doesn't have the same connotation with me as it does with Jerry. And to think I was dreaming of New York City, Chicago, Las Vegas, or The Broadmoor.

We trail the end of rush-hour traffic and exit onto I-70 west. It's a good thing I'm not psyched up for a fabulous weekend.

The resident gnome in my intestines kicks up his heels. "Oh no."

Jerry jerks his head my way. "What's wrong?"

"We can't go to the mountains!"

"Why not?"

"No cell service. Turn around, Jerry. We can't be out of contact with—"

He smiles.

This man has the nerve to smile at me while I'm suffering mother angst? "I'm not kidding, Revere."

Jerry out and out laughs. Well, I don't think this lack of judgment on his part is one bit funny. He reaches for my shoulder, and I hitch it up to avoid his touch. If he notices, he doesn't let on. "Don't worry, Lin. We're headed to the one spot in the mountains where cell phone service is pretty much guaranteed."

Really? I don't think such a place exists. "Where?"

He raises his eyebrows. "Do you want to guess?"

Doesn't he realize I'm not in a playful mood? "No."

I stare straight ahead, but in my peripheral vision, I see him shake his head. I'm along for the ride, but I won't pretend this is a celebration.

My lack of sleep catches up with me. I put on my sunglasses and lean my head back.

I don't know how long I slept, but it was long enough to give me a giant pain in the neck. I tip my head from shoulder to shoulder to ease out the kink.

Jerry passes me a bottle of water. "Hello, sleepyhead."

I accept his offering in silence. The scenery outside my window is amazing. We're driving above the tree line and are surrounded by bald mountains, as though we've landed on a distant planet. Because of the drop in temperature, Jerry has the AC turned off. Occasionally I catch a glimpse of an alpine flower, bravely thriving in this hostile environment. A sign approaches: "Independence Pass—Continental Divide."

"Do you want to stop, Lin?"

I'm dying to, but I won't give him the pleasure. "Nope."

We slow for the tourists bundled in jackets, walking alongside the road. Out of respect for the twisting highway, traffic has slowed considerably. Another sign passes my window: "Highway 82."

Where on earth are we? As we head away from the pass, I gaze at the line down the center of the road, my mind on Emma. I hope she wasn't putting on a brave face just so we would take our little weekend away. She doesn't need to be brave for me. I share her fear.

Something seems odd, and I realize the center stripe in the highway has disappeared. The road hugs the mountain, a wall of rock on our right, and a stone guardrail, hardly tall enough to provide comfort, skirts a drop to certain death on the left. It's not my imagination; the road has narrowed significantly. "Jerry?"

He adjusts his grip on the wheel. "This is a trip, isn't it?"

"Where did the road go?" No sooner are the words out of my mouth when the car in front of us slows to a crawl. We follow suit as an SUV driving in the opposite direction slowly squeezes beside us.

Jerry chuckles. "It looks like the road's run out of room."

I sit up to pay more strict attention. Not that it matters. I'm not behind the wheel. The road widens again, and I lean back, tension releasing from my knotted shoulders. Before I can catch my breath, the center line disappears again. "Oh, good grief."

We continue down the mountain, pressing as close to the right as possible when the road narrows. After a few more miles of white-knuckle driving, we pass a sign: "Welcome to the Roaring Fork Valley." This means nothing to me. I'm dying to know where we are, but I bite my lip and remain silent. We drive on for a few more minutes.

Jerry flashes me the grin that used to make my heart dance. "Have you guessed yet?"

I'm burning with too much curiosity to feign indifference. "Have we ever been in this area before?"

"Close but not exactly."

I get the impression he'd like me to pepper him with questions. That's not happening.

The mountain landscape gives way to a beautiful green valley. Houses dot the rolling vista. I can't imagine waking each morning to the awesome views outside those shining windows. Most of the buildings look more like mansions than the houses that populate my reality. We round a curve. Another sign reads "Aspen—5 Miles."

"Aspen? We're going to Aspen?" I've dreamed of visiting this town for years. A fantasy really, considering that the price of things here is quite beyond our budget.

Jerry smiles. "Give the lady a prize."

Despite my determination to dwell in my bubble of resentment, a frisson of excitement curls up my spine.

Soon, and as if by magic, we enter the beautiful Victorian city. Aspen's everything I dreamed it would be. Only better. And with more traffic. Okay, this much traffic tucked into a small mountain town is way more than anyone could believe.

Jerry pulls a map from between the bucket seats. "We're looking for Durant Avenue."

I glance at passing street signs to get my bearings. "Is that where the Hotel Jerome is?"

He bursts out laughing. "Dear, the Hotel Jerome is six hundred dollars a night. I don't think so."

Hmm. Swell. We navigate toward the address he's given me, passing amazing hotels with names I've heard on *Lifestyles of the Rich and Famous*—the Little Nell, the St. Regis. Our hotel is small and unassuming. There's a tiny gravel parking lot with room for about four cars. The side of the building has a deck with a hot tub. It looks clean and well maintained, but I'm not impressed.

We enter a lobby that looks like a family room furnished by Crate and Barrel. In the right corner is a desk, and to the left, a stone fireplace is flanked by comfy chairs and a couch. Jerry checks us in while I peruse the racks of area attraction brochures hanging on a wall.

"Lin?"

I follow him up two flights of stairs and down a narrow hall. Our room is small. Really, really small. Too small to have anything other than a bed and a corner armoire that conceals a television. Opposite the bed are a sink and vanity. The commode and tub are in a room so tiny you have to squeeze around the door to shut it.

"And how much are we paying for this?"

He pats my back. "Don't you worry your pretty little head. I've got it covered."

Humph. Whatever he's paying, it's probably too much.

Jerry maneuvers our suitcase onto a stand next to the vanity and sits on the bed. "What do you want to do?"

I suppose it would be unacceptable to say go home. "I don't care." I'd like to sit down, but there's no place except next to him. I'd rather stand until my legs are numb. The four walls of the miniature room begin to close in. "Let's go for a walk."

He gestures to the door, and out we go. We head east toward the center of town. I pull my cell phone out of my purse. Four signal bars. Amazing.

Jerry kicks a stone from the sidewalk. "God is good."

"What?"

"He knew you'd need to be able to contact the kids while we were away, and He arranged for me to choose Aspen for our anniversary destination."

That sure sounds like a God-thing, but I'm not going to give Jerry the satisfaction of saying so.

We wander around the trendy town and end up strolling along Main Street. My stomach is complaining about missing lunch, but I want to avoid sitting in a restaurant with my husband.

While we wait for traffic to allow us to cross the road, I spy the Main Street Bakery and Café. "How about some coffee and a snack, Jer?"

A bell jingles at the door as we push our way into the restaurant. The tables inside are nearly full, and beyond a screen door to the left is a small, welcoming patio. We place our order.

Jerry plays with coins in his pocket. "Want to sit in or out?"

"Can't we keep walking?"

He shrugs, trying to appear nonchalant, but I can see he's disappointed. *Good. I've been feeling that way about you for some time now.*

We step into the sunlight and turn on South Aspen Street. On our right is a park with a gazebo in the center. If this were a romantic weekend, that would be the perfect spot to picnic. Jerry grabs my elbow and steers me across the street. *Great.* I am not going to sit in a gazebo with this man.

A wooden bench anchors the corner of the park. I pull my elbow free. "This looks good." I plop down on the left side, giving him plenty of room to sit. The fragrance of my cranberry scone calls to me from the bag on my lap. I put my coffee by my feet and pull out my pastry. Jerry's shadow falls across me. I'd like him to move, but I resist being too much of a shrew by saying so. I don't want to argue with him. I don't even want to speak with him.

He shifts from one foot to another. I ignore his squirming and enjoy my repast.

He sighs deeply and finally sits next to me. Right next to me. As in three-quarters of an inch away from me. I take a sip of coffee, and I flit my eyes in his direction. He looks so smug that I'd like to spew my cappuccino at him. Unless I stand up, there's nowhere for me to go. And he knows that.

I pretend I'm infinitely interested in a man throwing balls to two Irish setters. I've never seen as many dogs in a town as I have the past hour in Aspen. And some of those dogs were dressed better than me. I always thought it was a faux pas to wear that much bling before sunset.

I feel a weight on my left shoulder and glimpse Jerry's hand. He's put his arm around my shoulders? *Eeww.* Now he's pushing it. "Would you please—?"

He wears a bold grin. "Shut up, Linda."

His words have the desired effect.

48

Only once has Jerry used that expression to me, and that was over twenty years ago. We didn't say shut up where I was raised. It's vulgar.

I'd have run away, but his grasp has me trapped. "Excuse me?"

He closes his eyes and bows his head. "Shhh, woman."

Prayer? He's going to pray?

"Dear Lord, bless Linda. Remove the fear from her heart and replace it with a peace that comes from fully trusting You. Bring to her mind the first prayer we prayed over Emma the moment she was born. Help Linda to recall that prayer when we thanked You for giving us our beautiful little girl and then placed her back into Your loving hands for safekeeping. Forgive Linda for snatching Emma from Your grasp and allow her to return our daughter to Your care. Thank You for Nick and for the blessing he is to us. . . ."

Jerry's prayer vibrates within my heart. The words are beautiful, but there's a disconnect in my mind. Is he blaming me for Emma's problems? I'm not the one who called Miss Boothe and started this disaster in motion.

"Amen."

I'm at a loss for words. If he thinks that's going to solve our problems, he's more naive than I ever imagined.

We sit in silence, he eating his turkey sandwich and me finishing my scone. I'm lulled by the warm sun. If I don't move, I'll fall asleep.

I gather my garbage. "Shall we walk again?"

We meander down the streets. I'm crazy about Aspen—the shops, the restaurants, the music drifting from open hotel windows, and the musicians on every other street corner playing like a dream. Oh, and the people—what can I say? They're gorgeous. Like the plastic kind from LA.

I stop dead in my tracks. An ambrosial fragrance drifts on the breeze and entices my senses. On the corner of the street, Lush seduces me into its open doors. Not only is the aroma amazing, but the shapes and colors of its soaps, lotions, and potions draw me into a world of sensory delight. "Oh, let's buy something for Em."

Jerry follows like an obedient puppy. I wander from aisle to aisle, touching, smelling, and reading about the wonderful products displayed before me. I load a basket with bath salts, shampoo, soap, and lotion. When we get to the cashier, I select a lip balm—unflavored of course—for Nick. I pass the bag with our purchases to Jerry, and we continue on our way.

One of the good things about Aspen is that you can walk throughout the entire city. One of the bad things about Aspen is that you can walk throughout the entire city—it's only five o'clock and we're finished exploring.

I'd be content to keep walking, but Jerry has a different idea. "Let's go back to the hotel."

I follow him along the Mill Street pedestrian mall, and we cut kitty-corner through Wagner Park. The city is alive with couples and families enjoying themselves. I wish my kids were with me.

We arrive back at our wee little room. *Now what?*

Jerry stretches out on the bed. "Lin?" He pats the bed.

I don't hide my suspicion when I glance at him. "Yes?"

"How about a nap before dinner?"

"Nap? Yes, I'm tired." I slip under the sheet, turn my back, and dissolve into slumber.

"Dear?" Jerry's shaking my shoulder.

"Hmm?"

"Let's get going. I've made dinner reservations."

I could have slept another five or six hours, but I drag myself from bed, reapply my makeup, and slip into a fresh pair of capris and a lightweight sweater. Jerry is handsome in his black polo shirt and jeans. Too bad he doesn't light my fire anymore.

He's always had an amazing sense of direction, and he leads us through the city to The Steak Pit. "Shall we order a glass of champagne?"

I shake my head. I wish he'd accept the situation. I'm here because I don't want to give Emma an emotional scar. Period. If the worst happens, I don't want Em to think she contributed to our marital problems. Thank goodness the restaurant isn't one of those quiet ones; this way our lack of conversation isn't too obvious.

The air has cooled when we make our way to the hotel again.

"Look at the stars, Lin. Aren't they beautiful hanging over the mountain?"

I can't muster up enough energy to match his enthusiasm. "Yeah."

In our petite room, we dance a bizarre waltz, Jerry trying to thaw my heart and me bringing on the chill. He gives up, and we settle into opposite sides of the bed in an uneasy truce.

● ● ●

I wake early. This mattress isn't nearly as sweet as my pillow top at home. I rise, shower, and dress. At seven, I kick the side of the bed. "Wake up. I've picked out our breakfast restaurant."

Jerry seems pleased. He's such an optimist. "Whatever you say, madam." He showers and dresses quickly.

We exit the hotel, and I lead the way. "I know exactly where to go."

He looks surprised. "Where?"

I smile. "You'll see." If he only knew my plan, that smile would fall off his satisfied little face. We walk toward Main Street and turn right to the Hotel Jerome.

Jerry raises his eyebrows.

Hold on to your hat, man, because I'm taking you for a ride. Since he practically forced me to go on this sham of an anniversary weekend, he's going to pay. Really pay.

The lobby is everything I imagined it would be. Quiet, elegant, plush. Our table is not quite ready, and the hostess invites us to wait in the room at the core of the hotel beneath an amazing three-story-high, glass-covered ceiling. I glide my hand over an antique buffet and drink in the beauty of the tile floor and luxurious sofas and chairs.

Jerry looks slightly uncomfortable. I'm sure he's doing the math and assumes this meal is going to put a dent in his wallet.

We're led to our table and greeted by a snooty waiter. Oh, I love this place. He starts to place menus on the table.

I take charge. "That won't be necessary. We know what we're ordering." I checked out the menu online in the lobby while Jerry was in the shower.

Jerry's jaw drops.

I continue. "We'd each like decaf coffee and orange juice and two eggs. Mine poached and his sunny-side up."

The waiter scribbles our order. I let him catch up with me. "Oh, and don't you have homemade sausage?" He nods agreement, and I finish, "And my husband would like a side of bacon, please." That was fun.

Our waiter turns in our order and returns with juice and a pot of French-pressed coffee. The aroma is divine.

I'm content to sit back and do a little people watching until our breakfast is served.

The haughty server whisks up to our table and places our meal before us.

Before the waiter can move away, Jerry speaks up. "Toast?"

The young snob pauses. "The meal is à la carte. Toast is extra. Shall I get you some, sir?"

Jerry blushes. "No, thanks."

We savor breakfast, myself probably a little more than Jerry. Our bill is placed on the table, and I snatch it up. "Oh, let me take care of this."

I hand one of our joint credit cards to Mr. Snooty Face. When the bill is returned, I write in a tip and pass the receipt to Jerry.

His eyes bulge. Who can blame him? Sixty-eight dollars for a simple breakfast of bacon and eggs. *Perfect.*

Jerry's decided we'll take a drive to a ghost town this morning. Ashcroft is a beautiful, ten-mile drive under a splendid Colorado sky. Jerry pays the fee, and we continue into town.

He reads from the crisp brochure as we walk down the dusty street. "'Founded in 1880, Ashcroft grew to a population of two thousand in 1883. By then there were two newspapers, a school, sawmills, a small smelter, and twenty saloons, making it a bigger town than Aspen.'"

"Uh-huh."

He reads more random facts. "'And by 1885 there were just one hundred summer residents and $5.60 in the town's coffers.'"

Blah, blah, blah. He loves history. I walk next to him while he babbles on about the dismal story of a dead community. Does he see the irony? The story of Ashcroft sounds like our marriage. Once vibrant, now a ghost town. Oh, I never imagined I would have such a thought. But that's exactly how I feel.

I'm relieved to head to the car for a bottle of water and the drive back to Aspen. We pull into the last space in front of our hotel. As I start to gather my things, my car door opens. For a moment, I'm disoriented. Jerry's standing outside my door, his hand extended toward me. The last time he did this was the morning Emma was born and he was depositing me at the ER entrance of the hospital. It's awkward. I have no choice but to grasp his hand and exit the car.

Back in our little room, Jerry sits on the bed. I lean against the windows. I see the tension play around his eyes.

He tosses the room key on the nightstand. "Give me the rest of the day. If you want to go home tomorrow, we'll leave first thing in the morning."

I'm dying to leave right now. I glance outside and see two young men and a young woman, a string trio, tuning up.

Jerry's perfectly still, as if he's holding his breath waiting for my answer.

If our marriage is on life support, I don't want to be the one to euthanize it. I'll let this weekend play itself out gracefully. I won't put an acrimonious ending to decades of good years. "Okay. I'll stay tonight."

Jerry's face lights up like he won a prize.

I don't want to lead him on. "But I still don't know where we stand. Please don't push me. The past few weeks have changed so much."

He looks as though he's about to speak and edits himself. He walks over to me, and for a moment I think he's going to try to kiss me. Instead he holds out his right hand. I place my hand in his, and he puts his other hand on top of mine. We stand silently, regarding each other.

"There's a place I want to take you, Lin. Will you come?"

I nod.

"Good. Put on some tennis shoes."

49

Jerry and I take our familiar route toward the center of town and then cut through the park and over to Cooper Avenue.

Jer turns right and leads me to the gondola at the base of Aspen Mountain. "Will you go to the top of the earth with me?"

"Yeah."

He disappears to purchase our tickets. A horse-drawn carriage clops by, holding a young family. I'm nostalgic for my children when they were young. We had a wonderful life.

Jerry bounds out to me, and we climb the stairs to the gondola entrance. We have a car to ourselves. It's breathtaking to see the city recede beneath us. The surrounding mountains look like pictures from an expensive, glossy calendar.

At the top of Aspen Mountain, a bluegrass band is set up under a tent. The music floating through the air gives the day a holiday feel. People mill around or sit in the seats placed on the grass.

Signs point to different hiking trails. Jerry gestures toward one, and I walk beside him up a wide trail. I'm in awe of the incredible scenery; we are surrounded by glorious mountaintops and waving fields of wildflowers. At a fork in the trail, we veer right and find ourselves on rock outcroppings facing a panorama of green mountains. I could gaze at this view forever and never tire of it.

"Shall we sit awhile, Lin?"

I choose a boulder and ease myself down.

Jerry sits beside me. He puts his hand into the pocket of his jacket, pulls out a thin devotional book, and begins to read. "'Shout with joy to God, all the earth! Sing the glory of his name; make his praise glorious! Say to God, "How awesome are your deeds! So great is your power that your enemies cringe before you. All the earth bows down to you; they sing praise to you, they sing praise to your name."'" He turns a page and continues, "'May the whole earth be filled with his glory. Amen and amen.'"

The wind whistles through the evergreens, and an eagle soars on the currents. It's a sight right out of *National Geographic*.

Pages rustle. "'How great is your goodness, which you have stored up for those who fear you, which you bestow in the sight of men on those who take refuge in you.'"

I tilt my face toward the sun and listen to Jerry worship. His faith is so transparent, so sure. He's blessed.

Laughter rises from beyond us. Tourists gape in wonder and snap pictures of friends and family with the backdrop of the snowcapped mountains.

Jerry's grown silent, and I know he's still praying.

What happens next, Lord? Despite the cool air from the high altitude, the sun is sweet and warm, yet my heart and soul are chilled. I've always dreamed that I would have an enduring marriage; it's still what I desire. But can that happen now? Can I return from this brink of disappointment?

The sound of gravel scraping over rock causes me to open my eyes. Jerry's on his feet. I start to rise, but he holds his hand up, palm facing me. "Can I take just a few minutes alone, Lin?"

Take all the time you want. "Yeah."

He drops his book by my lap and strides off. The pages flutter in the breeze. A few feet away from me, a small evergreen has taken root in the crack of a boulder. Only two feet tall, the plant is bright green and robust. It's a miracle it could grow or even thrive within the confines of its rock. I pull my camera out of my purse and take a picture.

I raise my eyes and see my husband in the distance, staring at the mountaintop. Jerry's like this little tree. He grows and thrives wherever he's stuck. Even in our declining marriage.

As if he knows I'm watching, he turns and waves. I lift my hand and salute. He tilts up his chin in response and strides toward me, his steps deliberate.

My heart trembles with an epiphany. This man, whom I have wronged in many ways, is joyfully returning to me.

He never walked away from me. I pushed him. He never stopped loving me. I shut him out.

In my mind, I see him sitting alone in the breast center, hanging in there in spite of the outcome. I see him standing strong in the midst of Emma's troubles, believing God will carry us through. I see him in the thick of an argument with me, fighting for our love. And I see him sitting beside me on a park bench, loving me with prayer.

My eyes well up with tears. How could I have been so blind? so stubborn?

As he gets closer, his peaceful expression dims, and his pace quickens. He rushes up the rock outcropping. "What's wrong?"

I stand to greet him. "Nothing. Absolutely nothing."

He wipes a tear from my face. "Happy tears?"

I grasp his hand in both of mine and bring it to my cheek. His arm comes around me, and I feel the familiar comfort of fitting perfectly into his embrace.

"Linda?"

"Uh-huh?"

His beautiful eyes lock on mine. "Do you think it's time to go back down?"

A warm, bubbling, healing giggle comes from deep within. I was so sure he was going to say something romantic. It would have been perfect timing. *What was I thinking? This is Jerry Revere.*

A moment later when we exit the gondola, the streets are alive with joy. Lovers stroll hand in hand, and children play with a puppy on the brick walkway of Hyman Avenue. The potted plants hanging along the street and from the well-kept facades of historic buildings are vibrant with color. The dancing fountain at Mill Street sparkles in the light and entertains a toddler with its erratic motion.

The afternoon sun is beginning to make its descent when we arrive at our cozy hotel. The play of light on the mountains that surround the town sings the majesty of the Creator. We enter our snug little room, and I kick off my shoes.

Jerry snores beside me. Everything about this moment is warm and sweet. He loves me inside and out, from top to bottom. This gift, this mystery, is a blessing.

All the months of daydreaming about romance seem silly now. Pretty words and extravagant gestures can't compare to being pursued by love and romanced with prayer.

Ah. What a man.

50

Jerry wakes me with a kiss on my shoulder. "The moon is shining like daylight."

I pry open an eye. Moon shadows lay in stripes across the comforter. "What?"

He's sitting next to me, his hair poking up like a child's drawing. "Let's put on bathing suits and go in the hot tub."

"What time is it?"

"Three forty-five. Come on."

Who is this man? "Are you kidding?" I'd much rather sleep.

He gives my hair a tug. "It'll be romantic."

Good point. And after all, isn't this what I longed for?

We put on our suits and tiptoe down the stairs and out the door, feeling like teenagers sneaking out of the house. A motion-detector light illuminates the small wooden deck, and the blue-green light from the hot tub and the steam that rises from the water cocoon us in a world of our own.

Am I dreaming? Jerry's smile makes my toes tingle. The canopy of stars looks magical, like the ceiling in Caesar's Palace Las Vegas.

He stretches his arms out. "Whatcha thinking?"

I smile and shake my head. *Are there words for this?* "I'm blessed."

Jerry tips his chin up and studies me. The intensity of his look makes me feel naked. "So am I." He breaks our gaze to glance at the stars and then locks eyes with me again. "Lin, when I thought

I might lose you, I felt like I would die too. I was powerless to do anything to help you, and I just didn't know what to do at all. I'm sorry if I let you down."

My heart sinks as if it's wearing a cement life jacket. I've been such a jerk. I never considered what he was feeling. "I should have told you what I was thinking, Jerry. We could have worked as a team. But I put myself in a cocoon. Can you forgive me?"

He grasps my ankle and pulls me to his side of the tub. I'm floating in his arms like a baby. His lips are close to my ear, and he laughs softly. "You are the luckiest woman in the world."

"Really, Jerry, I need you to forgive me."

He gently strokes my cheek. "Always."

In the morning, Jerry gives in, and we pack to go home. During checkout, we get alternate directions to Denver. I can't go over Independence Pass again. I'm finding enough gray hairs, thank you very much.

Although the scenery is breathtaking, the drive drags on. I'm desperate to be home with my children. My cell phone chirps from within my purse. I'm so anxious to answer it that I can hardly unzip my bag. It's a call from home. "Hello?"

"Mo— . . . cal—" Static fills the line.

I check the readout. Two signal bars. "Emma? Speak up. I can barely hear you."

For a moment, the signal improves. My heart constricts when all I hear is hysterical weeping. "Emma! Emma? What's happened?"

The call drops. No signal bars.

"No signal! She's crying, Jerry. Something terrible's happened."

Tears fall from my cheek to the hand holding my heart. Thank goodness we've got our seat belts on because Jerry's driving like a cowboy—accelerating on the straightaway and breaking hard around curves. I keep my eyes glued to my cell phone. As we approach Glenwood Springs, the signal bars begin to reappear. My hand trembles. I punch in our number.

It's answered on the first ring. "Mommy?" Emma's voice dissolves into tears.

"What's wrong? Is Nick with you?"

Her keening wail shreds what's left of my heart. "Emma!"

Jerry passes me a handkerchief; his face is wreathed with concern. I mop my tears.

Nick's voice comes across the miles. He seems to struggle for composure. "Mom?"

"Yes, I'm here."

His voice cracks as he explains about the phone call they just received.

We barely communicate through our shared emotion. I end the call and grab Jerry's hand. He pulls the car off the road.

I fall into his arms, weeping too vigorously to make any sense. I'm a crazy woman. Crying hysterically one moment and dissolving into laughter the next.

Jerry looks at me as if I've finally lost my fingernail grip on reality.

I wipe my eyes with a tissue. "It's over, Jer. It's over."

His expression displays his confusion. "What?"

"Our lawyer called. He said Miss Boothe is no longer interested in pursuing charges. It's over."

Jerry huffs out a breath. "Praise God!"

I'll remember this moment for the rest of my life. The moment my girl got her life back, the moment the crushing, black weight began to lift from my heart.

When we're close to Denver, Jerry pulls off the highway and into Arapahoe National Forest. He slaps my knee. "Let's do church."

Our car hugs the winding road bordered by spiking pine trees, and we park in the lot of a picnic area. The sign calls it Cloudland.

Jer leads me to a weathered table, and we sit together. The fragrance of pine, the melody of birdsong, and the whispering wind caressing the trees fill my senses. Jerry pulls out his worn devotional book and flips it open.

I close my eyes and listen to his warm voice bringing us into the presence of God. A soft breeze plays with my hair, the sun warms my back, and a peace I've not experienced in a long, long while fills my soul.

I replay Jerry's earlier accusation. In my next breath, my chest tightens like the mechanism that automatically winds the electrical cord on Betty, my vacuum cleaner. *Have I been a Sunday Christian?*

A brilliant spotlight searches the corners of my soul and finds it wanting. *Oh, Lord, forgive me. It had been so easy for me to pray and trust You until our trial with Emma came along. I snatched all the worries and fears and carried around my burden like a precious backpack filled with soiled river rock. I didn't trust You to see us through. I barely even prayed.*

I thought I knew what a broken heart feels like, but now I know the next degree of sorrow. I've utterly failed. Failed to trust God, failed to trust Jerry, failed to help Emma see divine love in the midst of her trouble. I'm ripe with the stench of unworthiness. From what seems like far away, Jerry praises God in his usual confident manner. I don't even deserve to be within earshot of such prayer.

Lord, forgive me. The tracks of my tears are cooled by the breeze. *Have mercy on me, Father.*

As I silently pour out my grief, Jerry rests his hand on my shoulder. "Lord, bless Linda. Show her Your hand throughout the past few weeks. Heal her heart. . . ."

His voice is obscured by the roaring ocean inside my ears. My heart races at the thought of what a pitiful believer I truly am. I should run away from this righteous man.

Jer squeezes my shoulder. "Father, how awesome are Your ways.

Thank You for Your compassion. Bind Linda's heart and give her Your joy. . . ."

"Yes, Father." I am poured out with grief at my shallow faith. My bones have turned to water. In my mind's eye I'm a puddle at the foot of the cross, clinging to a splinter of hope that I will experience forgiveness.

Jerry's strong voice continues, "Thank You that Your loving-kindness and Your truth have sustained us. Keep Your hand upon us and lead us in Your ways."

The pressure on my heart begins to yield. I suck in a deep, cleansing breath as though I had been swimming in fathomless, murky water and am finally breaking through to sunshine and fresh air. The blinding spotlight on my heart softens to a beautiful lambent, loving light. I am caressed by a warmth that loves me to the core of my being.

I don't recall Jerry finishing his prayers, but now he holds me tightly, blotting my tears with a tissue. I lift my head and rest against his chest.

For someone who is usually focused on his destination, Jerry allows us to sit in this beautiful place for a long while. I feel as though I'm being put back together like a puzzle whose missing pieces have been found. The fragrances of life—pine, soil, bark, fresh air—feed my soul.

Cloudland? It should be called heaven on earth.

Jerry stands. "Let's go home."

● ● ●

Emma must have been watching out the window because she greets us at the garage door. She's radiant. Her glow has returned, and her dazzling half-moon smile warms me to my toes. I nearly trip over the recycling bin to get to her.

I capture her in a bear hug. "Oh, I'm so happy!"

Nick joins us and helps Jerry with our luggage. We troop into the house and assemble in the kitchen. Our voices and laughter pile up on each other. Such a joyful sound. Even Belle gets in on the act, prancing on her rear paws and yipping.

The afternoon is glorious. Debbie has got to hear our wonderful news.

Her voice is filled with love for us. "Oh, honey. It's been a tough few weeks, hasn't it?"

She doesn't even know the half of it. "I'm just glad it's over. What's new with you?" I lean back in my Victorian chair and savor the feeling of normalcy as Deb chatters on about Randy and Andrea's wedding plans.

Emma's gone to bed early, exhausted from the excitement of the day. She looks like she's grown an inch, or maybe in her joy, she was floating with her feet an inch off the floor.

Jerry finds me standing in the door to her bedroom, watching her sleep. I never thought I would see her experiencing such peace again. Praise God.

"Shall we play hooky tomorrow, Lin?"

Oh yeah. We were still supposed to be in the mountains for another day.

"Uh-huh." I'm craving a day alone with my husband.

51

Jerry let me sleep in. When finally I stroll into the kitchen, he's reading the paper with a cup of coffee by his elbow. The kids have gone off to school, and Belle is sleeping in a pool of sunlight.

He peers over the rim of his reading glasses. "Coffee? I made decaf."

I heat my tall latte mug in the microwave and pour a cup. On my way to the table, I grab a few pieces of biscotti from the large glass jar that sits on the counter.

Jerry shares a section of the newspaper, and we sit in companionable silence, reading and dunking our biscuits. "Lin?"

I put my index finger on the article I'm reading to save my place. "Yeah?"

He smiles seductively. "You know, tomorrow's our twenty-fifth anniversary."

My heart soars. "I know."

"Let's go out to dinner. All four of us."

That would be something new. "Bring the kids?"

He reaches over and covers my hand with his. I don't even mind that he's made me lose my place in the story I was reading. "I want to include the kids. They should celebrate our marriage too. After all, they've been as blessed as we are."

"Oh, Jer." He's something, God bless him. "That's a great idea."

• • •

Jerry and I walk through the prairie. The Cherry Creek path is nearly deserted except for young mothers with their kids. Occasionally, groups of moms with children in strollers, on big wheels, or riding bicycles parade by.

Together our hearts sing a duet of praise, the Lord right with us. Could a day get any better?

When we get home, Jerry decides we need to run over to The Great Indoors to have our living room shade restrung. We work together to remove the window covering, and I toss it in the backseat while Jerry starts the car.

The Great Indoors is one of our favorite stores to window-shop. When we get there, Jerry hands over our shade to the clerk. She inputs our information into her computer. "We can do this while you wait. About fifteen minutes."

I follow Jerry out of the window covering department. His eyes twinkle. "Let's look at the wide-screen TVs."

I've been wondering when he was going to get around to that. "Sure, but we're just looking." He's been plotting to get a new television since he saw Steve's the day of Tammy's basement flood.

We enter the electronics department, and a salesman is on us quicker than a vulture on a rotting carcass. I catch Jerry's eye and hold my hand by my ear, mimicking speaking on the phone—a signal we've used in the past—and escape to the dinnerware department to browse to my heart's content.

I love the display tables with their beautiful place settings. The linens, the dinnerware, the crystal—such gorgeous colors and patterns. I walk around the department, making note of the designs and admiring the centerpieces on display.

A woman's voice in the next aisle rises as she speaks with a sales associate. Something about her tone seems very familiar. I'm not one to actively eavesdrop, but this sounds interesting.

"I was in here two days ago, and the associate told me that this wouldn't be a problem."

I peer through candlesticks on a display shelf and see the poor salesgirl. Her face is flaming red, and she's batting her eyes as if she's trying to withhold tears. "I'm sorry, ma'am. As far as I know this pattern only comes in complete sets. I'm not allowed to break open a box for a few pieces."

Her aggressive client, whose back is toward me, steps closer to the girl. "Well, then, I suggest you find someone else who can assist me."

Yikes. Poor girl. The hapless associate scurries off, no doubt grateful to escape further abuse.

Before I can walk away, the source of her torment turns and stares straight at me. My scalp begins to itch. It's Carol Wrecking Ball. Maybe she's not focusing on me. I rotate on my heel and begin to make my escape.

"Linda, is that you?"

I pause. *Should I keep going?*

The pause does me in. Carol's faster than she looks, and she catches up to me.

"Oh, Carol. Hi."

She smiles that weird, artificial smile. "What a pleasant surprise."

Surprise? Yes. Pleasant? No. I smile and nod. "Nice to see you."

We stand in awkward silence. Maybe she'll get bored and stalk away.

Carol bats her eyes at me. "I would love to buy you a cup of coffee to show my gratitude."

Now she's confused me. As usual. "Gratitude?"

She takes my elbow and points us in the direction of the Starbucks located in the front of the store. "Yes, my friend's daughter has been accepted into the internship program. You're going to love her; she's a delight. She'll be staying with me, you know."

Oh, crumbs. Now I'll have Carol's minion watching my every move this summer. "How wonderful."

She steers me past the electronics department, and I catch a glimpse of Jerry deep in conversation with an intense-looking salesman. "Oh, there's my husband. Thanks for the offer, but I don't think I'll have time for coffee."

How naive am I? Carol plasters her bizarre grin on her taut face and walks right up to Jer. "Mr. Revere? I'm Carol Ball, a friend of you wife's. Would you mind if I bought her a cup of coffee while you shop?"

My eyes widen in disbelief. I press my lips together and twitch my head at Jer. Surely after twenty-five years of marriage he can pick up on my clues.

Or not. He smiles and pumps her perfectly manicured, bejeweled hand. "Uh, nice to meet you." He glances at the salesman waiting impatiently for his attention. "Yeah, I'll probably be a few minutes."

I could just strangle him. Does this woman *always* get what she wants? I walk beside Carol, feeling defeated and slightly alarmed. What else does she want from me? I doubt she has an altruistic bone in her emaciated little body.

Carol orders a tall americano and steps aside for me to place my order.

I smile at the bored clerk. "May I have a grande, decaf, extra-wet cappuccino, please?"

Carol and I smile and nod to each other like two idiots while we're waiting on our order. My shirt is beginning to stick to the middle of my back, and my palms are sweating like a damp sponge. I'm nervous enough—what was I thinking, ordering a hot beverage?

We put cardboard collars around our steaming cups and make our way to a little table. I remove the lid from my coffee. The faster it cools, the faster I can drink it and make my escape.

Carol inclines her head. "I understand you've been out of town."

When I find out who at Dream Photography told Carol I went away, they'll wish they could disappear. "My husband and I just took a couple of days off for a long weekend."

"Oh, how lovely. Sometimes it's just so invigorating to get away. Don't you think?"

I nod and take a sip of my scalding coffee. *Get to it, Carol. What do you want from me now?*

Carol smiles as if I'm reciprocating her pleasantries. "And where did you say you went?"

I didn't. "The mountains. Aspen."

She leans in. "Splendid. It looks like you've been refreshed, Linda."

You have no idea. "Thanks. Things are going well."

Carol continues to incline toward me. I know what a salmon must feel like with a bear standing in the river. She takes a tiny sip of her calorieless beverage. "I wasn't aware we have a mutual acquaintance."

"Really?" *I can't imagine who.*

She sits back. "Yes, on Friday I had dinner with my sister-in-law. Her cousin joined us."

Get to the point. I smile. Her little game is making me nervous.

Carol folds her hands and places them on the table. "Yes, I believe you know her. Alice Boothe."

The hairs on the back of my neck stand up.

Carol nods. "She's one of your daughter's teachers, isn't she?"

If I weren't sitting, I'd fall to the floor. "Excuse me?"

She smiles, then folds her arms across her chest. "I understand Emma was having some troubles."

My head is spinning. *Is Carol Wrecking Ball responsible for setting my world right again?* A lump forms in my throat, and I start batting my eyes to keep from crying. It doesn't work. Tears stream down my face in a torrent. I can barely see through the river of gratitude. "Did you—?"

She scoots her chair in and puts a hand on my arm. "I'm a mother too. And I owed you a favor."

I can barely believe what I'm hearing. I mop my face with the stiff, brown Starbucks napkin. "God bless you, Carol." I leap up and gather this sweet bag of bones in an embrace.

I've somehow managed to pull her to her feet and rest my head against hers, crying like a baby. I expect her to pat my back in an okay-that's-enough gesture, but she puts her skinny arms around my shoulders and squeezes.

"It's all right, Linda. It's all right." She gently disentangles herself from my clutches and eases me into my seat.

I'm such a jerk. I've never had a kind thought toward this woman, and she's given my daughter her life back. "How can I ever repay you?"

Carol waves off my concern. "Don't worry about it. Besides, Alice's niece Robin has always been a nasty piece of work. She put Alice up to filing those ridiculous charges."

The remainder of my mascara smudges on the napkin. "You have no idea what this means to my family. If I can ever do anything for you, you just need to—"

She beams. "What are friends for? After all, I'm sure I can always count on you. Can't I, Linda?"

52

Although it's been only four days, I feel as if I've been away from work for weeks. When I left, my world was in ruins, my marriage was on the rocks, and my daughter would spend the rest of her high school years in juvenile hall.

I'm overjoyed to have my life back to normal again and thrilled to embrace the chaos that is my job. As usual, the lobby is full of customers. Even the high-maintenance ones can't bring me down today. *Don't like the color of the grass in that image? No problem, we'll redo it. Want that insignificant stray hair removed? No problem, we'll redo it. Want to change the pose choice on your completed order? No problem. . . .*

"Linda?" Jill stands over me with an armful of paperwork.

Bring it on. Nothing's going to slow my stride today. "What can I do for you?"

She plops a manila folder on my desk. "Luke wants you to take care of this."

I open the file. It's full of mortgage application forms. "What . . . ?"

Jill adds a few more papers to my stack. "It's for Pam." She looks at me as if I'm a few pixels short of a JPEG. "You know. What Luke's doing."

I haven't been gone *that* long. Have I? "What Luke's doing?"

Reality must catch up with Jill because she cracks a smile. "Oh, this all happened while you were out of the studio."

Yeah, not all of it. I know what I saw. *Those two snakes.*

She ignores my look of disgust. "I think it's just great. I never thought Luke had it in him."

Great? To cheat on your wife? To cause another woman to commit adultery? "Excuse me?"

"You haven't heard about Pam's troubles?"

"What troubles?"

Jill pulls up a chair and tells me a heartbreaking story. It seems that despite Pam's husband working three jobs, they've been short of money. The two of them are trying to make good on debts his mother incurred, and they're being hounded by creditors. It's a long and confusing story, but the bottom line is that if they don't help with the money, the old lady could go to prison. And the worst part is that they're in danger of losing their home. Luke's being the hero of the day by offering to cosign on a new mortgage for them. *Wow.* I would have never imagined it.

"So," Jill continues, "Luke needs you to fill out as much of his information as you know."

"Um, sure. I'll see what I can do."

Jill ambles out of the room and leaves me alone with my guilty conscience. *Could I have been any more wrong?* I jumped to the wrong conclusion. Again. It would have been horrible if I had blabbed my mistaken version of what I saw to my coworkers. Surely the Holy Spirit kept my slanderous lips sealed.

And what about me? The so-called believer? What was I doing to help? Nothing. I was too busy gossiping to my best friend. And I could have made a difference in Pam's life. I'm such a slug. The words on the papers before me sway through my tears.

I don't want anyone to find me at my desk crying. I jump up, grab a tissue, round the corner of the office, and run directly into Luke. My rebound is so forceful that if he hadn't grabbed me by my arms, I would be knocking art off the walls.

"Welcome back." He holds me at arm's length and scrutinizes my face. "Why don't you come into my office?"

I follow him down the hallway. There are a million places I'd rather be than here: the dentist, the breast imaging center, my ob-gyn, back-to-school night, the Department of Motor Vehicles, the IRS, the USPS bulk mail department. . . .

Luke enters his office and takes a seat. "Close the door."

Has he read my mind? Did he know my evil thoughts? Am I going to be fired? I perch on the end of the chair opposite him.

He takes a deep breath and holds it for a moment, looking like a puffer fish. "I've noticed you've been going through a difficult time lately."

I nod, and we sit in a painfully embarrassing silence.

Finally, he says, "You don't need to confide in me. I just want to know if there's anything I can do to help you."

Who is this man? "I'm fine. Thanks, Luke."

He studies me as if to force the truth out.

I try to create a smile. "Really. We had some problems, but they've been resolved."

His face relaxes. "Good, good."

I'm dying to escape this office. "I'll go work on those papers for you."

Luke smiles. I never noticed how warm his face can look. "I really appreciate your help with that. I hate paperwork."

I can't help my curiosity. "Why are you doing this?"

He leans back. "Several reasons. One of which is you."

"Me?"

"I never told you how impressed I was two years ago when you helped Jill get that car."

I almost forgot about that. "I knew someone who was donating one to charity and talked him into giving it to her. It wasn't such a big deal."

He grins. "That's where you're wrong. She became a different woman without the worries about transportation. Remember how freaked she was about possibly having an emergency with one of her kids and not having a car?"

I wouldn't have known he even thought twice about that. I put my hands on the arm of the chair to push myself up.

"One more thing. Was there something important you wanted to discuss with me a few weeks ago?"

"I don't know what you're talking about."

"I was talking to Pam in my office, and when you came in, you looked upset."

A blush rises from my neck. "Uh, no."

Luke seems to ponder my response. "I would hate to think that you felt neglected when I was trying to comfort Pam."

I reassure him that I'm okay and make my exit. It's nearly lunchtime, so I hike to the end of the property and sit underneath a maple tree. The ground is warm beneath me. I lie back and close my eyes against the mottled sunlight that falls across my face. I'm a horrible human being. All my failures of the past few months rise up and lodge in my throat. *Oh, Lord, forgive me.*

At the end of the workday, I drive home clinging to the bright spot of my month, my anniversary dinner with my family. Jerry's wanted to try the new steak house on top of the Holiday Inn for months. I hope he's made reservations.

When I approach the house, I see that Nick's car isn't in the driveway. Didn't Jerry remind him about our plans? I know I did. A bubble of irritation flows through my veins. This is so disappointing.

53

I charge into the house. "Where's Nick? Isn't he going to dinner with us?"

The house is too quiet. Where's Emma? and Jerry? Did everyone forget? "Jerry!"

"Hey." I hear him come down the stairs. "Why are you yelling?"

"Aren't we going out to dinner?"

"We'll be staying home tonight. I was given—"

My heart sags with regret. "I was looking forward to this dinner. It was going to be a—"

He steps toward me and places his index finger on my lips. His eyes are twinkling as if he's the only one in on a good joke. "Calm down, honey."

Something's going on. "Where are the kids?"

He puts his arm around my shoulders and leads me to the living room. "As I was trying to tell you, a colleague gave me two tickets to the Rockies game and—"

"And the kids deserted our dinner for a baseball game?"

He shakes his head. "There's a private party at the restaurant we chose, and there were no tables available. We'll go on Friday night."

"Oh. That's too bad."

Belle runs to the door barking. "Belle, no!" She leaps at the door just as the bell rings. Jerry pulls a check out of his pocket. *What the . . . ?* I grab the dog by the collar while Jer answers the door.

He transacts business with a deliveryman and is given a large plastic bag. And it smells delicious. He turns to me. "Get some matches."

"What?"

"We'll light some candles."

I like the sound of this. When I come into the dining room, Jerry has the lights on the dimmer switch. The table is already set with our good china, and an open bottle of champagne stands beside two flutes.

I would have never thought he had this in him. "Jerry?"

He pulls out my chair. "Dinner for two, madam."

I take my seat, and he disappears into the kitchen. I hear the refrigerator door open. He returns with a fresh red rose sitting in a crystal bud vase. "For you." He puts the flower in the center of the table.

Am I dreaming? Has my LAME plan somehow been successful? Okay, in my dreams I get twenty-five roses—one for each year, but I digress.

"Oh, Jerry. This is a wonderful surprise."

He unloads cartons of food and dishes up some fragrant beef stew over jasmine-scented rice. I'm mute with shock. We sit at the table, Jerry at the head and me to his right. He picks up a remote and aims it at the stereo. Soft music wraps us in romance. It's an instrumental CD with music from the seventies. Sweet. My heart dances in time with the mandolins in Rod Stewart's love song.

I need to say something to commemorate this perfect evening. "Jerry?"

He gazes into my eyes, and I place my hand on his.

"I don't deserve this beautiful evening or you or the life we share."

He leans toward me and gives me that smile that's always made me dizzy. "Shhh. You certainly do. After what we've been through, we both do."

"The first day I saw you, I knew you would take care of me, of my heart, for the rest of our lives. I love you."

He's usually not an emotional man, but I see a glimmer of a tear in the corner of his eye.

He guides my face with his hand and kisses my lips softly. *Oh, heaven.*

We turn our attention to the gourmet meal before us. "Jer?"

"Yeah?"

"Don't you think it would be nice if you said something to me?"

He puts down his fork and wrinkles his forehead in thought. I continue to eat. The song on the CD changes to another soft rock tune.

After a few minutes pass, I'm beginning to think I've wrecked the mood of our romantic evening. I shouldn't have made such a demand. "Never mind. It's okay."

Jerry perks up. "No, no. I've got it."

I give him my full attention.

"Remember that play we saw in Denver two years ago? *I Love You, You're Perfect, Now Change?*"

This sounds interesting. "Yeah."

He sits up, as though he's excited to share. "Remember the last vignette when the old couple was eating breakfast together?"

"Yeah." It was a sweet scene. The wife brought the coffee to the table and he passed the sugar; they didn't need to speak to communicate. And while the wife sat reading the paper, the male character sang about how he loves her more now than the day they married and how much more beautiful she had become to him over the years.

"Remember the song the old guy sang at the end of the play?"

"Yeah."

Jerry smiles and his voice gets softer. "Well, that's how I feel about you."

Now it's my turn to get misty-eyed. That's the sweetest thing

Jerry's ever said to me. Nothing could be more romantic. My knight in shining armor.

He reaches for my hand, enclosing it in both of his strong, steady ones. "Lin—"

He's interrupted by the ringing telephone. He releases my hand and rushes to the kitchen. "Hello? . . . Oh no. Where are you? . . . Okay. Got it. I can be there in thirty minutes."

Jerry comes back into the dining room and blows out the candles. "That was Nick. The car broke down. We need to pick them up. He called a tow truck and . . ."

We work together to put away our dinner, and I let Belle outside to do her business. It was a wonderful evening while it lasted.

I love my life.

ABOUT THE AUTHOR

Megan DiMaria has fond memories of the days when her mother would pile the kids into the car to take their weekly trip to the Troy, New York, public library. There under the mural of *Gulliver's Travels* and amid the stacks of books began a lifelong love of the written word.

Megan is an active member of several writers' groups and enjoys encouraging other writers in their pursuits. She volunteers her talents to her church and local nonprofit organizations and speaks to writers' and women's groups. When she's not tapping out another story on her computer, she loves to hang out with her husband and three adult children.

Megan holds a BA in communications, with a specialization in mass media from the State University of New York at Plattsburgh. She has been a radio and television reporter, a Web content editor, a contributing writer for local newspapers, and has worked for a weekly newspaper. Megan has sold magazine articles locally and nationally. In her day job, she works in the marketing department of an upscale Denver portrait studio.